T0148667

TO KISS A WILD SCOT

"*Maoth-chridheach,*" he murmured. "Tenderhearted, just as Dougal said."
She seemed not to know what to say to that, but her gaze met his. Both of them were quiet, the tension building between them as they stared at each other without speaking. The silence grew heavy with expectation until Logan, almost without knowing he did it, leaned toward her.

As he drew closer her green eyes darkened, and her lips parted...

He didn't leap upon her, or take her mouth hard, as if he had every right to it. No, he took his time, his mouth drawing closer to hers so gradually he was made achingly aware of how badly he wanted her kiss long before his lips touched hers.

But when they did...when they did...

A sigh unlike any he'd ever heard before left Juliana's lips. Her mouth was so warm, her lips softer than he ever could have imagined. He kissed her carefully, his lips gentle and teasing until she opened her mouth under his...

Books by Anna Bradley

LADY ELEANOR'S SEVENTH SUITOR
LADY CHARLOTTE'S FIRST LOVE
TWELFTH NIGHT WITH THE EARL
MORE OR LESS A MARCHIONESS
MORE OR LESS A COUNTESS
MORE OR LESS A TEMPTRESS
THE WAYWARD BRIDE
TO WED A WILD SCOT

Published by Kensington Publishing Corporation

To Wed a Wild Scot

Anna Bradley

LYRICAL PRESS
Kensington Publishing Corp.
www.kensingtonbooks.com

LYRICAL PRESS BOOKS are published by
Kensington Publishing Corp.
119 West 40th Street
New York, NY 10018

First Electronic Edition: September 2019
ISBN-13: 978-1-5161-0947-0 (ebook)
ISBN-10: 1-5161-0947-3 (ebook)

First Print Edition: September 2019
ISBN-13: 978-1-5161-0949-4
ISBN-10: 1-5161-0949-X

Printed in the United States of America

Prologue

Strathnaver, Scotland, 1814

The sun has not yet illuminated the morning sky, but the fires are already burning. The timbered roofs groan and hiss under the assault, but hours pass before the heavy beams succumb to the flames and collapse, still smoking, into the small farmhouse kitchens. It's not a place for women or children, but they're there, weeping quietly as they watch their homes reduced to cinders on the ground.

The men aren't quiet. This is the Scottish Highlands, where men wear the dirt of the land under their fingernails, just as their fathers did, and before them their grandfathers, digging a living from the soil. They've earned their fury, their hatred.

Greed, one farmer mutters as charred black fragments of his roof float upward in the hazy predawn sky. Patrick Sellar lit Will Chisholm's house up with his mother-in-law still inside. Murderers.

Murderers, another farmer echoes, his voice hoarse from the smoke. Robert MacKay's roof set afire, with his two sick little girls still lying in their beds.

There are no landlords here to witness the destruction. The Countess of Sutherland has sent her factor, Patrick Sellar, to clear the land for the sheepherders who will take possession as soon as the farmers have been driven away. Aside from a barn here and there, Sellar burns every building in his path, so the Cheviot sheep will be free to roam and graze at will.

The men who come to burn the houses, like Sellar, are Scots themselves— sheriff's officers, constables, and Sellar's own sheepherders. Their faces are hard, uncompromising as they set their fires in service to Sellar, to the Countess of Sutherland. They came from the south—from England, or the Scottish Borders—on horseback. These men here today with their blazing torches weren't the first to come, nor will they be the last.

Sometimes they wait until the families leave the farmhouses before they set them alight.

Sometimes they don't.

Every house in Rosal Township is set ablaze, one after the other. They all burn at once. A gray cloud envelops all of northern Scotland. People as far away as Thurso can taste smoke and ash on their tongues.

Margaret MacKay, Chisholm's mother-in-law, dies of her burns five days later. A day after her death, the last of the Rosal fires burn themselves out.

In 1814, Logan Blair is twenty-four years old. His father has been dead for a year now. Logan's clansmen now consider him Laird of Clan Kinross, and so he would be, if a lairdship were determined only by a man's love for his clan.

Logan has traveled north from County Ross to Kildare, and then further north to Strathnaver, to see for himself if the tales of the devastation of Clan MacKay are true. Before he arrives, he tells himself it can't be as terrible as he's been told.

Now, he watches as the haze of smoke from the fires billows against the horizon, turning the sun blood red. Rage coils inside him, hot and ugly, a serpent writhing in his chest. The confusion, the terror, the grief of the people defies description.

The smoke lingers much longer than the people do. The homes, their valued possessions—in some cases even their kin—are left behind in the ashes. Families, entire clans are disbanded. Some board ships to try their luck in North America. Others are relocated to coastal Scotland to scrabble out a hard living as kelp farmers, fishermen, or coal miners.

All of them are devastated.

Greed. Landlords, squeezing Scotland until English pounds fall out.

Highland chiefs, turning on their own people, their own kin.

Logan was raised on Kinross soil, like his father before him, and before his father his grandfather, reaching back for generations. But these lairds are nothing like his grandfather, who fought and died at Culloden. The chiefs today are more English than Scottish, and the laird of Clan Kinross is no different.

All of Logan's clan claim him as their laird. Not because they don't know better, but because in every way that matters to them, he *is* laird. But the Duke of Blackmore owns the castle, and all the land surrounding it. As far as the law is concerned the duke is the true laird, leader of a clan he's never seen, and doesn't understand.

A clan he has no love for, and feels no loyalty to.

The Duke of Blackmore is Logan's maternal uncle. Logan's twin brother is the duke's heir. Logan has never spoken to his brother, and he's never seen him. Years ago, the clan midwife told Logan he and his brother were indistinguishable from each other as newborns—that from the day they emerged from the womb until the day the Duke of Blackmore took his brother away to England, they slept with their tiny hands clasped together.

His brother is half English, half Scot, just as Logan is, but his brother has never set foot on Scottish soil. He's never worn the Kinross tartan, or chased a Scottish lass through the heather. He was raised as an Englishman, by an Englishman, with an Englishman's sensibilities. He and Logan share their parents' blood, but there is no history between them. There are no memories.

His brother has an Englishman's name.

He was christened Gavin Blair, but now he goes by the name Fitzwilliam Vaughan. When their uncle dies, Fitzwilliam Vaughn will become the sixth Duke of Blackmore.

That's when he'll come to Scotland.

It won't be today, or even tomorrow, but someday he'll inherit the land, and he'll come to assess his new properties. Measuring, calculating profits and losses with his every step over Kinross land.

No good ever came of an English aristocrat on Scottish soil. Logan isn't fool enough to believe Fitzwilliam Vaughan will prove an exception to this rule. Soon enough he'll discover Cheviot sheep are more profitable than people, and then the evictions will begin. If the future Duke of Blackmore chooses to be merciful, the people might lose only their homes. If he chooses not to be, the more vulnerable among them could lose their lives.

Logan sucks in a breath of air, coughing as smoke fills his lungs. Sellar's burning party moves on to the next farmhouse, then the next, until the air becomes so heavy with thick black smoke that Logan can't draw a clean breath.

By the end of it, all of Rosal Township will fall victim to the flames. The fire will devour more than two hundred fifty farmhouses, and scatter their inhabitants to every corner of Scotland and beyond. Later, long after the smoke has cleared, 1814 will be known as *an bhliain ar an dó*.

The Year of the Burning.

Logan doesn't stay to watch it happen. He turns his horse's head and leaves the scene of destruction behind him, but it's not the last time he'll see Patrick Sellar.

In 1816, he'll make the short journey to Inverness, to watch Sellar go on trial for the murder of ninety-year-old Margaret MacKay, burned to death in Rosal Township two years earlier. Despite the evidence against him, Sellar will be found not guilty of the charge.

There are other factors, after Sellar. Other greedy landlords eager to trade their history, their heritage, their kinsman's lives for a profit. The people will try to fight them, and they'll lose. The clansmen have no rights. Neither their landlords nor the law will protect them.

When Fitzwilliam Vaughan arrives in Scotland, there will be nothing to stop him from setting fire to every farm on Kinross land.

Nothing, that is, but Logan.

He won't let it happen. The duke owns the land, but he doesn't own the people. Whatever Logan has to do—lie, steal, fight—he'll do it. Laird or not, he's been raised to protect his clan at all costs.

He won't let an Englishman destroy Clan Kinross.

Not even if that Englishman is his brother.

Chapter One

By the time Lady Juliana Bernard realized something was amiss, her boots and the hem of her riding habit were already splattered with vomit.

Miss Findlay, who'd been looking a trifle green over the past few miles, slapped a hand over her mouth. "Oh, my lady! I'm so dreadfully—"

Sorry.

The word was lost in a faint gurgle, and poor Findlay once again cast up her accounts all over the floor of the carriage. Juliana jerked her feet back to save her boots from another dousing, but it was already too late.

"Oh, dear. I'm excessively mortified." Miss Findlay sagged back against the squabs, her forehead sheened with sweat. "Oh, and I've ruined your boots, and your favorite blue habit!" she wailed, looking as if she were about to burst into tears.

"Now, Findlay, you mustn't think on it. I have other riding habits. There's no real harm done." Juliana reached for her companion's hand and patted it soothingly. "Indeed, I blame myself. I thought you looked a bit off color. I should have realized you were ill."

"No, no. I'll be perfectly well in a moment," Miss Findlay protested weakly, but her face had gone from green to white, and she was obliged to swallow several times before she dared open her mouth again. "A brief rest, and I'll be as fit as ever."

Juliana didn't argue, but as soon as Miss Findlay's eyes drifted closed, she leaned out the window and told her manservant, Stokes to stop at the next inn. Miss Findlay had borne up well over the six days of travel between London and Gretna Green, but it was clear the poor thing was exhausted. As anxious as Juliana was to settle her business, she wasn't quite so wicked as to drag her poor companion another twenty-five miles to Dumfries.

Wicked enough, though.

Miss Crampton, her old governess—a woman of stern propriety and rigid ethical principles—had warned Juliana time and again that every lie was like another bar in a sinner's prison. Once a lie was told, one never escaped it. It might take years, even decades, but your lies would haunt you in the end.

Juliana shuddered. Miss Crampton had been a terrifying woman to be sure, but she hadn't been wrong. Juliana had told dozens of lies over the past few weeks—to her father, to her friends, and even to her six-year-old niece, Grace—and now she was being punished for it.

None of this was Findlay's fault. It was *hers*. Her toes were now resting in a puddle of vomit because she *deserved* it.

She dredged up a handkerchief, pressed it to her nose, and fell back against the squabs with a sigh. She must be mad to be chasing Fitzwilliam all the way to Scotland. When he'd left five months earlier he'd promised to write, and so he had—for the first month or so.

Since then he hadn't replied to any of the dozens of letters she'd sent him.

Not even the most urgent ones.

But Fitzwilliam was her dearest friend, and they'd been promised to each since birth. If a lady in desperate straits couldn't rely on her betrothed, whom could she rely on?

If she could only find him, all would be well.

But if I can't...if I can't...

The trouble was, she wasn't quite sure where he was. That is, she knew he was somewhere in the vicinity of the Sassy Lassie Inn in Inverness, because he'd told her to send his letters there. He'd answered the first few, so she knew he'd received them. Surely Castle Kinross wasn't so very far away from the inn? Surely, someone in Inverness would be able to direct her to the castle?

But if they couldn't, or wouldn't...

An image of Grace's face the day Juliana had left her in Buckinghamshire rose in her mind. Grace's dark eyes—so like Juliana's brother Jonathan's—had filled with tears. Since her niece was born, they'd never spent a single day apart. Juliana had done her best to explain to Grace why she had to go, but at six years old Grace understood only that her beloved Aunt Juliana was leaving her behind. She'd clung to Juliana's skirts, wailing, until her nurse had been obliged to drag her away.

Juliana squeezed her eyes closed and tried to hold off the familiar wave of grief and panic, but it was no use. Her chest tightened, her stomach heaved, and she might well have cast up her own accounts right then and there if Stokes hadn't signaled the post boys to stop the coach.

She stuck her head out the window to survey the inn, and her stomach gave another threatening lurch. The King's Head Inn was an indifferent looking place. Not dirty, precisely, but not clean, either, and cramped looking, with only a tiny inn yard and small stables. Juliana opened her mouth to instruct Stokes to go on, but Miss Findlay roused herself, and opened her eyes.

"Are we stopping, my lady?"

Juliana took one look at Findlay's pallid, clammy face and decided the King's Head Inn would have to do. "Yes, for a night. It's another half day to Dumfries. We're better off staying here and continuing our journey tomorrow."

Miss Findlay looked so relieved, Juliana's stomach knotted with guilt. She never should have involved poor Findlay in her mad scheme. "Stokes," she called. "Secure rooms for tonight, if you would, and order a light supper and bath for Miss Findlay. There." She gave Findlay a reassuring smile. "You'll feel much better after you've rested a night."

Stokes grumbled as he dismounted. He was a surly one, but he'd known Juliana since her birth, and was more like one of the family than a servant. Stokes wasn't at all pleased about their highland adventure, but of all the servants at Graystone Court, he was the least likely to reveal the truth about it to her father. Lord Graystone hadn't the faintest idea she was in Scotland. He thought she was in Buckinghamshire with Grace, and Juliana was determined to keep it that way. Stokes might grumble and scold a bit, but he'd keep her secret.

The proprietor of the inn was pleased to accommodate her ladyship's party. Within half an hour Miss Findlay was safely ensconced in an upper bedchamber, awaiting her bath and supper. Juliana saw her settled and bid her to go to sleep, then hurried back down the stairs in search of the inn's proprietor.

Surly servants, dusty roads, vomit, and ruined boots were unpleasant enough, but finding Fitzwilliam was a much stickier problem, and it became stickier the closer they got to Inverness. They were still several hundred miles away, but surely someone at the King's Head had heard of Castle Kinross? The innkeeper was the most likely person to help her, but when she stepped into the dining room she found only a handful of dusty travelers taking refreshment there. She hesitated for a few moments, hoping a servant might appear to direct her to her host, but she waited in vain.

"Where in the world is everybody?" she muttered crossly as she made her way down the hallway toward the entryway. Several carriages had arrived while she was upstairs with Findlay, and the ostlers were dodging about, trying to accommodate them all. She ventured out, hoping to find Stokes, but he wasn't in the yard.

Juliana stepped away from the bustle of guests and servants coming in and out the door, and leaned back against the side of the inn with a sigh. It was a warm day. She closed her eyes, let the sun caress her face, and tried to calm her mind. She'd spent so much of the past few months scurrying from one place to the next it felt strange to be still and let her thoughts go quiet.

She took a few deep breaths until her frayed nerves calmed a little, then began once again to ponder a way out of her dilemma. That is, the dilemma of having come hundreds of miles in search of a man who might not wish to be found.

Not even by her, his dearest friend.

Why hadn't he answered her letters? Oh, what a fool she'd been to go haring off to Scotland after Fitzwilliam! Even if she did find him, he might refuse to return to England with her. If he'd wanted to come home, he would have done so by now.

Tears gathered under her eyelids, but she fisted her hands and held them back, furious with herself. What good would tears do her now? She was at a shabby inn in Gretna Green, ankle-deep in vomit. It was too late to change her mind now, and even if she could, she wouldn't. In the end, her decision to come to Scotland had been a simple one. She needed Fitzwilliam's help, and as surely as she was his dearest friend, he was also *hers.*

She *knew* Fitzwilliam, from the exact shade of his blue eyes right down to the size of his boots. She knew every corner of his heart. She couldn't explain why he hadn't answered all her letters, but she knew he'd never turn his back on her.

She only had to find him.

Juliana opened her eyes and blinked against the sun. The commotion in the yard had died down, but Stokes still hadn't turned up. Perhaps she'd just go on to the stables then, and fetch him herself. That way she could be sure he'd secured a post chaise and horses for early tomorrow morning.

She straightened from the wall and had taken two steps toward the stables when a man walking across the inn yard caught her attention.

She had no reason to think he was coming toward her, yet she stilled, her breath held, unable to look away.

He was some distance still—far enough so she couldn't properly see his face, but he was tall and broad, with a headful of long, rather unruly dark hair. Perhaps he was handsome, but Juliana had spent too much time among the *ton* for a handsome face to unsettle her. London was rife with Corinthians, bucks and dandies, gentlemen of fashion and taste, of intelligence, grace, and uncommon beauty. She'd long since considered herself immune to even the most striking of male specimens.

But there was something about this man—

He looked up then, and Juliana froze, her heart stuttering in her chest. The angular jaw, the strong cheekbones, the square chin—there was only one man in the world with such an arresting face.

Fitzwilliam.

Had she said his name aloud? Had she shouted it, or whispered it?

He was coming toward her, and every part of her tensed to run to him. Every muscle, every nerve screamed at her to throw herself into his arms, but something held her back. Some instinct she couldn't explain kept her feet rooted to the ground.

He didn't call her name, or run to her. Why did he hold back? He'd be shocked to find her here, and perhaps angry with her for coming so far. She'd written and told him to expect her, but perhaps he hadn't received her letter yet, or...

Alarm darted down Juliana's spine. He didn't hold himself like a man who was angry, or one who was in shock. He wasn't stiff, but loose-limbed and graceful—the sort of man accustomed to physical activity, and comfortable in his body.

He didn't walk like Fitzwilliam.

He drew closer, and closer still. By the time he stopped in front of her, Juliana was so agitated she was sure he could hear her heart thundering in her chest.

He said something to her—something about assisting her—but she could only stare wordlessly up at him, a gasp frozen in her throat.

He wasn't Fitzwilliam.

He had Fitzwilliam's brow, his nose, his sculpted cheekbones, but this man was too rough, his features too aggressive, his manner too stern to be mistaken for Fitzwilliam, who was all smooth, polished charm.

He was speaking to her still, but Juliana didn't try to make sense of his words. She was staring at his hard lips.

His mouth is all wrong.

It was too wide, with a hint of ferocity in the lower lip. His voice was deeper, too, and though not unkind it was raw somehow, as if he were accustomed to barking commands, and had done so a few times too often.

Dear God, who was this man? She might have been looking at Fitzwilliam's mirror image, but through a cracked glass that distorted the reflection.

He was still talking, saying something about running away, and a missing bridegroom, and Gretna Green...

Gretna Green. The vowels lengthened in his mouth, and his tongue wrapped around the r's in a distinct Scottish burr. That lilt in his deep, smoky voice made her shiver, as if musical notes were darting down her spine.

He was Scottish. A Scotsman who looked just like Fitzwilliam.

What was happening? She'd never laid eyes on this man before. Fitzwilliam hadn't ever breathed a word about having family in Scotland, but it was beyond comprehension two men could be mirror images of each other without being related.

Indeed, they looked so much alike, it was impossible not to think they were...

Brothers.

She shook her head, trying to clear it. "I don't...it doesn't make sense," she muttered, dazed.

"He told you he loved you to get you to come with him to Gretna Green, didn't he, lass? But now he's gone and left you, hasn't he?"

Questions were tumbling through Juliana's mind, knocking everything about and leaving wreckage in their wake, but for some reason, this caught her attention. It penetrated the haze of shock, and a suspicion began to take hold.

Missing bridegroom...left her...Gretna Green...

Oh, no. This Scottish version of Fitzwilliam thought she was a runaway bride!

Well, how absurd. That is, she was aware she wasn't looking her best at the moment. Her hair was a nest of tangles, her riding habit was creased and dusty, and even the fresh air couldn't disguise the unpleasant aroma hanging over her like a noxious cloud. Even so, it was ungentlemanly in him to make such an assumption, no matter if she *was* at Gretna Green.

Juliana drew herself up and fixed him with the most dignified look a lady with vomit on her boots could manage. "Left me? No! I'm not a—" she began, but then clapped her mouth shut before she could do something stupendously foolish.

Like tell him the truth.

Perhaps I am a runaway bride, after all.

Fitzwilliam had a brother. By the looks of it, a twin brother. A twin brother who must know where he was, and who even now was likely on his way to Inverness, and from there, to Castle Kinross. She could ask him to take her along with him. That would be the simplest approach, but instinct held her back. Fitzwilliam's brother or not, Juliana didn't know or trust this man, and she hadn't the least intention of putting herself under his protection. She'd come too far to risk making a mistake now.

Still, this giant Scot was a precious gift, and he'd just fallen right into her lap. She intended to seize it—him—before he could slip through her fingers. She cast a frantic gaze around the inn yard, praying like she'd never prayed before that she'd find...yes! Thank goodness. There was Stokes, just coming out of the stables. "There's my husband now."

She bit her lip as Stokes inched his way across the inn yard. Oh, dear. He didn't look much like an eager bridegroom. He was hobbling along as if his gout were bothering him again, and even from this distance it was plain to see he was old enough to be her father.

"*Him?*" The man's tone was incredulous, but at this point Juliana didn't care if he found her pretend marriage scandalous. She only cared he *leave* so she and Stokes could follow him straight to Castle Kinross.

"Yes, indeed. He's, ah...that is, we're husband and wife."

A pair of dark brows too elegant for that rugged face drew together over his eyes. He gave her a long, measuring look. "Beg your pardon then, madam."

He bowed, and turned away with the sort of shrug generally reserved for stubborn children and barking dogs. Ah, good. He'd clearly washed his hands of her, just as she'd hoped he would.

Juliana kept an eye on him as he mounted a towering gray stallion. As soon as he rode out of the inn yard, she ran to meet Stokes. "Quickly, Stokes! Go back to the stables and secure two horses for us."

Stokes gaped at her as if she'd lost her wits. "I thought we were staying the night!"

"No, there's no time. I'll explain it all once we're on our way. Go on, hurry, while I run upstairs and have a word with Miss Findlay."

Stokes hurried off toward the stables while Juliana ran upstairs. She returned a few moments later to find him in the inn yard, waiting for the ostler to bring them fresh horses.

When he saw her, he shook his head. "You don't expect Miss Findlay to mount and ride today, I hope."

"No, she can't. I'm afraid she'll have to stay behind." Juliana didn't like to leave her companion alone at the King's Head Inn. Findlay was upset, and it wasn't proper for Juliana to travel without her. Then again, worrying about propriety at this point was rather like buffing a pair of riding boots stained with vomit—a wasted effort.

Poor Findlay was in no shape to chase a vigorous Scotsman from Gretna Green to Inverness. Juliana had no choice but to leave her behind with funds to hire a private coach to take her back to London.

As for her and Stokes...

For most people it was a four-day ride from Gretna Green to Inverness, but Fitzwilliam's brother looked as if he could do it in three. There was no way they'd be able to keep up with him in the coach. No, they had no choice but to do it on horseback, and take care he didn't notice they were following him.

It was going to be a long three days.

Still, for the first time since this ill-conceived journey began, hope unfolded in Juliana's breast. At last, everything was falling right into its proper place.

* * * *

If she hadn't smelled of vomit, Logan might not have noticed her at all.

If the wind had been blowing to the south rather than the north, or if she'd been standing a few feet further from the doorway, he would have passed by her without a second glance. It wasn't as if she was the first runaway bride he'd seen at the King's Head Inn. They all stopped here, the guilty bridegrooms and their ill-gotten spouses.

He'd been dismayed the first few times he'd noticed the brides, especially when they were weeping. It was a six-day journey from London to Gretna Green—more than enough time for a young lady to come to regret her clandestine marriage. Red eyes and tear-stained cheeks weren't an uncommon sight at the King's Head.

Like most men, Logan found a lady's tears deeply alarming, but he'd been back and forth between Scotland and England so many times these past few years, he hardly noticed the brides anymore.

But he noticed *her*.

She wasn't crying.

The unmistakable smell of vomit was surprising enough to make Logan pause to glance at her, but it was the absence of tears on that pale cheek that made him stop. What sort of lady was distressed enough to cast up her accounts, but not so distressed she couldn't squeeze out a single tear?

He didn't have time to spare for some foolish chit who'd wasted herself on a scoundrel, yet he found himself wandering closer to get a better look at her. English, of course—they always were. Fair hair, a delicate, heart-shaped face, stubborn chin. Her blue riding habit was creased and dirty, and yes, just as he'd suspected, she was the source of the sour smell. The hems of her skirts were stained with what looked suspiciously like someone's breakfast.

That she *was* a runaway bride was beyond question, but she was the most composed runaway bride he'd ever seen. Expensively dressed, too. Her riding habit looked as if it were worth a small fortune.

Or it had been, before she'd vomited on it.

An heiress then, lured into a Gretna Green marriage by some fortune hunter, though for a lady who'd been seduced and ruined, she was remarkably calm.

Logan glanced around the inn yard, but the lucky bridegroom was nowhere to be seen. No servant, either. He waited, but no one approached her.

It was damned odd, but it wasn't his concern, and he didn't have time to stand about and wait for the mystery to unravel itself. She didn't seem at all worried about her situation, so he didn't see any reason why *he* should be.

He turned away from her with a shrug and went to his horse, but his arse had hardly hit the saddle before he turned back for another glance at her.

She hadn't stirred a single step, and she was still alone.

Logan sighed, a curse leaving his lips as he dismounted. Damned if he knew why he should care what happened to the girl, but he had a weakness for creatures in need. Stray dogs, injured sheep, sick children, and now, apparently, runaway brides.

She hadn't noticed him the first time he passed, but this time he strode straight toward her. She saw him at once, and her eyes went wider and wider as he drew closer. They looked as if they'd swallow her pale face, the way the tender new grass swallowed the last patches of winter snow.

Green eyes.

Not just any green, he realized with a jolt of awareness, but an unusually bright green, like a spring leaf lit by the sun.

No doubt those eyes are what got her seduced in the first place.

Logan was so distracted by the color of her eyes he didn't notice at first that her body had gone rigid, and she was gazing at him in shock—far more shock than the situation called for.

He paused a few feet away from her, confused. "Are you all right, lass? Can I help you?"

Her mouth opened, then closed again. Color flooded her cheeks, and Logan saw she was shaking.

What the devil?

She'd been calm enough a moment earlier, but now she seemed to be fighting off a sudden panic. The flush in her cheeks receded as quickly as it had surged, and she was staring up at him as if she'd seen a ghost. Did she think he was going to hurt her? Logan held up his hands, palms out, to show her he didn't intend to touch her. "Miss? Is your husband nearby?"

She raised stricken eyes to his. She didn't reply, but managed a quick shake of her head.

No husband? What the devil was she doing in Gretna Green without a husband, or even a servant to attend her? Unless…

Was it possible the blackguard had already abandoned her? "Has he left you behind?"

This time she didn't appear to hear him. Her gaze was moving frantically over his face, as if she were mesmerized by his features. Logan wasn't sure what to make of this strange behavior, other than to assume she had indeed been abandoned, and the shock had addled her wits.

He tried a few more questions, but none of them elicited a coherent response. She only gazed up at him as if she couldn't credit her own eyes, until finally she murmured, "I don't…this doesn't make sense."

Ah! So, those dainty pink lips could form words, after all. He'd begun to wonder if they were merely decorative. Still, dull-wit or not, the lady was confused, and so he took care to speak gently to her. "He told you he loved you to get you to come with him to Gretna Green, didn't he, lass? Now he's gone and left you, hasn't he?"

This caught her wandering attention. Her wide green eyes went even wider, and her brow lowered. "Left me? No! I'm not—" she began, but before Logan could find out what ailed the chit she broke off, biting her lip.

Not what? Sane? Possessed of her wits?

Logan waited with as much patience as he could muster, but he never got an answer. In the next instant she caught sight of something over his shoulder and exclaimed, "There's my husband now!"

Logan turned, but the man she indicated was at least thirty years her senior, and dressed like a servant. "*Him?*"

"Yes, indeed. He's, ah…that is, we're husband and wife." Her words came out in a rush, as if she wished to be rid of them.

Rid of *him*, as well.

Logan, who'd begun to regret approaching her in the first place, was more than ready to oblige her. "Beg your pardon then, madam." He bowed, then strode out of the stable yard. Within minutes he was mounted, and riding away from the King's Head Inn, still shaking his head.

What an odd encounter.

Then again, Gretna Green was just the place one would expect to find a young lady who'd run off with her much older servant. Logan had seen more than one strange thing at the King's Head.

He doubted the green-eyed lady would be the last.

Chapter Two

Three days later
The Sassy Lassie, Inverness, Scotland

By the time Logan reined in his horse in front of the Sassy Lassie, the last thing on his mind was the green-eyed lady from the King's Head Inn. What *was* on his mind was a hot dinner, and a tankard of Fergus's special dark brown ale.

The past three days had been brutal. It was hotter and drier than early summer in the Highlands should be, and Logan's nose and throat were so coated with dust he would have sworn he'd come through a sandstorm.

As if that weren't enough to annoy a man, his horse had thrown a shoe several miles back. Fingal had been in a mood over it ever since, and when Fingal was in a mood he made sure Logan was aware of his displeasure. He'd been fretting and tossing his head since they left Bogbain, and Logan was ready to tear his hair out in frustration.

He was in a foul mood, and the mass of sweaty, smelly bodies crowding the inn's entryway didn't improve his temper. Where the devil had all these people come from? It was well past the dinner hour. Shouldn't these weary travelers have found their beds by now?

He leapt down from the saddle with a sigh, led his horse to the stables, then went off in search of Fergus McLaren, the inn's proprietor. Fergus had been a loyal friend of Logan's father, and he'd known Logan since he was too small to see out the bow windows.

Logan found him just outside the front door to the inn. He was scolding the ostlers for the delay in clearing the confusion of carriages and horses crowding the yard. His grizzled gray eyebrows rose when he saw Logan approaching. "That you, Logan? Good Lord, lad, ye look like ye been dragged through a knothole."

"Feel like it, too."

"Been in York again, have ye?"

"Aye." It was the second time he'd made the journey this year. He'd concluded his business, and he was happy enough to put England behind him.

Fergus spat on the ground. "Bloody nuisance."

Logan didn't argue the point. It *had* been a bloody nuisance, but it had been worth it. He'd been trying for months to persuade Alistair Campbell's widow to take her two sons south into York. They were both strapping lads and would find work easily, but Bonnie Campbell hadn't liked to leave the only home she'd ever known.

Logan didn't like it either, but neither did he like to see his clanswoman brutally evicted by a greedy landlord. Bonnie Campbell had a sister in York. She and her boys would be better off there. So, Logan had paid the necessary premium to secure an apprenticeship with a York apothecary for Angus Campbell, Bonnie's eldest son. It was a good start for the boy, and Bonnie had promised Logan if he could arrange it, she'd relocate to York for Angus's sake.

"I've not got much use for York, myself. London, neither." Fergus's mouth twisted with disdain. "Nothing but Englishmen there."

Logan grunted his agreement. "Any letters, Fergus?"

"Aye. I'll fetch 'em for ye. Go on into the parlor, and Alison will bring 'em."

Fergus shuffled off, and Logan made his way to the inn's private parlor. One of the serving lasses came with a glass of ale, and he drained it at once. He sent her off for another, then dropped into a chair to wait for Fergus's daughter Alison to bring him his letters.

His letters, and Fitz's, too. Ever since Fitz had appeared on his doorstep, Logan had taken it upon himself to collect *all* the letters sent to Castle Kinross. He had reason to congratulate himself on his foresight, if not his honesty.

He'd dreaded the task—had cringed every time he'd seen that thick, cream-colored paper, the daub of red wax. But now, for the first time in months, he waited with tolerable composure. God knew Fitz had thrown everything into a bloody mess when he arrived, but there hadn't been a word from Surrey since the last flurry of letters several weeks ago.

She's given up at last...

The serving girl appeared, slapped down a second tankard of ale in front of him, and bobbed a quick curtsy. Logan nodded his thanks and raised the tankard to his lips, but just as he was about to take a long draught, he was interrupted by a feminine drawl.

"Well, Logan Blair. Here ye are at last, snug as ye please, as if ye haven't been neglecting me these four weeks and more."

Logan lowered his glass, and a grin curved his lips at the sight of the girl leaning against the door jamb. "Hello, Alison."

"Hello Alison, he says." She tossed her mane of long dark hair over her shoulder. "Is that all ye have to say to me, Logan Blair?"

Her tone was scolding, but Logan could see the smile hovering at the corner of her lips. His own grin widened in response. "Tell me what to say, lass, and I'll say it."

Alison straightened away from the door and came toward him, swaying her hips as she walked. "Say ye missed me, ye half-wit. Say yer heart broke a little more every day we were apart."

Logan laughed. "I say any of that and your father will run me off with a pitchfork."

Alison McLaren was the eldest of Fergus's five girls, and according to Fergus she was the one most likely to send him into an early grave. Logan reckoned Fergus was probably right. The girl was far too pretty for any father's comfort, and to make matters worse, she was an incorrigible flirt.

"Ah well, then." Alison dropped a small bundle of letters onto the table in front of him, then flounced her way back over to the door. "If ye're not willing to risk a pitchfork to the ribs, then ye're not worthy of me, Logan Blair." She winked at him, then disappeared through the door with a final swish of her skirts.

Logan was still grinning when he reached for the bundle of letters, but just as he was about to pluck them up his smile faded, and his hand stilled over the packet.

There, at the top of the pile, was a letter on heavy, cream-colored paper, sealed with a neat daub of dark red wax. Across the front, the direction was written in dainty, feminine script.

His Grace Fitzwilliam Vaughn, the Duke of Blackmore, care of the Sassy Lassie, Inverness, Scotland.

Logan stared down at the elegant missive as if it were a coiled snake about to strike, then snatched it up, a dark cloud of foreboding descending on him as he held the corner of it pinched between his fingers.

There was every chance it was nothing. A harmless letter with an account of her recent marriage, or a simple query as to the recipient's health.

Logan was not the recipient, but that didn't stop him from breaking the wax, smoothing the paper flat against the table, and reading the dozen or so lines scrawled across the page. He read through it once, and then once again before he rose from his chair, crossed the room, and tossed it into the fireplace.

The letter was brief, but Lady Juliana Bernard didn't need more than a dozen lines to throw everything into chaos.

* * * *

"For pity's sake, Stokes, I already said I'd be careful. He won't even know I'm there, I promise you."

Lady Juliana glared up at Stokes, her arms crossed over her chest. It was times like these when she wished he'd behave less like an overprotective uncle and more like a servant.

"How can you be sure he won't see you?" Stokes's nose twitched. "Or—forgive me, my lady—smell you?"

Juliana sighed. Who would have guessed the smell of vomit could linger with such persistence? Even three days of hard riding hadn't managed to disperse it. Other smells had been layered over it, of course, but that could hardly be said to have improved matters.

In short, she smelled like an overflowing chamber pot.

Still, she was inclined to be optimistic. They'd trailed their quarry all the way to Inverness without him having the slightest idea they were following him, and now they were closing in on Castle Kinross.

It was near here. She could feel it.

"I'll stay downwind of him," she said, bringing her attention back to Stokes.

He grimaced. "Ten miles downwind? I don't understand why you need to see him at all. Why can't we just wait here until he comes out? It worked well enough at the other inns."

It had indeed, but she hadn't sent dozens of letters to any of those other inns. She'd sent them to the Sassy Lassie, and now she was here, she wanted a look inside the place. Perhaps they'd used her letters to paper their walls. It would explain why Fitzwilliam hadn't answered most of them. "Now we're so close, I don't like to let him out of my sight."

"I don't like to let *you* out of my sight."

Naturally he didn't, and she couldn't really blame him. Like her father, Stokes thought ladies were best suited to dancing, shopping, and paying calls, not running about all over Scotland and darting in and out of public inns.

Stokes wanted to protect her, but this journey had proved to her she was capable of far more than she'd ever imagined she was. She'd come nearly six hundred miles, the last third of those on horseback, chasing a man three times her size. She'd been blinded by the relentless sun, had her toe crushed under a horse's hoof, and swallowed at least a pint of dust. She'd been vomited on, for pity's sake.

Now, against all odds, she was on the verge of finding Fitzwilliam.

Juliana laid her hand on Stokes's arm. "I've made it this far."

Stokes glanced down at her in surprise, but then he smiled and shook his head. "So you have, my lady."

After that he ceased his grumbling and went off to the stables to see to their horses, leaving her to do as she wished.

Juliana glanced around the yard. No one was paying her the least bit of attention, so she walked over to the inn's entryway and peered around the corner. There was no sign of their quarry, but quite a number of people were bustling about, so she ducked in among them, kept her head down, and made it to a long hallway just in time to see a serving maid carry a tankard of ale through a door on the left.

A private parlor?

She waited for the serving girl to return, then crept down the hallway. Fortunately, the girl had left the door open a crack. When Juliana peeked through it she saw their dark-haired prey lounging in a chair with his long legs sprawled out. An empty tankard of ale sat on the table in front of him.

A vague feeling of disappointment washed over her. She wasn't sure what she'd been expecting to find, but certainly something more interesting than a man innocently refreshing himself. Still, she had no intention of letting him out of her sight. She wanted to be mounted on a fresh horse and waiting to follow him when he left the inn.

She took another peek, and this time she noticed a half-open window behind him that faced the back of the inn. Ah, perfect! She could see him easily from there, and with very little risk of him seeing her.

She hurried back down the hallway, through the front door, and around the side of the building to the back. As she drew closer she noticed a low murmur of voices floating through the open window. When Juliana peeked through it, she saw the man had company now.

A dark-haired girl stood in the doorway, a flirtatious smile on her lips, and a packet of letters in her hand.

Juliana's breath left her lungs in a sudden whoosh. There was no reason for her to think anything was amiss—they were only letters, after all—but for some reason the sight of that packet made every muscle in her body tense.

She rose to her tiptoes and squinted through the glass to get a better look at it, but the girl held the packet tucked against her side. She made no move to hand it over, and Juliana let out an impatient huff as the girl continued to stand there, talking and fluttering her eyelashes at the man. For his part, he seemed in no hurry to send her away. Juliana could hear a teasing note in his deep voice when he spoke to her, and when her gaze moved to his face she saw he was grinning.

Juliana rolled her eyes. For pity's sake, must they flirt *now*, when she was dying of curiosity to get a look at those letters? It was excessively tedious of them.

Finally, just when Juliana was ready to leap through the window and grab the packet herself the girl stepped forward, dropped the letters onto the table, and with a final playful flick of her skirts, left the room.

He turned his attention to the packet then, but just as he was about to take it up he paused, an odd, frozen look on his face as he stared down at it. Before Juliana could tell what that look meant, he reached for the packet, plucked one of the letters from the stack, and dropped the rest back onto the table.

Juliana's eyes widened.

Cream-colored paper, red sealing wax, and across the front, her handwriting...

It was the last letter she'd written to Fitzwilliam, right before she left Surrey for Scotland.

Relief washed over Juliana. He hadn't been ignoring her, then. He simply hadn't received the letter yet. It didn't explain why he hadn't answered the others, but—

But she soon had that explanation, as well.

Juliana watched through the window as the man broke the seal, opened a letter clearly *not* addressed to him, and as cool as you please, read the entire thing.

How *dare* he? Her mouth fell open, and she was seconds away from banging on the window when the man rose with her letter in his hand, and...

Juliana gasped.

Tossed it into the fire.

Then he snatched up the rest of the letters, shoved them into his coat pocket, and left the room.

Juliana remained outside the window for long moments, her hands clenched into fists, unable to stir a step. She could hardly believe what she'd just seen.

He'd burned her letter! Why, the man was a thief, a scoundrel, and a blackguard! Tears of rage filled her eyes, but she blinked them away and ran back toward the inn yard. She was intent on finding Stokes at once, but when she rounded the side of the building, she was obliged to duck back out of sight again.

The letter-thief was standing just on the other side, the inn proprietor with him.

"A favor, if you would, Fergus," the man murmured, so low Juliana had to strain to hear him.

"Aye, Logan. What can I do?"

Logan. So that was the scoundrel's name.

He led the older man away from the knot of people bustling about the entrance to the inn, closer to where Juliana was pressed against the side of the building.

"A lady may come here, asking for the way to Castle Kinross. See to it she doesn't find it."

An indignant hiss rose to Juliana's lips, and she had to slap her hand over her mouth to smother it.

"What sort of lady?" Fergus asked.

"English, and grand, most likely. I've no idea what she looks like, but I guess you'll recognize her easily enough. It's not as if there's dozens of aristocratic English ladies hanging about the Sassy Lassie."

"No, thank the Lord fer it. Those sorts are more trouble than they're worth." There was a pause, then the older man asked, "Problem with your duke, is there?"

Your duke...

He could only mean the Duke of Blackmore. Fitzwilliam was at Castle Kinross even now, and this hateful Logan was trying to keep her from seeing him!

"Won't be, as long as this lady doesn't find him. She comes here, tell her you never heard of the place, and send her back the way she came."

Juliana peeked around the corner and saw Fergus was shading his eyes from the last rays of the sun. "England's the best place for her, I reckon."

"There's no place for her at Castle Kinross, that's certain. You'll tell your people to keep quiet as well, aye?"

"Aye." Fergus's weathered face broke into a grin. "I warned ye not to get yourself a duke, lad. Now you got 'im, he's bringing all sorts of other odd ones your way. That's the way of it, with dukes."

"I wouldn't have taken him if I'd had a choice." Logan trudged over to his horse, shoved the packet of letters in his saddle bag, and swung up into the saddle. He kicked the big gray horse into motion, but then drew him to an abrupt halt again, and looked over his shoulder. "I don't want that English chit at Castle Kinross, Fergus. You'll take care to do as I asked?"

"Aye. I'll see to it."

Logan nodded and rode out of the stable yard. Juliana waited until Fergus went back inside, then she ran into the yard, hoping Stokes was waiting for her there.

He wasn't. Juliana swept a frantic gaze over the yard. Stokes was nowhere to be seen, but the horse she'd ridden into the Sassy Lassie was hitched to a post nearby, munching contentedly on some hay while she waited her turn in the stables.

Well, she'd have to wait a little longer.

Juliana hurried to the horse, took up her reins, and mounted. She hesitated only long enough to cast a single hopeful glance toward the stables, but Stokes didn't appear, and another anxious glance revealed the rapidly retreating figure of the scoundrel who'd just burned her letter.

Stokes was going to be beside himself when he found her gone, but she'd come back for him as soon as she could. He'd likely figure out what had happened, and anyway, there was no help for it. This might be her only chance to find Castle Kinross, and she didn't intend to lose it. If nothing else, she refused to let a vile blackguard like that Logan outsmart her.

"Go!" She tapped her heels lightly against her horse's flanks, and rode off in the direction he'd taken.

Juliana had always considered herself to be a practical lady, but she didn't allow herself to acknowledge all the reasons why it might not be wise to follow a strange man down a gloomy road, straight into the wilds of the Scottish Highlands.

Not just any strange man either, but a scoundrel. A thief. The sort of blackguard who didn't hesitate to rip open a letter not addressed to him, read it without so much as a by-your-leave, and without the faintest flush of guilt on his cheeks, consign it to a fiery grave.

Who the blazes did he think he was, trying to prevent her from reaching Fitzwilliam?

Logan. In the few letters she'd received from Fitzwilliam, he'd never mentioned that name to her. She didn't know the man, and she couldn't think of a single innocent reason why he'd be so determined to keep her and Fitzwilliam apart.

But she knew one thing beyond a shadow of a doubt. Fitzwilliam wasn't involved in it. He'd never do something so low—not to anyone, and especially not to her.

Whatever tricks this Logan was playing, Fitzwilliam didn't know a thing about it, and what's more, Logan wasn't going to get away with it. She was here now, and she didn't intend to leave without her betrothed. Grace's future depended on Juliana's securing a husband, and she would do so, no matter how many scoundrels she had to chase to make it happen.

She followed the man deeper and deeper into the countryside. Her determination to reach Castle Kinross never flagged, but as the ride dragged on into an hour, then an hour more, her energy did. It grew darker with every step they took—so dark, in fact, it took all of Juliana's concentration to keep track of the man in front of her. She dared not follow too closely behind him for fear he'd hear her horse's hooves trampling the dirt, but she also didn't dare to fall too far behind, in case she lost him entirely.

It had been easy enough to trail after a man on the public road, but it was much harder now she was obliged to be quiet. Horses were large, unwieldy animals, and this poor horse had been deprived of her rest at Inverness. As they plodded along, mile after mile, the horse's enthusiasm began to ebb. Juliana tried to soothe her with comforting caresses and murmurs, but at one point the horse let out a mournful whinny.

Logan, riding some distance ahead of them, came to a stop.

Juliana froze, her hand on the horse's neck to quiet her. She was too far back to see if he'd turned his head to search the darkness, or worse, if he was coming toward her. All she could do was remain as quiet as possible, her breath held as she listened for the sound of approaching hooves.

None came.

The silence persisted until at last Juliana allowed herself to gulp in a deep breath. He hadn't heard them creeping along behind him, after all. She was vastly relieved at it, but whatever comfort she felt vanished when she realized Logan had disappeared around a bend in the road, and she'd lost sight of him.

She urged her horse forward, her heart rushing into her throat. If she lost him, not only would it become impossible for her to discover Castle Kinross, but she would find herself out here alone in the Highlands. She'd been too focused on keeping up with Logan to mark her direction from the Sassy Lassie. She hadn't the faintest notion how to get back to Inverness.

At the very least, she'd be trapped here through the night.

Juliana didn't fancy a night alone in the pressing darkness of the Highlands. If hungry, wild animals lurked anywhere, it would be here.

She guided her horse around the bend and peered once again into the thick darkness before her, but she couldn't discern any shape or movement in the gloom. The man, Logan, seemed to have disappeared.

Apprehension raised the hairs on the back of her neck, but Juliana threw back her shoulders, straightening in the saddle. What nonsense. Men didn't simply disappear into the dark. He'd only pulled further ahead, that was all. She urged her horse forward again, this time with a bit more noise and haste than was perhaps prudent. Worse, her nervousness made her clumsy, and she flinched as the horse stumbled over an outcropping of rock.

She brought them to an abrupt halt. "Are you all right, sweet girl?"

But she already knew the answer. The horse was fatigued, and so was Juliana. Under such circumstances there was a high chance of injury to either one or both of them. She hadn't any other choice but to keep moving, but she couldn't charge forward without first checking to see if the horse had sustained some hurt.

She dropped the reins, threw a leg over the saddle, and prepared to jump down from the horse's back and check her legs for injury.

She never got the chance.

A long, hard arm snaked around her waist and jerked her from the saddle. Juliana let out a faint shriek and immediately began to kick and squirm to free herself, but it soon became clear she might as well have saved her energy.

Logan—for of course it was he, lying in wait for her—hauled her against a chest as hard and unyielding as a stone wall, and pinned her there with a pair of arms that felt like two iron bands squeezing her ribs.

"Sneaky bastard, aren't you?" His deep voice was heavy with menace. "But not sneaky enough."

Chapter Three

Logan had known for some time he was being followed.

A mile or so back he'd heard something—a horse's gentle snort, or a muffled nicker—and every one of his senses had sharpened in warning. He'd jerked Fingal to a quick halt and spun around in his saddle, but when he peered behind him he saw only darkness.

He waited, his ears pricked. He heard nothing, but Logan never doubted his instincts. The noise had attuned him to his surroundings, and he could sense someone was there, hidden by the darkness.

He hadn't heard them approach, and he didn't know from what direction they'd come, but now he knew they were there, he became aware they'd been following him for some time. He had a warning feeling in the pit of his stomach, one he'd long ago learned not to ignore.

The dusk was thickening, but Logan nudged his heels into his horse's flanks and eased Fingal into an easy trot, listening carefully for the sound of pursuit. Several long minutes passed in silence, but then he heard the faint thud of hooves hitting the dirt coming from behind him.

Whoever was following him was taking care to keep a careful distance between them, and that would be their downfall.

Logan and Fingal had trod this same pathway so many times before, they could easily find their way home in the dark. They knew every inch of turf between Inverness and Castle Kinross—every hill, every turn, and every outcropping of rock big enough for a mounted rider to hide behind.

His pursuer might know the road, but there was no way he knew it as well as Logan did. Logan simply had to get far enough ahead so the man would lose sight of him, then lie in wait, leap upon the scoundrel when he tried to pass, and drag him from his horse.

Careful not to show any haste that would betray him, Logan urged Fingal farther ahead of their pursuer, toward a curve in the road that wound sharply around a hill. Once they were on the far side, he dismounted, and waited. He didn't have to wait long.

The slow, hesitant hoofbeats drew closer, then so close Logan judged his pursuer was mere seconds from rounding the curve in the road...

A large, black shape emerged from the surrounding darkness. The rider, who was cautiously maneuvering the horse around the bend, didn't have a chance even to attempt an escape before Logan pounced. He snaked his arm around the rider's waist and with one hard jerk, dragged him from the saddle.

He was just about to throw the blackguard to the ground when a high-pitched scream made him freeze, his assailant still locked in his grip.

That scream. It had sounded almost as if—

"Unhand me at once, you...you...despicable villain!"

Even before the distinctly feminine cry met his ears, Logan realized something was amiss. The waist he'd grasped was far narrower than he'd anticipated, and the bundle now struggling in his arms weighed less than the saddle on the back of her horse.

Her horse.

His pursuer wasn't a man at all, but a woman, and judging by her slight weight and the soft curves pressed against his chest, she was a wee one at that.

Wee, and...pungent. Good Lord, she smelled even worse than he did, and after days of hard riding he smelled like the very devil. Still, it wasn't his practice to manhandle ladies, no matter if they did set his nostril hairs afire. "I'm not going to hurt you, lass," Logan said, tentatively loosening his grip on her waist.

It was a mistake. She began kicking and writhing like a rabid animal to escape him, and he was obliged to haul her higher against his chest and pin her there to prevent her from hurting both of them. "Be still, will you?"

"Go to the devil, you scoundrel!" she spat, digging her small fingers into his arm in a fruitless attempt to free herself.

Logan stifled a strange, sudden urge to laugh. She might be a tiny little thing, but she had a wicked mouth. "You were following me, *beag deomhan*. That makes *you* the scoundrel."

"Of course, I followed you! You made certain of that when you warned the innkeeper at the Sassy Lassie to conceal the location of Castle Kinross!"

Logan's head jerked back in shock. This wily little chit had been following him since Inverness, and he'd only just caught her? He was never so careless as that. He'd made a number of enemies over the past few years, and had good reason to stay aware of his surroundings. He'd outmaneuvered more than one blackguard intent on spilling his blood. How could this wee slip of a girl have managed to escape his notice?

Even more to the purpose, she must be desperate indeed to reach Castle Kinross if she'd follow a strange man into the isolated moors in the dark. "Who are you? What's your name?"

Her only answer was a furious huff, but she ceased her struggles, and after a moment she said, "Let me down, and I'll tell you."

"You'll tell me anyway, lass. You're not in a position to negotiate."

"No position to flee, either. If you do set me down, where do you suppose I'll go? It's dark, and I haven't the vaguest idea where I am."

Logan couldn't argue with that. After a moment's hesitation he lowered her carefully to her feet. She jerked free of him and her chin shot up, her furious gaze meeting his. As soon as he got a good look at her, his mouth fell open in shock. "You're the green-eyed chit from Gretna Green! The runaway bride!"

He stared at her, stunned. She hadn't followed him here from Inverness at all, but all the way from Gretna Green! It was a four days journey, but he'd made it in three on horseback. How the *devil* did a lady no sturdier than a hummingbird keep pace with him? She must hardly have slept in the past three days. Good God, she was a stealthy one, to have kept herself out of his sight for so long.

"How the devil did you manage to—" He broke off as something occurred to him. "What have you done with that old fellow...er, that is, what have you done with your husband?"

She gave him a scathing look. "You don't mean to say you believed he was really my husband?"

"Why wouldn't I? You said so, and I've seen stranger things. Beyond that, I didn't give it much thought. If he's not your husband, then who is he? More to the point, lass, *where* is he?"

She bit her lip. "He's my servant, of course. I left him at the Sassy Lassie in Inverness."

Logan raised his eyebrows. "He let you go off alone?"

A guilty look crossed her face. "Not exactly. He, ah...well, there wasn't time for me to tell him. I'll ride back to Inverness tomorrow and bring him back with me."

"You're saying you left your manservant without a word of explanation to tear off into the dark, alone, after a man you spoke to once? You must be eager to speak to me, to have taken such a risk."

She moved a step closer to him. "Very eager. You see, I need—"

"Sorry, lass. I can't help you with that," Logan said, shaking his head.

Her brow wrinkled. "What do you mean? I haven't even asked for your help yet."

"I'm not looking for a bride. The best thing you can do is head back to Inverness, collect your manservant, and get on back to England and beg your father's mercy."

Her mouth dropped open, and her cheeks flushed red. "For pity's sake! You think I came all this way because I want to marry *you*? Why you arrogant, conceited...No. You *must* be jesting."

"I can't think of any other reason you'd come so far."

She crossed her arms over her chest. "Can't you? Very well, then. I'd be grateful indeed if you'd explain to me how you reached such a startling conclusion."

Logan shrugged. "Some rake seduced you, lured you to Gretna Green, then took to his heels before you could get him up to scratch. I was kind to you, so you followed me, hoping I'd take the job."

She stamped her foot. "That's the most ridiculous thing I've ever heard!"

"It wouldn't be the first ridiculous thing to happen at Gretna Green. Just a few months ago some old English lord or other disguised himself as a woman to fool his grown children, and eloped with his housekeeper to Gretna Green. He was even wearing a bonnet..."

Her face was growing redder with every word out of his mouth. Logan wisely trailed off into silence.

"I've never heard such nonsense in my life. Of all the foolish, outrageous notions!" She paced back and forth, throwing her hands about and muttering to herself. At last she drew in a few deep breaths, and when she turned to face him again she was more composed. "I can assure you, sir, I wouldn't even follow you across a *street*, much less across half of Scotland! Indeed, you're the last man in the world I'd ever consider marrying."

Logan's lips twitched. "Not the *very* last. I'd wager you'd marry me before you would your manservant. I'm flattered, lass."

It wasn't at all funny, and it was never a good idea to tease a lady who was in a temper. Logan knew that well enough, but all at once the situation struck him as so ludicrous, he couldn't help himself. Here they were, two strangers, standing on the Scottish moors in the dark, arguing about which of them least wanted to marry the other. What else was there to do but laugh?

His companion didn't find it as amusing as he did. Not a flicker of humor crossed her face, and her green eyes were cold. "You're wrong. I'd marry him in a heartbeat if I had to choose between you. Stokes is an honorable man, and you're nothing but a thief."

Logan's grin vanished. He *was* a thief, and a liar too. The question was, how could some English chit he'd never laid eyes on before know it? "Oh? What did I steal, lass?"

She shot him an accusing look. "You stole my letter. I saw you through the window at the Sassy Lassie. It wasn't addressed to you, but you took it, you read it, and then you tossed it into the fire."

Logan stared at her, unable to utter a word. No, it was impossible. Except she'd clearly said "her letter." *Her* letter.

He'd only burned one letter when he'd been in Inverness.

The letter Lady Juliana Bernard had written to Fitz.

Logan had spent the better part of the ride from Inverness to Castle Kinross arguing with himself about that letter. A month ago, Fitz had received a letter from a friend in Surrey, and the man had mentioned Lady Juliana had become betrothed to some English marquess or other. That she'd found another gentleman to marry didn't excuse Logan's crime, but when his conscience pricked at him, he'd relieved the worst of his guilt by reminding himself she hadn't come to any harm because of what he'd done.

Then he'd read her letter today and discovered not only *wasn't* she married, but she was on her way to Scotland to claim Fitz.

Leaving Surrey on...arrive in Inverness in...keep your promise...

Had his dear brother Fitz promised to marry Lady Juliana Bernard if she came to Castle Kinross? If he had, he must have been urging her to make the journey in his earliest letters to her, before Logan started intercepting the correspondence between them.

If he hadn't been so distracted by that bloody letter, he might have realized sooner that someone was following him.

Not just *someone*...

He met her gaze. "What's your name?"

"I think you know very well who I am."

He did know, yet even as she stood before him, her green eyes flashing fire, he could hardly credit the evidence of his own eyes. He wanted to hear her say it.

"We had an agreement, lass," he murmured, moving a step closer to her. "I've set you down as you bid me. Now, what's your name?"

She raised her chin. "Lady Juliana Bernard."

Lady Juliana Bernard. The author of all those cream-colored letters, with the Marquess of Graystone's crest stamped into the red wax.

Fitz's betrothed, and the future Duchess of Blackmore.

At least, she had been once. Not any longer.

In the letter, she'd told Fitz she was coming to Scotland to find him, but as Logan had made his way over the moors tonight he'd come up with a dozen different arguments in his head as to why that would never happen. It was nearly six hundred miles from London to Castle Kinross. English heiresses didn't simply hop into carriages and travel hundreds of miles to retrieve their betrothed.

Even if she did take it into her head to scurry off to Scotland, the fact that she didn't know precisely where to find Castle Kinross should have deterred her. It wasn't more than twenty miles from Inverness, but the castle was tucked into a remote part of the moors, on the edge of Beauly Firth. It wasn't the sort of place one stumbled upon, least of all some English lass who'd likely never laid eyes on Scottish land in her life.

But then she'd solved that problem neatly enough, hadn't she? No wonder she'd seemed so dull-witted at Gretna Green. She'd been in shock. She must have known the moment she laid eyes on him it couldn't be a coincidence he looked so much like the Duke of Blackmore.

She'd been quick to capitalize on her good luck.

He stared down at her, not sure what to make of her. She looked like she should be sitting in a drawing room sipping tea, or lounging on a tufted silk settee, sketching baskets of kittens, or dancing a waltz in some stuffy English ballroom. Instead, Lady Juliana Bernard was here on the Scottish moors in the dark with a stranger, defiance written in every line of her perfect face. If he hadn't seen her with his own eyes, Logan never would have believed it.

Not many aristocratic English ladies would undertake a journey of ten days or more to chase her errant betrothed so far when she could have another marquess or earl with a snap of her pretty fingers. Lady Juliana was an heiress, after all, and there was nothing the English nobility loved more than money.

Unless it was a title.

Fitz could give her both.

Was there a chance Lady Juliana might venture so far if she believed Fitz would make her a duchess at the end of her journey? She must believe he'd marry her if she came to Scotland. No sane woman chased a man hundreds of miles unless she expected to become his wife at the end of it.

Well, there could be no question of Fitz's marrying Lady Juliana *now*. Still, an aristocratic lady of the sort Logan imagined Lady Juliana must be—that is, a lady accustomed to having her own way in all things—

would no doubt kick up some dust when she discovered her ambition had been thwarted.

"Who are you?" she asked suddenly. "Fitzwilliam is staying with you, you have access to his letters, and you look just like him. So much alike you must be his brother, but I've known Fitzwilliam all my life, and he's never said a word about having a brother. I've certainly never laid eyes on you before."

Logan didn't see any point in withholding his name from her. He had no choice but to take her to Castle Kinross now. Once they were there, the entire truth would come out.

"Logan Blair." *Laird of Clan Kinross.* The title rose automatically to Logan's lips, but he bit it back. He wasn't the laird anymore. Or, more accurately, he never had been. That title belonged to Fitz. Fitz was the elder of the two of them, by eighteen minutes. Incredible how much difference a mere eighteen minutes could make in a man's life.

"Well, Logan Blair, only a blackguard would steal a lady's private letter, read it, then toss it into the fire." She paused, then murmured to herself, "Though I'd rather it was that than Fitzwilliam ignoring me."

Her voice caught a little, and it occurred to Logan there was one other reason a lady might travel six hundred miles to retrieve her betrothed.

Love.

It was the simplest explanation of all. Love could move a certain type of lady to a greater degree of courage than either a fortune or a title ever could.

Whether Lady Juliana was such a lady or not…well, he'd find out soon enough, wouldn't he? He took in her disheveled hair, her creased, dusty gown, her ruined boots. She was a dainty little thing. Very English, with that pale skin, fair hair, and an angelic, heart-shaped face.

A perfect English rose, a belle, a diamond of the first water. In short, she was just what he'd imagined she would be.

Then again, how many belles rode from Gretna Green to Inverness with vomit on their boots? Then there were her eyes. They were too bright, too intelligent, and too apt to flash with temper for Lady Juliana to be mistaken for anything other than what she was.

A lady of courage, of spirit.

Right now, those eyes were narrowed on him, subjecting him to much the same inspection to which he was subjecting her. To Logan's surprise, he found himself wondering what Lady Juliana Bernard saw when she looked at him. Fitzwilliam's brother? A rough Scot with travel-stained clothes, wild hair, and lines of exhaustion bracketing his mouth?

But then she'd already told him what she thought of him.

A thief, a scoundrel, a despicable villain...

For the first time since this business with the letters began, real regret landed in the pit of Logan's stomach.

He hadn't chosen for the Duke of Blackmore to marry an Englishwoman, particularly not Lord Graystone's daughter. So, he'd set about making sure it didn't happen. He'd told himself he had far more serious concerns than some spoiled English chit who could have any man in London for the asking, but was in a temper at having lost the chance to marry a duke. He told himself he was doing what he must to protect his clan.

He'd been content enough with that reasoning at the time, but that was before he'd thought of Lady Juliana Bernard as anything more than an heiress, and the daughter of the bloody Marquess of Graystone. Before he'd been obliged to look into her eyes.

Six hundred miles was a long way to come to be disappointed.

But disappointed she would be, and bitterly so. If Lady Juliana had come all this way because she was in love with Fitz, then she'd end this night with a broken heart.

"You're a villain, Mr. Blair, but I've come this far, and I've no other choice but to rely on you now. I demand you take me to Fitzwilliam at Castle Kinross at once."

Logan had taken great pains to see to it Lady Juliana Bernard never set foot in Castle Kinross. He didn't want her anywhere near his home or his family, but he could hardly leave her out here alone on the dark moors. Fitz would be furious, and Logan's own sense of honor forbade it. He'd fought to keep her away, but she'd fought harder, and here she was.

He hated to admit it, but she'd earned the right to be taken to Castle Kinross.

"It's another half hour's ride." He went to her horse, nodding at her to mount while he held the reins.

She shot him a distrustful look, as well she might. "You'll take me with you, then?"

"I've not much choice, have I? I can't leave you here. Fitz won't like it."

"Fitzwilliam is there, then? At Castle Kinross?"

Logan waited while she mounted, then lifted himself onto his own horse's back. "You've come all this way not to be sure of even that much, my lady. Determined to become a duchess, are you?"

She didn't answer, or even look at him, but her face paled, and Logan immediately wished the words back.

They rode for some time in silence, but then a thought occurred to him, and he turned back to her. "Your father, Lord Graystone. Does he know where you are?" Having Lord Graystone appear at the door of Castle Kinross was, above all, the last thing Logan wanted.

"No. My father is in Bath, taking the waters. He believes me to be in Buckinghamshire with friends."

So, she'd ridden off to the Highlands of Scotland without her father's permission, or his knowledge. For such a proper lady, Lady Juliana seemed to tell a great many lies.

"Perhaps Fitzwilliam will ride back to Inverness with me tomorrow," she said hopefully.

Logan gave a slight shake of his head, but he didn't say anything. Lady Juliana would find out for herself soon enough things weren't going to turn out as she hoped as far as Fitz was concerned.

Or perhaps they'd turn out just as she wished. Fitz might take one look at her, and do precisely as she asked him to do. Perhaps Logan would be the one who was surprised.

He wouldn't be the only one.

He cast a quick glance at her, uneasiness tightening his chest. She was beautiful, an English heiress, and one of Fitz's dearest friends. When he spoke of her—which was often—it was with the tenderest affection. She came from the world Fitz had grown up in, a world he understood, and she and Fitz had been promised to each other for most of their lives.

Logan's chest drew tighter as they made their way in the dark toward Castle Kinross. This was what came of lies, wasn't it?

His lies...

If a heart did break tonight, it might not be Lady Juliana's.

Chapter Four

"You look surprised, Lady Juliana. What did you expect to find in a Scottish castle? Drunken clansman on every sofa, and sheep running around the hallways?"

Logan Blair had been so quiet during their ride to Castle Kinross Juliana had nearly forgotten him until his mocking drawl interrupted her thoughts. She glanced at him, and found him regarding her with a sardonic half-smile on his lips.

Once her gaze alighted on his face, she found it difficult to look away. His eyes were a much more vibrant blue than she'd first thought, and heavily lashed with such a thick, dark fringe it was a wonder he could keep them open at all.

He wasn't the most handsome man she'd ever seen. His features were too strong, too aggressive to be deemed classically handsome, yet it was his very roughness that held her gaze. Logan Blair was a thief and a scoundrel, but there was no denying his was the sort of face that caught a lady's attention.

"Scots aren't quite the savages the English aristocracy thinks we are." That infuriating grin flirted at the corner of his mouth. "You can rest easy during your stay at Castle Kinross, my lady."

A sharp retort hovered on Juliana's tongue, but she held it back. He was a dreadful, teasing thing, and she was determined not to gratify him by falling into a temper. "I've never been to a Scottish castle before. I didn't know what to expect."

Whatever it was she *had* expected, it wasn't this.

The road leading up to the castle was dark and isolated. She'd thought the castle would be as gloomy and forbidding as the thick copse of towering elms they'd passed under, but as soon as they were free of the tree line she'd let out a gasp of pleased surprise.

Light poured from a row of windows on the ground floor. Mr. Blair ushered her through the arched doorway, and she found the entryway was no less pleasing. It had a massive wood-timbered ceiling, rich tapestries on the walls, and thick carpets covering a spotlessly clean stone floor.

Castle Kinross didn't boast a grand, curving drive or elegant stone columns flanking the front entrance, but the place had a friendly, welcoming look about it, in the way only places that had sheltered generations *could* have. One had only to glance at the staircase to imagine the dozens of feet that had trod up and down it, or curl one's hand around the doorknob to feel the hundreds of fingers that had grasped the worn iron.

It looked like a home.

Fitzwilliam would like it here.

Juliana knew it instinctively with a sinking sensation in her chest. She stood blinking up at the carved wood staircase, and thought perhaps he never intended to return to England at all.

She had to see him, to talk to him. It was the only way to relieve the unbearable anxiety she'd labored under these past five months. "I'd like to see Fitzwilliam at once, if I may," she said, turning to Mr. Blair. "I daresay he'll be shocked to see me, since he didn't receive my letter."

She'd intended to give him a set-down, but it seemed Logan Blair was impervious to shame, because he only raised an eyebrow at her waspish tone. "He won't be the only one who's shocked."

He glanced over her shoulder, and Juliana turned to find a butler with a headful of white hair coming toward the entryway.

"There you are, Craig. His Grace has a visitor. Fetch him, please, and bring him to the library." Mr. Blair paused and glanced at Juliana. "Once you've brought him down, Craig, wait in the hallway. His Grace may need you again."

"Yes, sir. Right away." The old man assisted Juliana out of her cloak, bowed, and shuffled back in the direction from which he'd come.

"This way, my lady." Logan Blair took her arm and led her down a long hallway and into an enormous library. "You must be fatigued. Please, sit down." He guided her to a leather chair so massive it nearly swallowed her, then crossed the room to a sideboard and removed the stopper from a crystal decanter. "Sherry? Or Madeira?"

"Neither, thank you." Juliana glanced around the room, trying to gather her wits. It had been nearly six months since Fitzwilliam left England—months of uncertainty and worry, followed by days of exhausting travel. She could hardly believe she was here at all, moments away from seeing him at last. She twisted her hands in her lap and prayed he'd be pleased to see her. Or if not pleased, then at least not angry—

"Here. Take it."

Juliana looked up to find Logan Blair standing beside her chair, holding out a tumbler to her. She shook her head. "No, I don't care for—"

"Take it, Lady Juliana."

He didn't say any more, but Juliana noticed a flicker of sympathy in his eyes. She reached for the tumbler with a shaking hand, her stomach suddenly heaving with dread. If a hard man like Logan Blair could feel compassion for her, then she must be a pitiable object, indeed.

She didn't like this man. He'd stolen her letter and lied to Fitzwilliam. He was a scoundrel and a blackguard, but he was *here*, and she couldn't bear to go another minute without knowing whatever bad news awaited her. She grasped his arm, her fingers clawing desperately at his coat sleeve. "Something's wrong, isn't it? Quickly, tell me what it is at once, before he—"

But it was already too late. The door to the library opened. Fitzwilliam's voice carried clearly through the room. "Where the devil have you been, Logan? I expected you back here well before the dinner hour…"

He trailed off into silence as his gaze alighted on Juliana. His face paled, and he seemed to freeze halfway across the room. Juliana took a moment to squeeze her eyes closed and pray for strength, then she rose unsteadily to her feet and held her hand out to him. "Fitzwilliam. I—I've missed you."

"Juliana? My God, it is really you? Where did you…how did you…"

Just when Juliana thought she must faint, the smile she remembered so well lit up every corner of Fitzwilliam's handsome face. Oh, how she loved his smile. How she'd missed it! She couldn't remember a time when his smile hadn't been a part of her life, and to see it now was like holding a memory of her childhood in the palm of her hand.

"Juliana." Fitzwilliam hurried across the room and clasped both her hands in his. "I can't believe you're here. Why didn't you write? Only let me look at you. Ah, yes. A little travel weary, but as beautiful as I remember. You can't know how much I've missed you, Lina, and how happy I am to see you!"

Tears sprang to Juliana's eyes at the unmistakable affection in his voice, and his use of her childhood nickname. It felt as if a dozen lifetimes had passed since anyone had called her that. Her brother Jonathan and her dear friend Emma had used the nickname as well, but now Fitzwilliam was the only one left who ever called her Lina. "You're not angry I'm here, then?"

His face softened at the sight of her tears. "Angry? No. How could I be? Oh, don't cry, Lina! I only wonder you came such a long way without writing first."

Juliana shot Mr. Blair a dark look, but she didn't say a word about her stolen letter. She likely would have made it to Castle Kinross before her letter did, even if Logan Blair hadn't burned it. There didn't seem to be much point in fussing over it now. She had no idea why he'd taken it, or why he wanted to keep her from finding Castle Kinross, but there was a great deal going on here she didn't understand. Until she had the whole story from Fitzwilliam, she'd keep quiet about the letter.

"You haven't come alone?" An anxious frown clouded Fitzwilliam's brow. "Where is Lord Graystone? Surely your father must have accompanied you."

"My father?" Juliana shook her head, confused. Had Fitzwilliam not understood from her letters how dire the state of her father's health was? "No. He's in Bath, taking the waters."

"Taking the waters! Why should he? He's always been a picture of robust good health."

Juliana stared at him, a sudden chill rushing over her skin. She couldn't imagine how he could describe her father as robust after reading her letters. "I—I'm sorry. I thought I'd explained this, but perhaps I didn't...I might not have been..."

The color must have drained from her face, because Fitzwilliam took her arm and hurried her back to her chair. "It's all right, Lina. Sit down, take a deep breath, and tell me when you're ready."

Juliana struggled to catch her breath, but she was exhausted from her journey, worried about Stokes, and distressed over Logan Blair's treachery. The next thing she knew, she was blurting out the bad news. "My father is dying, Fitzwilliam. His friend Lord Arthur has taken him to Bath to try the waters, but the doctor warned us not to expect much improvement. I'm afraid it's quite hopeless."

Fitzwilliam went pale with shock. "But I don't understand this. How could he have deteriorated so quickly? He was healthy enough when I last saw him, and that was only a few months ago."

Juliana sighed. Fitzwilliam was fond of her father, and it would pain him to hear this. "He suffered a severe consumptive attack soon after you left. He recovered, but about a month ago he had another attack after returning from a trip to Buckinghamshire. Since then...well, you'd be shocked to see how feeble he's grown."

"Oh, no. Oh, Lina."

Tears threatened once again, and Juliana sucked in a deep breath to clear them from her throat. She and her father were both strong-willed, and they'd had a number of bitter arguments about Grace over the past few months, but he'd always been an affectionate parent, and she loved him dearly. "That's why I've come, you see. It's only a matter of time before I lose him, and I've got Grace to consider."

Fitzwilliam had taken her hands again. As soon as she mentioned Grace's name, his fingers tightened convulsively around hers. "Grace? What has she to do with this? Has something happened to her?"

Juliana had been fighting off a growing sense of dread since this conversation began, but it wasn't until Fitzwilliam mentioned Grace with such urgency that it swelled into full-blown panic.

She'd written to him weeks ago and told him all about her father's illness, Lord Cowden's threats, and Grace's situation. She'd been distressed, and her letters might not have been as coherent as she'd thought, but Fitzwilliam was behaving as if he were hearing all this for the first time.

Something is terribly wrong here...

He hadn't answered any of those letters. Not one.

She raised her gaze to Logan Blair. She couldn't explain why she needed to see his face, but some instinct made her seek him out. He was standing in front of the window, his back to them, his shoulders stiff. He'd withdrawn as soon as Fitzwilliam entered the room, but Juliana knew he was listening to every word that passed between them.

He didn't turn, and Juliana brought her gaze back to Fitzwilliam. "Nothing has happened to Grace yet, but it will if I can't find a way to stop it. I need your help, Fitz, rather urgently."

"Yes, of course. You know I'd do anything for you, Lina."

"My father is refusing to make me Grace's testamentary guardian as long as I remain unmarried." Juliana struggled to keep her voice steady. Whenever she thought of the fate that awaited Grace if she didn't secure a husband, her heart stuttered in her chest, and her entire body started trembling.

"You're not married? I thought...I had a letter from Lord Madsen several months ago, and he said you were betrothed to Lord Pierce."

Juliana stifled her groan. She'd been hoping he hadn't heard that particular piece of news, but she should have known better. She and Hugh hadn't announced their betrothal or had the banns read, but it seemed every person within ten miles of Graystone Court was intimately acquainted with her business nonetheless. "We were betrothed for a short time, yes, but he, ah...he isn't my husband. We didn't marry. He fell in love with another lady, and I couldn't bear to...well, she's lovely, and they're very happy together."

Fitzwilliam's face darkened. "You mean to say he jilted you?"

"No, no." The last thing she needed was for Fitzwilliam to fall into a fury over Lord Pierce. "Indeed, you can't blame Lord Pierce. He didn't jilt me. It was quite the opposite, really. I'm fond of him, as you know, and I couldn't bear to be the one who stood in the way of his marrying the lady he loved."

If she'd known what would happen when they returned to Graystone Court, she might not have taken such a romantic view of it. Those as desperate as she was had no business being generous.

Fitzwilliam was shaking his head, trying to make sense of it all. "Then you're not married?"

"No, I'm not, and I...I need to be, Fitzwilliam. As soon as possible. Otherwise I'm going to lose Grace."

All the color drained from Fitzwilliam's face. Juliana half-rose from her chair, alarmed. "Fitzwilliam? Are you all right?"

"Yes, of course. Perfectly well." He urged her back into her chair, but avoided meeting her eyes. "None of this makes sense, Lina. Why should your father wish to take Grace from you? Since Jonathan's death, you've been like a mother to that child."

Tears once again pressed behind Juliana's eyes, and she bit her lip hard to keep them at bay. Now she was back with Fitzwilliam at last, it was tempting to simply lay her head on the broad chest that had so often been her comfort when she was a child.

But she wasn't a child any longer.

She swallowed her tears, and raised her chin. "You don't understand. You know how grief-stricken he was after Jonathan died, but since his most recent attack, it's become much worse. He's not himself anymore. His mind is weak, and he falls prey to all sort of fears and delusions. I should have seen at once how it was, but it came on so gradually I didn't understand how much he'd deteriorated until he threatened to take Grace away from me."

Fitzwilliam dragged a hand through his hair. "I can't fathom it, Lina. I can't conceive of your father doing something so cruel."

"He doesn't understand he's being cruel. He thinks he does it for my own good. I'm his youngest daughter, Fitzwilliam, and his only remaining child. If he were in his right mind he'd never dream of taking Grace from me, but his wits often wander. He flies into rages, and he forgets things. Sometimes he talks about Jonathan and Emma as if they're still alive."

"Perhaps if I wrote to him, tried to reason with him—"

"No. Even when he's lucid he can't be reasoned with. He's afraid, both for himself and for me and Grace. He's made his wishes very clear in his will, and until I can present him with a husband, he refuses to change it. He can't be made to understand I could have any difficulty securing a spouse." Juliana didn't quite understand it herself. A lady who'd been betrothed not once but twice had reason to suppose she'd marry eventually, but with one thing and another...

With one thing and another, her first betrothed had fled to Scotland, and her second had fallen in love with another lady. Juliana couldn't make herself regret giving up Hugh to Isla Ramsey—how could she? Hugh was her friend, and no two people could be more in love than Hugh and Isla.

But it had been a rash thing to do, and now she was paying the price for it.

Her selflessness in releasing Hugh from their betrothal had not been rewarded. There didn't seem to be a single gentleman in England who cared to marry her—at least, not one she'd consider marrying—and now Grace's future was hanging in the balance.

Fitzwilliam rose from his chair with a jerk and began pacing in front of the fireplace. "What happens to Grace if you don't marry?"

Juliana paused. Dear God, how to explain it? This entire mess with her father's will had been a nightmare from the beginning, but this part was by far the worst of it. She dreaded telling Fitzwilliam, but there was no help for it. He must be made to understand how dire things were. She drew in a deep breath to steady herself. "Lord Cowden gets her."

Fitz stopped pacing and turned to her, horror on his face. "No, Lina. It can't be. Not *him*."

The now-familiar wave of helplessness rolled over Juliana, stealing her breath. It was the same thing she'd said to herself, over and over again.

It can't be him. Anyone but him...

But it *could* be. It *was*. "It's true, Fitzwilliam. If I don't marry, Benedict gets custody of Grace and guardianship over her fortune and her future."

Lord Cowden—or Benedict Reid, as Fitzwilliam and Juliana knew him—had been their neighbor and childhood playmate. The three of them had been inseparable at one time, but as they grew older Benedict had grown bitterly envious of Fitzwilliam. Fitzwilliam's fortune was greater, his title grander, and his future wife...

More than anything, Benedict envied Fitzwilliam Juliana.

As it always did, envy turned to resentment, and resentment to hatred. Their childhood playmate had become their nemesis, and he was a formidable one.

Lord Cowden was clever, charming. All the *ton* exclaimed over his elegance, his wit. But at his heart Benedict was a cold, brutal man. No one understood that better than Juliana and Fitzwilliam. A man couldn't hide his true nature from those who'd known him his whole life, and they knew Benedict for what he was.

Juliana resisted the urge to bury her face in her hands. It was a disaster. If it had been anyone but Benedict, perhaps she could have reconciled herself to it for Grace's sake. But to turn her beloved niece over to such a villain...no, it was impossible. She'd run away with Grace before she'd ever let Benedict have her.

"I don't understand this, Lina." Fitzwilliam looked dumbfounded. "Of all people, how could your father have chosen *him*? How did this happen?"

How? It was such a long, ugly story Juliana hardly knew where to begin. "About two months after you left for Scotland, Benedict came to me with an offer of marriage. He said—"

"Marriage!" Fitzwilliam's face darkened with fury. "When he knew you were betrothed to me? That *blackguard*. He's always wanted you, Lina, always schemed to get you for himself."

"He's always wanted my fortune, you mean." Her father's money, his properties—none of it was entailed. Even Graystone Court would go to Juliana.

Fitzwilliam's hands clenched into fists. "He wants *both*."

Juliana had been determined he'd get neither, and that was when the battle with Benedict had begun. "I refused him, but I was scared, Fitzwilliam. I knew he'd never give up as long as he thought he could get his hands on the estate, so I persuaded my father to secure everything in a trust for Grace, so my husband can't touch a penny of it. I thought it would dissuade Benedict—put him off the idea of marrying me."

"That wouldn't dissuade him. He still wants *you*, Lina."

A shudder wracked Juliana at the thought of either herself or Grace at Benedict's mercy. "It did dissuade him for a time, but then Benedict began paying frequent visits to my father. They'd spend hours together, closeted away in my father's study. I tried to put a stop to it, or at least to remain in the room while Benedict was there, but my father wouldn't hear of my interfering in 'gentleman's business,' as he put it."

Fitzwilliam laughed bitterly. "Let me guess. Once their gentleman's business was concluded?"

"Benedict had persuaded my father he couldn't possibly leave Grace in an unprotected woman's care. My father became frightened for me and Grace, and at Benedict's urging he added an amendment to his will, designating Benedict as Grace's guardian unless I'm married to a respectable gentleman by the time of my father's death. That's why Hugh and I became betrothed."

Fitz looked dazed. "I can't believe Lord Graystone would agree to such a thing."

"If he'd been in his right mind he wouldn't have, but his wits are befuddled, and he's easily worked upon. Benedict played on his fears. My father knows he's dying, and he's desperate to see me safely married before he passes away. Remember too that Benedict's father was my father's dear friend and neighbor, and we grew up with Benedict. My father trusts him."

Fitzwilliam dragged his hands down his face. "Does Benedict think to coerce you into a marriage with him this way?"

"No, he thinks to punish me for refusing him. There's no longer any question of a marriage between us. He recently married Lady Jane Abbott."

"Then I pity her." Fitz shook his head. "This can't be, Lina. No matter what, Grace can't go to Cowden."

Juliana didn't answer, but sat quietly, biting her lip. She knew of only one way to save Grace from Benedict. Fitzwilliam knew it as well as she did, but he hadn't said a word about their betrothal. That he hadn't brought it up said more than any other word he'd uttered.

Every one of her feminine instincts rebelled against introducing the topic herself. No lady wanted to offer her hand to a gentleman who hadn't asked for it, but neither could she allow Grace to be turned over to a monster like Benedict Reid.

"Do you intend to remain in Scotland much longer? My father's health is precarious. If we intend to…that is, the understanding between our families…" Juliana trailed off, her face heating. Oh, how awful this was! It didn't seem as if Fitzwilliam was still keen to marry her anymore, yet what was she to do if he didn't? He was her last chance.

Grace's last chance…

Juliana sucked in a breath, and plunged ahead. "We've been betrothed to each other from the cradle, Fitzwilliam. Our families always intended we'd marry. We're friends, moreover, aren't we?"

His gaze met hers, and his blue eyes softened. "Of course, we are, Lina. The best of friends."

Juliana's heart swelled with hope. "Then do this for me. Marry me, and return to England with me at once, before it's too late for Grace."

He didn't answer, but turned his head away from her, his throat working. Later, Juliana would wonder why, after seeing that, she hadn't realized his next words would devastate her.

That she'd made a dreadful mistake, coming here.

"I'm sorry, Lina," Fitzwilliam said quietly. "I should have realized something was amiss when I didn't hear from you again after I received your first few letters, but I've been quite preoccupied, I'm afraid. Selfishly so." Juliana drew her hands into her lap, pressing them tightly together to hide their trembling. "Grace and I need you, Fitzwilliam. We need you to do this for us."

"Oh, my beloved girl." Fitz strode over to her, and knelt beside her chair. "If there was any way for me to help you, any way at all, you know I would, but..."

But...

That one tiny word sent Juliana's last hope crashing to the ground.

Fitzwilliam grasped her hands in his, his eyes pleading for her to understand. "I wrote to you when I received Lord Madsen's letter about your betrothal to Lord Pierce, but you never replied."

Never replied? How could he say that? She'd written him letter after letter! He'd been the one who'd never replied. Unless...

Juliana's gaze shot to Logan Blair, and a dark suspicion rose in her breast as she gazed at that broad back. Had he taken all of the letters she'd written to Fitz and burned them?

All this time—weeks, months—had Fitzwilliam not seen any but the first few letters she'd written him? There'd been dozens. How many of them had been consigned to the flames at the Sassy Lassie, with Fitzwilliam none the wiser? Just the one? A dozen? Had Mr. Blair read them? If he had and was aware of her predicament, then he must be the wickedest, coldest man she'd ever encountered. If he hadn't, then he would be made to understand right here and now what grievous harm he'd done with his tricks.

"When I didn't receive any letters from you, I considered our betrothal to be at an end. I'm...this is more difficult for me than you can ever imagine, Lina, but I did write to you before I...to tell you..."

Juliana gazed down at him, into his clear blue eyes, and that was when she knew. She shook her head, as if by doing so she could make it not be true. "No. Don't say it. Please don't say it."

His fingers tightened around hers. "I can't marry you, Lina, because... because I'm betrothed to someone else."

Chapter Five

"Dear God, I've made a dreadful mistake."

Lady Juliana pulled away from Fitz. She wandered over to the window and stood looking out into the darkness, her arms wrapped around herself.

"We'll find a way, Lina, I promise you." Fitz took a few steps toward her, but stopped when she didn't turn around to face him.

Logan watched her reflection in the window. She kept her back to them, and he could see her struggling to compose her face. When she turned at last she was alarmingly pale, but her chin was high, and her voice steady. "I'm sorry, Fitzwilliam. I should have remained in Surrey. I must have been mad, coming here, but I thought if I…well, it hardly matters now."

She thought if she came to Castle Kinross, Fitz would marry her. No doubt he'd promised as much in his earliest letters to her.

Logan wasn't a man much given to regrets, but he'd had to look away from the despair on Lady Juliana's face when Fitz told her he was betrothed to another lady.

Perhaps she loved him. It stood to reason. They'd known each other since they were children, and there was no mistaking the tender affection between them. Perhaps Fitz had broken her heart, or perhaps her despair had more to do with this strange business regarding the child, Grace.

One thing was certain. It had nothing to do with Lady Juliana aspiring to become a duchess. He'd been wrong about that. He'd been wrong about a number of things.

Would it have made any difference if he *had* read her letters to Fitz? If he'd known there was a great deal more at stake than an English belle's fortune and a title? Logan wanted to believe it would have—that he would have been more careful with those letters—but he knew damn well whatever decision he'd made would have been in the clan's best interest, not Lady Juliana's.

He couldn't pretend otherwise, not even to himself.

It was useless to ask the question now. Logan hadn't read any but that last letter Lady Juliana had written to Fitz, the one he'd read today. He'd burned the rest without opening them. Maybe there was a part of him that had wanted to believe he was somehow less of a villain if he didn't read them.

"I left poor Stokes at the Sassy Lassie in Inverness without a word of explanation." Lady Juliana tried to smile. "He'll be worried about me. I'll return tonight to set his mind at ease, and we can be back on the road to London early to—"

"No." Fitz hurried across the room to her, alarmed. "Lina, I won't let you leave like this."

Lady Juliana appeared not to hear him. "I promised Lord Arthur I'd be back at Graystone Court within a month, before he and my father return from Bath. I have very little time."

"Lina, please—"

"You're not going anywhere tonight." Logan had remained quiet all evening, but he wasn't any more willing to let Lady Juliana tear off into the night than Fitz was. "You've been riding all day. You're exhausted, and it's too dark to make that journey."

Fitz looked between Logan and Lady Juliana, his face puzzled. "How do you know how long she's been riding?"

"Because she followed me to Castle Kinross from Inverness tonight, and before that from Gretna Green," Logan said bluntly, before Lady Juliana could speak.

Fitz's mouth dropped open. "*What*? She's been following you for *four days*? Why?"

"No. Three days. I didn't waste any time." Logan's gaze wandered over Lady Juliana, taking her in from the top of her head to the toes of her stained boots. She'd removed her riding jacket, but the white shirt she wore beneath was nearly as filthy as the jacket had been. It looked as if she'd tried to secure her hair, but half of it had come loose, and it hung in a tangled mess down her back. "I grant you it looks more like four."

It was an unforgivably rude comment, but even anger would be better than Lady Juliana's silence, that look of frozen despair on her face. It didn't goad her into a reply as Logan had hoped it would, but Fitz's face darkened, and he took a threatening step toward Logan. "What the devil's gotten into you? Apologize to Lady Juliana."

Logan didn't back away from his brother, but he did offer Lady Juliana a bow. "Beg pardon, Lady Juliana."

She didn't answer him, but for the first time since she found out Fitz was betrothed, she did look at Logan. He half-expected her to fly at him, to shriek and claw at his face, but she didn't. She simply stared at him, her green eyes hard, then looked away again without saying a word.

The moment when her gaze met his seemed to stretch and swell into the longest of Logan's life. The look in her eyes...

No one had ever looked at him with such quiet scorn before.

I'd rather she clawed me.

Fitz was still far from satisfied. "Would you care to explain to me why Lina would find it necessary to chase you from Gretna Green, Logan?"

"It was the only way she could be certain to find Castle Kinross."

"Why shouldn't she be able to find it?" Fitz was growing more impatient by the second. "I wrote to her with the direction, and anyway, Fergus could have told her the way. Why should she have to follow you?"

Logan raised an eyebrow at Lady Juliana. "Will you tell him, or will I?"

She didn't answer him. Her green eyes narrowed on his face, but it wasn't until she turned away that Logan realized she didn't intend to tell Fitz anything about the letter he'd stolen. He caught her arm and turned her back to face him, more upset by her silence than he should be. "Tell him. I don't need you to protect me, my lady."

"I don't do it to protect *you*!" She yanked her arm from his grip. "But to protect *him*."

She nodded at Fitz, who was looking between the two of them as if they'd both lost their wits. "What's going on here?" Fitz's voice had gone dangerously soft. "Why didn't Lina know the way to Castle Kinross? I'm not going to ask you again, Logan."

Logan didn't spare Fitz a glance. He kept his gaze on Lady Juliana. "Because she never received your letters. I took them, and then today I made Fergus promise not to give directions to Castle Kinross to any lady who asked for them."

Fitz stared at Logan, shocked. "You *took* my letters? I don't understand. Why would you...what did you do with them?"

"Burned them. Your letters to Lady Juliana, and hers to you."

Fitz's mouth dropped open. "*All* of them?"

"All but the first half dozen or so."

Silence fell as the two men stared at each other. Long, tense moments passed without a word between them, then Fitz slowly shook his head. "Why would you do that, Logan?"

Logan let out a short laugh. "You *know* why."

He didn't have to say anything more. Fitz's face fell, and Logan knew his brother understood exactly what he meant.

When Fitz had first arrived at Castle Kinross, he'd been everything Logan had feared he would be. Stiff, proud, distant—a lofty aristocrat who, despite the Blair blood flowing through his veins, had no understanding of the clan, the people, or the land.

Fitz owned this castle, and the land it stood on. He was the rightful Laird of Clan Kinross, and he was honor bound to protect his people. But when he'd first arrived at the castle there'd been nothing of the Scot in him—nothing of the laird. He was every inch the Duke of Blackmore, right down to his proper English accent.

In Logan's experience, English dukes were about as interested in the welfare of the Scots who worked their land as they were an insect that happened to land on a sleeve of their fine coats.

They'd flick them aside without a second thought.

Logan turned to Lady Juliana. "I never read any of the letters. Just the one you saw me read today."

Lady Juliana didn't look as if she thought much of this one restraint on his part, but before she could speak, Fitz blew out a breath. "I thought we were past all this, Logan."

"We weren't past it then. We may not be past it even now." Fitz hadn't turned out to be the villain Logan had dreaded he'd be, but that didn't mean Logan trusted him. Brother or not, Logan resented Fitz as much as he would any Englishman who owned his land.

Logan wasn't sure he'd ever get past that.

But as the months had passed, Logan found that under his new brother's haughty exterior, Fitz had a sincere wish to know his family. He wanted to learn about the clan, to understand the people. He'd gone from farm to farm with Logan, and when the people talked, he'd listened to them.

Then something miraculous had happened—something Logan hadn't anticipated.

He'd never even dared hope Fitz would fall in love with a Scottish lass, but from the moment Fitz first laid eyes on Emilia Ferguson, she'd taken his heart into her hands. There was only one thing standing between them.

Fitz's betrothed, Lady Juliana Bernard. She was a barrier, an obstacle to a happy ending not just for Fitz and Emilia, but also for Clan Kinross.

Logan saw his chance, and he took it. He began intercepting the letters between Lady Juliana and Fitz in hopes of putting an end to their betrothal.

"Should I assume, Logan, that you took the letters for my sake, so I could marry the lady I loved? How brotherly of you." Fitz's voice was heavy with sarcasm.

"No. I did it to protect the clan. It's better for us if you marry a Scot rather than an Englishwoman."

Especially *this* Englishwoman.

If Fitz married Emilia and they made their home in Scotland...well, even a cold-blooded English duke would think twice before tossing his wife's clan and family off his land. It was reason enough for Logan to want Emilia Ferguson to become the Duchess of Blackmore.

As for Lady Juliana...

Logan glanced at her. She wasn't at all what he'd expected, yet she remained, despite the spirit and courage she'd shown, the daughter of the Marquess of Graystone.

The marquess was no friend to the Scots. No, he was a friend to the Countess of Sutherland and her husband, the Marquess of Stafford, the two English aristocrats responsible for the Strathnaver Clearances. He was a friend to the thousands of English pounds he'd collected the following year, when he cleared his own lands to make way for the sheep herders who were better able to meet his exorbitant rents.

Logan could never forget the destruction he'd seen that day in Rosal Township. The taste of the thick black smoke in his mouth, the heat of the flames searing his eyes as one roof after another was set ablaze. The violence and confusion of it, the despair on the people's face as they watched their homes burned to the ground.

The Countess of Sutherland had sent Patrick Sellar to drive the people off her land, and he'd done a fine job of it. Sellar had brought Clan MacKay to their knees. Families had been torn apart that day, and then again only a year later, when the Marquess of Graystone cleared his land in Glengarry, and sent Clan MacDonnell scattering to the winds.

If Fitz married Lady Juliana, he'd go back to England with her. Once he was there, it would be the easiest thing in the world for him to forget what he owed to Clan Kinross. How long would it be before Lord Graystone convinced Fitz he could turn a far tidier profit by leasing Kinross land to sheep farmers? How long before Fitz decided to evict his own tenants, just as Graystone had done?

Logan wouldn't let that happen to his people, to his land. He'd been leading Clan Kinross since his father's death five years ago, before any of them had ever heard of the Duke of Blackmore. Logan wasn't the laird, but that didn't make him any less responsible for his clan. It made him more so, because he'd seen for himself how quickly a life could be reduced to ashes if a heartless man thought he could turn a profit by it.

"Well, then. It seems there's nothing more to be said. I wish to return to Inverness first thing tomorrow morning." Lady Juliana turned dull eyes to Fitz. "You'll take me, won't you?"

"So soon? No, Lina. You've only just arrived, and anyone can see you're exhausted from your journey. Next week, perhaps, or the week after."

"No, Fitz. I can't linger here for weeks. I haven't any time to lose. I've Grace to consider, and my father. I must return to London at once, and see what can be done to..."

To find another man to marry me.

The words hung in the air, unspoken, but there was no need for her to say them aloud. Each of them finished the thought in their heads.

She'd be forced to take whoever offered, and would end up married to a rogue, a fortune hunter, a gamester. She'd be wasted on some adventurer who'd steal every penny from her.

Fitz was already shaking his head. "No. I won't allow that. We'll think of something else."

Lady Juliana sighed. "What? It's too late, Fitzwilliam. You're betrothed to another lady."

Fitz didn't answer. He leaned an arm against the mantel and rested his head on it. He remained in this attitude for some time without speaking. When he shifted at last to face them, the look of misery on his face made Logan tense with foreboding.

He's going to jilt Emilia...

Logan knew it before Fitz could utter a syllable, but when Fitz did speak, his words slammed into Logan like a blow.

"I'm betrothed, Lina. Not married."

Logan thought of Emilia Ferguson, with her sweet blue eyes and her kind, quiet ways. Emilia wasn't the remarkable beauty Lady Juliana was, but she was a pretty, dark-haired lass, and she was devoted to Fitz. If he abandoned her now she'd never recover from the blow, and Fitz happened to be as madly in love with Emilia as she was with him. It made a marriage between them a joyous occasion for everyone.

Everyone, that is, but Lady Juliana Bernard.

"You're betrothed to a lady you're in love with," Logan bit out, his voice harsh. "Emilia's a worthy lass, and she loves you. Will you break her heart, Fitz?"

"What would you have me do? Abandon Lina to a disastrous marriage? What of Grace? Her father was my best friend, Logan. I've known Grace since she was born, and I won't turn my back on her now. No," he snapped, when Logan tried to interrupt. "Lina and Grace need me more than Emilia does. Emilia will..." Fitz drew a deep breath. "I'll find a way to make Emilia understand."

Logan let out an incredulous laugh. "Understand? You don't know much about women, brother, if you think Emilia will understand it when you throw her over for some English lady who's turned up out of nowhere."

"You *are* brothers, then. I knew you must be." Lady Juliana turned to Fitz, her lower lip trembling. "I don't understand. Why didn't you tell me? We've always told each other everything. To find out now, like this..."

Fitz shot Logan a furious glare, but his face softened when he turned to Lady Juliana. "I'm so sorry, Lina. I would have told you, but I didn't know it myself until recently. You remember when we were children, how cold my mother always was toward me? You haven't forgotten that?"

"No, I haven't. How could I?" Lady Juliana's mouth twisted with sadness. "You used to run away from home and come to Graystone Court just to escape her. You were just a young boy, but even so I recall your telling me once that your mother didn't love you. You could never understand why."

Fitz hesitated, then crossed the room to take Lady Juliana's hands in his. "I understand it now. She didn't love me, Lina, because I'm not her son."

The color fled Lady Juliana's cheeks. "Not her son?"

"No. I'm the son of the Duke of Blackmore's younger sister Sarah, and her husband, Gordon Kinross. As the Duke's eldest nephew, I *am* the legitimate heir to the Blackmore Dukedom, but I'm not his son, Lina."

"Dear God." She raised her palm to her forehead, her hand shaking. "He never told you the truth?"

"No. My mother...that is, the duchess told me after his death. Once he died, there was no longer any reason for her to carry the secret. She's always resented me, and when she saw her chance to be rid of me, she took it." Fitz stared down at their joined hands. "She said there was no reason for me to stay now the duke was dead, and sent me off here to find my 'real family.' My 'real family,' Lina. Those were her exact words."

"Oh, Fitzwilliam." Lady Juliana pressed her palm to his cheek. "How could she be so cruel?"

Fitz shrugged, but his mouth was tight. "It explains a good deal about her behavior toward me, doesn't it? She never wanted me, but the duke was desperate for an heir, and I was his last hope. The duchess lost a child early in their marriage, and it left her barren."

Lady Juliana remained quiet, waiting for him to go on.

Fitz swallowed. "Our mother, Lady Sarah, died giving birth to Logan and me. The duke came to Castle Kinross to see his sister buried, and while he was here he convinced my father it was best for everyone if the eldest son came to live with him in England, where he could see to it I understood my responsibilities as his future heir. So, he brought me home to Surrey with him, and raised me as his son while my brother remained in Scotland with our father." Fitz's gaze met Logan's then. "Some good came of finding out the truth, I suppose. I gained a brother."

"And Clan Kinross gained a new laird." Logan heard the bitterness in his voice, and cursed himself. No matter how hard he tried to bury his resentment, the same anger rose in his chest every time he thought of it. He tried not to blame Fitz for it, but the clan had been happy and prospering before he came here, and now all was thrown into uncertainty. Fitz's arrival put them all at risk.

"I left for Scotland soon after I found out. I never meant to abandon you, Lina." Fitz gave Lady Juliana a pleading look. "I always intended to come back to England, but once I got here…"

"Once you got here, you felt as if you'd come home."

Her voice was soft, for Fitz's ears only, but Logan heard her. He jerked his gaze to her, and was astonished to see she was gently caressing Fitz's cheek.

Logan watched the tender scene unfold, and something shifted in his chest. No one could look at them and deny Lady Juliana cared very much for Fitz. What's more, she understood him in a way only someone who's known you your entire life can understand you.

Logan knew it wasn't right, what he'd done to her. He'd known it all along, but tossing a few letters into the fire was far different than seeing the damage he'd caused with his own eyes.

Fitz was holding Lady Juliana's wrists in his hands, his forehead resting on hers. He was murmuring something to her, too low for Logan to hear. Lady Juliana was shaking her head, and Logan drew closer to hear Fitz's murmured words.

Emilia…back to Surrey with you…take care of Grace…

Logan grabbed his brother by the arm and wrenched him away from Lady Juliana. "You're not going to abandon Emilia and leave her here alone in misery!"

Fitz tore his arm free and pushed Logan away from him. "Do you think I *want* to leave Emilia? You've left me no choice. Don't forget, *brother*, this is all your doing. Once this business is sorted, I'll come back to Emilia. I'll explain it all to her, make her understand."

Logan looked his brother in the eyes and slowly shook his head. "No, Fitz. Emilia isn't going to understand. You're going to break her heart if you do this."

Lady Juliana studied Fitz for a long moment, taking in every detail of his shifting expression, then she turned that same piercing gaze on Logan. Without a word, she returned to her seat by the fire.

"Lina?" Fitz followed her across the room, pausing beside her chair. "I can't...you must know I can't let you—"

"No, Fitz. You'll remain at Castle Kinross and marry your betrothed, just as you planned."

Fitz shook his head. "No. I won't send you back to England alone. We have to consider Grace—"

"I *am* considering Grace. I always do. I won't be returning to England alone. I'll be taking my husband with me."

Fitz's head jerked back in surprise. "Your husband?"

Logan had crossed the room to stand in front of the fireplace, so he was close enough to see the look in Lady Juliana's green eyes when she turned them on him. They no longer looked like a spring leaf lit by the sun. They were as bright and hard as two glittering emeralds.

A strange feeling unfolded in Logan's chest as they gazed at each other. Even before she said a word, he knew...

"Yes. My husband. Mr. Blair is responsible for causing this mess, and Mr. Blair will be the one who gets me out of it."

Logan didn't expect what happened next, but before he could stop it a slow, appreciative smile rose to his lips. "Is that a proposal, my lady?"

"No, Mr. Blair." Her dark green eyes disappeared behind heavily lashed eyelids. When she opened them again, she wore a small answering smile on her lips. "It's a demand."

Chapter Six

Logan Blair was smiling at her, but it wasn't a warm, pleasant sort of smile. It was the sort of smile that made a shudder creep down Juliana's spine.

He may as well have been baring his teeth.

"It's curious, Lady Juliana. I remember you telling me I was the last man in the world you'd consider marrying."

Juliana didn't reply. She *had* said it, yes, and since he wasn't gentleman enough to refrain from reminding her of it, she braced herself for a recitation of every other insult she'd dealt him.

She didn't have long to wait.

"You said it was the most ridiculous thing you'd ever heard. A foolish, outrageous notion—yes, I think those were your words."

Juliana remained silent. She simply folded her hands in her lap and waited.

"You accused me of arrogance and conceit, and then…what was it? Oh, yes. This was the best part. You said you wouldn't even follow me across a street, much less half of Scotland."

Juliana raised an eyebrow at him. "Are you quite finished, Mr. Blair?"

He rested a casual arm against the mantelpiece and considered her with detached interest. "I only mean to remind you of how much you dislike me, lass. The last man in the world, remember?"

Behind her tight smile, Juliana's teeth were clenched. "Given my circumstances, you *are* the last man in the world, Mr. Blair. Unfortunate, isn't it? But here we are."

He shrugged. "Four hours ago, you were disgusted at the idea of marrying me. Have you changed your mind?"

"No, indeed. In fact, while you were speaking just now I was reflecting on the cruelty of fate. But beggars, alas, cannot be choosers."

A mocking smile drifted across his lips. "Are you *begging* me to marry you, my lady? How flattering."

"Oh, you haven't any reason to be flattered, I assure you. I haven't the slightest wish to marry you, Mr. Blair. I'd sooner take one of the stable boys. You are, quite literally, my last resort."

His full lips twitched. "I think you hold yourself too cheap. Shall we find out?"

He took a step toward the door, but Fitzwilliam stopped him with a hand on his shoulder. "Where do you think you're going?"

Logan turned to him in surprise. "To the stables, of course, to find a stable boy to marry Lady Juliana. There must be at least one who'll have her. She *is* the daughter of a marquess."

Juliana gave him a thin smile. "If I could persuade my father to accept such a match, I wouldn't hesitate. But alas, a stable boy won't do. No, as much as we both detest the idea, I'm afraid I'll have to have you, Mr. Blair."

"*Have* me, like you would a new bonnet, or a pair of slippers? No need to be afraid of that lass, because it won't happen."

Was that a trace of a smirk on his lips? Why, the gall of the man! Juliana's cheeks heated with anger, and her gaze wandered to the fireplace poker.

It was one way to knock that infuriating smile from his lips.

She clenched her hands together in her lap to keep herself from snatching up the poker. "A marriage between us would solve a great many problems. You must see that, Mr. Blair."

He raised one black eyebrow. "And cause a great many more. Or do you think we'd enjoy a lifetime of wedded bliss?"

Wedded bliss? Juliana nearly laughed aloud at the thought. "Oh, I've quite given up on any hope of wedded bliss."

He regarded her with cool blue eyes. "But I haven't, Lady Juliana."

"Perhaps not, but you forfeited it when you stole those letters. Don't forget, sir, you're the reason we find ourselves in this unfortunate situation."

"It will be more unfortunate still if we marry."

Juliana had sworn to herself she'd keep her temper in check, but she recognized the sharp words burning her tongue for what they were—the first sign of rising fury. "If I can lower myself to marry a man who stole from me before he'd ever laid eyes on me, then surely you can reconcile yourself to a marriage of convenience."

Logan Blair's arm dropped from the mantel, and he took a step toward her, still wearing that amused smile. "Would you rather I'd stolen from you *after* I laid eyes on you?"

Juliana stared at him, too angry to trust herself to reply. She'd never before been tempted to strike another person, but right now she'd give anything to forget she was a lady and deliver a stinging slap to that handsome cheek.

Did he find this whole thing amusing? Perhaps this was all just a game to *him*, but she didn't have the luxury of gambling with Grace's future.

Mr. Blair wasn't finished. "I don't think it would have made much difference if I had laid eyes on you beforehand. You've got a sharp tongue, lass—a much sharper tongue than most English belles. That must be why you've had such difficulty bringing your betrotheds up to scratch."

Oh, that was the outside of enough. Juliana's palm began to tingle. The next thing she knew she was on her feet with her hand raised, her furious gaze fixed on those mocking lips.

Before she could slap the smirk off him, Fitz grasped her hand and tugged her over to a sofa a good distance away from his brother. "For God's sake, Logan! Have you lost your mind? Leave off, will you? This situation is bad enough without you making it worse with your insults."

Juliana allowed herself to be seated on the sofa, but her hands were shaking with fury, and she was ready to tear her hair out with frustration.

Her hair, or Logan Blair's.

She darted a glance at him from under her eyelashes. His jaw was tight and his shoulders rigid. Logan Blair might affect a cool unconcern, but he was just as agitated as she was.

For her part, Juliana couldn't recall ever being so livid in her life, but there was no point in trying to calmly reason with Mr. Blair. Both of them were already as furious as two hissing cats, and she could see this wasn't going to end until one of them sank a claw deep into the flesh of the other.

It was going to be a brawl to the bitter end, and she'd just as soon Fitzwilliam wasn't here to witness it. He was already more distressed than she'd ever seen him, and this was about to get much worse. "Fitzwilliam, I want you to leave me alone with Mr. Blair."

Fitz crossed his arms over his chest. "No. I don't think that's a good idea."

"It's all right. I'm perfectly capable of speaking with your brother in private."

"Go on, Fitz. I give you my word I won't toss Lady Juliana into Beauly Firth, no matter how much she tempts me." Mr. Blair was talking to Fitzwilliam, but his hard gaze never left Juliana's face.

"Is that supposed to be amusing, Logan?" Fitzwilliam looked from one to the other of them, assessing their faces with tight lips. After a moment he rose to his feet, but he paused at the door, his brow creased with concern. "Are you sure, Lina?"

In truth, Juliana had no wish to be alone with Logan Blair, especially after she'd goaded him into a temper, but she wanted the business done, and they'd never get anywhere with Fitzwilliam in the room.

"Yes, quite sure. There's no need to worry." Juliana scraped together what she hoped was a reassuring smile.

"Very well, then." Fitz shot his brother a warning glance, then he left the library, leaving the door half-open behind him.

Silence fell over the room. Mr. Blair, who'd retreated to the sideboard and now stood with his back to her, seemed in no hurry to break it. Long minutes passed without either of them saying a word.

Juliana didn't fool herself into thinking a truce was forthcoming. They were each simply gathering their weapons and strength for the battle ahead.

It was a battle Juliana intended to win, and she knew just what she had to do.

"Well, Mr. Blair, you were right about one thing. I did need the Madeira." Juliana fetched her tumbler from the table in front of her and swallowed the last sip of the sweet wine.

He turned to face her, a slight smile on his hard lips. "Will you have another glass?"

"No. I think not. I fancy I'll need to keep my wits about me."

He took a healthy swallow from his own glass, then strode across the room and took a seat on the sofa across from hers. "I'm listening, Lady Juliana. What did you wish to discuss with me?"

Another brief silence fell as they took each other's measure, then Juliana cleared her throat. "I'll expect you to abide by one or two conditions once we're wed, Mr. Blair." Her cheeks warmed, but discussing their marriage as a foregone conclusion seemed as good a strategy as any. "It's only fair I warn you about them in advance."

The corner of his mouth twitched. "Call me Logan, lass. It's only proper, since we seem to be betrothed now."

Juliana scowled. For pity's sake, he looked as if he was actually enjoying himself. "This isn't a game. I'm quite serious."

He gave her an indulgent smile. "All right, then. What do I need to understand, my lady?"

"To begin with, there's Grace to consider. She's a very affectionate child. She'll likely be eager to spend time with you. I don't see any way to avoid that, but you will not, under any circumstances, attempt to interfere with any of my decisions regarding her. She's *my* niece. I'll decide how she's raised."

He regarded her in silence for a moment, then he asked, "Since you're to call me Logan, may I call you Lina?"

Juliana stared at him. For goodness sakes, had he even heard a word of what she'd just said? "No, you certainly may not call me Lina. Only Fitzwilliam calls me that."

"Julia, then? Lady Juliana is too much. It wearies the tongue."

Juliana huffed out a breath. "I'm sorry to have exhausted you, Mr. Blair."

He quirked an eyebrow at her sarcastic tone. "I'll call you Ana. Pretty name, that is. Simple."

Simple and pretty, yes, but not *her* name, for all that. "You still haven't assured me you accept my restriction regarding Grace, Mr. Blair."

He sighed. "I hope you're not this stubborn once we're married."

Juliana ignored this. "Do I have your word?"

He shrugged. "All right, but it's a pity. I'm good with children."

Juliana found that difficult to believe, but she held her tongue. "As for the second thing. Despite what you seem to think, I'm not a great heiress. I have my mother's fortune, but it's not the sort of money I suspect you're imagining."

Ah, he didn't care for that at all. It *was* offensive for her to insinuate he cared about her money. She intended it as a clarification of her circumstances, not as an insult, but Mr. Blair's lips went so tight they whitened at the edges.

"As for the rest of the money and properties, they will pass into a trust for Grace when my father dies," she went on, ignoring the ominous color rising in his cheeks. "Graystone Court, the various other country estates, the house in town—all of it belongs to Grace."

"That's enough," he warned in a low, hard voice.

"My mother's fortune includes an estate in Buckinghamshire. It's called Rosemount. I intend to remove there after…"

After my father dies.

She swallowed. "Rosemount is charming, but rather small. Not at all grand like Graystone Court."

"I don't give a damn about—"

"The trust with the rest of the fortune—which is considerable, I grant you—will be administered by the Marquess of Pierce. My husband won't be able to touch a penny of it. My father and I decided it was best that way, you see, to discourage fortune hunters."

Mr. Blair was reining in his temper with an effort. "Are you accusing me of being a fortune hunter?"

"Not at all. I simply wish to be honest with you."

"It's always about money with the English, isn't it?" His eyes flashed with temper. "Let me be understood, my lady. I don't have any interest in your fortune."

"Ah. It must be a love match, then. How romantic." Her voice dripped with sarcasm.

Logan Blair was no longer amused. His infuriating smile had fled, and he regarded her with narrowed eyes. "Your father wants you to become a duchess, doesn't he, Lady Juliana?"

Juliana's eyebrows rose. She hadn't any idea how Mr. Blair could know what her father wanted, but she didn't deny it was true. Her father had always dreamed she'd become the Duchess of Blackmore someday.

"I'm not a duke, or even a laird." He took a casual sip from his glass, studying her over the rim. "If he won't accept anything less than a title, then we can end this right now."

Juliana shifted uncomfortably in her seat. Not only did her father want a duke, he wanted Fitzwilliam. He hadn't mentioned title or fortune in his will, because he took it as a matter of course she'd become Fitzwilliam's duchess. She wasn't certain how he'd react when he discovered he'd have to make do with a duke's brother instead, but she didn't intend to reveal this to Logan Blair. He didn't need to know about all the lies she'd told. "He hasn't made any demands of that sort, no."

He eyed her, dangling his glass between long, surprisingly elegant fingers. "What of you, my lady? Are you determined to become a duchess?"

Juliana let out a short laugh. "I've never cared much about titles."

He studied her face, his blue eyes calculating. "Is that so? Yet your other suitor was a marquess."

She shrugged. "Lord Pierce is a dear friend."

"A friend who also happens to be a marquess, and another friend who happens to be a duke. You have quite a few aristocratic friends, my lady."

Juliana's chin rose. "Lord Pierce is Grace's uncle on her mother's side, Mr. Blair. He's as concerned with her welfare as I am. A marriage between us made sense."

He laughed softly. "He couldn't have been all that concerned. He went off and married another lady, didn't he?"

She smiled coldly. "Yes, well, I confess it would be easier if my betrotheds would stop falling in love with other ladies. It puts me in a dreadful position."

"I see that. Explain something to me, Lady Juliana. How is it your *dear friend* Lord Pierce allowed you to jilt him in the first place, given your niece's dire circumstances?"

"Well, as to that…" Juliana trailed off, her face heating. She'd lied to Hugh, too, and now all her lies were catching up to her with a vengeance.

"Shame on you, Lady Juliana," Mr. Blair murmured. "Lord Pierce thinks you're on the verge of marrying Fitz as well, doesn't he? You've told dozens of lies, and now you've made it worse by scampering off to Scotland without telling your father where you've gone. So deceptive, behind that pretty face."

"Yes, well, looks are deceiving, are they not? I wouldn't have guessed you were a thief, but there is the troublesome matter of my letters."

She half-expected him to fall into a rage, but to her surprise, a smile crossed his lips. "Another reason why a marriage between us would be madness. You can't wish to marry a thief."

Madness indeed, yet it was Juliana's only option, just the same. It was a pity her old governess Mrs. Crampton wasn't alive to see her lies return to haunt her. The old woman would have been thrilled Juliana had received her just desserts.

She studied the toe of her ruined boot. "Oh, I don't know, Mr. Blair. There's a certain symmetry to a liar marrying a thief, don't you agree? Perhaps we deserve each other."

He dragged a finger slowly around the top edge of his empty glass. "Is that why you let Lord Pierce go? Because you believe he deserves better than you?"

His blue gaze narrowed on her face with such intensity, Juliana looked away. Instead she watched his finger slowly trace the rim of his glass. *Around and around…*

"Lady Juliana? What made you decide to free Lord Pierce, when you knew your niece's future was at stake?"

She jerked her gaze back to his face. "I released Lord Pierce from our betrothal because I believed he deserved to marry the lady he loves."

"But you don't believe your dear friend Fitzwilliam—the man you claim to care so much for—deserves the same?"

"On the contrary. I believe it wholeheartedly." Juliana wished for Fitz's happiness as fiercely as she wished for Grace's, or for her own. To force him into a marriage would break her heart. The only difference between Hugh and Fitz was that this time she didn't have any choice.

Mr. Blair leaned forward and dropped his glass onto the table. "Come now, lass. You could have said all of this in front of Fitz. You sent him away so we could both speak plainly, so let's have it out. I'm refusing the offer of your hand. What do you intend to do about it?"

Juliana's heart began to pound, and she drew in a deep breath to calm it. Logan Blair wasn't the sort of man one liked to threaten, but she didn't have a choice. "If you refuse to agree to a marriage between us, I'll accept Fitzwilliam's offer to marry me, regardless of his betrothal."

They were some of the ugliest words she'd ever uttered. Even as they left her lips, Juliana shuddered at the thought of following through with her threat. She'd given Hugh his freedom because she cared for him, and she couldn't bear to be the reason he was kept apart from the lady he loved. Would she do less for Fitzwilliam? He was her oldest, dearest friend, the person she'd run to as a child to soothe her bruised knees, and later, when her girlish infatuations ended in disappointment, her bruised heart.

What sort of life could she make with him, if she forced him to abandon the lady he loved? How could he ever forgive her, if she demanded such a sacrifice of him? He'd make the best of it, because that was who Fitzwilliam was, but a marriage between them would destroy their friendship, and leave them with nothing but bitter regret.

She despised the idea of hurting him, but she couldn't afford to make another mistake this time. Her father had still been reasonably healthy when he, Juliana, and Grace had gone to Buckinghamshire to visit Hugh. When Juliana had discovered Hugh was in love with Isla, she'd thought she still had plenty of time to find another man to marry. She'd released Hugh from their betrothal thinking she'd simply wait until next season, and find a proper gentleman then.

Less than a week after they'd returned to Surrey she'd realized her mistake. Her father had had another attack, and this time instead of recovering, he'd continued to deteriorate. All at once it became imperative she marry at once, before her father…before it was too late.

If she hadn't given up Hugh to Isla, Juliana would be Lady Pierce even now, and Grace would be safe. Instead she'd tried to do the honorable thing, and she'd made a mess of it. She couldn't afford to do the same with Fitzwilliam.

A picture of her lively, dark-eyed niece flashed through her mind, and her heart swelled with pride and love. If Grace were sent to live with Lord Cowden, Juliana would never forgive herself.

She turned her attention back to Logan Blair, her face carefully blank. "Either you agree to marry me, or Fitzwilliam and I will leave Castle Kinross at once, and be back in England before two weeks have passed."

Mr. Blair's face remained expressionless, but his fingers tightened on the arm of his chair. "So, you wouldn't hesitate to rip Fitz from the arms of the woman he loves and force him into a marriage with you, even though you know he doesn't love you?"

"It's *you* who will be the cause of Fitzwilliam losing the lady he loves, not me. I don't like you, Mr. Blair. I don't trust you, and I don't want to marry you, but I'm willing to do it so Fitzwilliam can be with Emilia. It's a pity you aren't willing to do as much for your own brother."

"You don't have any idea what I'm willing to do."

Juliana suppressed a shiver. "Oh, I think I do. You've already confessed to being a thief, and you're guilty of a disgraceful invasion of my privacy. I can't suppose you'd hesitate to do worse. Indeed, even now you appear to be threatening me."

"No, no threats, but I do think you should be made aware of how many people you'll hurt if you insist on marrying my brother."

The tone of his voice, the look on his face when he said those words made the hair on the back of Juliana's neck rise. Her threat to take Fitzwilliam away should have ended this battle, but Mr. Blair wasn't finished.

He knew something. Something she didn't.

She swallowed. "I already told you, I have no desire to hurt Fitzwilliam or his betrothed, but—"

"No, I don't think you do wish to hurt them. But I'm not referring to Fitz or Emilia." He paused, his blue eyes glittering. "I'm referring, Lady Juliana, to their child."

Juliana went still, her heart shrinking in her chest.

Their child...

They were the last two words she heard before the roaring in her head drowned out every other sound, every thought.

Fitzwilliam was having a child. He was in love with his betrothed, and they were having a child together. A child as sweet and intelligent as Grace, perhaps, with Fitzwilliam's blue eyes and his beautiful smile. A child Juliana would love as much as she loved Grace, because Fitzwilliam's child would be her niece as surely as Grace was. Hadn't Juliana always considered Fitzwilliam her brother, as much as she did Jonathan?

A child who deserved a father...

Mr. Blair was saying something to her. She could see his mouth moving, but the words couldn't reach beyond the noise in her head. He reached for her, his eyes dark with concern, but Juliana shook her head and snatched her hand away.

Couldn't he see it was over?

He'd inflicted the deepest wound, drawn the most blood.

He'd won.

There was nothing left to say.

Chapter Seven

Fitz was waiting for him by the library door. As soon as he saw Logan, his face fell. "You don't look like a man who's happily betrothed."

"I'm not." Logan leaned against the door and tipped his head back against the wood. If he'd had any lingering hope he wasn't the blackguard he suspected himself to be, Fitz's anguished expression shattered it.

Logan had known he'd emerge from the battle of wills with Lady Juliana the victor. What he hadn't known was instead of feeling triumphant, he'd be heartily ashamed of himself.

"Unhappily betrothed, then?" Fitz asked hopefully.

"Not that, either."

Fitz's expression went bleaker still. "How's Lina?"

How was she? She was much as you'd expect a lady to be when her last hope had been brutally crushed. Logan thought of her pale, frozen face, the blankness in her eyes, and he couldn't prevent a shudder of remorse. "Worse than I am."

Fitz dragged a hand through his hair. "What a bloody mess. I realize things have been tense between us, but I never imagined you'd…stealing our letters, Logan? How could you do this?"

Logan could have offered any number of excuses for his actions. He could have told Fitz a few burned letters had seemed trivial enough compared to dozens of burned farmhouses. He could have said the lives of hundreds of people had been more important to him than the future of one lady who had her pick of every peer in London. He could have explained he hadn't understood how dire Lady Juliana's circumstances were—that he regretted the trouble he'd caused. He might even have said he'd done what he'd been taught to do since he was a child at their father's knee.

Whatever he must to protect the land, and the clan.

Instead, he remained silent. He'd had his reasons, but they didn't excuse what he'd done. He could argue all he wanted, but it didn't make him any less responsible for Lady Juliana's predicament. He'd been under no illusions when he stole those letters. He'd known it was a despicable thing to do, and he'd done it anyway. He hadn't bothered to consider that one bad act would have endless repercussions, like ripples of water after a tossed stone. He hadn't spared a single thought for Lady Juliana's future.

Fitz was pacing back and forth in front of the library door. "Lina has a claim on you, Logan. You're the reason she's in this mess. As a man of honor, you're obliged to see her out of it. A marriage between you—"

"Would be a disaster. You can't believe otherwise."

Fitz let out a bitter laugh. "You'll get no argument from me. I can't imagine Lina's any happier about a marriage between you than you are. You don't deserve her, after what you've done. But I don't see any way around it. If you have a better idea, please do enlighten me."

"She could marry one of the men from the clan." Logan had been turning this idea over in his head all evening. "Duncan Muir, perhaps, or Kincaid's eldest son, Brodie. They're both gentlemen, and men of education—"

"No. It won't do. If Lina's father doesn't approve her choice the marriage won't do her any good at all, and I can assure you the Marquess of Graystone won't settle for an obscure, untitled Scotsman for his only daughter's husband."

"If he won't settle for Duncan or Brodie, then he won't settle for me. I don't have a title, and I'm as obscure as either of them."

"Ah, that's where you're wrong." Fitz gave him a thin smile. "You're the brother of the current Duke of Blackmore, nephew to the previous duke, and your mother was daughter to a duke. Bloody dukes everywhere, going back for generations. You may like to think of yourself as an obscure Scotsman, Logan, but your bloodlines say otherwise, and of course our family's fortune is considerable. Lina has a far better chance of reconciling her father to a marriage with you than with any other gentleman."

"Even so, I doubt the Marquess of Graystone will find the Duke of Blackmore's brother as impressive as the duke himself."

"Oh, there's little doubt he'd rather have me, especially considering my long-standing betrothal to Lina, but a duke's brother is nothing to sniff at. With a letter of recommendation from me, you'll—"

"A letter of recommendation!" Logan scowled. "You think I need a recommendation from you to be considered a gentleman?"

Fitz shrugged. "It can't hurt."

Logan dragged a weary hand down his face. Christ, how had he gotten himself into such a mess? Why couldn't Lady Juliana have remained in England and married Lord Pierce as she'd planned to?

The trouble was, Fitz was right. She *did* have a claim on him. He'd dragged her into this, and she had a right to expect him to get her out of it. Before he sat down on the sofa across from her tonight he hadn't had any intention of marrying her. Now, he wasn't so sure

But a marriage, a move to England, so far away from his clan...

He owed his people far more than he owed Lady Juliana. He'd promised his father he'd do everything he could to ensure their safety, and a promise to his father outweighed any claims Lady Juliana might have on him.

He couldn't abandon the clan now, not when he'd finally found a way to help them.

After he'd witnessed the devastation in Strathnaver, Logan had purchased a large parcel of land in Cape Fear Valley, at the southern tip of North Carolina. For the past few years he'd been funding a migration of the heartier members of Clan Kinross there, setting them up to successfully pursue a new life in North America. For those not strong enough to make the journey he'd searched out places in the Scottish Lowlands and in northern England where they might settle.

Slowly, one family at a time, Logan was clearing out sections of Kinross land.

It wasn't what he wanted. Everything inside him rebelled at separating the clan, but after a good deal of internal struggle, he'd admitted to himself he hadn't any choice. At the time, he didn't know if the new Laird of Clan Kinross would evict his tenants to make way for sheep farms, just as the Countess of Sutherland and the Marquess of Graystone had done. If he did, there would be nothing Logan could do to stop him.

Even if the new laird chose to be merciful, there was little hope the clan would flourish if they remained here. There were simply too many people, and not enough food or land to sustain them all. The clan system had disintegrated after the Jacobite Rebellion—the British Crown had seen to that—and there was no sense in pretending otherwise. The best thing Logan could do for his people was to see them settled in prosperous circumstances.

Not everyone wanted to go. He had no intention of driving them off if they preferred to stay—there would be no forced evictions on Kinross land—but he'd managed to persuade about half of them to voluntarily relocate. Their land would then be enclosed to make larger farms for sheep grazing, and the profits used to sustain the rest of the clan.

The clan had warmed to Fitz since he'd become betrothed to Emilia, but in their eyes, Logan was still their laird. Fitz might try to persuade some of them to relocate, but what if they didn't trust him enough yet to rely on his word?

Logan straightened away from the door and faced Fitz. "I can see what a bloody mess I've made, but marriage to a lady I don't know, and a move to England, hundreds of miles away from Scotland, Fitz? There has to be another way."

Fitz's face went hard. "There is. If you won't marry her, then I will."

Logan shook his head. "She won't have you."

"What the devil does that mean? Of course, she'll have..." Fitz's eyes narrowed. "You told her about the child, didn't you?"

Logan flinched at the fury in his brother's eyes. "Yes. I don't know Lady Juliana well, but anyone can see she's not the sort of lady who'd take you away from your child."

She didn't have anything but frowns and scowls for Logan, but he'd seen the way Lady Juliana's face lit up when Fitz walked into the library tonight. He'd seen the joy, love, and fear in her eyes when she'd spoken of her niece, Grace.

They were the two people in the world most dear to her. She'd come all the way to Scotland for them, over hundreds of miles of rough roads. She'd risked her well-being, her reputation, and her safety for them. She might go as far as Scotland to protect her niece, but the one thing she wouldn't do was sacrifice one of them for the other. She wouldn't compromise Fitz's or his unborn child's happiness. Not even for Grace's sake.

"You'd better go to her." Logan tipped his head toward the closed library door. "She's...distressed."

"Yes, she would be, but you've got just what *you* wanted, didn't you, Logan? I hope you're pleased with yourself." Fitz didn't wait for an answer, but wrenched open the library door and went inside.

Logan waited for it to close behind Fitz before he turned and made his way down the hall to the stairs. He was halfway up before the words echoing in his head made it to his lips. "It's not what I wanted." His quiet voice sounded loud in the silence. "This isn't what I wanted at all."

* * * *

Juliana hadn't moved since Logan Blair left the room.

When Fitz found her, she was staring down at her hands clasped tightly in her lap. The fire crackled in the grate, the cheerful snap and hiss of the flames mocking the frozen silence of the room.

She was thinking of Grace, of how Grace had wept and clung to her skirts when Juliana left her with Lord Pierce in Buckinghamshire. Grace adored both Hugh and Isla, but nothing—nothing—could console her for the loss of her Aunt Juliana. For as long as Grace could remember, Juliana was the first person she saw when she woke, and the last one to kiss her goodnight before she fell asleep.

Until the moment Juliana learned about Fitzwilliam's child, she'd thought there wasn't a thing in the world she wouldn't do for her niece. Now she knew better.

She felt for Fitzwilliam's unborn child all the same love and tenderness she did for Grace.

Juliana stirred, and raised her gaze to Fitz's. "Is there a child, Fitzwilliam?"

Fitz dragged his hands down his face. "Lina," he began, sounding wearier than she'd ever heard him. "Just listen to me—"

"Is there a child?"

Fitz's head bowed, and his hands dropped limply to his sides. "Yes," he whispered. "There's a child."

She nodded. "It's gotten so late, hasn't it? I don't suppose I can leave tomorrow, but you'll ride to Inverness and fetch Stokes for me, won't you? We can leave from Castle Kinross together, the day after."

Fitz went to her. "Please don't leave like this, Lina. If you'll only give me a few days to think, I may be able to find a way—"

"No." Juliana turned her face away. "You should have told me the truth at once, Fitzwilliam. How can you think I'd trade your child's future for Grace's? Your happiness for hers? I never could, so there's nothing more to be done."

Juliana rose to her feet, but Fitz grabbed her hand. "Wait, Lina. I have an idea—something that might make Logan reconsider."

Juliana shook her head. "Mr. Blair may be a thief and a liar, but he's no fool. He might have agreed to marry me to keep you from having to, but he knows I'll never consider a marriage between us now. I no longer have any power to persuade him."

Fitz was staring into the fire, his brows drawn together. "What if I could give you that power?"

Juliana paused, a flicker of hope in her breast. "You think there's something else Mr. Blair may want enough to make him agree to the marriage?"

"I know one thing he wants more than anything, and it's in my power to give it to him. He won't like how I'll go about it. At least, not at first, but at the moment I don't much care whether he likes it or not." A faint smile rose to Fitz's lips. "If I can manage to work it out the way I want, it will be to everyone's benefit."

She shook her head. "I don't know, Fitzwilliam. Perhaps your brother is right, and a marriage between us is pure madness. I'm afraid I'm so desperate to have the thing done I can't tell anymore."

He squeezed her hands. "It's not ideal, a marriage between you. I don't deny it. But Logan is...well, I imagine you have a poor opinion of him, given what you've learned about him so far. I don't blame you for it. I'm furious at him myself. But there's a great deal more honor in Logan than you might suppose. I hadn't been at Castle Kinross more than a week before I realized that."

Juliana sighed. She trusted Fitzwilliam's judgment, but Logan Blair had been firm in his refusal. He wasn't the sort of man who could be made to do something he didn't wish to do. "I can't imagine what you can do to convince him."

"I don't like to say yet. Not until I'm certain I can manage the thing, but if I can, I promise you, Lina, there's not a chance of him refusing the marriage."

She blew out a breath. "Perhaps it would be better if I were to go back to England at once. There must be some gentleman or other in London I can persuade to marry me—"

"No. I won't send you off to London to become prey to scoundrels and fortune hunters. Logan hasn't shown himself to advantage, but I promise you, you're far better off with him than you'd be with any of those blackguards. Besides, you said yourself you must have your father's approval for the match. I know Lord Graystone, Lina. He may not be entirely lucid, but even so, I doubt he'll approve a fortune hunter."

"No," she agreed. "But there's no guarantee he'll approve Mr. Blair, either."

Fitzwilliam gave her a cryptic smile. "I think he will, especially once my arrangements are complete, but it's going to take a bit of time to get everything in order. Will you stay a little longer, and give me a chance to help you?"

Juliana looked into Fitz's anxious eyes, and her heart ached. She didn't have much hope Logan Blair would change his mind, but she couldn't refuse Fitzwilliam this—not when he wanted so desperately to help her. "I suppose a few days won't make any difference."

He pressed her hand. "Thank you, Lina. Now, you must be exhausted." He rang the bell, and after a short time the housekeeper appeared. "Ah, Mrs. Selkirk. Please show Lady Juliana to her bedchamber, and see that a hot bath is prepared and a tray is sent to her room."

"Of course, Your Grace." Mrs. Selkirk smiled at Lady Juliana.

"Oh, and Mrs. Selkirk? Once Lady Juliana is settled, send Miss Emilia to me, if you would."

Mrs. Selkirk nodded, and gestured for Juliana to precede her out of the room.

Juliana cast one last look at Fitzwilliam, but he waved her away with a smile. "Go on, and don't worry, Lina. I'll take care of it. I promise."

Juliana thought of Logan Blair's stiff face, the tightness of his mouth when he'd refused her, and she doubted anyone could take care of it. But she allowed herself to be led away by Mrs. Selkirk, her body weary from her long ride, and her heart filled with misgivings.

Chapter Eight

Juliana's first thought when she woke the next morning was that a wiser lady would give up this mad scheme. She'd go back to England and do whatever she must to dig up a likely husband. It would be easier than trying to reason with Logan Blair. Easier than marrying him, as well.

Fitzwilliam didn't intend to let her give up, however. He'd guessed she'd succumb to her doubts this morning, and had appointed her a guardian to keep her from fleeing.

"More tea, Lady Juliana?"

Juliana nodded, and held out her teacup. "Yes, thank you."

Emilia Ferguson poured the tea into the dainty porcelain cup, set it on the tray, and pushed it across the table toward Juliana. "There. Isn't this cozy?"

"Yes, very." Juliana was well aware Fitzwilliam's betrothed was her gaoler for the day, but as far as prisons went, she couldn't deny Emilia had created a remarkably cozy one.

Juliana had woken later than usual. She'd thought to find the breakfast room deserted, but Emilia had been waiting for her there, despite the advanced hour. She'd cheerfully informed Juliana that Fitzwilliam had ridden to Inverness much earlier to tend to some business there. He expected to be gone all day, but he'd promised to stop at the Sassy Lassie and bring Stokes back with him to Castle Kinross that evening.

There was no sign of Logan Blair, and Juliana wondered fleetingly whether Emilia had taken her to this secluded back parlor to keep the two of them apart.

"I don't mind saying I'm glad to have you to myself today, Lady Juliana," Emilia said, as if she'd read Juliana's mind. "Fitzwilliam has told me so much about you, I'm anxious to know you."

Emilia offered her a shy smile, and Juliana's own lips curved in response. Emilia Ferguson had one of those infectious smiles that made everyone around her smile in return. It was easy to see why Fitzwilliam had fallen in love with her.

She was very pretty, certainly, with her dark hair and dark blue eyes, and she had a sweetness about her, a loveliness that radiated outward from her heart.

In some ways Emilia reminded Juliana of herself when she was younger. Oh, she'd never been as shy as Emilia was—every time their gazes met Emilia's cheeks flushed a becoming pink—but she'd had that same sort of naiveté about her, that same cheerfulness that came from knowing everything in her life was just as it should be, and would remain that way forever.

Until, of course, it didn't.

Perhaps if she'd been forced to overcome some challenge before then, she wouldn't have been so shocked when everything fell apart, but up until Emma's death, and then Jonathan's a year later, Juliana had had very little in her life to vex her.

Juliana let out a weary sigh. She must have looked desolate indeed, because she felt a soft touch on her arm and looked over to find Emilia's brows drawn together with concern.

"Won't you tell me a little about your niece, Lady Juliana?"

Juliana, who was more than happy to have the distraction, gave Emilia a grateful smile. "It's so kind of you to ask. Grace is the dearest little thing you can imagine. So bright, so inquisitive. Naughty occasionally, as all children are, but with a tender, loving heart. I'm certain you'll meet her yourself someday. Fitzwilliam is very fond of her, and will want you to know her."

"Oh, I should like that more than anything. Does she look like you?"

"Not at all. She's got dark hair and big dark eyes. My late brother Jonathan wasn't as fair as I am. Grace resembles him, but she looks much more like her mother than anyone else. She'll grow up to be a beauty, just as Emma was." Juliana smiled, but it was tinged with the sadness she always felt whenever she spoke of Emma and Jonathan.

Emilia saw it, and quickly changed the subject. "What sorts of things does she like to do? Does she ride yet?"

"She does, indeed. She has her own mare at Graystone Court, and she's fond of riding her. She likes the outdoors, so we spend a good deal of our time tramping about the grounds, studying plants and flowers. She adores fairy tales and stories. I read her a new one every night at bedtime, and then I tell her a story about her parents. I don't want her to forget them, you see."

"No. No, of course not." Emilia hesitated, then said, "I can tell you love her very much."

"I do. More than anything."

Emilia patted her hand. "Fitzwilliam tells me this man—this Lord Cowden—isn't a fit guardian for Grace. Is he as bad as all that?"

"He's worse than unfit. He's dangerous."

"Dangerous?" Emilia echoed, her hand going to her throat. "How?"

Even thinking of Benedict made Juliana's heart race with fear. "He's the sort of man driven to extremes by bitterness and jealousy."

"W—what sort of extremes?"

Juliana sighed. "For as long as I've known him, he's never been satisfied with what he has. He's an earl, but he holds his own title in contempt. His fortune is substantial, but no amount of money is ever enough for Lord Cowden. He's always envied Fitzwilliam. Despised him, even, because Fitzwilliam outranks him, and his fortune is much greater than Lord Cowden's."

Emilia recoiled. "He sounds dreadful."

"He is, but he's very good at hiding his true nature. He's a handsome man, and extremely clever and charming. He recently married, and his wife is very young, enamored of him, and a great heiress. Last night Fitzwilliam said he pitied Lord Cowden's bride, and I can't help but feel the same. I haven't the faintest doubt he's after her fortune, and doesn't care a fig for her."

Emilia looked horrified. "But how could your father appoint such a man as his granddaughter's guardian? It doesn't make sense!"

A day didn't go by Juliana didn't have the same thought, but as angry as she was at her father, she still found herself leaping to his defense. "My father isn't well, and hasn't been for some time. You must understand, Fitzwilliam and I grew up with Lord Cowden. His father was a dear friend of my father's, and we've known the family all our lives. Lord Cowden can be very charming when he wishes to be. My father is utterly taken in by him."

Emilia's face had gone pale. "Your niece, Grace. She's an heiress as well, isn't she?"

"Yes." Juliana's tone was grim. "Grace's money is reserved for her in a trust. Legally, her guardian can't touch a penny of it, but a man like Lord Cowden…well, I've no idea how he'd contrive to get his hands on it, but

I'm sure he'd try. He doesn't care a whit for Grace, that much is certain. I don't want him anywhere near her."

"No, of course you don't! Why, nothing could be worse!"

Juliana stared down into her teacup, her stomach churning. No, nothing could be worse than Grace being left at Lord Cowden's mercy. Not even marriage to Logan Blair.

It was a timely reminder.

Juliana set her teacup aside and rose to her feet. She was wasting precious time, sitting here chatting when she could be trying to persuade Mr. Blair to marry her.

Or failing that, threatening him into it.

"Have you seen Mr. Blair today?" Juliana asked, taking care to keep her voice casual. "I, ah…I have a question to ask him."

"Not since this morning, no. Perhaps Mrs. Selkirk knows where he is." Emilia rose to pull the bell, but paused as she passed the window. "There he is. It's looks like he's going for a ride."

Juliana hurried to Emilia's side. She peered through the window into the stable yard below, and there was Logan Blair, his dark hair ruffling in the breeze. He was wearing tight-fitting buckskin breeches, and his thighs looked like tree trunks.

Not that *she* had any use for his thighs, but really, he was the most imposing man she'd ever seen. Dreadful too, of course, but imposing. His sheer size alone…

Juliana's eyes narrowed as she watched him take the reins of his enormous gray stallion from a waiting stable boy and swing himself up into a saddle burdened with two bulging saddlebags, one on each side.

"Where do you suppose he's going?" It didn't look to Juliana as if he was off on a mere ride. No, he was outfitted for a journey, and a long one, at that.

"Off to visit some tenants, perhaps. He often does so."

A knot of suspicion was tightening in Juliana's chest. "I see. Is he usually gone for quite some time?"

Emilia shrugged. "It varies. Sometimes just a day or two, but I've known him to go off for several weeks before."

Several weeks! Without another word, Juliana whirled around and rushed to the parlor door. Why, that despicable coward was running away from her!

Emilia startled, then hurried after her. "Lady Juliana! Where are you going?"

"I'm going after Mr. Blair."

Emilia's eyes went wide. "Going after him! But *why*?"

"Don't you see, Emilia? He knows very well I can't hang about Castle Kinross for weeks, waiting for him to return. He thinks to escape a marriage to me this way!"

"Oh, no, Lady Juliana! I'm sure that's not so!" Emilia looked appalled. "Logan isn't like that. He'd never do something so cowardly!"

Juliana didn't see why not. He was a thief, wasn't he? Why shouldn't he be a coward as well? "Perhaps not, but I'm not willing to take that chance. Mr. Blair is going to have company today, whether he likes it or not."

Emilia was growing more distressed with every word out of Juliana's mouth. "Oh, dear. Perhaps I should send a servant to Inverness to find Fitzwilliam?"

"No, there isn't time. I'm sorry, Emilia. I don't like to upset you, but I'm going after him. Will the groom be able to give me his direction?"

"Yes, but you're not going *alone*?" Emilia was wringing her hands.

Oh yes, she was. If she was alone when she caught up to Mr. Blair—and she *would* catch up to him—he'd be forced to bring her back to Castle Kinross himself.

If Logan Blair thought he was going to just ride blithely off into the distance and remain there until she was forced to leave Scotland, he was very much mistaken.

* * * *

She couldn't feel her backside anymore.

Juliana shifted this way and that on the saddle, but it was no use. Her poor posterior had gone completely numb. She was an accomplished rider, but a ramble around the grounds with Grace wasn't quite the same thing as a mad dash across the Scottish Highlands.

Perhaps she should have listened to Emilia and waited for Fitzwilliam to return home. He'd warned her to let him deal with his brother, but Juliana was reluctant to let Mr. Blair out of her sight. Why, even now the man might be running off to some far-flung firth, or some out-of-the-way castle to escape her.

She'd paused only long enough to confirm with a stable boy that Mr. Blair was heading for the Robertsons' farm, and that if she rode due east, she'd catch up to him before he arrived. It had taken several hours of hard riding, but twenty minutes ago she'd caught sight of him ahead of her, perched on the back of his gray stallion.

He'd since become aware she was following him, but so far, he hadn't acknowledged her by so much as a glance. He was so intent on ignoring her, in fact, that Juliana was tempted to charge after him, leap onto his horse's back, and tackle him to the ground.

Let him try and ignore *that*.

Upon further thought, though, she decided a less confrontational approach would be best. No man wanted a bride who wrestled him into the dirt. No, it would be far better if she kept her temper in check, and tried to charm him instead.

She'd been charming, once upon a time.

Juliana tapped her heels into her horse's flanks, her gaze locked on Mr. Blair's broad back. He was still some distance ahead of her, but she urged her horse into a canter, and soon she drew close enough to him it became ridiculous for him to refuse to notice her.

At last, he turned to her with a resigned sigh. "Is it a habit of yours, Lady Juliana, to chase after men who don't want your company?"

She arched a brow. "If they *did* want my company, I wouldn't have to chase them, would I? Besides, following you has proven to be quite a productive use of my time. You did lead me straight to Castle Kinross last night, if you recall."

She took care to keep her voice pleasant, but all she got for her efforts was a dark frown.

She tried again. "The moors are quite beautiful." The sun cast its afternoon rays over the gently rolling hills, picking out what seemed to Juliana thousands of shades of brown and green. "What's it like when the heather is in full bloom?"

He glanced briefly at her. "Purple."

"How pretty that must be!" Juliana exclaimed, with resolute cheerfulness.

Mr. Blair didn't reply.

Juliana frowned. Goodness, what a stubborn man. The more determined he was to ignore her, the more determined she became to make him talk to her. "You're not at all like Fitzwilliam, for all that you two are brothers. He's *never* cross."

"I'm not cross," he snapped. "But if I *am*, it's only because—"

"That sort of bad temper won't do when we're married, you know," she went on. "I won't have you biting my head off every morning at the breakfast table."

He spun in the saddle to face her, his cheeks flushed with irritation, but as soon as he caught the mischievous grin on her face, his lips gave a reluctant twitch. "Very clever, *mo bhean uasal*."

Mo bhean uasal? "What does that mean?" Something insulting, no doubt. Insufferable Englishwoman, perhaps.

He shrugged, but wouldn't answer.

She huffed out a breath. "I don't see any reason for us to quarrel, Mr. Blair."

"Don't you, lass?" The sarcasm in his voice was slightly offset by the hint of a smile still lurking at the corners of his mouth.

She studied his lips, a tingle of awareness lifting the fine hairs on her neck. He had quite a nice mouth. Perhaps he should put it to better use and smile more.

But then his mouth was no concern of hers. Juliana cleared her throat. "How much longer until we reach the Robertsons' farm?"

He stiffened in the saddle. "*We* aren't going to the Robertsons' farm. *I'm* going, without you. You made it this far on your own, and you can make it back the same way. Castle Kinross is due west. Keep riding until you run into it."

Juliana didn't believe for one minute he'd send her back to Castle Kinross alone. "No, I don't think so. I've already been that way. I'd rather go along with you, and see more of the eastern countryside."

"This isn't a pleasure ride, Lady Juliana. A half-dozen or so of the Robertsons' sheep have gone missing. He can't account for it, and suspects a poacher. It's going to be an exhausting day." He swept a derisive look over the pristine riding habit she'd borrowed from Emilia. "Filthy, too. We'll be clambering over hills and under bushes searching for the sheep. You won't find it amusing."

Juliana's mouth tightened at his mocking tone. He imagined she lived only to be amused, did he? Perhaps that had been true once, but she couldn't recall the last time she'd been at liberty to pursue frivolous entertainment. Logan Blair, for all his smirking and innuendo, hadn't the vaguest idea what she was capable of. "You might be surprised, Mr. Blair, at what I'd find amusing."

He gave her a skeptical look, as if to say he'd be shocked if he found anything she did surprising. "You won't be able to keep up with us. You'll only slow us down."

Juliana ran an uneasy eye over the rough terrain surrounding them. The truth was, she hadn't intended to ride today. She'd slept poorly, and her body was still fatigued from yesterday's adventures, but she'd be damned if she'd admit any of this to Logan Blair. "Nonsense. I kept pace with you from Gretna Green to Inverness, didn't I? Why should this be any different?"

"Because we're chasing sheep today. You're bound to get in the way."

Juliana shrugged. "Even so, I don't like to let you go without me. Who knows how long you'd decide to be gone from Castle Kinross? It would be a pity, indeed, if I was obliged to leave Scotland without saying goodbye to you."

Juliana's voice was pleasant, but he understood at once what she was implying, and his face darkened with anger. "All right then, my lady. If you want to watch my every move, I can't stop you. But there's no harm in taking you along, is there, lass, since you're so certain you can keep up?"

Juliana eyed him, her gaze narrowing. He didn't believe for one moment she could keep pace with the men. She could see by the smug smile on his lips that he was only humoring her. He was just waiting for the moment when she admitted she couldn't keep up, and was forced to plead for mercy.

Juliana fisted the reins, anger burning in her chest. Logan Blair could keep her out here all night, and that moment would never come.

"One more thing, Lady Juliana. The men out here don't have much use for aristocratic English ladies. You're not in any danger from them—that is, not as long as you stay close to me."

Juliana smothered a snort. *Danger, indeed.* He was only trying to intimidate her.

They didn't speak at all after that, but rode across the moors at a quick pace. It was another hour before they reached the farm, which was a little more than twenty-four miles to the east of Castle Kinross. Juliana's legs, still weary from yesterday's ride were groaning in protest by the time they rode into the farmyard, but she maintained a stoic silence.

She'd dismounted and was trying to shake some feeling back into her legs without attracting Mr. Blair's attention when the door to the farmhouse opened, and the most enormous man she'd ever seen came out. That is, he was the most enormous man she'd ever seen until she got a look at the two other men who followed him into the yard.

She stared, her mouth agape. All three of them had bright red hair, darker red bushy beards, and shoulders so muscular and wide they put her in mind of a team of oxen.

"Hallo, Logan." The first man out the door offered Logan a brief nod, but he wasn't looking at Logan. He was looking at *her*, and he didn't seem at all impressed. He stared at her for a moment, as if he couldn't quite decide what sort of creature she might be, then jerked his chin in her direction. "Who've ye got here?"

Logan leapt down from his horse's back and strode across the yard to shake hands with the red-headed giant. "Robertson." He nodded to the other men, then turned and waved a hand toward Juliana. "This is Lady

Juliana Bernard. She's a friend of Fitzwilliam's, and has come to Castle Kinross for a visit."

It took every bit of Juliana's composure not to blanch when the three pairs of hard blue eyes turned on her. None of the three of them said a word, but they stared at her for so long her knees trembled underneath her skirts. Dear God, each of them was more enormous than the next, and they looked as if they'd welcome the chance to squeeze the life of out of her.

"Lady?" One of them asked, just when Juliana was ready to sink under the weight of those cold blue gazes.

"Yes." Juliana gathered her courage and took a step forward. "How do you do?"

Three sets of red eyebrows shot up. One of the men turned and spat on the ground, then dragged a massive hand across his mouth. "She's *English?*"

This wasn't asked in the spirit of friendly curiosity. He fairly seethed with menace, and Juliana, whose courage had failed her, was unable to say a word in response.

Logan cast her an impatient look, but he did take pity on her. "Aye, she's English, and under my protection." He didn't say anything more, but the other men seemed to understand him readily enough.

The Englishwoman—as undesirable as her presence might be—was to be treated if not with courtesy, then at least with forbearance.

"But what's she doing 'ere?" The smallest of the three giants shoved his way past his brothers, and gave Logan a baffled look. "What're we meant to do with 'er?"

"That's a foolish question, Callum," Logan said, that smug smile once again playing about his lips.

The other men didn't seem to find it foolish in the least. They blinked at Logan, then exchanged glances with each other.

Logan raised an eyebrow. "She's come to help us search for the sheep, of course. Or the poacher. Whichever comes first."

"*She?*" Callum swept a doubtful look from the top of Juliana's head to the toes of her riding boots. "But she's no bigger than a sheep 'erself!"

"I beg your pardon!" Juliana folded her arms across her chest, piqued. "I'm much bigger than a sheep, I assure you!"

"An English sheep, maybe," Callum muttered.

Juliana huffed out a breath, but before she could offer a word in her defense she was interrupted by a hearty laugh from Logan. She jerked her gaze toward him, and her eyes widened.

Yes, a very nice mouth, indeed.

He'd put it to good use at last, too, with that smile. Mocking as it was, it wasn't the sort of smile a lady could dismiss with a shrug. But then it wasn't aimed at *her*, was it?

Logan slapped Callum on the back. "You never know, Callum. She may surprise you, and prove a useful member of the search party."

It was plain by his arrogant grin Logan thought it unlikely she'd prove anything but a nuisance, and if she could judge by their discontented mumbling, his tenants thought the same. Juliana regarded them all with narrowed eyes, her determination rising right along with her temper. Logan Blair might go to the devil, and take that infuriating smirk with him! She was going to make him swallow those words. She'd find a damn sheep today if it took until midnight, or she died trying.

She marched over to her horse, swung herself up into the saddle, and turned a cool look on the four men still standing in the yard. "Well? Do you intend to stand about all day, discussing the size of English sheep, or will you actually come and find them?"

Callum Robertson's red brows drew together. "*Bhig galla*," he muttered.

Logan threw back his head in a laugh. Whatever Callum had just said, he seemed to find it very funny, indeed.

Juliana's lips pinched together. "What does that mean?"

No one answered her, but Logan let out another chuckle that made Juliana want to tear his hair out. The Robertson brothers—for indeed, brothers they must be, for no three men could look more alike—mounted their own horses, and in the next moment they were all off, clouds of dust rising from ten pairs of hooves as they thundered from the farmyard.

Once Robertson had pointed out the general area where the sheep had gone missing, Logan pulled out a tattered map and marked off a large section of land with that spot in the center. They split up into two groups, with Juliana, Logan, and Callum going in one direction, and the two other Robertson brothers in the other. They spent the rest of the afternoon riding in an ever-narrowing circle around the place where the sheep had disappeared. They met up at the close of each circle to confer, then set off again, moving a little closer to the center each time.

By the time they'd gone around twice, Juliana had begun to understand the enormity of her foolishness in insisting on accompanying Logan on the search. It was back-breaking, exhausting work—far more strenuous than anything she was used to. Her legs were screaming with pain, and her bottom, which had been courteous enough to remain numb for the earlier part of the ride, suddenly awoke, and made its fury known. She'd gone cross-eyed from peering under bushes and scrub brush for a glimpse of white wool, and her back was soaked with sweat.

Still, not a single whisper of complaint crossed her lips.

As the afternoon wore on she caught Logan watching her with a measuring look in his eyes, but she only raised her chin and rode on. She'd fall off her horse in a dead faint before she'd gratify him with even a murmur of protest.

After the third time around without any sign of a sheep they paused, and the men bent their heads over the map. Juliana stayed a little apart, half-listening to the four of them argue about which direction to take next when a faint noise caught her attention.

They'd stopped near the edge of a small wood, and the noise seemed to be coming from the trees. She stilled, listening, and after a moment she heard it again.

It sounded like...bleating.

Juliana straightened in the saddle, her ears pricked. Yes! It was definitely bleating, but she couldn't tell which direction it was coming from.

"Did you hear that?" She brought her horse closer to the men, but they were gathered in a tight circle, and they didn't shift to make space for her. "I heard a sheep or a lamb bleating!"

No one paid her the least bit of attention.

"We've already been 'round the south edge three times." Callum tapped a finger against the map. "They wouldn't 'a come all this way."

Logan was shaking his head. "They have before. I say we circle back one more time."

Juliana raised her voice. "I beg your pardon, gentlemen, but I'm quite certain I heard—"

"I say we 'ead back toward the farm." Robertson scratched his beard, frowning. "They don't usually wander so far."

"For pity's sake, will you listen to me? I tell you, there's a bleating sheep not five yards from—"

"If they were that close to the farm, they'd 'ave made their way back by now," Callum insisted.

Juliana looked from one man to the next, but none of them spared her a glance. "Oh, bother this." She wheeled her horse around and headed in the direction from which she thought the sound had come.

No one tried to stop her, and no one asked where she was going.

By the time they remembered her presence and looked up to find her, she was gone.

Chapter Nine

It was some time before Logan realized Lady Juliana had disappeared.

He and the Robertson brothers had been deep in discussion about which direction their search should take when Callum Robertson, who'd dismounted and wandered off to take care of his personal business, sauntered out of the wood, looked around, and asked, "What's happened to yer wee English lass, Blair?"

"Nothing's happened to her. She's right…"

But she wasn't right there. Lady Juliana had been a few paces behind him, prattling some nonsense about bleating lambs, but she and her horse had vanished. Logan glanced around, shading his eyes from the sun. There was no sign of either of them.

Lady Juliana was gone.

Now he'd noticed her absence, he suddenly became aware at least ten minutes had passed since she'd ceased blathering in his ear. He peered around again, uneasiness tightening his stomach.

There was no telling how much trouble Lady Juliana could get into in ten short minutes. Her father had lost track of her for only a few weeks, and she'd made it all the way to Scotland.

"She's wee, but she's hearty." Brice, the eldest of the Robertson brothers, nodded at Logan. "She's that look about 'er like a brisk wind could blow 'er off 'er horse, but she's sturdy like. Wee, but stronger than she looks."

This was high praise indeed coming from Brice Robertson, but Logan wasn't interested in Brice's philosophical musings about women. "She may be small, but she's not small enough to disappear. Come on, then. She can't have gone far. We'll have to go find her, and then we can carry on searching for the sheep."

Logan kicked Fingal into a trot and headed for the woods, and the other men fell in behind him. When they found Lady Juliana, he was going to wring her delicate white neck. What did she mean, running off like that without a word to anyone? It had already been a grueling day, and it promised to become more so before it was over. They'd been riding for hours without any sign of the missing sheep, and now they were obliged to halt their search to chase after a troublesome chit who was too foolish to know better than not to scamper about the Highlands by herself. He should never have let her come with him today. As soon as he noticed she was following him, he should have taken her right back to—

"That lass don't carry on much," Callum Robertson offered suddenly, as if he'd been considering the matter for some time. "She looks like the sort who would, ye ken. English sorts do, especially the smallish women." He nodded wisely. "But that lass never moaned once all day, not even when Brice's horse kicked that cloud of dust in 'er face."

His brothers nodded their agreement. Logan kept quiet, but he silently admitted to himself it was nothing but the truth. By midday he could see the rough terrain and the relentless pace were wearing her down, but she hadn't uttered a single word of protest all day. She'd listened to his instructions, and though she'd struggled at times, she'd kept pace with four men three times her size.

"Aye, she seems a good lass. Bonnie, too." Dougal, who was the second youngest of the brothers and a favorite with the ladies, winked at Logan. "Just as well she came out today. I'd rather look at 'er than any of you."

His brothers laughed, but Logan, who was far more irritated by this comment than he had any right to be, scowled at him. "Never mind looking at her. She's not here for *you*, Dougal Robertson."

"No," Dougal agreed, mildly enough, but his eyes were glinting with mischief when they met Logan's. "I 'spect she's yours, innit she, Blair?"

Logan gritted his teeth. If the offer of her hand made her *his*, then she was damn well *his*, all right.

Then again, Lady Juliana hadn't offered her hand so much as demanded his. Not that it would make any difference to the Robertson boys. They'd consider any offering or demanding of hands a betrothal, and the last thing Logan needed was the entire clan gossiping about how he was going to marry an English lady.

"She won't be anyone's unless we find her, so stop your blathering, Dougal, and put your eyes to work instead of your mouth."

Dougal chuckled, but he obeyed this command, and they searched along the edge of the tree line without speaking. For the first mile or so Logan was distracted by fantasies of tossing Lady Juliana onto her horse and riding her straight back to Castle Kinross, but as they continued on without any sign of her, his irritation began to give way to concern. It was only another hour until the sun set, and there was a chance a poacher was nearby.

Where could she have gotten to? Had she gone down the far side of a hill, and lost her way? It seemed unlikely she'd get so easily turned around. Lady Juliana's mind was even sharper than her tongue.

Was it possible she'd lost patience with him and had returned to Castle Kinross on her own? Again, it didn't seem likely, but he hadn't been particularly kind to her today. He'd let his temper get the best of him this morning, and he'd been surly with her ever since.

Guilt stabbed at him as he recalled that she'd been trying to tell him something right before she disappeared. He hadn't paid any more attention to her than he would a streak of dust on his boot.

What had she been saying? Something about a lamb bleating—

"Did ye hear that?" Callum pulled his horse up with a quick jerk and sat still for a moment, listening. "It sounds like—"

"Like a lamb bleating. Just before Lady Juliana disappeared she was trying to tell me something about a lamb. She must be nearby." Logan called the words over his shoulder as he rode deeper into the woods.

By now he'd grown desperate to lay eyes on her and assure himself she was still in one piece, but as soon as they got into the woods their progress slowed to a crawl. There'd been a violent storm the previous week, and they were obliged to pick their way over fallen branches and downed trees.

Logan followed the sound of the lamb, whose frightened bleating had taken on a new sense of urgency. It was squealing and carrying on as if some wild animal were about to pounce on it, a circumstance that did nothing to ease Logan's mind.

As they drew closer, Logan heard rushing water. He turned to Brice with a puzzled frown. "Is that Ruthven Burn? Jesus, it's flowing fast."

Brice nodded. "Aye. It's like to have swollen past its banks from the storm."

For the most part Ruthven Burn was wide and shallow—more a creek than a river—but some parts of it were deeper than others, and it was known to overflow its banks after a torrential rain.

"That could be where your sheep have got to, couldn't it?" Logan was more concerned about Lady Juliana than the sheep, but he had a suspicion where they found one, they'd find the other.

"Mayhap they wandered here to drink from the burn." Brice frowned. "Every now and then they come down this far, but not often, and they find their way back to the farm quick enough."

"They may have come down and gotten trapped in the deeper water." Logan's tone was grim. Sheep weren't the stupid creatures many people believed them to be, but their intellect wasn't such that they could assess the depth or speed of the burn. And where one sheep went, others would follow. Instinct told him they were about to find a half-dozen drowned sheep in the Ruthven Burn, but when they cleared the woods at last and emerged onto the bank, what he saw instead was far, far worse than drowned sheep. He stared, the blood going cold in his veins.

The burn had indeed swollen past its banks, and an enormous tree had torn loose and fallen across the rushing water. Three or four sheep who'd gone down to the bank to drink had gotten trapped amongst the tree roots and drowned. The sight of their helpless, swollen bodies was enough to unnerve even stalwart farmers like the Robertson brothers, but it wasn't the sheep that made Logan go numb with panic.

A tiny lamb was perched on the thick trunk of the fallen tree, halfway across the width of the burn. It was stranded there, bleating piteously, its fleece smeared with mud and its spindly legs shaking.

And there, her arms flung wide to balance herself was Lady Juliana, creeping along the trunk toward the lamb, one tiny step at a time.

"What the *devil* is that lass about?" Callum Robertson was the last to make it to the edge of the bank. He took in the scene with one glance, and was startled into an ill-advised shout.

"Shut it." Dougal slapped a hand over his brother's mouth. "Ye'll make 'er fall!"

Logan held his breath, his heart crowding into his throat. His body tensed to leap for Lady Juliana, but she didn't fall, or even stumble. She only paused, and said in a steady voice, without turning to look at them, "Quiet, if you please. If the poor thing takes fright, she'll tumble in and drown in an instant."

"*She'll* drown?" It took every bit of Logan's control not to shout at her to return to the safety of the bank at once, but he managed to keep his voice calm. "You'll *both* drown if you fall in, lass. You should have thought of that before you crawled out there!"

This warning didn't make any impression on Lady Juliana, who continued to make her way across the trunk with no more concern for her own safety than if she were moving through the figures of the quadrille. "Nonsense. I know how to swim."

Logan was tempted to ask her if she'd ever gone swimming in a fast-moving burn in boots and a riding habit. Instead, he held his tongue. She was less likely to panic if she didn't stop to consider the real danger she was in.

He was forced to admit she looked very far from panicking. Logan couldn't imagine how the indolent life of an English aristocrat could have produced a lady of such nerve, but there was no question she was as steady as the massive tree trunk under her feet.

Brice was watching her creep along the trunk, shaking his head. "Ach, the wee thing's mad, innit she? Brave, though," he added, with unmistakable admiration.

"Aye. She's brave. Bloody foolish, too." Logan tossed his coat to the ground and dropped onto his arse on the bank to tug off his boots and stockings. Then he picked his way over loose branches and protruding roots to the end of the fallen tree trunk resting on the side of the muddy bank.

"Don't come after me, Mr. Blair," Lady Juliana ordered. "The trunk is a bit tippy, you see, with only the mud on either bank to support it."

Logan swallowed. "Tippy?"

"Yes. Your weight may throw it to one side or the other, and I'll lose my balance."

Logan opened his mouth to argue, but he could feel the cold, slimy mud seeping through his toes even now, and he knew she was right. There wasn't a thing he could do aside from wait, and prepare to jump in after her if she did fall into the burn.

None of them spoke while she crept along the tree trunk. When she at last made it to within reaching distance of the lamb, Logan let loose the breath he'd been holding. "I beg your pardon, *mo bhean uasal,* but how do you plan to snatch up the lamb without both of you tumbling over the side?"

"I have a plan."

Logan wasn't at all surprised to hear it. Despite his growing anxiety, he couldn't help the small smile that rose to his lips. "Of course, you do. Do you care to share it with us, lass?"

She didn't answer, but in the next moment she crouched down and braced her hands on the trunk in front of her.

"Juliana!" Logan leapt forward, certain she'd lose her balance and fall, but Brice restrained him with a hand on his shoulder.

"She's all right. Stay where ye are."

She *was* all right. She'd reached down with her hands to steady herself, dropped to her bottom, then flung her legs onto either side of the trunk so she was straddling it. Once she was steady, she reached out her arms and gathered the lamb against her chest.

"Don't cry." She ran a gentle hand over the lamb's head. "Yes, I know you're frightened, but you're all right now, sweetheart. I've got you."

There was no question of her turning around with such a squirming, bleating bundle in her arms, so as cool as you please she began to shimmy her way back across the trunk with her back to them. It wasn't at all ladylike, as her skirts were hiked up to her knees, but Lady Juliana, who was still cooing soothingly to the lamb, didn't seem to notice.

Logan and the Robertson brothers watched her in silence, their mouths open, identical expressions of amazement on their faces. None of them said a word until Dougal, overcome with admiration, breathed, "I think I'm in love with that lass."

"Aye. Me too." Callum gave a vigorous nod. "She's a verra fine lass."

"Yer both eejits." Brice cocked his head, watching as Lady Juliana scooted her way toward them. "Not but what she *is* a fine lass. Tenderhearted, too, the way she went after the poor wee creature. A tender heart's a fine thing in a lass, don't ye think so, Logan?"

Logan didn't reply. His whole attention was fixed on Lady Juliana. She'd made it far enough so he could reach out and grab her without too much effort. He was debating whether it was wiser to do that or just let her come along on her own when the lamb, seeing itself within leaping distance of the safety of the bank struggled free of her arms and jumped over her shoulder, wailing and bleating like a banshee.

The sudden movement upset Lady Juliana's balance, and with a little cry of dismay she lost her grip on the slippery bark, and tumbled into the burn with a splash.

The Robertson brothers let out a startled shout. Dougal and Callum both leapt forward, but Logan was already there. He jumped in after her, caught hold of one of her arms, and pulled her back to the surface. She was gasping with shock and cold, and Logan didn't waste any time. He wrapped one arm around her back, the other under her knees, hauled her against his chest, and struggled against the rushing water until he fell onto the bank, with Lady Juliana still in his arms.

"Give 'er here before ye both drown." Brice was there, holding out his arms for her.

Logan was strangely reluctant to let her go, but before he could protest that he had her, Brice grasped her under her arms and dragged her further up the bank to safety. Dougal and Callum each took Logan by an arm and yanked him out after her. He crawled up the bank, his chest heaving with effort.

Lady Juliana lay on her back with her eyes open. She was alert, but her breathing was labored, and her face pale. Logan hung over her, the

Robertson brothers at his back, and waited with growing alarm for her to say something.

It was a while before she did, but at last she fixed her gaze on Logan, opened her mouth, and asked, "Is the lamb all right?"

Logan stared down at her, unsure whether to laugh or shout at her until her ears bled. In the end, he did neither. Instead he staggered to his feet, plucked up the lamb, who was shivering on the bank a few feet away, and laid her gently on Lady Juliana's chest.

* * * *

Logan had never before seen any of the Robertson brothers move as fast as they did when Lady Juliana entered their farmhouse.

They scurried about as if Queen Charlotte herself had just honored them with her presence. Logan thought sourly that if they'd made half as much effort searching for the sheep, Lady Juliana might not have fallen into the burn in the first place.

"Take a seat right 'ere, my lady." Callum dragged the best chair in the room closer to the fire and patted the seat.

"Wait! Callum, you eejit, let me take Logan's coat off 'er first. It's wet." Callum shot Logan an accusing look as Dougal tenderly removed the coat from Lady Juliana's shoulders. "Yer coat is *wet*, Logan. Muddy, too."

Logan scowled. "That does tend to happen when a man jumps into a burn, Callum. My shirt and breeches are damp as well, so if you don't mind, a blanket would be wel—"

"A blanket, 'o course! Dougal, go fetch the lass a blanket."

Dougal darted out of the room as if his heels had caught fire. He returned a moment later, draped a thick blanket over Lady Juliana's shoulders, then tossed another one across the room to Logan. "Here. Stop yer moaning."

Logan caught it and used it to dry the last of the droplets from his hair. It had taken them the better part of an hour to ride back to the Robertsons' farm, so his clothes were mostly dry.

He tossed the blanket aside and threw himself into the chair across from Lady Juliana's. She was still holding the lamb on her lap, just as she'd done the entire ride back to the Robertsons' farm. None of them had tried to take it from her, not even when she entered the farmhouse. It snuggled against her, its white, woolly head resting on its curled legs.

"Aw, look at the wee thing." Brice paused with a tea tray in his hands and grinned down at Lady Juliana. "Ye should keep 'er, my lady. Take 'er back to the castle with ye."

"How kind you are, Mr. Robertson. Thank you." Lady Juliana beamed at him.

Logan could have sworn he saw Brice Robertson blush.

"Ach, well, it's nothing at all, lass." Brice fumbled with the teapot, his big hands clumsy, but at last he managed to pour a cup of tea. "Here ye are. This'll warm ye up."

Lady Juliana took it with a grateful smile, but Logan noticed once she finished it she was still shivering under her blanket. He reached over and fingered a fold of her heavy riding habit.

Still damp. Likely her hair was, too.

He grabbed the bottle of whisky from Brice's tray and poured a generous measure into a glass. "Here. Drink this."

She accepted the glass, took a tiny sip, and wrinkled her nose. "It burns."

Logan chuckled. "Drink it. It'll warm you faster than tea will."

She sipped obediently from her glass, and after a little while her eyelids began to droop. When she dropped into a doze, Logan gently drew the glass from her slack fingers and set it on the table.

"Poor lass," Brice murmured. "She's too weary to keep 'er eyes open."

Logan studied her in silence. Her heavy, dark lashes rested on her pale cheeks, and the fair hair that had escaped its pins hung in damp curls around her face. One hand rested on the chair's arm, but the other was still cupped around the lamb's head.

She looked very small sitting there, half-buried in the blanket Dougal had put over her, but in every way that mattered, there was nothing small about Lady Juliana Bernard.

Brice was right. She *was* a brave lass. A bit mad too, perhaps, certainly sharp-tongued and impatient. *Bhig galla*, just as Callum had said. She was as troublesome a lady as Logan had ever known, but he also didn't know many ladies who'd risk their own safety to rescue a terrified lamb from drowning.

Shouldn't someone do the same for her?

For all her bravery, for all her tenderness of heart, Lady Juliana was drowning, and by some strange twist of fate, he was the only one who could pull her back to the surface again.

Logan hadn't slept at all the night before. He'd been up pacing from one side of his bedchamber to the other, haunted by the despair on Lady Juliana's face when he'd left her alone in the library last night. The hurt and disappointment on Fitzwilliam's.

He might have been able to brush aside his pangs of conscience again this morning, but then Lady Juliana had gone and saved that blasted lamb...

To some people, it would have been a small enough thing. It was just a lamb, hardly worth anything really, but to Logan, compassion wasn't a small thing at all. He'd seen the lack of it too often to think of it as insignificant.

He leaned back in his chair with a sigh and turned his attention from Lady Juliana to Brice. He'd been distracted by her all day, but now it was time to get down to business. "I want to talk to you, Robertson." He nodded at the other two men. "Dougal and Callum, too."

Logan hadn't come here today just to search for sheep. That had been a convenient excuse to visit the Robertsons' farm. He glanced from Brice to Dougal, and from Dougal to Callum. All three Robertson brothers were big, strong, healthy men—the sort of men with the brawn and the heart to make a success out of a chance at a new life.

It was a chance he wanted to give them.

If he did decide to go to England with Lady Juliana, this would be his last opportunity to do so. If the Robertson brothers went, other members of the clan would follow.

One of Brice's red eyebrows rose. "All right, then. What do ye want to talk about?"

Logan leaned forward in his chair and fixed his gaze on Brice's face. "I want to talk to you about Cape Fear Valley, in North Carolina."

Chapter Ten

Logan and the Robertson brothers did talk, for far longer into the night than Logan thought they would. By the time he and Lady Juliana were mounted and riding west toward Castle Kinross the sky had darkened to a midnight blue, and thousands of frosty silver stars were winking above.

They hadn't gone more than three or four miles before Logan realized his companion wasn't going to make it as far as the castle. She'd never admit it, but he could see she was chilled to the bone, and swaying in the saddle as if she was one yawn away from toppling to the ground.

The Robertsons' farm was the closest, but Logan couldn't bring her back there for the night. Lady Juliana's reputation would never recover if anyone found out she'd spent a night alone with four unmarried men, especially if one of those men was Dougal Robertson.

No, he'd have to take her to the Macaulay farm. He'd planned to stop there on his way back to the castle in any case, to leave some supplies Mrs. Selkirk had given him to take to Widow Macaulay, but it was well past midnight now. Agnes Macaulay wasn't going to be pleased to find Logan and an exhausted, half-drowned English chit on her doorstep in the middle of the night.

But he didn't have any better ideas, so he turned Fingal's head and set a slow, steady pace northward. The farm was about an hour's ride away, but they'd only made it half that distance before Logan was obliged to reach for Lady Juliana's reins and bring her horse to a halt.

He leapt down from Fingal's back. Lady Juliana startled awake when he wrapped his hands firmly around her waist. "Are we there already?" She squinted into the darkness around them, puzzled. "Where's Castle Kinross gone?"

Logan hid a grin. "I expect it's right where we left it. Here, let me help you down. Hold the lamb steady." He gave her a gentle tug, and she slid down from her horse's back without a word of complaint. Logan caught her easily in his arms, his grin widening. Her wits were definitely befuddled with fatigue, otherwise she never would have jumped into his arms without an argument.

Instead, she hugged the lamb to her chest and tucked her head under Logan's chin. She smelled like Ruthven Burn and damp wool, but Logan didn't mind it. That is, he didn't *like* it—certainly not enough to bury his face in her hair for a quick sniff. No, the very idea was ridiculous, and he'd deny it to his dying breath.

"Steady, Fingal." Logan lifted Lady Juliana onto his horse's back, then swung up behind her. She had the lamb in her lap, and Logan had *her* in his. There was very little room for the three of them in one saddle, but Lady Juliana was too fatigued to ride any further. He couldn't just let her fall from her horse, could he?

No, there was nothing for him to do but spread his legs a little wider and wedge her curvy backside between his thighs. His body roared to life, and he forced a half-dozen breaths of cold air into his lungs to discourage it.

It didn't work. An ice-cold plunge into Ruthven Burn wouldn't have worked.

He gritted his teeth, and wrapped an arm around her waist.

It was going to be a long ride...

Logan sighed, and set Fingal to a brisk walk. The swaying of the horse beneath them soon lulled Lady Juliana into another doze. She murmured something in her sleep, and her body relaxed against his. He instinctively gathered her closer against his chest and angled his head to get a glimpse of her face.

Her green eyes were closed, her thick eyelashes shadowing her cheeks. Her lips were slightly parted, her mouth soft. Her fingers had gone slack, but even in her sleep she kept the lamb safely wrapped in her arms. Logan shook his head, a reluctant smile on his lips. Damned if he knew how she was going to get the animal back to England with her.

Logan struggled with his eager body the entire ride to Macaulay's, but strangely enough, the time seemed to fly by. Before he knew it, they were riding past the fence he and his father had helped build years before and into the small farmyard. The house was dark and silent, but one of the stable boys startled awake when they rode into the yard.

He came out of the stables rubbing his eyes. He fixed his bleary gaze on Logan, Lady Juliana, and the lamb, then rubbed his eyes again. "That you, laird?"

"It's me, Douglas. Beg pardon for waking you, but can you take care of Fingal and Domino here?" Logan tipped his head toward the black-and-white horse Lady Juliana had been riding. "They've both been ridden hard today. Oh, and take the lamb, too."

Douglas scrambled to Logan's side. "'Course I will. Ye just leave 'em here with me, and I'll tuck 'em up tight fer the night."

"Good man, Douglas." Logan dismounted carefully, one hand on Lady Juliana's waist to steady her. He reached up with the other to scoop the lamb from her arms, but it didn't care for the idea of being wrenched from its warm cocoon. It began bleating piteously and kicking its skinny legs in protest. One of its little hooves landed on Lady Juliana's chin, and she woke with a start.

At first, she gazed down at the lamb as if she were surprised to find it there, but after a moment understanding dawned, and she settled it back down on her lap. "There now, don't fuss."

Once the lamb was quiet again, Lady Juliana raised her head and took in her surroundings. Her eyes widened as she glanced around the unfamiliar barn, then widened further when they rested on Douglas. "This isn't Castle Kinross. Where are we, Mr. Blair?"

"Widow Macaulay's farm. You're in no shape to ride another three hours. We're spending the night here."

Logan expected an argument, but Lady Juliana only raised an eyebrow. "Fitzwilliam won't like it."

No, he wouldn't. Even with Widow Macaulay as chaperone, Fitz was going to be furious. "We'll deal with Fitz tomorrow. Here, now hand the lamb down to me."

Lady Juliana clutched the lamb to her chest. "No. I want to keep Fiona with me."

"Fiona?" Logan rolled his eyes. Of course, she'd name the lamb Fiona. The English thought all Scottish lasses were named Fiona. "How do you know it's a girl?"

"It's a girl," said Douglas, who was watching the scene with interest. "If ye just lift 'er tail, ye can tell by the—"

"Never mind lifting her tail, Douglas. What do you intend to do, Lady Juliana? Bring the animal to your bedchamber and tuck her into bed beside you?" Logan reached up and plucked the lamb from her arms. "Douglas will take good care of the troublesome little…that is, er…Fiona. Won't you, lad?"

"Aye, sir." Douglas grinned as Fiona burrowed her small, soft head into his shoulder. "She's a sweet wee thing, innit she?"

Logan reached up to lift Lady Juliana down, but she shifted away from him before he could wrap his hands around her waist. "I'm perfectly capable of dismounting without your assistance, Mr. Blair."

"*Dùr bhean*," Logan muttered, and Douglas grinned.

Lady Juliana frowned down at him suspiciously. "What does that mean?"

"It means stub—" Douglas began, but Logan cut him off.

"Are you coming down, or not? We haven't got all night, Lady Juliana." Her legs were likely numb and would collapse beneath her as soon as her feet touched the ground, but Logan dropped his arms and stepped back.

Lady Juliana swung one leg over the saddle and attempted a graceful leap to the ground. She made it down well enough, but her last claim to dignity disintegrated as her legs buckled beneath her.

She let out a faint cry and would have fallen to the stable floor, but Logan caught her and swept her up into his arms. "I think a tumble into Ruthven Burn is enough excitement for one day, don't you?"

"Mr. Blair!" Lady Juliana gasped as the floor disappeared beneath her feet. "Put me down at once! What do you think you're doing?"

"Carrying you to the farmhouse. The Widow Macaulay will have my head if a young lady under my protection crumples into a heap on her doorstep. Be still," he added sternly, when she began to wriggle to get free. "If you can't manage to get down from a horse, what makes you think you can walk to the door?"

"The fact that I've walked to hundreds of doors throughout my lifetime, all without your assistance?"

Logan grinned at the note of pique in her voice. If there was one thing Lady Juliana despised, it was having her abilities questioned. "This one door won't make any difference then, will it?"

He balanced her against his shoulder and pounded on the door with his fist, but there was no answer. The house remained dark and silent.

"She's a bit deaf." Logan raised his fist and pounded again, harder this time.

"Oh, dear. This is dreadfully rude of us." Lady Juliana was biting her lip. "Perhaps we should go on to Castle Kinross after all. You'll frighten the poor thing to death with all that banging!"

Logan let out a short laugh. "Nothing frightens Widow Macaulay."

"You mean to say she's not afraid of someone breaking down her door in the middle of the night? Why, that's utter non—"

The door flew open then, and Lady Juliana's words died away.

The Widow Macaulay stood on the doorstep in a brown-and-white spotted dressing gown. Her hands were on her hips, her hair flew in wild gray tufts around her head, and she wore a scowl fierce enough to frighten the devil himself.

"Good evening, ma'am." Logan hitched Lady Juliana higher on his chest and managed an awkward bow. "I beg your pardon for disturbing you at such a late hour, but—"

"Well, now ye've done it, haven't ye, Logan Blair?"

Logan had learned long ago never to admit any wrongdoing to Widow Macaulay. He blinked innocently at her. "Done what? What did I do?"

She jerked her chin toward Lady Juliana. "Ye gone and stolen yerself an English lass."

Logan didn't even bother to ask how she knew Lady Juliana was English. By the time he'd turned five, he'd already decided the Widow Macaulay knew everything. "I didn't *steal* her."

"Well, where'd ye get 'er, then?"

"She's a guest at Castle Kinross. This is Lady Juliana Bernard, a friend of the duke's, visiting from England."

"Humph. Why does she look like she's been trampled by a herd o' sheep?"

Logan sighed. They weren't going to get through the door until Widow Macaulay was satisfied. "We went out to the Robertsons' to search for some missing sheep. Lady Juliana fell into Ruthven Burn when she rescued a lamb. She's too cold and exhausted to make it back to the castle, but we couldn't stay at the Robertsons'."

"No. Not with that rascal Dougal Robertson there." Widow Macaulay regarded Juliana with shrewd gray eyes for a moment, then jerked her chin toward the hallway behind her. "All right. Bring 'er in. Can she walk?"

Lady Juliana scowled up at Logan. "Of course, I can."

She tried to wriggle free again, but Logan's arms tightened around her. "Better not risk it. She fell when she tried to dismount."

"Take 'er to the back bedchamber. I'll fetch her a drink and some dry clothes."

Widow Macaulay disappeared around a corner, muttering to herself, and Logan made his way to the back of the house. When they reached the bedchamber, he laid Lady Juliana down carefully on the bed.

She glanced up at him, her cheeks flushed with embarrassment. "I, ah—I thank you for your…solicitousness, Mr. Blair."

Logan frowned down at her. "There's no need for you to be embarrassed, *mo bhean uasal*. You're exhausted, and your limbs are stiff from being so long in the saddle. I've seen burly farmers experience the same."

Her brows rose, as if the last thing she'd expected was for him to make excuses for her.

"You're not used to such a hard ride as we had today," he added, when she remained silent.

"Well, I confess it was a bit more strenuous than a jaunt through Hyde Park." She stole another glance at him. Her face relaxed a little when she saw he wasn't laughing at her.

"There's no shame in accepting help, Lady Juliana."

She snorted. "No, but you're hardly one to deliver that particular lecture, Mr. Blair."

Logan thought of the many times he'd refused Fitz's help since his brother came to Castle Kinross. "No, maybe not."

"Stubborn." She let out a long sigh. "We have that in common."

She went quiet, but before Logan could withdraw from the room she surprised him by saying, "I'm afraid if I ask for help too often, I'll forget how to help myself. It wouldn't be so surprising, really. I was raised to be decorative, not useful."

Logan stared down at her, too astounded to say a word. *Decorative?* Is that all she thought she was? He'd never known a more determined, independent woman in his life. He'd also never known a more obstinate, willful, maddening one, but one thing Lady Juliana Bernard was *not* was useless.

He sat on the edge of the bed, careful to keep a respectable distance between them. "You rode for hours today—a good part of it after taking a swim in Ruthven Burn. You saved Fiona, and made the three Robertson boys your devoted slaves. Would you have believed you could do all that before today?"

She shook her head, a rueful smile on her lips. "No. None of it. I wouldn't have believed myself capable of journeying to Scotland to coerce a reluctant gentleman into becoming my husband, either."

His lips twitched. "You don't need me anymore, you know. Any one of the Robertson brothers is yours for the asking."

She laughed. "What nonsense."

"No. Dougal in particular is smitten. Your daring rescue of Fiona sealed his fate." He was quiet for a moment, studying her face. "What made you do it? You must have realized how dangerous it was. It's a miracle you and Fiona didn't both end up at the bottom of the burn."

"Yes, I suppose so. I didn't really think about that at the time, though. She was cold and frightened, and...*crying*, and she'd watched her poor mama drown. I couldn't just leave her there to die. I never would have forgiven myself if I hadn't at least tried to help her."

"*Maoth-chridheach*," he murmured. "Tenderhearted, just as Dougal said."

She seemed not to know what to say to that, but her gaze met his. Both of them were quiet, the tension building between them as they stared at each other without speaking. The silence grew heavy with expectation until Logan, almost without knowing he did it, leaned toward her.

As he drew closer her green eyes darkened, and her lips parted...

He didn't leap upon her, or take her mouth hard, as if he had every right to it. No, he took his time, his mouth drawing closer to hers so gradually he was made achingly aware of how badly he wanted her kiss long before his lips touched hers.

But when they did...when they did...

A sigh unlike any he'd ever heard before left Juliana's lips. Her mouth was so warm, her lips softer than he ever could have imagined. He kissed her carefully, his lips gentle and teasing until she opened her mouth under his.

Logan went still, but only for the space of a single heartbeat. Then he buried his hands in her hair and surged between her lips with a groan, his tongue flicking and teasing the tender pink skin. She braced her hands on his chest, her fingers curling around his coat to pull him closer. He shifted until his body was pressed against hers, and he could feel every soft, warm curve of her against him.

A deep growl vibrated in his chest, and his mouth became more desperate. She clung to him, meeting every one of his hungry kisses, every sensuous stroke of his tongue. Logan's control slipped further with every taste of her sweet, eager mouth. His restless hands moved over her back, then lower, down to her hips.

He'd forgotten where they were—had forgotten everything but her taste, her touch. He was seconds away from dragging her across his lap when footsteps coming down the hallway penetrated the haze of his desire. Just before the door opened, he managed to tear his mouth from hers.

He leapt up from the bed and hurried to the other side of the room just as Widow Macaulay bustled into the bedchamber. She had a tray in her hands and some clothes thrown over her arm. "All right, here we are, then. A wee dram of whisky will warm ye, and here's a night rail and a dress for tomorrow, and...Logan? What ails ye, lad?"

Logan backed toward the door, his chest still heaving with his ragged breaths. "Nothing at all, just...I'll leave you alone."

He fled into the hallway, closing the firmly behind him. He wandered into the kitchen, fell heavily into one of the wooden chairs at the table, and dragged a shaking hand through his hair. He was still struggling to catch his breath, and his heart was pounding.

Christ, he'd kissed her.

He hadn't *planned* to kiss her. He hadn't thought about it beforehand. They'd been talking about Fiona, and then the next thing he knew he was leaning toward her, his gaze on those parted pink lips, and...

Had he even *wanted* to kiss her?

He'd hardly had a chance to think the question before the answer was there, echoing inside his head.

God, yes.

He'd spent the past few hours in a saddle with her, with the sweet curve of her arse pressed between his legs. He'd had to force himself to imagine Brice Robertson's red nose hair to keep from embarrassing himself.

Damn right, he wanted to kiss her. She was beautiful, and he was a man, wasn't he? What man *wouldn't* want to stroke that soft skin, or tangle his hands in that thick, silky hair? His tastes usually ran toward lush, dark-haired Scottish lasses, but he'd have to be mad not to want to taste that sharp tongue of hers, plunge between those warm, pink lips and—

"Yer English lass wants to see ye."

Logan leapt to his feet and turned to find Widow Macaulay standing in the kitchen doorway. "She does?"

"Aye." She crossed the room and shook a warning finger in his face. "She's half asleep already, and I won't have ye standing in there all night long gawking at her. Ye make it quick, and ye mind yer manners with that lass, Logan Blair."

"Yes, ma'am." Logan couldn't think of any reason why Juliana would want to see him, but he made his way down the hallway to the back bedchamber and knocked softly. "Lady Juliana?" He pushed the door open and tiptoed to the bed.

She was lying on her back, her eyes half-closed, a mass of loose curls spread out across her pillow. When she saw him standing there, her lips curved in a sleepy smile.

Logan stared down at her, swallowing.

Mind your manners, mind your manners, mind your—

"You're a heroic sort of man, aren't you, Mr. Blair?"

Her voice was so soft Logan had to draw closer to hear her. "Heroic? No, I'm not heroic, lass."

"Yes, you are. You pulled me from the burn, then you carried me here on your horse, and when I nearly fell in the stables, you caught me. Whenever I'm about to take a tumble, you seem to be always there, waiting with open arms."

Logan wasn't sure how to reply to that, but Lady Juliana didn't seem to expect an answer. "I'm not looking for someone to save me, you know.

All I need is a husband. I'd hoped for a quiet one, with no heroics or drama about him, but that's not you, is it?"

Logan's lips quirked. "If you promise to stop falling down, I promise to stop catching you."

She raised a hand, but then let it flop back down onto the bed. "It's not just that. I want a dull husband, but you're not…you're all fierce glowers and broad shoulders and dark blue eyes and soft lips…"

Soft lips? She thought he had soft lips? Logan leaned over her, eager to hear what else she thought, but she trailed off, and her eyes drifted closed.

He waited, but she didn't stir, and after a moment he reached down and drew the coverlet over her.

He was about to turn away when her fingers closed around his wrist to stop him. "It wouldn't have to be like a real marriage. You wouldn't need to stay in England for long, just…I only care that Grace is safe. My father is…he's very ill, you see, and once he…" Her voice hitched, and she drew in a deep breath. "Once my father is gone, you could return to Scotland."

"Return to Scotland?" Did she mean she and her niece would return to Castle Kinross with him, or—

"If you wish it. I'd agree to a divorce, once my father—"

Logan drew his hand away and strode over to the window before she could say any more. He was more upset by her offer than he could explain. A divorce would shame and humiliate her. Her fine friends, even her family might shun her if her husband divorced her.

Had he really driven her to such extremes?

He leaned his hands against the windowsill and stood there for some time, peering out into the darkness, his thoughts a baffling mix of remorse and confusion. By the time he returned to the side of the bed, Lady Juliana had fallen asleep. He felt a quick, sharp stab of disappointment, but perhaps it was for the best.

He didn't have any answers for her.

Logan slipped quietly into the hallway, intending to sleep on one of the settees in the sitting room, but any hopes he'd had of avoiding Widow Macaulay died a quick death.

"Stop right there, Logan Blair."

Logan froze. He might be the laird, but Agnes Macaulay had known him since he was a drooling infant. She hadn't the slightest qualm about flaying the skin from his bones with that barbed tongue of hers.

She stared hard at him for long enough to make him squirm, then asked, "Ye going to marry that lass?"

Logan opened his mouth, then closed it again.

Yes? No? I'm going to marry her, then divorce her?

He hadn't any idea which answer was the truth, so he said nothing.

His expression must have said it all, though, because Widow Macauley let out a delighted cackle, as if he'd given her just the answer she wanted. "That's what I thought. Ye were a naughty little lad, Logan Blair, but even then, I never took ye for a fool. Glad to see I was right."

Chapter Eleven

The next day dawned cool and sunny. Despite their late night, both Logan and Juliana rose early, and were on the road to Castle Kinross only an hour after the sun peeked over the horizon.

There was no more talk of soft lips or blue eyes, and no more talk of marriage. There was no more sharing a saddle, either. Lady Juliana and Fiona rode Domino, and Logan did his best to convince himself it was much more comfortable having Fingal's saddle to himself.

Neither of them mentioned the kiss.

Logan thought about it, though. He spent most of the ride playing over those moments in his mind. His stomach leapt every time he recalled her warm lips pressed against his. He would have sworn Juliana was thinking of it, too. She took care not to look at him, but every time she felt his gaze on her face, her cheeks reddened.

Logan reconciled himself to a quiet ride, but after a few more miles passed, Juliana surprised him by saying, "You never intended to be gone from Castle Kinross for longer than a day, did you?"

"No. I meant to return last night."

"When I saw your saddle bags, I assumed..." She trailed off, biting her lip.

Lady Juliana had been there when he'd unpacked his saddle bags this morning, and turned over to Widow Macaulay the medicine, cloth, and other supplies Mrs. Selkirk had sent.

"You assumed I was a dishonorable scoundrel and a coward, as well as a thief." Logan's temper sparked, but then he noticed the mortified flush on her cheeks, and his anger softened. "You had cause to think so, I suppose." He hadn't given her any reason to trust him.

"Perhaps, but I'm sorry I...that is, I beg your pardon, Mr. Blair."

Logan glanced at her. He hadn't expected that. "I accept your apology, and I beg your pardon for taking your letters. I regret it." He blew out a breath, relieved to have that weight off his chest.

"Why did you do it?"

"I told you why, the night you arrived. I thought it was better for the clan if Fitz married Emilia." He still thought so, but he didn't say it.

To his shock, Lady Juliana said it for him. "Because of who my father is, you mean."

Logan tensed. There was no anger in her voice, yet he still hesitated to bring Lord Graystone into it. It would only be natural for her to defend her father, and he didn't want to open another rift between them. Then again, if they did marry, they'd have to have it out sooner or later. "Yes."

She was watching him carefully. "Then thievery is not your general habit, Mr. Blair?"

Logan's gaze jerked to her face. "No."

"You mean to say, then, that you wouldn't have taken my letters for any reason other than to protect your clan?"

"I—yes. That's what I mean to say." He hadn't had to say it, though, because again, she'd said it for him. Logan stared at her, amazed. He'd expected her to defend her father, and instead she'd defended *him*. He would have said he couldn't be more shocked than he was at that moment, but then she said something that made his mouth drop open.

"If it had been Grace's welfare at stake, I would have done the same thing. We're not so different, Mr. Blair."

That startled a smile out of him. "No. Odd, isn't it?"

Her lips quirked. "Very."

They fell into a surprisingly comfortable silence after that, but as soon as they arrived at Castle Kinross, their peace was shattered.

Fitz must have been watching for them, because he was waiting in the entryway when they entered, his arms folded over his chest and his lips pressed into a thin, angry line. Emilia was there as well, looking anxious.

"Where," Fitz began, his voice colder than Logan had ever heard it. "Where the *devil* did you two spend last night, Logan?"

"Fitzwilliam!" Emilia cried, shocked at the curse.

Fitz didn't reply. His gaze remained locked on Logan, his eyes like blue ice. "Logan?"

Logan was as anxious to have the explanation out as Fitz was. "We rode out to Robertson's farm. By the time we left it was too late to make it back here, so we spent the night at Widow Macaulay's."

"Widow Macaulay's?" Emilia breathed a sigh of relief. "Well, that sounds perfectly respectable, so—"

"Why is Lina wearing that dress? It doesn't even fit her!" Fitz turned to Emilia. "Didn't you tell me she was wearing your riding habit when she left yesterday?"

Emilia shot Juliana an apologetic look. "Well yes, but—"

"Well, Logan? If it's as simple as you claim, why was Lina obliged to change clothes? It looks like she's wearing one of Widow Macaulay's gowns!"

Fitz was glaring at Logan, but before he could say a word in reply Juliana marched up to Fitz and poked her finger into his chest. "That's because I *am* wearing one of her gowns. And I beg your pardon, *Your Grace*, but kindly stop speaking of me as if I'm not here."

Logan smothered a grin. Lady Juliana hardly reached Fitz's shoulder, but that didn't stop her from scowling fiercely up at him.

Fitz blinked down at her. "You don't understand, Lina. Logan should never have taken you to Robertson's farm to begin with. He's risked your reputation—"

"My reputation! Oh, for pity's sake! What does that matter now? And Logan didn't *take* me anywhere. I followed him to the Robertsons' farm, and then I fell into Ruthven Burn, and Mr. Robertson gave me the lamb I rescued, and we ended up at Widow Macaulay's for the night, and if you don't believe me, then you can go to the stables and see Fiona for yourself!"

No one said a word after this outburst. Fitz and Emilia were gaping at Juliana, and Logan, who couldn't make much sense of her tale despite having witnessed the entire thing, was trying not to laugh.

The silence stretched on until at last Fitz cleared his throat. "I want to speak to Logan alone. Emilia, will you please take Lina upstairs? Logan, I'll attend you in the library in five minutes."

With that, Fitz turned on his heel and strode away.

Logan looked at Juliana. "That went well. See? I told you we'd manage him."

Her eyebrows shot up, but then she caught his grin and a smile curved her lips. "You did say that, didn't you?"

She didn't have a chance to say any more, because Emilia took her by the hand and dragged her up the stairs. Logan watched them go, then wandered off to the library, threw himself into a chair before the fire, and rested his muddy boots on the ottoman.

He already knew what Fitz was going to say to him. He could hear the words in his head as clearly as if he were reading them aloud from a page. *Stolen letters...ruined reputation...an honorable man would...*

The worst of it was, it was all true. Juliana wouldn't be in this mess if he hadn't taken her letters, and that made him guilty of everything else that followed.

Then there was the child, Grace, to consider. He was fond of children. Fonder than he was of adults, truth be told. He'd noticed the way Juliana's eyes lit up whenever she spoke of Grace, and he didn't like to think of the child being sent off to live with a scoundrel because of something he'd done.

Then there was that kiss...

Logan's lips curved. Well, he wouldn't be the first man who'd married to gratify his lust.

"That's a satisfied smirk you're wearing. I can't think of a single reason why you should be so pleased with yourself. Plenty of reasons why you shouldn't be, however."

Logan glanced over his shoulder to find Fitz standing just inside the library door. "I don't suppose it would do any good to ask you to keep those reasons to yourself, would it?"

"None at all." Fitz came into the room, paused at the sideboard to pour himself a glass of port, then strolled over to the fireplace. He threw himself into the chair across from Logan's and fixed him with a cool stare.

Logan shifted uncomfortably. It was unsettling to see his own face staring back at him. Fitz had been at Castle Kinross for months, but Logan still wasn't used to seeing his image in anything other than his mirror.

"Well?" Fitz crossed an ankle over his knee and raised one dark eyebrow at Logan.

Logan scowled. It wasn't just Fitz's appearance, either. It was his voice, his gestures—everything about him. It was damn unnerving they could look so much alike, yet still be so different. "Well, what?"

Fitz's eyebrow went up another notch. "Even if your adventure with Lina last night was as innocent as you say, it doesn't make a damn bit of difference. You know that, right?"

Logan didn't try to deny it. If it got about that he and Lady Juliana had spent a night together away from Castle Kinross, her reputation would be ruined. "I know."

Fitz waited for him to say something more. When Logan remained quiet, Fitz considered him for a long moment, his eyes slightly narrowed. For the first time it occurred to Logan that the brother who'd been so agreeable since he arrived at Castle Kinross could be pushed too far. He'd make a worthy adversary once he was.

Fitz studied the glass of port dangling from his fingers. "Given the circumstances, perhaps you'd like to reconsider the question of your marriage to Lady Juliana?"

Logan was already considering it, but he stiffened at the commanding note in Fitz's voice. "That sounds like an order, brother. Every bit the duke, aren't you?"

"I'm the laird, as well. Or have you forgotten that?"

Logan recrossed his ankles, uncaring that his boots left a muddy streak on the pale-yellow silk ottoman. Fitz might be his elder brother, but Logan had been his own man for twenty-eight years, and he wasn't going to start answering to someone now. "Do you think to issue commands to me, brother?"

He expected an angry retort, but Fitz only gave him a calm shrug. "Lina's reputation has been compromised. I don't blame you for it, but I do want to know what you intend to do about it."

Logan had just been asking himself that same question, but that did nothing to prevent the spark of temper rising in his chest. "I haven't decided yet, but when I do, you can be sure I'll speak to Lady Juliana about it, not *you*. It's none of your concern, Fitz."

"Lina's my dearest friend. Everything to do with her is my concern."

Logan thought he heard a proprietary note in Fitz's voice, and his brows lowered. Fitz might have grown up with Juliana, but they were no longer betrothed. He didn't have any claim on her. "You should have thought of that before you fell in love with Emilia."

As soon as the words left his lips, Logan wished them back. "I beg your pardon. I didn't mean—"

An angry flush rose to Fitz's cheeks. "Perhaps I would have, if you hadn't hidden Lina's letters from me, but I'm afraid it's rather late for that now. So, let's get back to the point, shall we? What do you intend to do about Lina?"

It was a bloody good question. Pity he still didn't have an answer.

Logan dragged a hand down his face. He never should have kissed her. If he'd never kissed her, he wouldn't know those tempting pink lips were even more delicious than they looked. He'd have no idea that the sensation of Juliana's fingers dragging through his hair was enough to bring him to his knees at her feet.

Those green eyes...

Try as he might, he couldn't think of a single thing to dislike about her wide green eyes. He'd avoided looking directly at her today, but more than once, when his gaze caught hers, he'd struggled to look away again.

He liked her eyes best when they were flashing with temper. Which they often did, when he was around. Would it be the worst thing in the world to gaze into those flashing green eyes every day? He'd have to keep her in a temper, of course, but that would be easy enough.

And that kiss...good Lord, that kiss.

Logan thought of her lips opening under his, and a lust unlike any he'd felt before unfurled in his belly. Juliana hadn't said a word about consummating the marriage, but the union wouldn't be legal otherwise. She'd be his *wife*, after all.

But was a single, knee-weakening kiss a good enough reason to leave Scotland? This was his home, and his father's home before him. The Blairs had lived at Castle Kinross for as far back as anyone could remember. Logan had always imagined he'd marry a sweet, blue-eyed Scottish lass someday, and raise a half-dozen or so dark-haired Scottish children here.

And if he'd started to dream of green eyes instead of blue, and fair hair instead of dark?

Christ, he didn't know. He couldn't make sense of how he felt, or what he wanted. He knew the right thing to do was to marry Lady Juliana and pull her free of the chaos he'd plunged her into, but knowing it was right didn't mean he wasn't plagued with doubts.

He thought of what Juliana had said last night, about accepting help from others. Leaving Scotland would mean accepting Fitz's help—trusting him—and he wasn't sure he could do that. He wasn't sure he'd ever trust Fitz, no matter if they were brothers.

There was a chance the clan would thrive under Fitz's leadership, and all might yet be well. There was also a chance Fitz would grow bored with Scotland. He could begin to find life here tedious, and start to yearn for his friends in England. He could choose to move Emilia back to Surrey, and leave the clan behind.

"You'll have to make a decision soon, Logan." Fitz's voice was gentler now, and Logan wondered if his brother had seen the struggle on his face. "Lina's father needs her, and that's to say nothing of Grace. She can't remain in Scotland much longer."

Logan dropped his head into his hands. "I know. I'm trying to...I'm doing everything I can, Fitz."

Fitz was quiet for a moment, then he rose from his chair and dropped a hand on Logan's shoulder. "Do everything you can to make up your mind to marry her, Logan. Meanwhile, I'll do everything I can."

Logan frowned up at Fitz. "If I choose not to marry her, there won't be a thing you can do about it."

Fitz looked down at him, an enigmatic smile hovering at the corner of his mouth. "We'll see, brother. We'll see."

Chapter Twelve

Three days later

"Kiss me, Kate, we shall be married o' Sunday…"

Juliana tossed Shakespeare aside with a derisive snort. Well, it was perfectly delightful a kiss should have led to Kate's wedding, but not every lady was so lucky.

A kiss hadn't led to anything at all for Juliana, other than three long days of silence. After their adventures at the Robertsons' farm, she'd hoped she and Logan had reached some sort of…well, if not an agreement, at least a truce. She'd even half-convinced herself he'd eventually agree to marry her, but since they'd returned to Castle Kinross, she hadn't exchanged more than a half-dozen words with him.

He'd become more distant than ever.

He rode out early each morning without telling a soul where he was going. Even his valet wasn't privy to his whereabouts. He did return in the evenings, but only in time to change his dress and join the family at the dinner table.

Then he'd take his place across from her and sit through five or more courses without addressing a single word to her. He did look at her a good deal, with a raw intensity in his gaze that made her breath catch. She was hard-pressed to describe his expression, but she thought it was more analytical than anything else. He studied her the way a mathematician studies a particularly complex problem, as if she were a knot to be untied. It wasn't at all flattering, yet those blue eyes sweeping over her never failed to make her flush with heat.

It was disconcerting, to say the least.

With every day that dragged on, she became more and more convinced marriage to a London fortune hunter would have been much easier than this. What a pity the easiest thing never proved to be the most effective. She hadn't used to think so—she hadn't used to think of anything in terms of ease or difficulty. One didn't, when they were so rarely faced with a challenge.

But then adversity was meant to build character, wasn't it? A lady never knew what she was capable of until she was forced to rise to a challenge. Or not rise to it, as the case may be.

Well, she'd risen to it. She'd risen all the way to northern Scotland. As little as three months ago she would have shrunk from the idea of such a journey, but now here she was, scheming to marry a man who'd taken to fleeing his home every morning to escape her.

This time, he was succeeding.

She'd made her way down to the stables just as the sun was rising this morning, intending to coax some information about Logan's daily jaunts from one of the stable boys. As luck would have it, she arrived just in time to see Logan Blair himself riding out of the stable yard, his gray stallion's massive hooves kicking up a thick cloud of dust behind him.

Logan must have taken the stable boys to task after she'd followed him to the Robertsons' farm, because no plea, threat, or bribe could induce any of them to divulge his direction. Juliana, more disheartened than ever, had returned to the library for another empty, endless day of worry and anguish.

Precious moments were ticking by. She still had no idea how Fitzwilliam planned to bring Logan around to the marriage, or if he'd even made any progress on it. All she knew was Fitzwilliam left every morning to conduct some sort of mysterious business in Inverness, and was usually gone for most of the day.

She was going mad, sitting about the castle all day with nothing to do but wait. Emilia had done her best to entertain Juliana for the first two days, but she'd left for her father's farm yesterday morning to spend some time with her family before her wedding.

Aside from Stokes, who hadn't yet forgiven Juliana for abandoning him at the Sassy Lassie, she had no one to talk to, and nothing to distract her.

Juliana gave up pretending to read and crossed the room to peer out the window. As if the day weren't gloomy enough already, it had begun to rain. She stood and watched the drops strike the glass. Well, it was some consolation at least to imagine Logan Blair soaked to the skin and shivering.

She turned from the window with a sigh, and crossed to one of the bookshelves. Sir Walter Scott had seemed an apt choice for today, but the novel wasn't holding her attention. She needed something a bit more scandalous to distract her. Richardson, perhaps, or Henry Fielding. Ah, yes—there was a copy of *Tom Jones*, just one shelf above her head.

Juliana rose to her tiptoes and reached for the first volume, but just as her fingertips grazed the spine a sudden loud knock made her jump back, a startled cry leaving her lips.

What in the world?

Her eyes widened as the knock came again, this time followed by a mysterious scuttling sound. The noises seemed to be coming from the other side of the bookshelf.

Rats, perhaps?

Juliana shuddered at the thought of a rat large enough to make such a loud noise. She wasn't a squeamish, missish sort of lady, but any sane person drew the line at rats.

She started to back slowly away, intent on putting some distance between herself and the giant rats, but then another sound met her ears. It sounded like...

A sniffle, followed by a muffled sob.

A weeping rat? No, surely not.

She was now certain the sounds were coming from behind the bookshelf, and they were so close it was as if someone was standing just on the other side of it. "Hello? Is anyone there?"

The only reply was a childish hiccup.

Juliana's mouth fell open. Dear God, there was a child trapped on the other side of the bookshelf! There must be an alcove of some sort there. She'd heard some of these ancient Scottish castles had secret rooms and passageways.

She began pushing and pulling at anything she could reach, her hands moving frantically over the edges of the shelves, the spines of the books. There must be some sort of switch or mechanism to swing the shelf aside. She only had to find it, and—

Yes! Just there, on the edge of one of the lower bookshelves was a place where the wood was a bit more worn. She pushed her hand against it. It felt loose, as if there was nothing supporting it from behind, so she pressed harder, and all at once the entire shelf swung heavily inward.

It was as dark as pitch on the other side.

She stuck her head into the narrow opening, and a blast of cold air hit her in the face. She immediately burst into a series of violent sneezes, and the smell of must and mildew nearly knocked her back again. She paused at the threshold, uncertain what to do, but in the next instant a frightened whimper met her ears. Her eyes adjusted to the dark just in time to see a very small boy with tears running down his cheeks dart down a passageway and disappear around a corner.

"Wait!" Juliana scurried after him, her heart in her throat. The musty passageway looked like just the sort of place where every rat in the castle would hide, but she couldn't just leave that child alone in there. Why, he'd looked terrified! There was no telling how many passages there were, either. He could be lost for hours. The poor thing would cry himself sick.

Juliana scurried after him, following the faint sound of his footsteps. She called to him once or twice, but he ran on, too frightened by now to do anything but flee. She followed him around one corner after another, and down too many narrow passages to count, but at some point, he got far enough ahead of her she could no longer hear his footsteps, and she was forced to stop.

She leaned one hand against the rough stone wall and tried to catch her breath. She waited until her heart ceased its pounding, then she looked about, squinting in the gloom.

And squinting, and squinting…was that…it almost looked like…

Oh, no. Juliana's eyes went wide. The rats were the least of her worries. She'd been so intent on following the boy, she hadn't realized someone else was following *her*. Someone much larger and broader than she was.

Juliana held out a shaking hand as he advanced on her. "D—don't come any closer, or I promise I'll make you regret it!"

The man froze and raised his hands in front of him. "I've no doubt of that, *dùr galla*. I regret it already."

Juliana let her hand drop back down to her side. The voice was deep, a little rough, and more than a little amused. She would have recognized it anywhere.

Logan Blair.

"What are *you* doing here?" She wasn't sure whether she was comforted or alarmed by his sudden presence, and her confusion made her voice sharper than she intended.

"What am *I* doing here? Well, let me see. One of the housemaids told me you hadn't left the library all day, but when I came searching for you I found the room empty, and the door to the underground passageway open."

He'd come searching for *her*? For the past three days he'd gone out of his way to avoid her, but today, for some unknown reason, he was so anxious for her company he'd chased her into a tunnel? Juliana shook her head. It didn't make any sense, but at least he'd returned to Castle Kinross before nightfall. She'd learned over the past few months to seize any advantage fate happened to hand her.

"I knew you must have gone through it," he went on, "And you see, I was right. So, *alainn galla*, the more pressing question is, what are *you* doing here?"

Juliana frowned at the Gaelic. He often used Gaelic words when he spoke to her, and she was sure he was making fun of her. One day soon she was going to find out what all these words meant, but at the moment she had other things to worry about. "I heard a noise, and there was a child, and he was crying..." *Oh, for pity's sake.* The whole story sounded so absurd, Juliana had begun to wonder if she'd imagined the entire thing.

But to her surprise, Logan seemed to know exactly what she was talking about. "A little boy?" he asked. "About six, with red hair?"

"He ran away before I could see his hair, but yes, he was very young."

Logan nodded. "Ah, that's Duncan Munro. His older brothers must have put him up to this. They tease him mercilessly. Mischievous little imps, the both of them."

Juliana let out an indignant huff. "Well, they both deserve a firm lesson, then. That poor child was beside himself."

"Aye, I'm sure he was. We'd better go after him. If he panics, he'll end up running in circles down here for hours. Go on." Logan waved a hand toward the tunnel in front of them. "I'm right behind you."

Never having crept through a secret underground passageway with a large man before, Juliana soon realized it wasn't scuttling rodents that should be her first concern.

It was proximity. Proximity to Logan Blair, to be specific.

It was tighter than a tomb in here. She couldn't see a thing, and as a result her other senses sharpened to supply the information her eyes no longer could.

Senses like touch, and sound, and smell.

Logan was directly behind her, so close she could feel the warmth of his big body running the length of hers, hear each breath he gathered into his lungs. Under the mustiness and mold of the disused passageway she could detect a faintly woody scent, with the barest hint of something else, something warm, like...woodsmoke?

Logan Blair smelled like fresh wood in a warm, crackling fire.

"Perhaps this wasn't a good idea, after all." Juliana winced at her own cowardice, but, well...it didn't seem at all wise to venture into a dark tunnel with a man whose scent made her want to curl up next to him like a lazy cat.

"You're giving up already? What about poor Duncan? There's no need to be frightened, lass. I'll go first."

"I'm not a bit frightened," she said, nettled, but then jumped when a large, warm hand pressed into the small of her back.

He chuckled, stirring the loose tendrils of hair at her temple. "Oh, no. Not at all."

He didn't give her a chance to reply, but eased her gently aside so he could squeeze past her in the narrow passageway. Juliana was still trying to gather the wits his nearness had scattered when his long fingers closed around hers.

"I…what are you doing? Why are you holding my hand, Mr. Blair?"

He stiffened slightly and dropped her hand. "I was going to guide you through the tunnel. You can hold on to a fold of my coat, if you'd rather."

Fierce heat rose to Juliana's cheeks, and she was glad for the darkness that hid her blush. She sounded like a nervous schoolgirl. Still, she didn't take his hand again, but grasped his coat, as he'd suggested. Neither of them had bothered with gloves, and it seemed wiser not to touch his bare skin.

"This tunnel connects to more of the rooms on the ground floor than you'd think. It's a complex one, as far as secret passageways go. From here we can get to the library, the kitchens, the dining room, and even under the grand staircase in the front entry, in case the safest route out is through the front door."

"Is Clan Kinross a wicked one then, to need so many secret doors to escape their enemies?"

"The English might say so. The Scots would say it's a brave one." He edged around a tight bend in the tunnel that took them off toward the right. "Where should we search first? This tunnel we're in leads to the kitchens."

"I expect you know every inch of this tunnel, don't you? Did you used to sneak into the kitchens through the secret passageway when you were a boy and steal sweets from the cook?"

"Naturally, I did. How did you know?"

She laughed. "Young girls aren't so very different from young boys. If we'd had such a fascinating passageway at Graystone Court, you can be sure I'd have used it to steal sweets from the kitchens, and I expect you were a much naughtier child than I was."

He laughed. "Naughty enough. Here we are."

Juliana peered over his shoulder. He'd stopped in front of a low wooden door with iron fittings. "Can Duncan have gone through it? Does it open?"

"No. Not since Mrs. Craig came to Castle Kinross." He grasped the heavy iron door and gave it a tug, but it didn't budge. "She put an end to the pilfering by locking the door, and ordering a massive set of shelves to be placed in front of it."

"Why, what a clever way to manage naughty boys."

"Mrs. Craig is clever, all right. Bad-tempered, too."

Juliana didn't miss the note of affection in his voice, and her lips curved in a smile. Logan Blair was an entirely different man when he talked about his home. It was obvious he cared deeply for this place and the people. Juliana found herself eager to hear more. "How long has Mrs. Craig been at Castle Kinross?"

"Since I was in short pants. I was terrified of her when I was a child. The children are still terrified of her now, but she makes a delicious cranachan, so she stays."

"A delicious *what*?"

He'd taken a few steps away from the door toward another narrow passage to their left, but now he stopped and turned to face her. "Cranachan. Don't tell me you've never had cranachan?"

"I've never even heard of it." It was too dark for Juliana to make out the expression on his face, but she heard the outrage in his voice, and her grin widened. Logan's cool reserve was melting like an icicle in the sun. "Is it a sweet?"

"Aye, it's a sweet. Cream, honey, oatmeal, and Perthshire raspberries. Pity it's too early for raspberries. I'll ask Mrs. Craig to make it with the early gooseberries instead, though it's likely to earn me a clout to the side of the head."

"Well, then don't suggest it! Why should you?"

"So you can try it."

"Well...oh." Juliana thought this a sweet gesture on his part, and wasn't sure what to say in reply. He didn't seem to expect any response, because he turned and began to make his way down the passage to their left.

Juliana caught at his coat and followed along, her thoughts in more of a turmoil than they'd been since she arrived at Castle Kinross. If she did persuade Logan to marry her, it would be far easier if she could continue to be wary of him. She'd thought that would be easy enough, but now here he was, entertaining her with his stories and offering her raspberries and sweets.

The blasted man was making it difficult for her to dislike him. She didn't care one bit for it, but there wasn't much she could do about it while she was trapped in a tunnel with him. Perhaps it would be best if she suggested they find their way back out as soon as—

"Oh, *no*. Did you hear that, Mr. Blair?"

He turned. "What?"

It was a furtive scuttling, like little claws scrabbling across a stone floor. An involuntary shudder ran down her spine. "It sounded like—" Her words dissolved into a screech as one—no, *two*—sets of tiny feet scurried over the toes of her shoes.

Juliana didn't pause to think or utter a single word, but ran instinctively toward Logan. Later she'd congratulate herself for not leaping into his arms, but instead contenting herself with standing on the tops of his boots, so her own feet were off the floor and away from those loathsome creatures.

Logan gave a faint exclamation of surprise to find himself suddenly in possession of a panicked female. To his credit, he didn't send them both sprawling, but closed his arms around her waist to keep her steady.

Juliana had wrapped her own arms around his torso to keep from toppling over, but now the first alarm had passed, she was ready to sink to the floor in mortification. She wasn't afraid of much—snakes, stinging insects, heights—but rats made her lose her wits.

And now...oh, for goodness sakes, she'd actually *thrown* herself at him! How in the world would she excuse herself? He was going to laugh himself silly at her—

"Let me guess, Lady Juliana. Rats?"

There wasn't a hint of laughter in his voice. It should have comforted her, but somehow his gentlemanly forbearance made it even worse. At least if he'd laughed at her, she could have defended herself.

As it was...

"Yes, I...oh, dear. I do beg your pardon, Mr. Blair," she muttered, her face once again in flames. She felt his chest vibrate and was certain he was suppressing laughter, but when he spoke his voice was remarkably grave.

"Don't apologize. I'm happy to help you. Are they gone now?"

It wasn't until then Juliana realized she was still standing on top of the poor man, and clutching at his waist. "Yes, I—I think so." It didn't matter if they were still there or not. Even if there'd been dozens of them waiting to fly up her skirts, nothing could be more humiliating than to carry on molesting him.

Juliana swept one suspicious glance over the floor, then climbed down off him. "Do you think Duncan's found his way out by now? Shall we go back up and see?"

"You don't want to see the room where Bonnie Prince Charlie is rumored to have hidden from the English? It's just over there." He waved a hand behind him.

Over his shoulder Juliana could just make out a spot where the tunnel walls widened into a room of sorts. "No, thank you. That is, I'm sure it's fascinating, but..."

But unless Bonnie Prince Charlie was still in residence, she'd leave the room to the rats.

"Aye, all right, but are you *sure*, Lady Juliana, you don't wish to see the wine cellar? It's just up a short flight of stairs. Some of the bottles are hundreds of years old."

Was he teasing her? Juliana gave him a sharp look, but he only gazed back at her with innocent blue eyes. "No, I think not, Mr. Blair. It's kind of you to offer, but..."

But if there was a place rats tended to gather, it was in a wine cellar.

He sighed, as if disappointed. "All right, but first I want to show you the timbered alcove. It's haunted by the ghost of a Jacobite soldier who lost his leg at Culloden, and later died in this very tunnel. I couldn't let you leave without seeing where he bled out."

He was teasing her, all right, the devil. He was trying to hide it, but Juliana could see just the tiniest grin lurking at one corner of his lips. She crossed her arms over her chest and fixed him with the sternest look she could muster after having climbed him as if he were a tree, and she a squirrel. "You're an odious, wicked, teasing man, Mr. Blair."

His grin widened. "Not at all, lass. There really is a ghost in the tunnel. It isn't a soldier, though, but my great-great-great uncle Mackenzie Blair, who's said to haunt the cellars in search of a bottle of his favorite whisky."

Juliana did her utmost to stifle her answering grin. "I never cared much for whisky. Now, Mr. Blair, if you're quite finished, I'd be grateful if you'd take me above ground again. I'm certain Duncan must have gone out by now."

He bowed. "We'll go back through the library. It's the closest."

Juliana took up the fold of his coat she'd already ruined with her frantic clutching, and let him lead her through what felt like dozens of narrow passageways. Just as she was able to discern the light spilling into the tunnel from the library, Logan came to an abrupt halt.

Juliana's fingers tightened on his coat. "What is it? More rats?"

He didn't answer. He was advancing toward another of the shallow alcoves tucked into the wall at the end of an adjacent passage.

"Come out, Duncan." Logan's voice was kind, but firm.

There was a brief silence, then Juliana heard the unmistakable sound of a child's sniffle. The little boy she'd seen earlier crept from the alcove. His small face was red, his eyes swollen, and his cheeks wet with tears.

"Don't cry. It's all right now." Juliana darted forward, her arms stretched out instinctively for the child, but he wasn't looking at her. He was looking at Logan.

Logan beckoned the boy forward, and knelt down so he could see his face. "Finlay and Brodie again?"

The boy nodded, and then, as if he couldn't bear to contain his misery a moment longer, he let out a pitiful sob. "They laughed at me, an' called me a baby, and then I said I wasna a baby, and they said prove it, an'—"

Logan sighed, and drew the little boy closer to stand between his knees. "And they sent you into the tunnel to prove it, and you got lost. Do you remember what I told you about Finlay and Brodie, Duncan?"

Duncan drew his sleeve across his running nose. "Aye, sir."

"What was it?"

"Ye said to tell 'em the laird says I'm their brother an' they best behave decent to me, sir."

"Good. And what else did I tell you, privately?"

"Ye said they'd come 'round, an' I 'spect they will, but it's taking ever so long, an' I don't have anyone to play with."

Logan chucked the little boy under the chin. "They'll come 'round, Duncan, but until they do, why don't you play with Isobel?"

Duncan stared at him, horrified. "But she's a *girl*!"

Logan's lips twitched. "A lad can't have too many friends, and Isobel will be good to you." He took Duncan by the shoulders and turned him to face Juliana. "See this lady here? She's Mr. Fitz's best friend."

Duncan stared doubtfully up at her. "His *best* friend?"

The little lad had a mass of unruly red hair, and his big blue eyes were still swimming with tears. Juliana's heart just melted for him. "His very best." She sank down onto her knees so her face was even with the boy's. "Girls make very good friends, Duncan—quite as good as boys, I daresay. I'm sure Mr. Fitz would tell you the same."

Duncan rubbed the heels of his hands into his eyes, drew a shaky breath, and nodded.

"Go on and see if you can't find Isobel, Duncan, and then next week you and I will go fishing in Ruthven Burn together."

"Ye mean it, sir?" Duncan asked.

"Aye. We'll bring a picnic, if you like."

A radiant smile replaced the last of Duncan's tears, and after a few more reassuring words from Logan, he allowed himself to be coaxed out of the tunnel. Logan gestured for Juliana to follow after him, then pushed the door that led from the library into the tunnel firmly closed behind them.

He reached down to tousle Duncan's hair. "When you see Finlay and Brodie, tell them the laird's looking for them."

"Are you gonna thrash 'em?" Duncan asked hopefully.

Logan winked. "No, but they don't know that. Now, off with you."

"Yes, sir."

Duncan skipped out of the room, much cheered. Logan watched him go, then turned to Juliana. Her expression must have given her away, because a faint smile rose to his lips. "Why do you look so surprised, *galla*? I told you I was good with children."

"So you did." She watched Duncan race down the hallway with a bemused smile, then turned back to Logan. "You haven't said why you came looking for me this afternoon, Mr. Blair."

His smile disappeared. "I, ah…I need to speak with you alone, Lady Juliana."

Oh, no. Juliana's heart twisted with dread. There was only one thing he could possibly need to say to her privately, and he didn't look like a delighted prospective bridegroom. No, he looked like a man about to disappoint a lady—to crush her last hope, shatter her fondest dream.

Logan Blair had made up his mind. He was going to refuse to marry her.

Chapter Thirteen

Logan's palms were sweating, and a bead of moisture dotted his forehead. He hadn't thought he'd be nervous. It wasn't as if he were a lovestruck suitor, offering for his beloved's hand. That is, he *was* offering, but only because she'd offered hers first. He wasn't about to bare his heart, or fall to his knees with desperate protestations of love and devotion on his lips. Their marriage was a necessity, not the passionate conclusion of a budding romance. He hadn't any reason at all to be nervous.

"Mr. Blair? What do you wish speak to me about?"

Her eyes were greener than usual today. She was wearing a pale green dress made of some sort of light, floating material, and a wide green ribbon nestled amongst the shining tendrils of her hair. No dusty riding habit today. No soiled boots. Not a whiff of vomit or Ruthven Burn about her.

Somehow, she'd emerged from the musty passageway looking as if she'd just climbed out of the bath. He leaned toward her and took a cautious sniff, and his stomach tightened.

She smells like springtime.

He'd never seen her look more beautiful, and all at once he became painfully aware his coat was rumpled, his hair was damp with sweat from his ride, and his boots were streaked with mud.

She looked like a breath of fresh air, a warm spring day, and he... he looked like he'd spent the morning mucking out the stables. Likely smelled like it, too.

Logan blew out a breath. Damn it, this wasn't even a real proposal, but it was already turning out to be a devil of a business. He hadn't the first idea how to go about it. If he hadn't already known she'd say yes, he'd probably have fallen into a swoon by now. He huffed out a breath, disgusted with himself.

"You seem distressed, Mr. Blair. Perhaps now isn't the best time to talk." She tried to dart past him, but Logan caught her by the elbow. "No, no, I'm…will you take a walk in the gardens with me, Lady Juliana?" It had rained all morning, but now the sun was peeking through the clouds.

To his surprise, her face paled. "The gardens? You chased me down a tunnel to ask if I'd walk in the gardens with you?"

Another bead of sweat trickled down Logan's neck. He had a vague idea the gardens might be the right setting for a proposal, but she looked faintly ill, much as she had when she'd seen the rats in the secret passageway.

Still, he couldn't propose to her *here*. For all he knew, Finlay and Brodie Munro could be hiding behind the library shelf right now, listening to every word he said and laughing themselves sick. "A short walk only, my lady."

Her shoulders slumped. She took the arm he offered and let him lead her out into the formal gardens, but she looked like a prisoner being led to her execution rather than a lady out for a stroll among the roses.

Once they were outside and Logan could drag in a few breaths of fresh air, his confidence returned. It was a simple enough thing, really. All he had to do was tell Lady Juliana he agreed to the marriage, wave off her gratitude, and then they could go on much as they'd done before.

Except hopefully there'd be more kissing…

He turned to her, determined to have the thing done, but as soon as he got a close look at her, the words died on his tongue. Her eyes were downcast, her lips turned down, and an anxious furrow rested between her brows. She'd hardly spared the garden a glance, and she'd gone suddenly quiet once they left the library.

This wasn't a promising start, and Logan's nerves came rushing back. Should they have remained in the library? He thought she'd find the masses of rosebuds spilling from the neat rows of arbors romantic, but she didn't even seem to notice them. "Don't you like the gardens, Lady Juliana?"

She started, and glanced up at him. "They're lovely, of course. I especially like the, ah…the lavender."

Logan didn't think she could be that impressed with the lavender, given every garden from Exeter to Perth was smothered in it. "Aye, the lavender is…" Damn it, he didn't care about the cursed lavender. He couldn't think of a single word to say about it. "I wanted to speak to you about our—"

"Wait, Mr. Blair! I mean, these gardens don't interest me. Will you take me to the wild gardens, instead? I've been longing to see the blue poppies the Highlands are famous for, and I believe they're in bloom now."

"Aye, if you'd rather—"

Logan didn't get a chance to finish before she snatched his arm and dragged him through the formal gardens and onto a graveled path that wound toward the back of the castle. They crossed through the thick hedge that separated the wild gardens from the pathway. When she caught sight of the rough trails and riotous profusion of flowers, she let out a forlorn little sigh.

"It's lovely here, isn't it?" She wandered ahead, heedless of the unevenness of the ground at her feet, and approached a patch of overgrown azaleas and rhododendron spilling onto the walkway. "What rich colors. This garden reminds me a bit of Rosemount. The gardens at Graystone Court are very grand, but the formal arrangement is off-putting, somehow, with rows upon rows of roses, all of them perfectly aligned. They're beautiful in their way, of course, but I never much admired them."

Logan didn't care about the roses at Graystone Court, but this was the longest speech she'd made since they left the house, so he pasted on an encouraging smile. "I thought all English ladies loved roses."

She shrugged. "Roses are fine, really. It's not the flowers, but the rigid lines and fussy, manicured look of them I don't care for. Flowers should grow in wild profusion, just like this. Don't you think so?"

"Aye. I like this garden better than any of the others at Castle Kinross. Here are the blue poppies." Logan took her arm again and guided her carefully over the rutted pathway toward a blur of vibrant blue flower heads rising above a carpet of glossy green leaves. "The shade of blue varies. Some poppies are much paler, but we tend to get the deeper blue color in this garden."

Lady Juliana ran her fingertips gently over the delicate blooms. "I can't imagine a prettier blue than this."

That pleased Logan, but she lapsed back into a pensive silence after that, and his smile gradually faded. He watched her as she wandered down the paths, stopping here and there to study a plant or caress a flower she particularly admired.

The grim line of her mouth had relaxed, but she wasn't smiling. Her lips were turned down, and her eyes were dull. She looked...sad.

He'd seen Lady Juliana in a temper, her green eyes flashing. He'd seen her smile and scowl, and he'd watched her face as she drifted off to sleep. He'd seen her dirty, creased, and covered with dust, and he'd seen her soaked to the skin.

But he'd never seen her sad before.

It was...oddly unbearable.

It shouldn't matter to him. If he'd been asked to explain why it did, he couldn't have. He only knew he couldn't offer her his hand while she looked so melancholy. It didn't mean anything, of course. Really, his hesitation had nothing to do with Lady Juliana at all. It was just...well, what man wanted to propose to such a dejected-looking lady?

He drew in a deep breath. Perhaps she'd smile again, once they'd settled this marriage business. "You've been patient these last few days, Lady Juliana. I've made a decision, and I want to speak to you about—"

"Ruthven Burn!" she shouted suddenly.

Logan's head jerked back. "Ruthven Burn? I don't...what about it?"

"Doesn't a section of it flow just beyond the walled garden? I long to see it again! Won't you take me?"

Logan stared down at her, baffled. "I don't think it's a good idea. The bank is slippery, and neither of us wants to take another swim in the burn."

She waved this away. "You needn't worry about that. I'm very sure-footed, Mr. Blair. You've seen so yourself."

"Sure-footed, yes—right up until you tumbled into the burn." He'd never get this damned proposal out if she fell into the burn again. He couldn't ask for her hand when she was soaked and shivering. It wasn't gentlemanly.

"Nonsense. I wouldn't have fallen at all if Fiona hadn't jumped." She tugged on his hand. "Come now, Mr. Blair. Take me to the burn."

This proposal was turning decidedly odd. Logan had a vague idea it wasn't meant to go this way, but he allowed her to drag him through the wild garden to an old stone wall covered with moss and climbing ivy. A thick wooden door was set into a shallow recess in the wall, and he pulled back the sharp branches to clear a pathway for her.

This section of the burn wasn't as deep or as fast as the one by the Robertsons' farm, but Lady Juliana seemed to be delighted with it. They wandered at the edge of it for some time, and she exclaimed over the enormous trees and lush greenery growing alongside the bank. She seemed happy enough to duck under branches and crawl over roots, no matter if her hems grew wet, and her shoes muddier with every step.

She was interested in everything around her, and asked a number of questions, but she didn't chatter at him, and she didn't insist on foolish points of propriety. She never blinked when she was obliged to hike up her skirts and clamber over a branch or root. Logan, who was walking behind her, caught more than one breathless glimpse of a pretty ankle and calf.

He had no idea how they'd ended up mucking about out here, but despite his confusion, he couldn't prevent the smile that curved his lips as he studied her. Her dainty, pale-green dress was spoiled by a streak of dirt across the front of the bodice from an errant tree branch, and there was a tiny tear in one of her sleeves. She hadn't been wearing a bonnet when they left the library, and now...he peered more closely at her, and his grin widened. Long tendrils of hair were tumbling over her shoulders, and several leaves had gotten tangled in the silky strands.

Lady Juliana seemed reluctant to leave, so they wandered for a while, until at last she agreed to leave the burn behind, and they made their way from the woods back into the walled garden at one side of the castle. Logan had intended to take her back to the formal gardens and force his proposal out, but then he hesitated, recalling something.

There was a place in the garden—a special place, enough out of the way he was sure Juliana hadn't seen it before—and all at once it struck him as the only place in the world he could ask for her hand. It was a foolish, romantic notion, so much so he was surprised at himself, but once the idea was there he couldn't shake it free. "I have something else to show you I think you'll like, if you're not fatigued."

Her gaze met his. He thought he caught a flash of apprehension in the green depths, but she looked away before he could be certain. "I'm not fatigued," she said in a small voice.

"All right, then. Follow me." He led her back toward the wild garden and down a path they hadn't explored the first time. When they neared the end, he took her arm. They were coming up on the arch, and he wanted to see her face when she first caught sight of it.

She paused at the end of the pathway, and a soft gasp escaped her lips.

Logan hadn't realized he'd been holding his breath until he saw her reaction, and it left his lungs in a quick burst. "Do you like it?" He could see she did, but he wanted to hear her say it.

"Like it? It's beautiful." She gazed up in wonder at the mass of bright yellow flowers dangling in clusters over her head. "My goodness. I've never seen anything like it before. What sort of flowers are these?"

"Laburnum. This is the Laburnum Arch. The trees are trained to grow over the arched frame underneath. See?" Logan brushed a few flowers aside to show her. "When the flowers bloom they fall in a cascade, and it creates a tunnel effect."

She reached up and dragged a finger across one of the lacy golden blooms. "They're so pretty."

"They are. You'd never guess they're poisonous, would you?"

She snatched her hand back. "Poisonous! Are they, indeed?"

"Very, but only if you eat them. Poisonous enough to kill a small child."

She gasped. "Surely that's never happened? No child ever died, did they?"

"No, but there was one child foolish enough to defy his father's orders to never put any part of the tree near his mouth."

She cast a sidelong glance at him, and a small smile crossed her lips. "Well, he sounds like a very naughty little boy. How old was he at the time?"

"About eight. Old enough to know better."

"Hmmm. Why do you suppose he'd do something so foolish?"

Logan reached up, plucked one of the clusters of yellow blooms and held it in his palm. "Because he'd been warned against it, of course. He was the sort of stubborn lad who'd do a thing for no other reason than he'd been told not to."

Her smile faded. "Was he also the sort of child who'd *refuse* to do a thing, simply because someone asked him to?"

Logan shrugged. "Sometimes, yes."

"A child as obstinate as that must have grown into an equally obstinate man," she said, watching him intently.

"Some say so. I think *you* would."

Her face fell, and she looked away from him. "I see. Well, what happened to him after he ate the flowers? Did he become very ill?"

"He spent the next few days frothing at the mouth and casting up his accounts, but that was nothing to the thrashing his father gave him when he recovered at last."

"Ah. Did he learn his lesson? I hope he wasn't so foolish again."

He crushed the flowers in his palm, then tossed them to the ground. "No, he generally stays far away from this tree."

She titled her head back to gaze at the flowers and let out a little sigh. "Well, aside from the poisoning, I think it must have been wonderful to have been a child here. I suppose there were always a great many of you running about?"

There had been. Logan had never been lonely, despite having grown up without his twin brother, and without any other siblings. The children he'd played with had grown into adults, and now they had children of their own, all of whom romped in this garden just as he had when he was a boy. It was the reason the people of Clan Kinross were so connected to each other, and to this land. They were bound together by generations and centuries of shared history, with the land bred into their very bones.

Whether Fitz could become a part of that shared history remained to be seen. For the clan's sake Logan prayed he would, because soon he wasn't going to be here to act as their laird.

He glanced down at Lady Juliana. Her face was turned up to his, her expression oddly wistful. "Yes, there were always children running about. But you look sad, *bòcan*. Were you a lonely child?"

"Lonely? No. I had my brother Jonathan. I was very fond of him, and of course I also had Fitzwilliam. But mine wasn't a carefree childhood, either. My father is a stern man, Mr. Blair. A good man, but stern, and conscious of propriety. We weren't permitted to run free."

An unfamiliar tightness seized his chest at the forlorn look on her face. Without thinking, he impulsively reached up, plucked another yellow bloom from the tree and offered it to her. "Here. Will you have a taste? It's never too late to behave like a wicked child, Lady Juliana."

She accepted the flower from his hand, but she didn't smile. "No, thank you. I prefer to confine my wickedness to something that won't poison me." She twirled the flower between her fingers, staring down at it as if lost in thought. "I do worry about Grace, though," she murmured after a moment.

Her voice was so soft Logan had to lean closer to hear her. "What do you worry about?"

"That she'll be lonely. I love Rosemount above all other places, but it's quiet there. Nothing like Castle Kinross. There aren't dozens of children running about, and it's unlikely Grace will ever have a sibling." A blush rose in her cheeks.

"You can't know that." Neither of them could. The thought should have terrified him, but instead some unexpected emotion swelled in his chest. He couldn't name it, precisely, but it felt like…hope.

She drew a deep breath, tossed the flower aside and met his gaze. "I don't think you came looking for me today to take me for a walk in the garden, Mr. Blair. I think you brought me here to tell me you won't marry me. I suppose you'd better get on with it."

Logan went still. She thought he was going to *refuse* her? Was that what had put the shadows in her eyes? It had never occurred to him she'd think so, but now, looking back over the past few days he realized she couldn't have believed anything else.

Being near Juliana muddled his thoughts. He'd been avoiding her so he could untangle them, but she didn't know that. All this time he'd been sorting himself out, she'd been giving way to despair.

He placed two fingers under her chin and tipped her face up to his. "I didn't ask you to walk with me today so I could refuse you, Juliana."

She swallowed. "You didn't?"

"No. I came looking for you to tell you…to ask you to be my wife."

For a moment she seemed not even to breathe, but then a soft sob escaped her lips. "I don't...I don't know what to say."

He smiled, but his heart was threatening to leap from his chest. "Say yes, lass."

But she didn't say yes. Not at first. She didn't say a word. She gazed at him for a moment, and then...

Then she did something he didn't expect.

She reached up and laid her palms against his cheeks.

Logan stared down at her. Her hands were soft and warm. A shiver ran through him at her touch, but it was nothing compared to what he felt when she rose to her tiptoes and pressed her mouth to his. It was the briefest brush of her lips, so soft he might have thought he'd imagined her kiss if it hadn't echoed inside him, setting fire to everything it touched.

Jesus, his knees went weak. "Juliana?"

She looked down, took his hand, and closed it tightly between her small ones. When she raised her gaze to his again, her green eyes were filled with tears. "Yes, I'll be your wife. Thank you, Logan. Thank you."

Chapter Fourteen

Stokes stood in front of the horse the stable boy had saddled for Juliana, his arms crossed over his chest. "I don't like it, my lady."

Juliana sighed. No, Stokes wouldn't like it, would he? Between her disappearance the night she'd followed Logan to Castle Kinross and the Robertson farm debacle the next day, Stokes had taken to muttering darkly every time Logan crossed his path. "I see that, Stokes, but I can assure you despite appearances to the contrary, Mr. Blair is perfectly trustworthy."

"He doesn't look trustworthy. He looks like a scoundrel."

"Hush, will you?" Juliana peered around the stable door into the yard. Logan was waiting for her, ready to escort her to the Sassy Lassie to retrieve whatever letters might be waiting there. "He'll hear you."

"Don't care if he does hear me. I don't like the way he looks at you."

Juliana bit her lip, but she couldn't help herself. "How does he look at me?"

Stokes scowled. "Like a thief looks at a silk purse."

Did he, indeed? Juliana suppressed a shiver. "Nonsense. You're being ridiculous. Mr. Blair is a perfect gentleman."

Perhaps that was just a *tiny* exaggeration, but Juliana wouldn't admit that to Stokes. He wouldn't hesitate to kick up a dreadful fuss if he thought she was putting herself into a rake's hands. Logan wasn't a rake, of course, but that's how Stokes would see it, especially if he knew about that kiss.

"I can fetch your letters just as easily as you can, my lady." Stokes's lips were pressed into a stubborn line.

"Yes, yes, of course you can, Stokes, but..."

But I'm going to marry the man, so there's no sense in drawing the line at riding to Inverness with him.

She hadn't mentioned the betrothal to Stokes yet. Not that she was *hiding* it from him, of course. No, nothing so devious as that. She'd tell him soon. Just as soon as...

As soon as she and Logan were wed, and it was too late for Stokes to object.

"But what?" Stokes regarded her for a moment with narrowed eyes, then threw his hands up in the air. "If you're up to any tricks, my lady, you'd better 'fess up right now, or—"

"Lady Juliana?" Logan peered around the side of the stable door. "If we're going to get back to Castle Kinross by this afternoon, we'd better go."

"Did you hear that, Stokes? If you keep me here arguing much longer, Mr. Blair and I will be riding back at dusk. *Alone.*" Juliana lowered her voice, so only Stokes could hear her. "Surely that's not what you want."

Stokes shot a dark look at Logan. "Don't want you riding with him at all."

Stokes didn't make any effort to lower his voice. Logan heard him and looked from Juliana to Stokes and back again, a sly grin lifting one corner of his lip.

That wicked little grin was *not* helpful. Juliana shooed Logan back into the stable yard with a wave of her hand before Stokes could see it. "Now then, Stokes. Mr. Blair is the duke's brother. Do you suppose His Grace would let me ride off with him if he wasn't a proper escort?"

Stokes cast another threatening look in Logan's direction, but this was the right argument to make. Stokes had known Fitzwilliam for years, and he wouldn't dream of questioning His Grace's judgment. He relented, and helped Juliana mount Domino. "If you're not back by the afternoon, I'm coming after you."

"Yes, yes. Very well," Juliana called, keeping her impatient huff to herself as she rode out to meet Logan.

Once they'd cleared the stable yard and turned down the road toward Inverness, Logan said with a grin, "You know, my lady, I have the oddest feeling your manservant doesn't like me."

For pity's sake. Between Logan and Stokes she'd be driven to madness before she made it halfway to the Sassy Lassie. "He doesn't. He thinks you're a scoundrel."

"Ah. Well, he'll be delighted when I become your husband then, won't he? It's going to be a long journey back to England."

"He'll settle down once we're wed." A lie, of course, but she wouldn't allow herself to think about that now. Her marriage would secure Grace's safety, and that was all that mattered. As for everything else, well, it would all come right in the end.

Somehow.

"You're a terrible liar, Lady Juliana." Logan's grin widened, but he didn't argue further. As they rode along in a comfortable silence, Juliana's spirits lifted. Logan Blair certainly knew how to hold his tongue when the occasion called for it. Surely that was a desirable quality in a husband? Perhaps it wouldn't be so unpleasant, being married to him.

He had other redeeming qualities, as well. He'd fished her out of Ruthven Burn, instead of letting her drown. He'd done his best to protect her by taking her to Widow Macaulay's instead of leaving her at the mercy of Dougal Robertson's wicked reputation. He'd saved her from the rats in the secret passageway. He'd even helped her get Fiona from the Robertsons' farm to Castle Kinross. Surely these were all points in his favor?

He'd agreed to marry her...

Juliana glanced at him and her throat closed, just as it always did when she thought of that moment under the Laburnum Arch. She'd never forget the flood of relief and gratitude she'd felt when instead of refusing her, Logan asked her to be his wife.

Fitzwilliam had told her Logan was an honorable man. Juliana hadn't believed it at the time, but over the past week she'd seen another side of Logan. Yes, he'd stolen her letters, but he'd done it for the most unselfish reason—to protect his clan. That didn't excuse his actions, yet Juliana understood the sort of love that drove a person to do something they otherwise wouldn't have done.

It was the kind of love she had for Grace.

In some ways, she and Logan Blair were very much alike. Whether or not it was enough to build a friendship on remained to be seen, but Juliana was determined not to dwell on the early rancor between them.

He was to be her husband. She hadn't made a promise to love him or to remain with him forever, but she'd privately vowed she'd do her best to become his friend.

She could manage that much, couldn't she? She'd been raised to be appealing to gentlemen, and for all his rough edges, Logan Blair was a gentleman.

He could even be downright charming when he chose to be. She liked the way he'd talked to her of that Scottish sweet, cranachan, and of Castle Kinross's cook, Mrs. Craig. Perhaps if she could get him talking about his home again, they'd eventually become more comfortable with each other.

She turned to him with a determined smile. "Tell me, Mr. Blair. Do you ride often to Inverness?"

His eyebrows rose at this formal enquiry, and Juliana's cheeks flushed. She sounded absurd, addressing him as if they'd just been introduced at a ball, but how else did a lady become more familiar with a gentleman, other than polite chitchat? "You're well acquainted with the proprietor at the inn there."

He nodded. "I've known Fergus since I was old enough to ride to Inverness with my father. On very cold days, Fergus used to sneak a tiny splash of whisky into my teacup when my father wasn't looking."

Whisky, for a child? Juliana tried to hide her shock. "My goodness. What would your father have done, if he'd caught you?"

"Thrashed me, maybe. Or maybe he'd have thrashed Fergus."

He smiled at the memory, and Juliana pushed on, encouraged. "What was your father like? Was he a very stern man?"

Logan's brows drew together thoughtfully. "I never thought of him like that, but he was, in his own way. He was…it's difficult to do justice to him in words, but I worshipped him when I was a boy."

"And as a man?" Juliana asked.

"As a man, I loved him," he said simply. "I miss him. I wish Fitz had had the chance to know him."

Juliana thought of the Duchess of Blackmore, how cold she'd always been to Fitzwilliam, and a small sigh escaped her. "I'm sure he wishes it, too."

"What about you, Lady Juliana? Did you drink whisky as a child?"

Juliana laughed. "Whisky? No, certainly not."

"What, you mean you didn't have some wicked uncle or other who used to slip whisky into your tea?"

"No whisky for me, I'm afraid. If I'd had an uncle perhaps he would have made the attempt, but neither of my parents had any siblings."

"No uncles, or cousins?"

"Not one. It was just me and my brother Jonathan."

He frowned a little, as if that answer troubled him, but all he said was, "I think your brother must have been a fashionable gentleman, and you the belle of your season."

"No, indeed. If I'd been the belle of my season, I wouldn't have had to come all the way to Scotland for a husband." Juliana paused, confused at the note of bitterness in her voice. She'd meant to say that lightly, but it hadn't come out that way at all.

"You came here for Fitz, Lady Juliana. It's not the same thing."

Logan's voice was unexpectedly gentle, and Juliana jerked her gaze to his face. Did he *pity* her? That didn't sit well with her, and she forced a tinkling laugh. "No, it's not the same, I suppose."

They rode on for some time after that without speaking. Juliana tried to distract herself by admiring the early-blooming heather growing wild on the green hills of the moors, but even those pretty splashes of purple color didn't lift her spirits.

Before she could stem the rush of emotion, an aching sadness washed over her.

She'd never had a season—never had a chance to be a belle. She'd been betrothed to Fitzwilliam from her cradle, so her father had deemed a season unnecessary. She hadn't minded it, really. She'd never aspired to be a *ton* darling.

Still, she hadn't imagined it would be so *very* difficult to secure a husband. For all her supposed charm, she hadn't been able to bring either of her suitors up to scratch. There wasn't, it seemed, a single gentleman in England who wanted to marry her.

England, or Scotland.

She jerked her reins, impatient with herself. It was pure vanity to fuss over it. She cared for Fitzwilliam and Hugh very much, but she hadn't been in love with either of them. Neither of them had broken her heart.

But then neither of them had been in love with *her*, either. Perhaps that *did* bother her just a bit, as selfish as it was. Losing one betrothed to another lady was bad enough, but two? That was enough to make any lady question her appeal.

Now here she was with her third betrothed—a man she'd had to beg to marry her—and the best she could hope for from him was that he might become a friend.

A friend with firm lips, and captivating blue eyes…

Never mind his eyes.

Juliana pushed the thought aside before she could begin thinking of all his other…pleasing attributes.

Like his broad shoulders and long legs, his muscular chest—

No, no. This wouldn't do at all. At best, Logan would become her *friend*, and one didn't dwell on the firmness of her friend's chest.

Not that a friend was anything to sniff at. She'd welcome another friend right now. Jonathan was gone, and so was his wife, Emma, who'd been Juliana's dearest friend since childhood. She had Grace, of course, and Hugh and his wife, Isla, but she didn't see the two of them much, and now it looked as if Fitzwilliam didn't intend to return to England.

And it was only a matter of time before her father…

Juliana set her face forward, ignoring the telltale sting behind her eyes.

The doting father she'd loved had slipped away so gradually she hadn't realized it was happening until one day she woke up and discovered she didn't know him anymore. The nightmare over Grace had begun soon after that, and since then she'd been so angry with him, she almost felt as if she'd already lost him.

Since then she'd told herself over and over again all she needed was Grace, but the truth was, she'd be grateful for the chance to have Logan as a friend. She drew in a deep breath to steady herself. She wanted to know him better—to talk to him about whatever nonsense he liked—whisky, or the Robertson boys, or Mrs. Craig—it didn't matter what.

She turned toward him, but the words stalled in her throat.

He was staring at her with darkened blue eyes, a flush of color on his high cheekbones. Juliana thought he'd glance away when she caught him staring, but he didn't. Instead his gaze swept over her face, lingering on her eyes and lips.

All at once the kiss they'd shared in Widow Macaulay's bedchamber came rushing back to her. The warmth of his mouth against hers, the surprising softness of his lips. His hands tangling in her hair, his hot tongue teasing and stroking hers. Intense heat washed over her, staining her neck and rushing into her cheeks.

He hadn't tried to kiss her again since that night. Once or twice she thought she'd seen a heated expression in his eyes when he looked at her, but she'd dismissed it as her imagination.

If he *did* want to kiss her again, he was doing a wonderful job resisting temptation. He hadn't even kissed her hand when they'd become betrothed. She'd kissed him, but it had been quick—no more than a peck, really—and he hadn't tried to take it any further than that.

Perhaps he didn't want to kiss her again. Perhaps she'd done it wrong, or made a mess of it, despite having kissed other gentlemen before. She'd kissed Hugh once, when they'd become betrothed, and Fitzwilliam half a dozen times, when they were much younger and trying to determine whether the affection between them was simple friendship, or something more.

But never before had she been kissed the way Logan Blair had kissed her that night at Widow Macaulay's. If anyone had asked her she couldn't have explained it, except to say his kiss had been commanding, possessive, as if he knew she'd been kissed before and wanted to erase the memory of every other man's lips, so only he remained.

Kissing Logan had been like falling into Ruthven Burn. One moment all was firm and steady beneath her feet, and then in the next she was flying, struggling for purchase and finding nothing but air to cling to. It had been wild and terrifying and overwhelming, but exhilarating, too, until the water closed over her head and she wondered, in the split second before Logan pulled her free, if she'd ever surface again.

"When do you intend we should wed?"

Juliana jerked her attention back to Logan. "Soon."

"How soon?"

Juliana glanced at him, surprised at the huskiness in his voice. His jaw was rigid, and his big hands were tight around his reins. Was it possible he was as nervous about their upcoming nuptials as she was? "At the end of the week, perhaps?"

"The end of the week? That's ages from now!"

Juliana's eyebrows shot up. "Ages? It's four days, Logan."

He cleared his throat. "I thought you wanted to return to England at once."

She did want to get back to Surrey as soon as possible, but at the same time every one of her maidenly instincts shied away from a marriage to a man she'd only known for a week. Surely it would be best if they could take another few days to get to know each other before she was obliged to turn herself, body and mind, over to Logan's protection?

Well, not her mind. She fully intended to keep possession of that herself, but the rest of her person would legally belong to Logan once they were wed, and that didn't seem quite...well, it was a bit intimidating to think... that is, she'd just as soon not—

"Four days feels like ages to me, *beag bòidhchead*."

Beag bòidhchead...

Juliana didn't know what the words meant, but his low, hoarse murmur drifted up her spine, leaving shivers in its wake. "But we haven't even told Fitzwilliam yet." She and Logan had agreed to take a day or two to get accustomed to the idea themselves before informing him of their betrothal. "I thought another few days to get to know each other would be welcome. If we could become friends—"

"Friends? We're not going to be friends, Juliana. We're going to be husband and wife."

The last word lingered on his tongue like a rough caress, and another shiver darted up her spine. "I know, but—"

"Are you trying to delay the wedding night, lass? You'll only become more nervous about it if you do."

Juliana turned to him in alarm. How in the world had he known what she was thinking? "I didn't...I wasn't...how did you know I was—"

"Thinking about our wedding night?" He laughed softly. "You're as red as a gooseberry, Juliana. Nothing else could make you blush like that."

"Well, I was just thinking...that is, I wondering if we...it's not as if we have to—"

"Consummate? Oh, we'll consummate the marriage, *bòcan*."

Juliana worried nervously at her lower lip. He seemed to be following her thoughts with distressing accuracy.

"It's not legal otherwise," he added.

She'd been afraid of that. No, that wouldn't do. The thing had to be done right. Very well, then, once she and Logan were wed they'd consummate the marriage. Only once, of course, to make the thing legal—

"There are other reasons to consummate too, aside from that."

Dear God, did he actually want to *discuss* the other reasons? Wasn't the whole business nerve-wracking enough without having to reflect on it beforehand?

"Are you eager to share my bed, Juliana?" His low, husky voice brushed against her nerve endings. "Because I find myself very eager for our wedding night."

Eager? Juliana's cheeks went hot. The thought of sharing a bed with Logan Blair made her feel...

She didn't know how it made her feel, aside from strange—a touch fluttery in the belly, and oddly breathless. It was worrying, to say the least. If she couldn't even *think* about it without her wits scattering, how did she propose to *do* it?

"You don't need to look so worried. It won't be as bad as all that." He gave her a teasing smile. "There's even a chance you'll find the whole thing...*pleasurable*."

Juliana's eyes widened. Pleasurable? My goodness, was he flirting with her?

Her gaze caught on his curved lips, and once again the memory of his mouth on hers overwhelmed her, making her stomach leap. If the rest of it was anything like his kiss, she might find it pleasurable, indeed. She wasn't sure if that made it better, or worse. "I daresay you're right, and there's not a thing to worry about. Why, I'm sure it'll be over before it's hardly begun."

Logan choked back a laugh. "*Fuilteach ifrinn*, lass."

She stared at him, puzzled. What had she said? More to the point, what had *he* just said in reply? At this rate she was going to have to learn Gaelic.

"For my own part," he added with a slow smile. "I hope it lasts all n—"

"Logan!"

Juliana was burning with curiosity to hear his next words, but she never got the chance. They'd reached the Sassy Lassie's inn yard, and a young lady with dark hair rushed toward Logan, a welcoming smile on her red lips.

It was the girl from the other day. The one who'd brought Logan the packet of letters.

The one he'd been flirting with.

Juliana had never seen a man leap from the saddle as quickly as Logan did when he saw her running across the inn yard. "Hello, Alison."

She came barreling toward him, and he caught her just in time to keep her from crashing into him. "Here again after only a week? Why, Logan! Did ye miss me, lad?"

Logan cast an uneasy glance at Juliana. "Well, ah…I'm always happy to see you, Alison, but we came for our letters."

The girl drew back and pursed her lips in a pout. "Letters! Is that all? How can ye be so cruel? One of these days I'm going to throw ye over for a man with a warmer heart, Logan Blair!" She slapped him lightly on the arm, and her pretty pout dissolved into a smile even more alluring than her sulk had been.

Juliana sat frozen atop her horse, an unpleasant weight settling on her chest as she watched the girl tease and flirt with him.

She was young—not more than eighteen or so—with abundant, shining raven hair piled in an untidy knot atop her head. Her translucent skin shone like a pearl, and she had the widest, most thickly lashed blue eyes Juliana had ever seen.

The beauty of the girl's eyes didn't seem to be lost on Logan. He was looking down at her with a smile unlike any Juliana had seen on his face before. He looked as if he'd been asleep all this time, and had only awoken now, when this beautiful girl rushed into his arms.

Juliana quickly averted her eyes, aware she'd been staring at the two of them. She slowly dismounted, unsure what to do next. Courtesy demanded she wait for Logan to introduce her, but he was far too busy gazing admiringly at the girl's smiling lips and generous curves to remember his manners. At least, that was how it appeared to Juliana.

All at once, she wished herself anywhere but here.

Was this ravishing girl the reason Logan hadn't wanted to marry her? Was he in love with her? It looked as if the girl was besotted with him, but while there was clearly admiration and affection in his gaze, if he felt anything deeper, his expression didn't betray it.

Not that it mattered to her if Logan *did* love the girl, Juliana thought dully. Once he'd served his purpose in England he'd return to Scotland quickly enough. This girl could have him all to herself then, with Juliana's compliments.

It was nothing to her what he did.

She straightened her shoulders and went to move past them, courtesy be damned, but before she could disappear through the entryway of the inn, Logan caught her arm. "Wait, Lady Juliana. I want to introduce you to

Miss Alison McLaren. Alison here is Fergus's eldest daughter. The Sassy Lassie is named after her. Alison, this is Lady Juliana Bernard. She's…well, she's…she's the Duke of Blackmore's friend, visiting here from Surrey."

Well, how very odd. It must have slipped Logan's mind Juliana was also his *betrothed*.

The girl dipped into a hasty curtsy, her flirtatious smile replaced by a curious one. "How do you do, my lady? You're quite a way from Surrey, aren't you?"

The girl's smile was friendly, and she spoke cheerfully enough, but Juliana's own smile felt as if it were frozen to her lips. "How do you do?" She returned the girl's curtsy, but she didn't linger. "I'm pleased to meet you, Miss McLaren, but if you'll excuse me, I'll go and see if your father has any letters for me."

Logan's fingers tightened around her arm, but Juliana freed herself from his grip with a subtle tug. He was welcome to stand here in the inn yard and flirt with Alison McLaren if he liked, but she didn't have to stay here and watch it.

She could feel his gaze on her back as she walked away, but she disappeared through the inn's doorway without turning around.

There weren't many people about, but Juliana saw a man in the dining room dragging a damp cloth across the bar, and she recognized him at once as Fergus McLaren. "I beg your pardon, Mr. McLaren, but do you have any letters here for Lady Juliana Bernard?"

He looked up from the bar, and his furry eyebrows shot up. "Lady who?"

"Lady Juliana Bernard, Mr. McLaren. Surely that name must be familiar to you? I'm the English lady Logan Blair warned you about. The lady you were meant to keep away from Castle Kinross."

He ran a grimy sleeve across his forehead. "Are ye now?"

"Indeed. As it happened, I found the castle in spite of you."

He took her in from the top of her head to the tips of her boots, and a grin rose to his lips. "Did ye now? How did ye manage that, lass?"

She shrugged. "It was simple enough. I saw Logan leave the inn and I followed him."

Fergus seemed mightily amused by that. He slapped a hand down on the bar, cackling. "And what did Mr. Logan Blair do when 'e found ye sneaking after 'im?"

"There wasn't much he could do, aside from take me to Castle Kinross with him. He wasn't at all pleased about it, if that's what you're asking."

Fergus cackled even harder. "Aye, I bet 'e wasn't, at that. Ye English lassies are wily ones. All right then, Lady Juliana Bernard. Ye just wait 'ere, and I'll fetch the letters for ye."

He shuffled off, still chuckling, and Juliana wandered over to the window to wait. Logan was still talking with Alison McLaren in the yard. What was the girl saying to him, to put such an amused smile on his face? He was so wholly absorbed by her he didn't even seem to notice Juliana had disappeared. She turned her back on them with an irritated huff. It looked as if she'd have to fetch the castle's letters, too, since Logan was too preoccupied to do it himself.

"Here ye are, my lady. There's a few here fer the duke, and one fancy one on fine paper fer you." Fergus handed the letters over with a sly wink. "Nothing but the finest paper fer yer ladyship, eh?"

Juliana snatched the letters from him, but Fergus didn't seem offended by her rudeness. He only cackled again, and shook his head. "Wily, and sassy, too. Logan'll have 'is hands full with this one."

He went back to his work. Juliana placed Fitz's letters safely in the pocket of her riding skirt, and wandered out into the hallway to read hers.

It was postmarked from Bath, and Lord Arthur's crest was stamped into the dark green wax. Juliana stared down at it, her stomach suddenly in knots. Lord Arthur had said he'd write if her father's health made a drastic change for the better, or for the worse.

Except there was no better for her father. Not anymore.

Juliana's hands shook as she slid the tip of her fingernail under the wax and opened the sheet. The letter was brief, but in the few moments it took for her to read the half-dozen lines, her entire world fell apart.

Rapid deterioration...father very ill...leaving Bath for Surrey today... Come at once.

Lord Arthur must have written the letter just after she'd arrived in Inverness. She stared down at it, the words and lines blurring in front of her eyes. Then she shoved it into her pocket and ran out the front door of the inn.

Logan turned when she came out into the yard. He took one look at her and the smile Alison McLaren had put on his face vanished. "Juliana? What's happened?"

Juliana didn't answer him. She hardly heard him. Lord Arthur's words were echoing in her head, and her only thought was she must get back to Castle Kinross as quickly as she could.

"Juliana!" Logan caught her by the shoulders as she raced across the inn yard and held her still, his blue eyes dark with worry as he gazed down at her. "Juliana, what is it? Tell me what's wrong."

"My father," she whispered, the words torn from a throat suddenly gone dry with panic. "I must return to England at once."

Chapter Fifteen

Juliana didn't say a word on the way from Inverness back to Castle Kinross, but Logan could see she was quietly panicking. Each time her face began to crumple or she bit her lip to hold back tears, his chest cracked open wider.

It was torture, watching her struggle with her grief.

She hadn't shown him the letter she'd received from Lord Arthur, but it was plain the news from England wasn't good. Logan didn't know what to say to her, or how to comfort her. All he could do was stay close beside her as they rushed through the longest ride he'd ever taken.

When they arrived at the castle they found Fitz pacing the entryway, waiting for them. Logan was too distracted by Juliana to notice it, but later he'd wonder why he didn't find this odd at the time. Fitz never waited unless he had a reason for it. Logan should have realized then something momentous was about to happen.

"Logan, Lina. I'm glad you're both here. I need to speak…" Fitz trailed off when he caught sight of Juliana's face. "Lina? What's the matter? You're as white as a ghost."

"I've had a letter from Lord Arthur." Juliana pulled the letter from her pocket and held it out to Fitz, her hand shaking.

Fitz took it, but he didn't look at it. He kept his gaze on Juliana's face. "Your father. Is he—"

"He's had a turn for the worse. Lord Arthur writes to say he's taken him back to Surrey. They're likely there, even now." Juliana grasped Fitz's hand, her face going even whiter. "What if he…what if I'm too late, Fitzwilliam?"

"No. You're not to think like that. Do you understand me, Lina?" Fitz's voice was firm, but he gathered Juliana against him and gently stroked her back.

Logan stood there, his chest tight as he watched his brother offer Juliana the comfort *he* longed to give her. Even as he cursed his own selfishness, his jealousy was like a fist squeezing his heart.

Fitz held Juliana for long, quiet moments. When she raised her face from his chest, the tears she'd fought on the ride from Inverness were streaking her cheeks. "I'll leave for England at once—tomorrow, if we can manage it."

Fitz nodded. "I'll see to everything. Go up to your bedchamber, Lina. I'll send Emilia to you, and one of the maids to help you pack your things."

"Thank you." Juliana started for the stairs, but just when Logan was certain she'd disappear to her room without a word to him, she paused. "Mr. Blair?"

Logan practically leapt across the space between them. "Aye. What can I do?"

She'd dried her cheeks, but her green eyes were still swimming with tears. "You'll speak to Fitzwilliam about…our plans? You'll need to warn Stokes, as well, and tell him we're leaving for Surrey as soon as we can."

Logan ached to gather her close, but he only nodded. "Yes. I'll make all the arrangements."

To Logan's surprise, she took his hand. "Thank you." A grateful smile drifted across her trembling lips, then she turned for the stairs.

Logan and Fitz watched her until she reached the landing and went down the hallway toward her bedchamber. "Christ," Logan murmured, once she was out of sight. "I hope it's not too late."

Fitz's face was somber. "So do I."

Logan drew in a deep breath. "I need to speak with you privately, brother."

"What a coincidence. I need to speak to you as well. Shall we go to the library? I need a drink."

Logan followed Fitz down the hallway to the library and closed the door firmly behind him. Fitz went straight to the sideboard, sloshed some whisky into two tumblers, then joined Logan, who was seated in a chair before the fireplace.

They didn't speak until they'd both tossed back half the whisky in their glasses, then Logan placed his tumbler on the table in front of him, and met Fitz's eyes. "Juliana won't have to make the journey back to England alone."

Fitz's eyebrows rose. "No?"

"No. I'm going with her. I'm marrying her, Fitz."

For a split second, Fitz's face remained blank, but then his mouth twisted, and a chuckle escaped his lips. The chuckle deepened and swelled until Fitz gave into it, and threw his head back in a hearty laugh. Logan's mouth dropped open. He wasn't sure what reaction he'd expected, but it wasn't *this*. "What the devil is so funny?"

"You, Logan. You're what's so funny." Fitz wiped the tears of laughter from his eyes. "Jesus. I've been waiting for days to hear you say that, and now *today*, of all days, you tell me you're marrying Lina."

Logan stared at him. "What difference does it make what day it is? This is what you wanted, isn't it?"

"It's what I wanted, all right, and if you'd made the decision a day earlier, I would have been able to say I knew you'd marry her all along, and my faith in you was totally justified. As it is…well, let's just say what's done can't be undone."

"Well, what the devil's been done?" Logan didn't have the faintest idea what his brother was going on about, but he didn't like the sound of it.

Fitz didn't answer right away. His brows drew together, as if he were pondering the best way to explain himself, but when he did speak, his words only added to Logan's confusion. "You know, I never asked to be the laird. Never wanted to be either, if you want the truth."

Logan gaped at him. "What does that mean?"

"Never asked to be duke, either, come to that. I certainly never asked to be both at once. God knows being a duke is enough trouble for one man."

"Enough tr…for God's sake, Fitz, what are you talking about?"

"But then I guess our uncle must have known that, since he never intended for me to become the Laird of Clan Kinross."

Logan stiffened. "He left the land to *you*. Whoever owns the land is laird. Our uncle knew that well enough."

Fitz shrugged. "Yes, I expect he did, but then he also knew the Kinross land wasn't part of the entail. It belonged to our grandmother on our mother's side, as I'm sure you know. It became our grandfather's when they married, and then our uncle's when he became duke, but it was never part of the Blackmore dukedom."

"So? What does it matter? The land is yours now. That makes you the laird."

"Ah, but as I said, I don't want to be laird. Never did. *You* do, though, don't you, Logan? Want to be Laird of Clan Kinross, I mean."

"You know damn well I do." As far as Logan was concerned, he was now and always would be Laird of Clan Kinross, regardless of who owned the land. He'd been raised to act as laird—had expected to lead the clan since he was old enough to balance on his father's knee, the law be damned. The law might say he wasn't laird, but the law couldn't erase a man's history.

"Yes, I do know that." Fitz's tone remained casual, but he was watching Logan closely. "But there's something you don't know. You see, our uncle always intended for you to have the land, Logan. He left it to me, yes, but I can dispose of it if I wish, to whomever I choose. Why do you think I came to Castle Kinross in the first place?"

Logan's mouth opened, then closed again. He stared at Fitz, too stunned to say a word.

"It's a fair trade, really, once you consider it rationally. Our father's eldest son in exchange for a large parcel of land. The Duke of Blackmore gets to raise his heir, and Gordon Blair's second son gets the land and becomes the rightful Laird of Clan Kinross."

"A trade?" No, it wasn't possible. His father would have told him.

Fitz sipped at his whisky, watching Logan over the rim of his glass. "I didn't think you could have known. If you had, you'd have been pleased to see me arrive at Castle Kinross. I'm surprised our father never said anything to you about it, but then he and our uncle didn't much care for one another. Maybe he thought the duke would go back on his word. Then again, our father did raise you as if he knew you'd become laird someday."

Logan was thankful he was sitting down, because if he'd been standing his knees would have buckled beneath him. "You mean to say you came here to turn the land over to me?"

His heart was pounding with hope, but Fitz dashed it with his next words. "I did indeed, but then I changed my mind."

"What do you mean, you changed your mind?" Logan's voice lowered to a dangerous growl. "You just told me our uncle always intended to turn the land back over to the clan."

"He did, but that doesn't mean I have to honor his wishes. I'm the duke now, you see, and the land is mine. I can do whatever I choose with it."

A roar filled Logan's ears, and the next thing he knew he'd shot to his feet, grabbed Fitz by his coat and jerked him out of his chair. "You're a bloody cheat, *brother*."

"No need to threaten me, *brother*." Fitz grasped Logan's wrist and calmly detached his coat from Logan's grip. "You'll get your land, now you've made up your mind to marry Lina."

It took Logan a moment before he could make sense of Fitz's words. When he realized what Fitz meant, he dropped back down into his chair, stunned. "You've given the land to Juliana."

"I have, indeed. I thought you'd come to the decision to marry Lina on your own, and I was right about that, but you dithered on about it for so long I got nervous, and decided to force your hand. My solicitor brought me the paperwork earlier today, and I signed it. The land belongs to Lina now, and—"

"And once I marry her, it will belong to me."

Fitz nodded. "Just as our uncle intended, albeit with one added step."

Logan stared into the fire, his thoughts in turmoil. On one hand, he couldn't help but admire his brother's cleverness. Fitz was well aware Logan would do anything he must to protect the clan, and the best way to protect them was to have control of the Kinross land.

On the other hand, it infuriated him Fitz had been so damned high-handed about it. If he'd only waited another day this all would have sorted itself out, but now, once Juliana found out Fitz had given her the land, she'd think Logan had only agreed to marry her so he could get his hands on it himself, and become the laird.

It shouldn't matter. He was going to be Laird of Clan Kinross, just as he and his father always wanted. What could be more important than that? In any case, this wasn't a love match on Juliana's side, any more than it was on his. She was marrying him as a means to an end, so what did it matter if she believed he was doing the same?

Except it did matter. It mattered very much.

"Juliana's going to think I'm only marrying her to get the land," Logan muttered, avoiding Fitz's gaze.

"Hmmm." Fitz studied him with narrowed eyes. "Would that bother you, if she did think so?"

It *would* bother him, but Logan wasn't ready to admit to Fitz he cared what Lady Juliana thought of him. "Well, it's not true, is it?"

"Then tell her it's not true, Logan. I'll tell her, as well. Despite what you might think, Lina doesn't want to believe the worst of you."

"Why shouldn't she? I stole her letters, remember? I tried to keep her away from Castle Kinross. I accused her of chasing a duke all the way to Scotland just so she could become a duchess. If you were in her place, wouldn't you believe the worst of me?"

Fitz shook his head. "She's not like that, Logan. Listen to me. You don't know her very well yet, but Lina's as sweet and loving as she is beautiful.

She's not the sort of woman who'll hold your past mistakes against you. She's everything a man could want in a wife."

"Every man but you." Logan was ashamed of the words as soon as he spoke them, but he'd hoped over time he could persuade Juliana to trust him, and he was furious with Fitz for putting him in this position.

Fitz's face hardened. "You're wrong. I would have married her in a heartbeat, and considered myself lucky to have her."

Logan stiffened. "You sound as if you're in love with her."

"Of course, I love Lina. I always have."

Logan snatched up his tumbler and downed the rest of his whisky before he could give in to the urge to slam his fist into Fitz's jaw. Christ, he was more jealous over his brother's shared history with Juliana than he'd ever been over Fitz owning the Kinross land.

What's happening to me?

He didn't think anything could ever mean as much to him as the land, but now—

"What about the wedding?" Fitz asked. "I suppose it'll have to be tomorrow morning. You and Lina can leave right afterwards. You should be able to make it as far as Dalwhinnie if you leave by—"

"No. The wedding has to be this evening."

"This evening! But that only leaves us a few hours to make the arrangements."

"It's not going to be a grand wedding, Fitz. Send Stokes off to the Andersons' farm. Their cousin Fraser is visiting, and he's a minister. We'll do it in the castle chapel, with you, Emilia, Craig and Mrs. Craig as witnesses."

Fitz was frowning as he considered it. "It could be done this evening, I suppose, but I don't know that Lina's in a frame of mind to—"

"She won't be in a better frame of mind by tomorrow morning."

"No," Fitz admitted. "But I still don't see why you insist on rushing—"

"She's an innocent, Fitz," Logan said quietly. "I won't have her spend her wedding night at some inn in Dalwhinnie. We'll wed this evening, spend tonight at Castle Kinross, and leave for England tomorrow morning."

Fitz looked surprised, but then he smiled. "Good man, Logan. I knew I couldn't be mistaken in you. You may not believe it, but I haven't any doubt you'll take good care of Lina." He hesitated, then said, "There's one other thing you could do for me while you're in England. A favor, of sorts."

Logan gave him a wary look. "What sort of favor?"

"Now I've signed the Kinross land over to Juliana, I don't have any Scottish land of my own. I want some."

"You just told me you never wanted to be a laird."

Fitz scowled. "I don't. I mean...oh, for God's sake. I don't know what I bloody want, all right? In any case, I'm acquainted with an English earl who might be persuaded to sell his Scottish land, if the price suits him. He'll want far more than it's worth, but I'm willing to indulge his avarice to get his land."

Logan straightened in his chair. He hadn't expected this. "Where's his land?"

"It borders Kinross land to the south, in Perth."

"Clan Murray territory?"

Fitz nodded. "My guess is this earl of mine is thinking of clearing it. He won't hesitate to turn the people off if he thinks he can squeeze an extra penny out of it." Fitz's mouth pulled tight. "If he does want to clear it and the people resist, it'll be a massacre. Worse than Strathnaver, even. He's not a merciful man, Logan. To make matters worse, he bears me a grudge."

"Who is he? What's his name?" Suspicion was gathering in Logan's chest, cold and heavy. But no, surely it couldn't be *him*—

"It's Lord Cowden, Logan."

Ice filled Logan's veins. Somehow, he'd suspected it was Cowden. "The blackguard who manipulated Lord Graystone into giving him custody of Grace when Juliana refused to marry him? Why would he agree to sell you his land? He despises you, doesn't he?"

"He does. Always has. But he needs the funds—gaming debts, you know—and I'll give him an exorbitant amount of money for it."

Christ. Logan would be far happier bloodying Cowden's nose than offering to buy his land, but if Fitz owned that piece of Perth it would prevent another round of devastating clearances.

Save another clan from destruction...

"You'll have to approach him carefully, Logan. Cowden's not your average scoundrel. He's smart, and dangerous. Terrible snob, too." Fitz smirked. "Like all Englishmen."

Logan shot Fitz a guilty look. "I never said you were a snob."

Not aloud, that is.

Fitz laughed. "Of course not. Why would you? I'm no more an Englishman than you are, brother. Speaking of Scots, that little red-headed lad Duncan Munro was here today, looking for you. He wanted to remind you of your promise to take him fishing next week."

"Damn." In all the upheaval, Logan had forgotten his promise to Duncan. He hated to break it, but he'd be halfway to England by next week. "I'll find him this afternoon and explain why I can't—"

"No, never mind. I'll take him, if he'll have me in your place."

"You will?" Logan asked, surprised.

Fitz shrugged. "Why not? I like fishing, and Duncan's a good little lad. Don't want to disappoint him."

Logan studied his brother, a grin on his lips. "Spoken like a true laird, brother. Maybe there's hope for you, after all."

Chapter Sixteen

"No, Emilia. You're wonderfully kind, but I can't take it."

Juliana stood in the middle of her bedchamber, staring at the lovely cream-colored gown draped over Emilia's arm. Even as she refused it, she couldn't keep her fingers from reaching out to stroke the delicate skirt. The gown was simple but elegant, made of a very fine, thin muslin, with dainty puffed sleeves.

"Of course, you'll take it. There's no sense in arguing with me, Juliana. I insist on your having it."

A lump rose in Juliana's throat. "But it's your wedding gown."

"Yes, but today is *your* wedding day, and we can't have you wearing your riding habit, can we? My wedding isn't for several weeks. There's plenty of time for me to make up another gown for myself."

Juliana tried to return Emilia's cheerful smile, but between Lord Arthur's letter, her worry over her father, and now Emilia's heartbreaking kindness, the best she could manage was a dejected twist of her lips.

"Oh, dear. That smile won't do for a bride on her wedding day." Emilia laid the gown carefully across a chair, then took Juliana's hand and led her to the bed. "I daresay this isn't how you imagined your wedding day, but I promise you, Juliana, you can trust Logan with your life. He's a good man, and he'll take care of you."

Juliana shook her head. "It's not just Logan."

No, it was everything. Her father, Grace, the suddenness of her wedding, Alison McLaren—

Alison McLaren? For pity's sake, how had that thought managed to sneak in? She wasn't thinking about Alison McLaren. Of course, she wasn't. Why, it was utter nonsense.

Except…

Wasn't it possible Logan was in love with the beautiful dark-haired girl? Juliana couldn't think of a single reason why he wouldn't be. He'd known her all his life, and he'd been delighted to see her today. No man looked at a woman the way Logan had looked at Alison unless he was in love with her.

Juliana met Emilia's concerned gaze. "It's just…what if we're too late, Emilia? What if my father…what if I'm dragging Logan away from Alis… from everyone he loves, and it's all for naught?"

Emilia gave her hand a reassuring squeeze. "You needn't worry about *that*. Logan's not the sort of man who'd allow himself to be dragged into anything. If he's marrying you, it's because he's made up his mind it's the best thing to do. You can be sure of that much."

But Juliana wasn't sure of that, or of anything else. Everything had become so tangled in her mind she couldn't make sense of it anymore. "He feels responsible, Emilia, because of the letters."

"Well, isn't he responsible? He never should have taken those letters." But Emilia bit her lip, and Juliana could see she was struggling between her loyalty to Logan and her innate sense of fair play.

Juliana sighed. "No, but we both know he didn't do it for selfish reasons. He was trying to protect the clan. How can I hold him responsible, when I'm sure I would have done the same thing in his place? Yes, it was wrong—I don't deny it. But isn't it just as wrong to force him into a marriage he doesn't want when he was only doing what he felt he must?"

Emilia rose from the bed and crossed the room. She plucked absently at the folds of her wedding gown, thinking, then turned back to Juliana. "What if he wasn't being punished at all, but rewarded? Would that reassure you, and reconcile you to the marriage?"

Juliana blinked. "Rewarded? How?"

"I told Fitzwilliam I wouldn't mention this to you. Logan wants to speak to you about it himself, but I think it might bring you peace of mind. You're going to find out soon enough anyway, so I don't see that it makes much difference."

Juliana's heart started to pound. "What is it, Emilia? Please, you must tell me."

Emilia drew a deep breath. "Fitz is going to give you the land. Indeed, he already has."

"The land?" Juliana repeated stupidly. What land?

"The Kinross land," Emilia said patiently. "Kinross Castle, as well. It all belongs to you now."

All the air left Juliana's lungs at once, leaving her fighting to catch her breath. "To me? But I don't...that doesn't...*why*, Emilia? Why would Fitzwilliam do such a thing? I don't want it!"

"Hush now, and listen to me. Fitzwilliam was never going to keep that land. His uncle, the previous duke, always intended for Logan to have it. Fitzwilliam came to Scotland to give it to him, but then you arrived, and there was all that confusion with the letters, and everything became dreadfully tangled, and—"

"And Fitzwilliam knew if he gave the land to me, Logan would marry me," Juliana finished quietly. That sweet moment under the Laburnum Arch when Logan had asked her to be his wife hadn't truly been a proposal, then. It had been the culmination of a business arrangement.

Wasn't that what she'd asked him for? A marriage of convenience? Well, now it would be convenient for both of them. They'd each get the thing that was most precious to them. She'd get Grace, and Logan would get the Kinross land.

What right had she to begrudge him that?

If she'd managed to persuade herself there was something more between them, then she'd been a fool. His nervousness that day, the hope she thought she'd seen in his eyes, the tenderness of that kiss between them...she'd imagined it all.

Juliana closed her eyes against the pain flooding through her. It was so intense she wrapped her arms around herself, afraid it might tear her apart. "I—I see. Well, I suppose that does give Logan a reason to marry me, doesn't it? Fitzwilliam's very clever."

Emilia came back to the bed and took Juliana's hands. "I know what you're thinking, but you're wrong. Logan just found out about it this afternoon. He didn't agree to the marriage to get the land, Juliana. He'd already promised to marry you before he knew anything about it. It's the truth, but if you don't believe me, then ask Fitzwilliam. He'll tell you the same."

"Of course, I believe you, Emilia," Juliana said dully, more to put an end to the discussion than anything else. Perhaps it was true. There was a part of her that believed if Logan had agreed to the marriage to get the Kinross land, he would have told her so at once. Oddly, though, that didn't diminish her pain. Instead it spread from her stomach to her chest until it felt as if her heart were being clawed to bits.

"I think I'd like to rest now." Juliana drew her hands free of Emilia's grip. "I'm to be married this evening, after all. I don't want to drop into a doze before I can say my vows, do I?"

Emilia studied her for a moment, then rose from the bed with a sigh. "You'll wear my gown? Please, Juliana. I want you to have it."

Juliana caught Emilia's hand and pressed it gratefully. "You're a lovely friend. Yes, of course I'll wear it, if you truly wish me to."

"I do wish it. Nothing would please me more." Emilia squeezed her hand, then crossed the room to the door. "I'm off to see the chapel is made ready, and to gather some heather for your hair. I'll come back in a few hours to help you dress, shall I?"

Juliana lay back on the bed and let her head fall against the pillows. "Yes. Thank you."

Once Emilia was gone she closed her eyes, but it was some time before her troubled thoughts calmed enough for drowsiness to overtake her. Memory after memory rolled through her mind, almost as if she were flipping through images in a picture book. Grace's dark eyes, her father's face, and Logan's slowly curving lips...

She was poised on the edge of sleep before the truth came over her, and her eyes fluttered open.

It hurt to think Logan might only be marrying her to get the Kinross land, but there was more to it than that. Deep down, she'd hoped he'd decide to stay in England with her. Now he was to become laird, that dream was shattered. As he soon as he fulfilled his promise to her, he'd return to Scotland at once.

Since she'd come to Castle Kinross, she'd told herself time and again all she needed was Grace. That if she could only have Grace, she'd be happy.

Now she knew the truth.

She'd been lying to herself the entire time.

* * * *

If someone had been peeking through the chapel window during Logan and Juliana's wedding, they would have described it as a lovely ceremony.

Emilia had outdone herself with the chapel. It was a small room with a high, wood-timbered cathedral ceiling, gray stone floors, and an arched alcove behind the altar fitted with a beautiful stained glass window.

As it was an evening wedding it might have been a trifle dark, even gloomy, but Emilia was determined to make Juliana's wedding as beautiful as it could be. She'd seen to it that every candle was lit. The flames flickered against the stone walls and caught at the bright reds and yellows of the stained glass saints kneeling at the foot of the cross. Only Emilia and

Fitzwilliam, Mr. and Mrs. Craig, and Stokes attended. The ceremony was simple, brief, and intimate, with a quiet beauty about it that soothed even Juliana's frayed nerves.

Logan wore a kilt in the black and green Kinross tartan, with a tight-fitting dark green jacket and a tartan cape draped over his left shoulder. His dark hair was brushed back from his face, and from the first moment Juliana caught sight of him standing at the altar waiting for her, she couldn't tear her gaze away.

He didn't smile as he watched her coming toward him, but those blue, blue eyes took in every inch of her, lingering on her muslin-draped curves. When she took her place beside him at the altar and his gaze met hers, Juliana would have sworn he caught his breath. It was one of the few moments that stood out for her in what was otherwise a confusing blur.

There'd been a late supper. Not a wedding supper—there hadn't been time for Mrs. Craig to prepare such an extravagant meal, but she had made one sweet especially for Juliana.

Cranachan.

Juliana glanced shyly at Logan when the dainty glass dish was set before her. He was looking down at her, an uncertain smile on his lips. "It's not proper cranachan without the raspberries, but since it's our wedding supper I persuaded Mrs. Craig to make do with gooseberries instead."

Juliana's eyes widened. "*You* asked her to make this for me?"

A faint flush rose on his cheekbones. "I did say I couldn't let you leave Scotland without trying it."

Juliana picked up the dish and turned it this way and that, admiring the bright red berries drowning in generous drifts of cream. "You also said you'd earn a clout to the head if you asked for cranachan with gooseberries."

"My right ear is still ringing." Logan nodded at her dish. "Taste it."

Juliana loaded her spoon with gooseberries, cream, and toasted oats, and slipped it between her lips. The taste of tart berries and rich, sweet honey and cream exploded on her tongue, and her eyes slid closed. "Oh, my goodness." It was thick and smooth and crunchy at once, with a little bite from the whisky that lingered on her tongue.

When she opened her eyes again, Logan was watching her. His lips were parted, and the look in his eyes...Juliana's body flushed with heat, and all at once she became very aware tonight was her wedding night.

Logan cleared his throat, but when he spoke his voice was still thick, husky. "Do you like it?"

He was staring down at her, his hot blue eyes darting between her eyes and her lips. As always, once he caught her gaze, Juliana couldn't look away. She swallowed. "I—yes. Very much. It's, ah…well, I've always been fond of gooseberries."

His lips curved in a slow smile, his dark blue gaze darting to her mouth. "Such a pretty red, and tart and sweet at once."

Juliana caught her breath. Were they still talking about berries?

She didn't dare look at him again after that, but she could feel him beside her, his powerful body thrumming with the tension that snapped and hummed between them.

The supper courses came and went. Then, before she was prepared for what came next, it was over. Emilia rose from her seat and motioned to Juliana to withdraw and leave the gentlemen alone with their port. Juliana rose unsteadily and followed Emilia out of the dining room. Once they reached the hallway, Emilia took her by the hand and led her up to the family wing of the house.

Not to her own bedchamber, but to Logan's.

"Here are a few of your things." Emilia waved a hand toward a massive mahogany dressing table. "Everything else is already packed, but I had my maid gather what I thought you'd need for tonight and bring it here for you."

"Thank you." Juliana wandered over to the dressing table. Her brush, comb, and silver mirror had been laid neatly across the top. She took up the brush and was absently stroking her fingers across the bristles when something else caught her attention.

A sheer white night rail and matching dressing gown were draped over the back of the chair.

Her gaze collided with Emilia's. Her friend smiled, and came closer to take her hands. "This is a trifle awkward, but I did think I should…I wanted to ask if you…I know your mother died when you were very young, and it did occur to me you might not know—"

"It's all right, Emilia. My sister-in-law Emma spoke to me about it, after she and my brother Jonathan were married." It had been a brief enough conversation, Juliana being unwilling to pry into the intimate details of her brother's marriage, but she knew enough to understand the basic mechanics of the thing.

Anything beyond that, well…she'd soon find out, wouldn't she?

Emilia blew out a relieved breath. "Thank goodness. Shall I help you undress, or send for one of the maids?"

"No, no maid." Juliana was already nervous enough. The last thing she needed was a maid hovering about. "If you could just unfasten the row of buttons down my back and unlace me, I'm sure I can manage from there."

Emilia obliged, then took Juliana by the shoulders and turned her around so they were facing each other. "The wedding gown suits you. I knew I'd made the right decision persuading you to wear it. You looked beautiful this evening, Juliana. Logan thought so, too. I could see it in his face when he looked at you."

Juliana drew in a shaky breath, then leaned forward and pressed a kiss to Emilia's cheek. "Thank you for all you've done for me, Emilia. You can't know how much I…I never hoped to have another friend as dear to me as my late sister-in-law was, yet here you are."

Emilia's pretty blue eyes shone. "We're sisters now, or nearly so. It's all going to come right between you and Logan, Juliana. I know it is." Emilia squeezed her hands once last time, and then she was gone.

The room felt empty and quiet after she left.

Juliana turned in a circle, unsure what to do.

What did a bride do on her wedding night, while she waited alone in her new husband's bedchamber for him to join her? She didn't have an answer, so she wandered about aimlessly for a bit, until she found herself back at the dressing table.

The night rail—yes, she'd change into that. Logan could walk in at any moment, and she'd just as soon be prepared when he arrived. She stepped carefully out of her wedding gown and petticoat, slipped out of her corset, then paused, unsure what to do next.

Was she meant to wear her chemise under the night rail? It seemed silly, given that Logan would remove whatever she was wearing. Unless… *would* he remove it? Or was the thing meant to be done quickly, without removing one's clothing?

She didn't know! It was too late to ask Emilia now, so she'd simply have to do what she thought best, and hope it was the right thing.

She dragged her chemise over her head and hurried into the night rail, but when she caught sight of herself in the dressing table mirror, she gasped. Dear God, she could see right through it! It was so thin and sheer she could see the curves of her breasts, the darker pink of her nipples, and even the shadow between her…

Juliana snatched up the matching dressing gown. She tugged it on, wrapped it tightly around her body and studied herself in the mirror. It was a bit better, but the dressing gown was as sheer as the night rail. It didn't hide her curves so much as reveal glimpses of them, half-hidden under two entirely insufficient layers of fabric.

Very well, then. She'd wait for Logan in the bed, with the covers pulled up to her chin. Climbing boldly into his bed made her nearly as anxious as the night rail did, but it was better than standing nearly stark naked in the middle of his bedchamber.

She rushed to the dressing table and snatched the pins from her hair, then hurried through an arched doorway, hoping to find the bed on the other side of it.

She found it, and the sight of it brought her to an abrupt halt.

It was enormous.

Juliana stared at it in dismay. Four massive posts rose from each corner. They were so tall they nearly met the ceiling, and sumptuous dark green silk hung from a heavy, carved wood canopy. It was gigantic, imposing, aggressively masculine, and so high she'd need a step stool to get into it.

Either that, or a running start.

She was still staring at the bed, biting her lip and debating whether or not she should drag the dressing table chair over when she heard the outer door open behind her.

"Juliana?"

Logan's deep voice sent a shiver up her spine. "I'm in here," she called, then cringed at the telltale squeak in her voice.

She heard some rustling from the other side of the door, then Logan's footsteps drawing closer. "Are you—" he began, but then trailed off with a rough breath.

Juliana turned to find him standing in the doorway. He'd already removed the tartan cape, his jacket and his cravat. That alone would have been enough to disconcert her, but it was the look on his face that made her eyes go wide.

He was staring at her, naked heat in his blue gaze. He'd looked at her with desire before, but this...

Juliana swallowed. He looked as if he wanted to drag her to the bed and devour her as if she were a dish of cranachan. Why was he—

Oh, no. He could see the outline of her body through the dratted night rail! The candlelight behind her was shining through the fragile muslin, revealing every curve and hollow.

Scalding heat washed over her cheeks and neck. She snatched at the edges of the dressing gown to wrap it more tightly around her, but Logan's husky voice stopped her.

"Don't."

She froze, her fingers twisted in the sheer fabric.

He came across the room and stopped in front of her. "There's no need for you to be shy, *mo bhean.* I'm your husband now, and I think you're..."

He glanced down her body, and his throat moved in a rough swallow. "*Àlainn.* Beautiful."

"You do?"

He laughed softly and reached out to drag a finger over the narrow band of ribbon at her neckline. "I didn't think I'd been subtle about it, but you sound surprised."

He continued to stroke that finger over her, the tip of it brushing against her skin. Juliana's breath quickened, and her eyelids became so heavy they sank to half-mast. She wouldn't have thought such a big, powerful man could touch her so gently.

"Get in the bed," he murmured. "I'll join you there in a—"

"No. I can't."

Logan had been gazing down at her with sleepy eyes, but that made him frown. "You can't? We talked about this, Juliana. The marriage isn't legal unless we consummate it."

"No, no, it's not that. I mean…it's too high." She waved a hand toward the bed, her cheeks heating. "It looks like it was made for a giant."

Logan's lips curved. "My wee wife."

Juliana let out a relieved breath. That smile, the glint of humor in his blue eyes—this was the Logan she knew, the man she'd begun to trust. "I'm *not* wee, though I confess I could use a little help getting—" She gasped as Logan slid an arm across her back, another under her knees and swept her up into his arms. "Logan!"

"You *are* wee, but I don't mind." He carried her to the bed, his chest and shoulder muscles shifting against her as he lay her gently on her back.

He stood for a moment, gazing down at her. "*Fhìnealta. Uaine air leth-shùil bòcan,*" he murmured, his blue eyes glowing.

Juliana didn't know what that meant, but the look in his eyes when he said it…

She tried not to sigh.

He'd said he'd join her in a moment, so Juliana thought he'd leave her there while he went off to do some mysterious bridegroom preparations, but to her surprise he stretched out on the bed beside her.

When he moved closer and draped an arm over her waist, Juliana's nerves came roaring back. The next thing she knew, she was babbling. "I thought you wanted to…what I mean is, didn't you say you—"

"Juliana." He pressed a finger to her lips to quiet her.

His blue eyes roamed over her face. He paused at her mouth, seeming fascinated by the sight of his fingers against her lips. He stroked her with a fingertip, tugging gently on her lower lip, opening it for him.

Then…then he kissed her. He was careful with her, his mouth sweet and gentle against hers. One kiss blended into the next until Juliana couldn't tell where one ended and another began. Then, when he parted her lips with his tongue, she stopped thinking altogether.

His kisses were slow, drugging—more seductive than anything she'd ever felt. He kissed her until she went boneless against the bed, her limbs heavy with a delicious languor. He kissed her until she was arching against him, her fingers frantically tugging at his hair, the sound of her own panting breaths echoing in her head.

This was what she'd been so nervous about? Why, it was glorious! She couldn't get enough of his kisses, his caressing fingers. She whimpered when he dragged a hand down her neck and pressed his lips to her throat. She needed to bring him closer, as close as she could get him…

When she thought it over later that night, she couldn't pinpoint the moment when things started to go wrong. By the time she realized it was happening, it was already too late to stop it. One moment Logan was kissing her and her head was dizzy with wonder and desire, and the next…

Cold air rushed over her skin. Logan had dragged her night rail over her head, and the chill had been just startling enough to remind her she'd never been unclothed in front of a man before, much less one who was intimately touching her. His body felt enormous against hers, his weight heavy, the smattering of crisp dark hair on his chest surprising her. It tickled her breasts, and she stiffened slightly. It wasn't unpleasant, just…strange.

"Juliana?" Logan pulled back, concerned.

Juliana laid a hand on his cheek and brought his mouth back to hers. He'd soon kissed her into quivering, needy mindlessness again, and things might have gone on well enough from there, but then he'd put his hand in a place where no man's hand had ever been. It was a place a husband might be expected to put his hand, but she'd tensed again, and this time Logan went still above her.

"So small…don't want to hurt you." He tried a second time, gently probing with his fingers, but he soon withdrew his hand again. "Not ready for me," he muttered, his breath harsh against her neck.

Not ready? She was naked and lying beneath him. What else was required?

She was doing something wrong, and it must be terribly wrong indeed, because Logan was drawing away from her. Did he not intend to consummate the marriage, then? The thought threw her into a sudden panic, and misgivings careened wildly through her head. Doubts flooded her, each more disordered than the last, but there was only one that made her gasp with pain.

Alison McLaren. Logan was in love with Alison, so in love he couldn't take his own wife...

Before she knew what she was about she was clutching at him, wrapping her limbs around him and whispering at him to finish it—to take her. She squirmed beneath him, urging him on until at last he pushed inside her with a defeated groan.

There was pain—ripping, wrenching, stinging pain, so acute she lost her breath for a moment. Logan made a tortured sound, hot, sticky warmth gushed between her legs, and then...

It was over.

They didn't speak afterwards. He didn't leave her, but it was as if an invisible line had been drawn down the center of the bed. Logan kept to his side, and she kept to hers. She wanted to say something to him, but she was too busy struggling with her own discomfort to think of a word to say to ease his.

How had things gone so wrong?

She'd been nervous, yes. That was to be expected. But Logan had been nervous as well, and she *hadn't* expected that. Surely, he'd had dozens of women before? He was strong, handsome, and irresistible when he smiled, but he'd been so hesitant, almost as if he were afraid to touch her. Somehow, they'd gone from those sweet, drugging kisses to painful self-consciousness, and then, that bit at the very end...

Juliana wasn't so innocent she hadn't known it would be painful.

For *her*, that is.

She hadn't thought it would be painful for *him*, but there'd been no mistaking his look of anguish when he jerked away from her. And then there'd been so much blood. Even now she could feel it coating her thighs.

But for better or worse, it was done. They'd consummated the marriage, and now she could put the entire business out of her mind. But even as she tried to reassure herself, Juliana knew there was no putting *that* out of her mind. There was no looking her husband in the eye now, either.

She lay awake all night, listening to him breathing. Part of her wanted him to try and make love to her again, but he didn't.

He remained on his side of the bed, and she remained on hers, staring up at the massive carved canopy above her, wondering where they'd go from here.

Chapter Seventeen

The room was dark when Logan woke the next morning. He reached out a cautious hand, expecting his palm to meet warm flesh, but Juliana's side of the bed was empty.

He came fully awake with a start. Memories of the night before assaulted him, and he dragged his hands down his face with a groan. Jesus. He couldn't have made more of a mess of things if he'd tried.

It was early still—so early the servant hadn't yet appeared to tend to the fire. He threw the covers back, swung his legs over the side of the bed and went to the window, snatching the drapes aside. Just enough light spilled in for Logan to see the bedclothes on Juliana's side of the bed had been neatly arranged, and her pillow plumped and smoothed.

But there was no sign of Juliana. He padded out into the other room in his bare feet, hoping to find her there, but the room was empty.

His wife was gone.

The house was dark and still, the sun had yet to peek over the horizon, and his wife was nowhere in sight. Logan wandered back to the bed and sank down onto the edge of it, uncertain what to do.

Where the devil could she have gone?

She's likely halfway to Surrey by now...

A chill washed over Logan as memories of their wedding night came crashing down on him. Her green eyes, wide and anxious, staring up at him as he hovered over her. The startled cry that left her lips when he'd pushed inside.

He shuddered. *Mo Dhia.* It had been an utter disaster.

He let his forehead drop into his hands. How could he have made such a mess of it? It wasn't as if he'd never had a woman before. He wasn't a debaucher, but he also wasn't a saint. He knew how to give a woman pleasure. Up until last night he'd flattered himself he was a skilled lover. But he'd never taken a woman's innocence before, and Juliana wasn't just any woman. She was his wife.

His wee, dainty, delicate wife.

And he was a huge beast of a man, big and rough and clumsy...

Logan hissed out a curse. Now the marriage had been consummated, he doubted she'd ever let him near her again. She'd probably fled their bed the moment he'd fallen asleep, and crept back to her own bedchamber. Even now she was likely there, her cheek resting on her tear-stained pillow, having nightmares about the lecherous fiend she'd married.

Logan's jaw tightened. Damn it, he wouldn't have his own wife afraid of him. He rose from the bed, tugged on a shirt, a pair of breeches, and his boots, and made his way into the hallway and down the stairs, muttering to himself all the while.

Won't have her hiding from me...fetch her back to my bedchamber... won't lay another finger on her unless she asks...

"I beg yer pardon, sir!"

Logan came to an abrupt halt in the middle of the hallway. A chambermaid was kneeling on the floor near Juliana's bedchamber, picking up a few pieces of coal she'd dropped from her scuttle. He'd been so distracted he'd nearly run right over her, and she was staring up at him with wide, frightened eyes.

It wasn't even dawn, and he'd already terrified two women.

"Is her ladyship inside?" Logan nodded toward the door of the guest bedchamber where Juliana had been staying since she arrived at Castle Kinross.

"No, sir. Mrs. Selkirk says 'er ladyship's gone back to England. She sent me up 'ere to fetch the coal."

"Gone to England? What, already?" Was it possible she'd actually gone *without* him?

No, she wouldn't do that. Juliana hadn't gone to such great lengths to secure a husband only to leave him behind now.

The girl shrank back, her eyes wider than ever. Logan drew in a deep breath and forced himself to speak calmly before the chit scurried off like a frightened mouse. "What makes you think her ladyship has left Castle Kinross already?"

"Saw 'er creeping out to the stables a while back," the girl said, her voice shaking. "She were dressed for travel."

Logan stared at her, panic tightening his chest. He could only think of one reason Juliana would creep off to the stables alone.

Jesus, was she actually leaving him? His chest grew tighter with every breath as he raced down the stairs, through the door, and into the stable yard. He was about to burst into the stable when he caught sight of Stokes lingering by the doors. "Where is she?"

Stokes's face darkened when he saw Logan, but he jerked his head toward the open stable doors. "Inside."

Logan pushed past Stokes and raced into the stables, searching for Juliana in the dim light. He couldn't have said whether he was relieved or furious, but some powerful emotion was clawing at his throat. He wasn't sure if it was a plea or a tirade—he only knew it was going to burst free with some violence the moment he saw her. "Juliana?"

"I'm here."

Her voice came from a far corner of the stables. He stalked toward her, his confused emotions burning their way up his throat to his lips, but as soon as he saw her, they dissolved on his tongue.

She was sitting on a hay bale, her blue riding skirt spread out in a pool around her, holding Fiona in her arms. Tears were streaming down her cheeks.

"Juliana." Logan forgot his anger and his panic, forgot their disastrous wedding night, and forgot he'd believed less than a minute earlier that she'd left him. He rushed to her side. "Don't cry, *mo bhean*."

"It's foolish of me, I know." She dragged her sleeve across her eyes to dry her tears, but they kept falling. "I shouldn't have taken her from Mr. Robertson. I knew all along I'd have to leave her behind."

"If you don't want to leave her, we'll bring her with us." The words landed in the dusty air between them, surprising Logan. The last thing he wanted was to share a cramped carriage with a nervous lamb, but he would have promised anything to make Juliana stop crying.

He shook his head, amazed at himself.

"No, we can't bring her with us. She'll slow us down, and it isn't fair to her to drag her all the way to England. I won't be so silly as that, though I don't deny I'll miss her." Another tear rolled down Juliana's cheek, and she pressed her face against the lamb's woolly head. "My father always kept hunting dogs, but I never had a pet of my own."

I'll find you another lamb, dozens of them...

The words jumped from Logan's head to his lips with alarming speed, but before he had a chance to say them Juliana rose, and with a final sniff put Fiona down on top of the hay bale. "I'm sorry, Fiona, but it can't be helped." She leaned down and pressed one last kiss on the lamb's head, then turned to Logan.

"I've asked Stokes to ready the carriage for the ride to Inverness. I'm prepared to leave whenever you..." She trailed off, appearing to notice for the first time he was wearing only a shirt and breeches. Her gaze seemed to linger on his bare neck, but she quickly averted her eyes, her cheeks flushing pink. "But perhaps you're not quite ready to leave yet."

Logan's gaze followed that wash of pink color as it swept down her throat, absurdly pleased by it. If a hint of his bare skin could make her blush like that, perhaps all hope wasn't lost, after all. "I'll be back in a moment."

By the time Logan washed, dressed, and returned to the yard, Stokes was mounted, their baggage was secured, and Fitz and Emilia were waiting in the stable yard to bid them goodbye.

"Promise me you'll stop often to rest, Lina. You won't be much good to your father if you're ill when you arrive in Surrey." Fitz pressed a kiss to one of Juliana's cheeks, then the other. "There's one for Grace, as well. You'll give it to her for me?"

Juliana smiled and squeezed his hands. "Yes, of course."

Fitz took Logan aside while Juliana and Emilia said their goodbyes. "She's yours now, Logan," he murmured, looking at Juliana. "Take care of her."

After last night Logan wasn't sure he knew how to take care of a wife, but he nodded.

"Goodbye Logan. I'll miss you." Emilia pressed her cheek to his. "Promise me you'll bring Juliana back for a visit soon."

Logan thought it was much more likely Juliana would send him back to Scotland alone, but he nodded again. He took Juliana's hand to help her into the carriage, then climbed in after her and shut the door behind him.

The carriage rolled quietly out of the stable yard, Stokes following them on horseback. They stopped at the Sassy Lassie, where they left Fitz's carriage and hired another to take them as far as Dalwhinnie.

They didn't speak much. Juliana's face gave nothing away, and Logan wondered what she was thinking. Was she worrying about their disastrous wedding night? Grieving over Fiona still? Fretting about her father and Grace? Or was she thinking of their wedding ceremony the previous evening?

Until Juliana arrived at Castle Kinross, Logan had never given his wedding day, or his bride, much thought. Both had always been hazy in his mind—something that would happen with some unknown lady, in a far distant future.

A Scottish lady, that is. He'd have laughed at anyone who told him he'd marry an English heiress in a rushed ceremony without any of the Scottish traditions he'd always assumed would take place on his wedding day.

There were no bagpipes. He and Juliana didn't exchange rings. The bells at the kirk in Inverness remained silent. There was no dancing, and no brandy-soaked wedding cake. If he hadn't been wearing the Kinross tartan it could have been any ceremony, taking place anywhere, between any two people.

Logan glanced at Juliana, tucked into a corner of the carriage. The pretty pink color he'd seen this morning hadn't returned to her cheeks, and she was drooping with exhaustion.

"Try and sleep, Ana," he murmured, after they'd traveled a half-hour in silence. "It will make the time pass more quickly."

A wan smile lit her face. "Yes, perhaps I will." She lapsed back into silence, and it wasn't long before her head dropped against the window and her eyelids fluttered closed.

Logan didn't sleep. He sat in his own corner watching her, listening to her deep, even breaths and worrying at a stone he held in his pocket.

He'd carved their names into the stone yesterday afternoon. Even now he didn't know why he'd bothered, other than it was a Scottish tradition for a wedded couple to have an oathing stone. Juliana wasn't a traditional Scottish bride, but he'd thought she should have one memento of her wedding day.

He'd intended to give it to her this morning, but then he'd woken up alone. He'd found it in his sporran when he retired to his bedchamber to change for the journey. He'd considered tucking it into a drawer and leaving it behind, but at the last minute he'd snatched it up and dropped it into his coat pocket.

Foolish of him, really. This wasn't a real marriage, and given the drastic decline in Lord Graystone's health, it was likely to be over before it began.

But it wasn't over yet. When they retired to their bedchamber this evening they'd still be husband and wife, yet legally speaking there wasn't a single reason Logan should ever bother Juliana with his attentions again.

All that fine, pale skin he'd imagined worshipping with his hands and mouth, left untouched, unkissed.

His throat went dry as his gaze moved over her thick, fair hair. He could remember just what it felt like, tangled in his hands. Was the delicate curve of her neck as delicious as her sweet pink lips were? Would she cry out for him, beg him?

He'd dreamed of her standing naked before him, her pale skin flushed, the heavy curtain of her hair tumbling down to her waist. Since she'd come to Castle Kinross he'd spent more than one lonely night in his bedchamber lost in fevered imaginings of her. Even when he hadn't liked her he'd wanted her, and his need for her had grown deeper with every day that passed.

It had nothing to do with her sensuality, or her beauty. No, it was something else altogether. He couldn't describe it, but it was the same thing that made her tongue so sharp, her dainty little chin so stubborn. It was the same thing that made her hold her own with the Robertson boys—the same thing that had sent her out onto that tree trunk to rescue Fiona.

A faint smile crossed his lips. *Bhig galla*, just as Brice had said.

The surprise of her...

Maybe that was all it was. Logan didn't know. He knew only he wanted her, badly.

But not like this.

He let his head fall back against the squabs. He'd imagined her in his bed over and over again—had imagined taking her, making her his—but in every one of these heated fantasies she'd been in his bed for one reason only: because she desired him as desperately as he desired her.

Not because they had to consummate their marriage to make it legal, or because she was his wife, and it was her duty. He'd never taken a woman to bed for any other reason than she wanted him, and he didn't want to begin with Juliana.

She was his wife. His *wife*.

Beads of sweat popped out on Logan's forehead as he thought of how small she was, how fragile her body was compared to his. He was experienced with women, but Juliana wasn't anything like the hearty, lusty, Scottish lasses he'd bedded.

Still, she was a woman, not a child, and much stronger than she looked. Wee, but hearty.

He glanced at her again to reassure himself of this, but that turned out to be a mistake. She was lying across the seat now, her folded hands tucked under her cheek, and if anything, she looked even smaller than she had when she'd gotten into the carriage. Her entire body fit easily on the narrow cushion.

Mo Dhia, was she shrinking?

Logan dragged his sleeve across his damp forehead.

Christ, he was nervous. An enormous, nervous husband with a fierce, burning desire for his tiny, innocent wife wasn't a promising combination.

If she did let him near her again, he'd just have to be careful, that's all. So very careful. No letting his weight rest on her. No rubbing or squeezing. Certainly, no squeezing—

"Logan? What's wrong?"

Logan jerked his gaze toward her.

She hadn't moved, but her eyes were open now, and she was regarding him with a furrowed brow. "You're grimacing, as if you're in pain."

It's not my pain I'm worried about, but yours.

Unfamiliar heat crept into Logan's cheeks. "It's just the carriage. It's cramped."

Juliana straightened in her seat and concealed a yawn behind her gloved hand. "Yes, I expect it is, for you. Will we stop to change horses soon?"

They'd already stopped once, but Juliana had slept through it. "Yes, at Aviemore."

"How far is it from Aviemore to Dalwhinnie?"

Her voice was strained, and Logan knew she was thinking about her father. "Another thirty miles or so. We'll travel as quickly as we can, and with any luck we'll reach Guildford by the end of the week."

They changed horses at Newtownmore and again at Etteridge. By the time they pulled into the inn yard at the Castle Arms in Dalwhinnie, dusk had fallen. Logan shook some life back into his stiff limbs, then descended from the carriage and approached Stokes, who was just dismounting. "Secure three rooms for tonight, Stokes, if you would."

Juliana was overwhelmed, exhausted, anxious for her father, and likely dreading a repeat of last's night amorous fiasco. Only a savage would bother his wife with his attentions under such circumstances. Since he wasn't certain he could keep his hands off her, it was best if they each had their own bedchamber.

Stokes raised an eyebrow, but he said nothing, only tossed his reins to the waiting ostler, then disappeared into the inn.

Logan returned to the carriage and offered Juliana his hand. She placed her gloved fingers in his palm, and he couldn't help but notice his hand swallowed hers.

Juliana decided against dining in the bedchamber. Logan tried not to take this as an indication his wife didn't wish to be alone with him, and escorted her down to dinner without complaint. After they'd dined he took her back upstairs, but he didn't venture into her bedchamber. Instead he offered her an awkward bow as he hovered in the doorway. "I'll bid you goodnight now, Juliana. I wish you a pleasant evening."

She'd passed by him to enter the room, but now she jerked around to face him. "You'll bid me good...you mean you're not staying with me tonight?"

Logan's eyebrows shot up. She almost sounded disappointed. "After last night I thought you'd prefer it if I—"

"No. I don't prefer it."

If it hadn't been for the furious blush in her cheeks, Logan might have thought he'd misheard her. "You, ah...you want me to stay here tonight? With you?"

She turned toward the looking glass, biting her lip and stealing glances at his reflection. "You're my husband, Logan. Of course I want you to stay with me. That is, if you want to. I understand it if you prefer to have your own bedchamber."

She thought he'd rather sleep without her? Logan shook his head, stunned. "I *don't* prefer it."

When he met her gaze in the mirror she looked quickly away, and tenderness swelled inside him. She was nervous, and he...well, he was the *man*, for God's sake. It was his responsibility to reassure her. If he couldn't find a way to help his bride relax, tonight was sure to end in disaster, just as last night had.

He closed the bedchamber door, came up behind her, and rested his hands gently on her shoulders. "Are you anxious, Ana? There's no need to be." It wasn't quite the truth, but this was one of those rare instances where the truth wouldn't do either of them any good.

Juliana met his gaze in the mirror. "I, um...well, aren't all new brides anxious?"

Logan, encouraged by this reply, ventured to press a chaste kiss to her temple. She smelled delicious—like something fresh and green. He inhaled deeply, his head swimming as her scent flooded his nose. "Aye, I think they are, but I'll do my best to see it isn't as terrible as it was the first time."

"Oh, no! I don't think...I didn't mean for you to think...it wasn't *terrible*."

"Unpleasant enough, though?" Logan grinned to take the sting out of his words.

Her cheeks reddened. Logan was still half-dazed by the scent of her skin. He didn't step back when she turned to face him. She was so close she was nearly in his arms. He gathered her gently against him, tightly enough so she could feel his body brush against hers, but not so tight she could feel anything...distressing.

She laid her hands on his chest. "Not unpleasant, no. Just..." she swallowed, and her gaze lowered so she was staring at his cravat instead of into his eyes. "I don't know what I did wrong."

Logan stared down at her in astonishment. Jesus, is that what she thought? That *she* was at fault? "You didn't do anything wrong, *bòcan*. Last night was *my* fault, not yours. I should have taken care of you, and I failed." He touched his lips to her forehead. "I'd never intentionally hurt you, Juliana. You know that, don't you?"

She looked surprised. "I know you wouldn't. It's just that I was anxious, and when I get anxious I stiffen up. I don't suppose that helped matters much, and I kept thinking of…well, it doesn't matter."

"What? What were you thinking?"

She tried to hide against his chest, but he touched his thumb to her chin and raised her face to his. "Juliana? What were you thinking?"

"I was thinking of Alison McLaren."

"Alison McLaren?" For a second, Logan couldn't even remember who Alison McLaren *was*. "What, you mean Fergus's daughter? Why in the world would you be thinking of Alison while we were…"

Oh. *Oh.*

He'd completely forgotten they'd met Alison at the Sassy Lassie earlier that day. Alison had flirted outrageously with him, just as she always did, and he'd laughed at her, just as he always did, but to Juliana it might have looked like a great deal more than that.

Her next words confirmed it. "I saw you with her, and it occurred to me your affections might already be engaged. She's very pretty, and you looked so happy—"

Logan pressed a finger to her lips. "Juliana, listen to me. I'm *not* in love with Alison McLaren. She's a good lass, and I'm fond of her, but it's not romantic. We're friends, nothing more."

A shy smile curved her lips. "Oh. Well, I suppose it's all right, then."

Logan gazed down at her, admiring the way the candlelight played over her golden waves. It struck him as unbelievable Juliana could think he'd even look at another woman. Since she'd come to Castle Kinross, he could think of nothing but her.

"I think you're beautiful, Ana," he whispered, his lips close to her ear. "I can't take my eyes off you long enough to even notice another woman."

A soft, sweet sigh left her lips, and she reached up to wrap her arms around his neck.

"I'll promise I'll take care of you tonight." His voice lowered, deepened. "Do you trust me?"

She nodded, her eyes searching his.

When he bent to brush his lips over hers she met him halfway, and returned his kiss with the same innocent passion she had the first time he'd kissed her at Widow Macaulay's. He was determined to build her desire slowly, however, and he spent long moments nibbling and teasing at her lips. When at last he slipped his tongue inside, she dug her fingertips into his shoulders and sighed into his mouth.

She was already trembling for him, but Logan held himself ruthlessly in check as he kissed and stroked her. By some miracle she'd given him a second chance, and he wouldn't squander it.

He gathered her in his arms and carried her to the bed, taking care to smooth her skirts down her legs before he joined her. He trailed his knuckles across her cheek before he took her lips again. Logan kissed her and kissed her, his mouth growing just a bit hungrier as she tangled her tongue with his.

He rested a hand on her waist as he plundered her mouth. She whimpered when he dragged the tip of his tongue across the inside of her upper lip. The breathless little sound made him dizzy, and he slid a hand up her back. *Slowly, slowly...*

He paused to kiss and nuzzle her as he bared her, worshipping every inch of that smooth, pale skin. He tasted her throat, her neck—kissed each of her shoulders and ran his tongue across one delicate collarbone, then the other. She whimpered when he pressed passionate kisses to the curves of her breasts, and cried out when his mouth found her sweet pink nipples.

"*Logan.*" She arched against him, her fingers tugging at his hair, but Logan took his time, rubbing his rough cheek against the hard peaks, then sucking them between his lips to soothe them. It wasn't long before she was writhing beneath him.

And still, he didn't stop. He held her shoulders against the bed, always gentle with her even as he tongued her relentlessly, licking at the stiff peaks. His cock was straining against his falls. He ached to sink into her damp heat, but he also thought he could stay here all night, teasing her nipples and listening to her sighs and moans.

He kneaded the slight curve of her belly, and traced light circles on her abdomen with his fingertip. He stroked her hips and sides, his palms gliding over her supple flesh. He pressed dozens of kisses between her breasts. He caressed and played and coaxed her body until at last he dragged his hand down her belly and slid his fingers between her legs.

Logan's lips parted and his eyes slid closed when he felt how wet she was. "Ah, God, sweetheart, you're so ready for me."

"Yes. Please, Logan." She arched against him, and her core rubbed against his hard length. Logan groaned and nudged between her legs as his mouth closed around a nipple.

She gasped and curled her fingernails into his shoulders, then leaned up and pressed her lips to the hot skin of his throat. Logan threw his head back with another moan, stunned to find how badly he wanted her mouth on his bare skin.

Juliana tugged on his shirt, trying to reach more of him. "Take this off."

Logan didn't need to be told twice. He leapt up from the bed, shed his boots and tore his shirt over his head.

But then he hesitated, his fingers hovering over the buttons of his falls. He was painfully hard for her, his eager flesh rigid and straining, and she was watching him, her heavy-lidded gaze taking in every inch of him. Would the sight of his engorged cock distress her? They'd been under the covers last night, so she hadn't gotten a good look at it, but she'd certainly felt it when he'd entered her, battering at her tender flesh, making her bleed—

"Logan." She held her arms out to him. "Come here."

He stared down at her, his mouth opening in wonder at what he saw. Her skin was dewy, and she was trembling. Her hard, pointed nipples were flushed a dark pink from his mouth, and the curls between her legs were damp with her arousal.

He sucked in a quick breath. She wanted him. Against all odds, and even after last's night disaster, she wanted him.

He tore at his buttons, then ripped off his pantaloons, his stiff cock bobbing eagerly as he joined her on the bed. He rested his hands on her inner thighs and gave a gentle push. "Open your legs for me, *breagha bhean*."

She obeyed him at once, putting to rest any lingering doubts he had about her desire for him. "That's it, Ana." Logan took himself in hand and carefully nudged his head against her entrance, but he didn't slide inside. Instead he hovered there for long moments, his body shaking with the effort to keep still.

Then, so slowly he wasn't sure he was actually moving, he pushed the tip inside.

His back bowed with pleasure when her warmth closed around him. He was barely inside her, and already he was in danger of releasing. He slid in another inch, gritting his teeth. "You feel so good, *bòcan*. So good. Am I hurting you?"

She shook her head, wild tendrils of her hair tumbling over her bare shoulders. "No. I want all of you, Logan. Please."

He groaned at her breathless murmur, that sweet plea on her lips. He moved forward another inch, then another, a bead of sweat rising on his forehead. He could feel her stretching, her body working to accommodate him, yet still he hesitated.

Slowly, slowly...

"Logan." Juliana arched under him, her hips meeting his.

Logan swallowed as he slid deeper inside her. Christ. He was going to explode.

Another inch. Another. He was so deep now her body was working him, pulling him in. "Ah, God. Juliana."

With one final push of his hips, he was buried inside her. Then he stilled again, panting as he waited for her to adjust to him. "Are you all right, *bhean*?"

"Yes." She gave a tiny thrust of her hips to urge him on.

He drew back slowly, then thrust into her again. Then again and again, until she took up his rhythm. "*Yes*, Ana. Move with me."

She pressed her face to his neck with a moan. "Logan, I—I—"

"Let go, Juliana. Come for me." Logan's neck corded with strain as he struggled to hold on, his hips working quickly now to give her what she needed. Right before she shattered she let out a breathless cry, and wrapped her legs around his hips.

Then she was tightening around him, her body squeezing him—

Logan threw his head back with a groan as the tingling in his spine spread to his legs, his belly, his cock. His own release took him hard, then left him dazed and shaking in its wake.

He looked down at Juliana to find her staring up at him, a dreamy smile on her lips. He leaned down and pressed kisses to her forehead, eyelids, and finally her mouth.

He shifted away to relieve her of his weight, but this time he didn't retreat to his own side of the bed. He caught her in his arms, pulled her close, and eased her head down to his chest. "Sleep, Ana."

"Mmmm." She let out a contented sigh, kissed his chest, then curled closer. Within minutes her breathing deepened and she melted against him.

Logan buried his face in her hair and followed her into sleep.

Chapter Eighteen

The journey from Dalwhinnie to Surrey took ten days, and they were the most confusing ten days of Juliana's life.

She worried about her father every day, and when she wasn't worrying about her father, she was worrying about Grace. She startled awake before dawn each morning, torn out of her nightmares by her own gasping breaths. In the darkest of her dreams—the one that left her clammy and shaking with horror—they arrived at Graystone Court only to find her father dead, and Lord Cowden dragging Grace away.

She'd known it would be this way. She'd known she'd spend every moment of every day between Inverness and Surrey agonizing over Grace and her father, and every night trapped in nightmares of grief and loss.

What she hadn't known was that somehow, between the nightmares and the long, tedious days on the road, she'd fall in love with Logan Blair.

But that was what happened. The most anxious ten days of her life were also the most breathtaking, because of Logan.

There was no more talk of separate bedchambers. They spent every night of the journey together. She fell asleep each night with his arms wrapped around her, his big hands folding her to his chest, and every morning when she came hurtling out of her nightmares he was there, waiting to catch her.

He didn't speak much in those moments. He simply held her tightly, stroking her hair and murmuring to her in Gaelic until her shaking stopped and she relaxed against him. He'd kiss her softly then, and whisper that he wanted to make love to her, if she wanted him.

Juliana always wanted him.

Yet he still asked her, every time.

It went on that way until very early in the morning on the day they were due to arrive at Graystone Court. That was the day Juliana didn't wait for him to ask.

Instead, she asked him.

For the first time since they'd left Castle Kinross, she'd woken calmly. Logan was still asleep beside her, sprawled across the bed with his arms flung wide.

She lay there for a long time with her eyes closed, thinking she'd never before felt as warm and safe as she did when she was cradled in his arms.

The next thought came upon her slowly, softly, as naturally as following one breath with another.

I'm in love with him.

He was her husband, she was in love with him, and she'd never again let him wonder if she wanted him.

Juliana reached across the bed, searching for his warm, solid form. Her hand landed on his chest, and she slid her palm up to stroke his collarbones and throat. Her fingertips dancing across his bare skin made him stir, but he only rolled onto his back and threw an arm over his head.

He didn't wake.

Ah, good. She didn't want him to wake just yet.

Taking care to be quiet and not to jostle him, Juliana rose to her knees and dragged her chemise over her head, shivering a bit as the cold air drifted over her bare skin.

No matter. She'd be warm soon enough.

She leaned over him, intending to wake him with a kiss, but seeing his body spread out before her, like a feast just waiting to be devoured made her pause. She bit her lip, her gaze lingering on his broad chest, the long, muscular length of his thighs.

Did she dare?

Well, she'd dared any number of other things, hadn't she? She'd ended her betrothal to Hugh, and chased Fitzwilliam hundreds of miles to Scotland. She'd trailed Logan for days, and demanded he take her to Castle Kinross. She'd ridden across the Highlands with the Robertson boys, and she'd saved Fiona.

She'd coerced a wild Scot into marrying her, and dared to fall in love with him.

It didn't make much sense to stop now, did it?

Her mind made up, Juliana swung one leg over his torso. Logan slept on, oblivious to the fact she was now straddling him. That is, until she sank lower, and let her bottom rest on his thighs.

That woke him up.

"Juliana?" He tried to sit up, realized she was on top of him, and fell flat against the bed again. "Juliana, what are you—"

"Shhh." She fumbled around until she found the hem of his shirt, then dragged it over his head. When he was naked beneath her, she ran her eager hands over his bare chest and then lower, stroking her palms over the hard planes of his stomach.

She'd woken him from a deep sleep, but if Logan was groggy, he shook it off the moment he realized his wife was on top of him, bare as the day she was born, and had just stripped him of his clothes.

Juliana leaned over him and dropped a tiny, teasing kiss on one corner of his mouth. "I want to make love to you," she whispered, her tongue grazing his earlobe. "Do you want me?"

His lips curved. "What do you think, lass?" He took her hand and pressed her palm against his rigid length, hissing softly when her fingers curled instinctively around him. "Stroke me, Ana."

He'd explored every inch of her body—touched her everywhere, with both his hands and his mouth—but he'd never before asked her to touch him. "Like this?" Juliana gripped him carefully and moved her hand up his hard length, then back down again. She stroked him once or twice, and then, emboldened by his panting breaths, caressed him in a steady rhythm until Logan's neck arched, and his head fell back against the pillow.

"Yes. God, yes. Just like that." His voice was husky, strained. Juliana continued to stroke him, her lips parting in surprise when he twitched and pulsed against her palm. A tortured groan left his lips, and his hips jerked beneath her.

"Come here, *bhig galla*." He grasped her hips and held her steady as he shifted to sit up against the pillows. Then he tugged her closer. "Wrap your legs around my hips."

Juliana did as he asked, her breath leaving her lungs in a heated rush when he dragged his hands up her sides and filled his palms with her breasts. The faintest hint of light was now peeking into the room. Logan's gaze remained riveted on her face as he stroked and teased her nipples into hard, straining peaks. "Jesus, you're so beautiful, Ana. Do you want my mouth on you, *mo bhean*?"

Warmth pooled between her legs and her hands twisted in his hair. "Yes. I want everything."

Logan's hands slid from her hips up her back. He held her steady and leaned forward to nuzzle her neck and the soft skin between her breasts.

Juliana's head fell back, and Logan groaned as her long hair brushed against his thighs. He took one of her nipples into his mouth and darted his tongue over her before sucking at the tender peak. He tormented her like this for what seemed to Juliana to be hours, his hot mouth nipping and teasing until she was writhing against him and whimpering.

Her soft, pleading sounds seemed to madden him. He trailed his hand down her stomach and slid his fingers between her legs. He parted her soft folds, and a harsh groan tore from his chest. "You're so ready for me. So slick and hot."

His fingers tightened around her hips and he lifted her up. Juliana expected him to ease her flat against the bed and move over her, but he didn't. Instead he took himself in hand and positioned her over him. "Sink down onto me, Ana."

Juliana's eyes went wide. She hesitated, but Logan was guiding her down, and she could feel his hard length easing into her. She wanted him so much, loved him so much...

"Yes, *galla*. Move with me. *Dia tha*. Yes, just like that." He teased and coaxed her, his hands steady on her hips, easing her down onto him each time he thrust upwards until they were moving in perfect sync.

"Ah, Logan. Please." Juliana had never felt him so deep inside her before. Her fingernails curled into his back as he drove her closer and closer to the edge with each thrust of his hips.

"Come for me, Ana. Now, *galla*. I want to see you." He jerked her down hard over his length, surging up into her at the same time. Juliana cried out as the pleasure slid closer and closer. She was right on the edge when Logan's mouth closed over the tip of her breast. He dragged his teeth lightly over her nipple just as his hand slid between her legs and his clever fingers found her center.

One stroke was all it took. Juliana's entire body drew taut, and she unraveled with a sharp cry. Logan buried his face in her neck with a harsh groan, his hips arching helplessly as her body sent him hurtling to his own pleasure.

They were quiet afterwards as they waited for their breathing to calm. Juliana held him as tightly as she could, her heart thundering, her fingers tangled in his hair.

* * * *

"We're less than two hours from Guildford, Ana. You should try and rest before we reach Graystone Court."

Juliana turned from the window toward Logan, gazing at his mouth as he spoke. He had such a lovely mouth, with full, firm lips. They were soft, too. Much softer than such a fierce man's lips should be, and he kissed her so gently. Just the memory of the way he'd nibbled and teased at her lips made her breath quicken even now. His kisses left her dizzy, and the touch of his big, rough hands made her ache with a desire that stunned her.

"You'll need all your strength to see your father," he added, his forehead creased with concern.

Her father. Shame washed over Juliana at finding her father hadn't been uppermost in her thoughts. Since she'd received Lord Arthur's letter, she'd spent nearly every moment thinking about him, praying she wasn't too late, both for her father's sake, and for Grace's.

"I love him, you know," she said suddenly. "My father. I love him, but I'm angry at him still, and I don't want to be. I want to forgive him, but…"

But she couldn't, and how unfair, how selfish that made her. To resent a father who was afflicted with a disease that made him a stranger to himself. A father who'd always loved her with such tender affection. To withhold forgiveness from him now, as he hovered on the verge of death—

Logan didn't speak, but he reached for her, his large, warm hands closing over both of hers. She met his gaze, and the compassion in his face made tears rush to her eyes. "He gave me everything, Logan. His love, his attention, everything I could have asked for—"

"No, he didn't. He didn't give you his trust."

"His trust? What do you mean?" Juliana clung to his hands, her voice thick with tears.

"He didn't trust you to take care of Grace, or to take care of yourself. That's a difficult thing to forgive in someone you love, but you will, in time."

Juliana frowned. "Of course he trusts me. He's my father, Logan."

He studied her in silence. She didn't understand the look in his eyes, but it made her want to hide her face from him.

He didn't argue with her, but he drew his hands away. "You need to rest, Juliana. You're pale and shaky. Come, you won't be any help to your father if you're ill."

Juliana waited for him to say more, but he remained silent, so she turned her gaze back to the window. At some point she must have fallen asleep, because when she came to again the coach had rolled to a stop, and Logan was leaning over her, gently shaking her shoulder. "Wake up, Ana. We're here."

Juliana gazed groggily up him, then jerked awake as the meaning of his words sank in. She struggled upright and glanced out the window. They'd drawn up in front of the entrance to Graystone Court. "We have to find Lord Arthur at once." Juliana fumbled for the coach's door, but Logan got there first. He opened the door, leapt out onto the drive, then offered his hand to her.

Juliana scrambled out, intending to rush for the entrance, but her body was fatigued and her legs numb from so much time spent in the carriage. She was grateful for the solid strength of Logan's arm supporting her.

Before they could reach the door, it swung open. Her father's butler, Pinkerton, and Lord Arthur stood there.

Juliana froze halfway up the stairs, her blood going cold. Lord Arthur's skin was gray, his face lined with worry and exhaustion. He looked as if he'd aged ten years since she saw him last. "Is he…is my father…" She trailed off into silence, afraid to finish her question.

Lord Arthur hurried down the stairs to meet her. "We put him straight to bed when we returned from Bath. The journey weakened him, and he hasn't risen since. He's very ill, my lady, and his mind wanders. You must prepare yourself."

Juliana ran up the rest of the stairs, still clutching at Logan's arm. "Grace? Where is she?"

Lord Arthur hurried up the stairs after them. "On the road from Buckinghamshire. I wrote to Lord Pierce from Bath. He and Lady Pierce are on their way. They should be here tomorrow with Grace."

They'd reached the entrance hall. Pinkerton held out his hands for their cloaks. "How do you do, Pinkerton?" Lady Juliana asked, with a sympathetic glance at the butler. She'd never seen him so distressed. Her father was a stern, uncompromising master, but Pinkerton had been with him for decades, and they'd grown fond of each other over the years.

"It's kind of you to ask, my lady. I'm as well as I can be, under the circumstances. Your father has always been good to me, as you know." Pinkerton's gaze slid to Logan, and he offered him a stiff bow. "I beg your pardon, sir."

It was taking all of Juliana's strength not to give in to the tears pressing behind her eyes. She'd known since she received Lord Arthur's letter that her father was gravely ill, but she could see by the grief on Pinkerton's and Lord Arthur's faces it was even worse than she'd thought.

They would lose him in a matter of days only. Perhaps a matter of hours.

The small girl inside her that would always revere her father wanted to collapse to the floor, to weep and rail at fate. Logan's quiet, solid presence beside her was the only thing keeping her upright. "This is my husband, Logan Blair, Laird of Clan Kinross."

Pinkerton was too well-trained to show any surprise, but Lord Arthur's eyes went wide with shock. "Blair? But I thought you meant to marry—"

"Mr. Blair is the Duke of Blackmore's brother." Juliana's fingers clutched at Logan's coat sleeve. "It's a long story, Lord Arthur, and I'd like to see my father at once."

"Yes, of course." Lord Arthur gave her a hasty bow. "Pinkerton, if you could show Mr. Blair to the drawing room—"

"No. My husband will accompany me to my father's bedchamber."

Given that Logan had never met the marquess, it was highly irregular for to him to appear in his lordship's bedchamber. Even Logan seemed surprised at it. "Are you certain?"

"Yes. You're my husband. I want you there," Juliana said, without a trace of hesitation. She didn't want him to leave her side.

"Very well." Lord Arthur gave Juliana a measuring look, but he didn't offer further argument. He followed them up the stairs to the family wing on the third floor, and down the hallway to the end, where the marquess's apartments were.

Juliana opened the door to her father's bedchamber. The drapes had been drawn across every window, and only one lamp burned. The dimness was a shock after the bright sunshine outdoors, and an odd, musty smell hung in the air—a smell of closed apartments, and decay.

Juliana crossed the room, but stopped before she reached her father's bed, fear clawing at her throat. He hadn't stirred when they entered, and he was so quiet and still. If he'd passed, and she hadn't had a chance to say goodbye to him—

"It's all right." Logan's warm hand settled in the small of her back. He urged her gently forward. "The coverlet over his chest is rising and falling."

Juliana swallowed and crept forward again until she was standing beside her father's bed. A choked gasp left her throat as her gaze settled on his face. It had been less than a month since she'd last seen him, but he was so altered she wouldn't have recognized him. His once noble cheekbones were sunken, and his aristocratic nose was a sharp blade rising from his shrunken, waxy face. He was covered with what looked to be dozens of blankets, but even their bulk couldn't disguise how feeble he was, how diminished his frame.

"Father?" Juliana perched gingerly on the edge of his bed and took his hand. "Father, it's Juliana."

He didn't stir, and his eyes remained closed. Juliana, unsure what she should do, gave Logan a helpless look. "Should I wake him?"

Later, she'd wonder why she'd asked Logan that question instead of Lord Arthur, but in that moment, she didn't try to explain it to herself. Her heart was shattering in her chest, and she turned instinctively to Logan.

He drew a step closer. He looked down into her face and brushed a stray hair from her cheek. "You should forgive him," he murmured, his voice so soft only Juliana could hear him.

Forgive him.

Juliana gazed down into her father's face, no less beloved for the ravages of age and disease, and whispered, "I—I already have."

She had. Of course, she had. If the words felt awkward leaving her lips it was only because she was in shock.

Her father's demands regarding her marriage, the dreadful risk he'd taken with her own and Grace's happiness—surely none of it mattered now? How could it, compared to all the love he'd given her? Everything he'd done, whether misguided or not, had been done out of love for her. She couldn't be so wicked as to withhold forgiveness from her dying father.

She laid a hand against his wasted cheek. His skin felt hot and dry to her touch, and her heart gave a miserable throb in her chest. He might slip away without waking, and then he'd never know she was here, that she'd come to him—

"Juliana?"

Juliana started, and blinked the tears from her eyes. She leaned closer to the bed and saw her father's eyes were open. "Yes, Father. I'm here." She clasped his hand between both of hers. "I'm right here next to you."

"I knew you'd come. Always been a good girl…always been so proud of you, Juliana." His voice was weak, but the ghost of a smile drifted across his cracked lips.

"I know, Father. I know." Juliana wasn't certain he could focus on her face, but she forced a smile to her lips.

Her father struggled to inhale few wheezing breaths. "Is Jonathan with you? Jonathan, and Emma?"

Juliana drew in a shuddering breath. Her father had never recovered from the blow of losing his only son. No parent should have to live through losing a child, and Juliana couldn't bear to speak of it to him now. "Jonathan and Emma…send their love, Father, and promise they'll see you very soon."

This soothed him, and his eyes dropped closed. Juliana hung anxiously over the bed, fearing he'd lost consciousness, but after a short time he opened his eyes again, and fixed on Juliana's face. "You're married?"

The now-familiar wave of anger and sadness washed over Juliana, but she made herself smile down at him. "Yes. Just as you wished." She drew Logan forward. "Father, this is my husband, Lo—"

"Fitzwilliam." Her father reached out a feeble hand to Logan. "Fitzwilliam. Thank God."

Fitzwilliam? For a second Juliana was confused, but then she realized what had happened. The room was dark, her father's mind was wandering, and Logan looked so very much like Fitzwilliam it was only natural her father would mistake one for the other.

But it wasn't just that. Her father *wanted* to believe it was Fitzwilliam standing there. That it was Fitzwilliam she'd married.

"You'll take care of her, Fitzwilliam. Of her, and Grace."

Logan shot Juliana a questioning look, as if he were waiting for her to say something. Juliana opened her mouth, but somehow the words froze on her lips. Marriage to Fitzwilliam was the last thing her father would ever ask of her. All he wanted was to know his last living child was safe, that someone he knew and trusted would take care of her.

How could she take that away from him?

When she remained silent, Logan stepped closer to the bed and took her father's hand. Her father patted it weakly. "Knew you'd be a duchess, Juliana. Duchess of Blackmore."

Her father's dearest wish, that she'd become a duchess someday.

It had never been her wish.

A peaceful smile lit her father's face. He sank against his pillows with a contented sigh, and dear God, he looked so happy, so relieved to know she'd married Fitzwilliam at last.

He's dying...

"Yes, Father. The Duchess of Blackmore at last, just as you wanted. Fitzwilliam and I are...very happy."

She couldn't bear to look at Logan when she said it. She thought of how they'd been this morning—how she'd felt when he'd told her she was beautiful. The soft catch in his voice when he called her *mo bhean.*

My wife...

What a coward she was.

She'd dared to fall in love with him, only to betray him when it mattered most.

Another tear rolled down her cheek. Of all the tears she'd shed, it was the bitterest.

Logan didn't say a word or withdraw his hand from her father's, but Juliana sensed his entire body go rigid. The air around him shifted, grew colder.

They didn't speak again. Juliana remained on the bed with her father, one of his hands clasped between hers, and Logan withdrew, melting into the shadows. Lord Arthur remained by the window, a respectful distance away.

Juliana wasn't sure how much time passed. It was dark, and the moments both contracted and stretched around them until time no longer made sense.

When Logan took her out of the room much later, her father was dead.

Chapter Nineteen

Graystone Court
Eight days later

Logan knew he was being watched.

He wasn't sure how long she'd been there, but ten minutes or more had passed since he'd sensed the wide, dark eyes on him and glanced up just in time to see her duck back behind the library door.

He slowly turned over the pages of his book, waiting. Sooner or later she'd gather up the nerve to approach him. Grace was shy, but she had a good deal of her Aunt Juliana's backbone in her. So he sat quietly, his legs stretched out in front of him. He kept his gaze fixed on the book in his hands and did his best to look harmless.

It must have worked, because a few seconds later Grace gathered up her courage enough to creep around the edge of the door and venture a few steps into the library. Logan pretended not to notice her, and she gradually made her way closer, creeping like a wary mouse, one hesitant step at a time.

Soon enough, she was hovering beside his knee. "Mr. Logan?"

Logan looked up from his book and raised his eyebrows, feigning surprise. "Hello, Grace. Where did you come from?"

"From 'round the door. I was hiding there," she said with a shy smile.

Logan's lips quirked. Grace had the sweetest smile. "Were you? You must have been quiet, because I didn't see you there. Do you need something?"

"It's pretty outside, and warm, too."

Logan glanced across the room to see the late afternoon's rays illuminating the window. They were into July now, and the sun continued to promise a warm summer. "It is."

Grace fiddled with her skirts. Logan noticed she was dressed for riding in a dark brown skirt and jacket that vaguely resembled a lady's riding habit. This time he didn't have to feign his surprise.

She'd never asked him to take her riding before.

As promised, Lord and Lady Pierce had brought Grace to Graystone Court the day after Logan and Juliana arrived. The child had kept a careful distance from him that first week. Whenever she did happen to encounter him, she'd either run away or hide behind Juliana's skirts.

Logan hadn't pushed her. Grace had just lost her grandfather, the house was in turmoil as mourners came to pay their respects, and her beloved Aunt Juliana was pale and withdrawn, caught in a crushing wave of grief.

By the end of the week it grew calmer. Lord and Lady Pierce had taken their leave yesterday, after Lord Graystone's body was interred in the family tomb beside his beloved son's. Juliana had spent the better part of today alone in her bedchamber, and the house was quiet.

Grace had been consigned to the tender care of her nanny for the day. Mrs. Culpepper was a worthy woman, but not a terribly amusing one. Grace soon grew bored with her company and turned her attention to Logan who, while far more terrifying than Mrs. Culpepper, was also a great deal more interesting.

She didn't speak to him at all at first, but she took to following him about from room to room. She'd kept a wary eye on him all morning, but when she'd reassured herself the only alarming thing about him was his size, she'd bravely invited him to play at paper dolls with her.

Logan wasn't very good at paper dolls. The fragile bits of paper were too tiny for his big hands, but Grace was patient with him. After a morning of playing at Cinderella and the Glass Slipper a tentative friendship had sprung up between them. Soon enough Logan found himself drinking tea from miniscule china teacups and helping Grace rock her dolls to sleep.

She hadn't yet ventured outside the house with him, but it looked as if that was about to change. Grace had evidently given this invitation some thought, because she was shrewd enough to begin with flattery. "My aunt Juliana said you have a big gray horse at your house, and that you're a very good rider. Is that true?"

"I do have a gray horse, and I suppose I'm a decent enough rider, though I'm no better than your Aunt Juliana is." Logan smiled, but saying Juliana's name caused him a pang in his chest.

"What's your horse's name?"

"Fingal. It's a Scottish name. *Fhiongail*. It means 'fair stranger' in English."

"We have a big horse in our stable named Finnegan. He's not gray, but maybe you'd like to ride him still?" Grace turned big, hopeful dark eyes on him.

"I would like it, Grace, but does your aunt Juliana know you're going out for a ride?" Logan didn't want to disappoint Grace, but he wouldn't take her out without Juliana's knowledge.

Grace nodded eagerly. "Oh, yes. She said a ride would do her good. She's coming down now."

Juliana was coming down? Logan tossed his book onto a table and jumped to his feet. He'd hardly seen her since the day they arrived in Surrey. She'd come down for dinner when Lord and Lady Pierce were here, but last night she'd taken a tray in her room.

Since she'd lied to her father about marrying Fitzwilliam, neither she nor Logan seemed to know what to say to each other. His new wife had told her dying father she'd married his brother. What was there to say, after that? They could hardly even look at each other now.

So, Juliana avoided him, and Logan brooded over it.

He wanted to tell her the lie didn't matter to him. He wanted to reassure her he understood why she'd done it, but he couldn't make the words leave his lips.

It *did* matter. It mattered so much he hadn't been able to make himself forget it.

He had no right to be angry with her. No right to be seething with hurt, and…yes, damn it, jealous, but that lie had been echoing in his head since the moment he'd led her from her father's room the night Lord Graystone died.

Over the following week he'd made dozens of excuses for her. He'd told himself Juliana was overwhelmed with grief and shock—that she hadn't meant what she'd said. He'd reasoned that she'd only been trying to ease her father's final hour. But no matter how much he argued with himself, Logan couldn't quite convince himself there wasn't more to that lie.

Lord Graystone had died believing Juliana was married to Fitz—that she'd become the Duchess of Blackmore—and there was a part of Logan that wondered if she wished it were the truth. She'd loved Fitz her whole life. For as far back as she could remember, she'd always imagined she'd become his wife. Instead she'd had to settle for Logan, a man she'd been forced to marry because he'd stolen her letters, and nearly destroyed her niece's future. A man she hardly knew.

He'd known from the start of this if she had a choice, she wouldn't have chosen to marry *him*. It hadn't bothered him much at first. It wasn't as if either of them regarded this as a love match. They were each marrying the other as a means to an end. Logan did regret taking those letters, but once he'd made up his mind to marry Juliana, he'd accepted whatever would follow.

But that was before...

Before he'd spent every night of the journey from Castle Kinross to Graystone Court holding her in his arms, her head nestled against his chest. Before he'd tangled his hands in the heavy silk of her hair and brought it to his lips. Before he'd heard her sigh his name, her mouth pressed to his ear, her arms around his neck. Before he'd met Grace, who was every bit the sweet, loving child Juliana had told him she was.

Before he'd fallen in love with her—

"Grace? Where are you?"

Logan's head jerked up as Juliana's voice floated down the hallway.

Grace ran across the library to the door. "Here, Aunt. Mr. Logan says he'll come riding with us!"

"That's very nice of him." Juliana appeared in the doorway, but she didn't come into the library. She hovered there, half-hidden by the door, much as Grace had when she'd been peeking at him earlier.

Was this what he and Juliana had come to, then? Was she afraid of him now? Had they gone from making love and sleeping in each other's arms every night to *this*? The thought was so painful Logan opened his mouth to tell them he'd changed his mind, and wouldn't accompany them riding after all, but he didn't get the chance.

Grace darted across the library, grabbed his hand, and led him down the hall to the entryway. "Can we ride to the woods, Aunt? I want to see if there are any bluebells left."

"Wait, Grace," Juliana said, stopping her before she could dash out the door. "You've forgotten your hat. Fetch it, please."

"Dratted thing! You won't go without me?"

"No, of course not." Juliana nodded at the staircase. "Go on. We'll wait right here for you."

Grace darted up the stairs, leaving Logan and Juliana alone in the entryway.

Juliana went quiet, but Logan caught her watching him from the corner of her eye. She looked pale still, and she was anxiously biting her lip. He could see she was distressed. A part of him wanted to gather her against his chest and soothe her, but he kept his hands fisted at his sides. He didn't dare touch her anymore.

When the silence had stretched Logan's last nerve to the breaking point, he cleared his throat and stiffly enquired after her health. "Are you well? You look tired still. I hope you're sleeping?"

His manner was colder than he'd meant it to be, and Juliana seemed to flinch away from him. "Not as well as usual, perhaps, though I expect it's the strain fatiguing me, rather than lack of sleep."

Logan nodded. "It will get better in time."

She was quiet for a moment, her throat working, then, as if she couldn't bear to hold them back another moment, a flurry of words burst from her lips. "Logan, I—I want to thank you for…for everything. I don't know how I could have managed without you this past week. I'm truly grateful."

Logan's throat tightened. "I'm your husband, Juliana. I did what any husband would do for his grieving wife. Did you expect any less of me?"

"No! No, I didn't mean to suggest…I only wanted to thank you."

Logan glanced at her, cursing himself when he saw her stricken expression. "I'm glad I was here and able to help you. I don't like to think of you going through that alone."

"No, neither do I." She swallowed. "Indeed, about your being here. I wanted to know if you—do you intend to remain in England much longer?"

Logan's body went rigid. Was she trying to hint he should return to Scotland, now he'd served his purpose? Grace's future was secure, so there was no reason for Logan to linger here, was there? Juliana was married, and by the terms of Lord Graystone's will, she was now Grace's legal guardian.

As for Logan, he had no legal claim to Grace, despite being Juliana's husband. But why should he? Lord Graystone had never even heard the name Logan Blair. Bitterness welled inside Logan, and he didn't try to hide it. "If you're so anxious to be rid of me, my lady, I'm happy to oblige you."

Juliana jerked her head up, appalled. "No! That's not why I…indeed, I only asked because I know you're anxious to return to the clan, and I wanted to make it clear I—"

"I'll be gone within the week." Logan still had to take care of that business with Lord Cowden that Fitz had asked him to settle. He didn't intend to leave England until it was done, but if Juliana wanted him gone from Graystone Court, he wouldn't linger afterwards.

It was for the best. The sooner he left, the better off they'd both be.

Julian sucked in a breath. "You don't understand, Logan. I want—"

"Here I am!" Grace came charging down the stairs, waving her hat over her head. "*Now* can we go?"

"Forgive me, Grace. I forgot I have some business this afternoon." Logan forced a smile. "I'm afraid it can't wait."

Grace's face fell.

Logan flinched. Damn it, he didn't like to disappoint a child, particularly this one. He knelt down and took her by the shoulders. "I beg your pardon, but I'll take you riding another time—later this week, if you like."

"This week? You promise?" She brightened a little.

He had no business promising the child anything. He'd be gone from her life soon enough. It wasn't fair to Grace to encourage her attachment. But the promise fell from his lips, just the same. "Aye, I promise."

To Logan's surprise, Grace leaned forward and pressed a kiss to his cheek. "All right."

Logan ruffled her hair, then rose and opened the door. He paused on the threshold, but didn't turn to face Juliana. "I don't know how long I'll be. You should plan to dine without me."

He waited, but she didn't reply. He left without looking back.

* * * *

It was well past calling hours when Logan arrived at Lord Cowden's estate, but as he'd expected he was admitted at once, and taken to the drawing room to await his lordship.

Lord Cowden left him alone for longer than was polite, but again, Logan wasn't surprised. Fitz knew Lord Cowden far better than most people did, and he hadn't hesitated to share his knowledge with Logan.

Logan already understood a great deal more about the man than Cowden realized. He knew, for instance, that Cowden was the sort of man who liked to wield power over others—even such paltry power as keeping a visitor waiting. He also knew Cowden would appear soon enough, if only to satisfy his curiosity regarding the man who'd married Lady Juliana Bernard.

The man who'd succeeded, where Cowden had failed.

When Cowden strolled into the drawing room at last, he was just what Logan expected he'd be.

Tall, handsome, scrupulously elegant.

Cold, with icy gray eyes and a cruel edge to his mouth.

"Well, Mr. Blair. How do you do?" He gave Logan a charming smile. Useful, that smile. That and Cowden's unrelenting gentlemanliness was what kept in him good standing with the *ton*, despite the ugly whispers that followed him.

"I confess I'm surprised you've called," Cowden went on. "Pleasantly surprised, of course."

190   *Anna Bradley*

Logan doubted Cowden was at all surprised, but he only nodded politely. "It's kind of you to receive me at such an hour."

"Yes, well, I wouldn't dream of turning away Lady Juliana's husband. She and I are dear friends, you see. But I suppose she's told you that already?"

Logan stretched his lips into a thin smile. "She did. I think you'd be surprised at how much she's told me about you, my lord."

Lord Cowden's own smile remained fixed in place, but his eyes narrowed. "Indeed? Well, we've known each other since we were children, and as I said, we're dear friends. I did, of course, hear of Lord Graystone's recent passing. Unfortunately, I've been out of town and was unable to pay my respects."

Logan already knew Cowden had been out of town. He also knew where he'd been—in London, squandering his new bride's money at Boodle's. Cowden was a skilled gamer, but these past few months his luck had been out. Dozens of aristocrats in London held his vowels, debts of honor Cowden was obliged to pay with his wife's rapidly diminishing fortune, unless he fancied a hasty trip to the Continent.

"You'll pass my condolences on to Lady Juliana, won't you?" Cowden took a pinch of snuff from a silver snuffbox embossed with his crest, then sneezed daintily.

"I didn't come here to talk to you about my wife, Lord Cowden." Logan didn't like hearing Juliana's name in this man's mouth. "I have business to discuss with you."

Lord Cowden waved Logan over to a settee near the fireplace. "Do you? I can't imagine what it could be."

"Your land in Perth. I want to buy it," Logan said bluntly, determined to get the thing done with as quickly as possible.

"The Scottish lands? I'm afraid they aren't for sale, Mr. Blair."

No, but they would be soon enough. "I'm prepared to pay you handsomely for them."

Lord Cowden's eyebrows rose. "You, or your brother, the Duke of Blackmore?"

Logan's expression didn't change, but Lord Cowden had managed to surprise him. Either his connection to Fitz was more widely known in England than Logan thought, or Lord Cowden had made it his business to pry into Fitz's private affairs. "Does it matter?"

Cowden laughed. "My dear man, of course it does. As I'm sure you know, Fitzwilliam is another old and dear friend of mine."

Christ, he could almost admire Cowden. If he hadn't already known the man despised Fitz, Logan never would have guessed it from Cowden's bland expression. "If he's one of your oldest friends, then you must be anxious to oblige him."

"I wish I could, Mr. Blair, but alas, I've other plans for that land. Plans I've already set in motion."

Logan shrugged. "Plans change."

"But I hate to alter them now. It took me ages to find a proper man to act as my factor, but I managed to secure one at last, and he's anxious to begin his work. He's in Scotland even now, arranging matters to my satisfaction."

"You've hired a factor? You intend to clear the land, then?" Logan fought to keep his voice steady.

"Of course. Sheep farming is quite lucrative, as I'm sure you know."

"What of the people there? Clan Murray has held that land since the twelfth century. Where do you expect them to go once you've cleared it?" Logan asked, though he already knew the answer.

Cowden didn't give a bloody damn where they went, as long as they got off his land.

"Clan Murray? Is that who they are? How quaint." Cowden waved a languid hand. "Clan Murray isn't really my concern, Mr. Blair. I imagine they'll find *someplace* to go."

Logan clenched his hands into fists to keep from wrapping them around Cowden's neck. "Sheep farming is lucrative enough, but yours is a small property. Hardly worth the trouble, particularly when the duke is prepared to pay you far more than the land is worth."

Lord Cowden's cold gray eyes were filled with triumph. "Fitzwilliam always did have deep pockets. It's no wonder, really, that Lord Graystone chose him for Lady Juliana. Only a duke will do for a diamond of the first water, hmmm? But as I said, the land's not for sale—not even to the Duke of Blackmore."

Especially not to the Duke of Blackmore.

Cowden didn't say so, but he might as well have.

Revenge. That was Cowden's true motive, and likely the only thing in the world more important to him than money.

Cowden had always hated Fitz—had always bitterly envied him. If he'd ever had any affection for Juliana it had turned to hatred when she'd rejected him, then thwarted his attempt to gain control of Grace.

Now he also hated Logan, for being Fitz's brother and Juliana's husband. Logan could feel the animosity pouring off of Cowden, even as his charming smile never faltered.

"Forgive me, Mr. Blair, but if that's all, I must bid you goodbye. I've an engagement this evening. You will give Lady Juliana my best regards, won't you?" Lord Cowden rose from the settee. "I do hope it's not too much trouble for you to see yourself out."

Logan waited until Cowden left the drawing room before rising to his feet. He'd show himself out, but he'd be back tomorrow, and again the day after that.

He'd pry that land free of Cowden's grasp, no matter how many days it took.

Chapter Twenty

Three days later

It had been three long, empty days since Juliana's argument with Logan in the entryway. Three days of misery on her part, and three days of mysterious disappearances on his.

He never said where he was going, and when he returned he never explained his absences. Juliana knew only that he rode off every afternoon without a word to her, and each time he went, he stayed away longer than he had the time before.

He'd gone again the previous night, and hadn't returned to Graystone Court until the early morning hours. He'd taken care to be quiet when he entered his bedchamber, but Juliana had been wide awake, praying for him to come home.

Waiting for him, her heart a heavy stone in her chest.

She hadn't closed her eyes once the entire night, not even once she knew he was back. She'd lain awake, hoping against hope the door connecting their bedchambers would open, and he'd come to her. But the door had remained closed, just as it had every night since they'd arrived at Graystone Court.

Juliana rubbed her gritty eyes and threw her bedcovers back, but she couldn't summon the energy to drag herself out of bed. She'd have to, soon enough. The day was advancing, and she'd promised Grace she'd ride with her and Logan this morning.

What business could he have that would take him away from Graystone Court day after day, and for hours at a time? He'd been in England for less than two weeks. Juliana couldn't think of a single reason he'd be obliged to stay out all night.

Well, no. That wasn't true. She could think of two reasons, and both of them made her numb with despair.

Either he had a mistress, or he was arranging his return to Scotland. Since that dreadful argument three days earlier, Juliana had been in anguished expectation of the moment he'd bid her goodbye, mount his horse, and leave Graystone Court without a backward glance. It was, after all, what they'd agreed would happen. He'd fulfilled his end of their bargain. She had no right to ask him to stay, and God knew he had reason enough to wish to escape her.

As for a mistress...

Juliana threw an arm over her head and stared up at the green silk hangings above her. It was absurd to imagine Logan could have secured a mistress in the short time he'd been in England, but that didn't stop her from imagining it. Nor did it stop her heart from twisting miserably in her chest when she did. It was odd how the heart came to completely overrule the head, once you fell in love.

Well, she'd fallen. She was hopelessly in love with Logan Blair.

She couldn't imagine her life without him now, and yet as surely as she loved him, she'd also hurt him, so badly she was terrified she was going to lose him. Every time he looked at her or spoke to her she was certain he'd tell her he was leaving, and her heart would shrivel in her chest.

Not that he spoke to her often. He looked at her even less. Since she'd told that lie to her father, it was as if Logan could hardly bear to be in the same room with her. Whenever her gaze did happen to meet his, words tried to rush from her mouth. Pleas for his forgiveness, promises of love, an explanation for why she'd lied...

But she didn't *know* why. The words would hover there, trembling on her lips, but she couldn't speak them. She didn't have any answers for Logan, or for herself. She tried over and over again to untangle her thoughts, but somehow her love for Logan and her pain over hurting him were tangled up with her anger at her father, and her grief over his death. Nothing made sense anymore. Everywhere she turned she found only sorrow, confusion, and regret.

"Aunt Juliana!" A sharp knock on her door pulled Juliana from her thoughts. A moment later Grace dashed into the room. "Why are you still in bed? Have you forgotten we're meant to ride with Mr. Logan this morning?"

Grace had been looking forward to this ride all week, and she was outraged at the idea Juliana could have forgotten such a momentous occasion. Despite her dark mood, a smile rose to Juliana's lips, and she held out her arms for Grace. "Yes, I know. Come, I'm fatigued this morning. You'll have to help me up."

Grace made a running leap and landed in the middle of the bed with a grin. "There! Are you awake now?" She tried to snatch Juliana's hands and pull her from the bed, but Juliana caught her niece in her arms and gathered her tightly against her chest.

Out of this whole tangled mess with her father and Logan, this was the one thing that had gone right—the only thing in Juliana's life that made sense. *Grace.*

Her niece was hers now. No one—not her father, and not Lord Cowden—could take Grace away from her. No matter what happened with Logan, Juliana would always be grateful to him for giving her such a precious gift.

She buried her face in the springy dark hair under her chin, but Grace wasn't in the mood to be cuddled. She squirmed free from Juliana's arms. "No, there isn't time! Mr. Logan told me he has to go out this afternoon and won't be home until after dark. If we don't ride now, we won't get to go with him at all. *Please*, Auntie Juliana!"

Logan was off again today, then, and likely wouldn't return until close to dawn, just as he had last night. Juliana's heart sank, but she forced a smile for Grace's sake. "Yes, all right. Fetch my dark green riding habit, won't you? I'll be ready in a moment."

Grace pranced about like an overeager puppy while Juliana gathered her hair up into some pins and donned her riding habit. "Mr. Logan," was a decided favorite with Grace, and he was becoming more so every day. She was going to be devastated when Logan went away. Juliana's heart sank another notch thinking about it, but Grace didn't give her time to wallow. She grabbed Juliana's hand and tugged her toward the stairs.

Logan was in the entryway waiting for them, and Juliana's breath caught at the sight of him. He was wearing a dark blue coat that made his eyes appear bluer than ever, and his tight buckskin breeches accentuated the long, muscular line of his legs. A lock of his dark hair hung over his forehead, and a hat and riding crop were dangling from his elegant fingers.

She'd been so ashamed of her lie she'd hardly dared look at Logan these past weeks, but as he stood there below them, his face turned up to watch them descend, Juliana felt a hint of that same determination that had helped her coax him into marrying her. Her chin inched up a notch, and for the first time in days, she forced herself to hold his gaze.

He didn't look away, but he didn't smile, either. His face was cool and set as she came down the last stair. "Good morning, my lady. Are you ready for our ride?"

Juliana flinched. His tone was perfectly polite, his bow proper, but his eyes were hard. Her throat went dry, and her murmured "yes" was so soft she wasn't sure Logan even heard her.

If he had, he didn't acknowledge it. Instead he turned to Grace, and the polite smile melted into a playful grin. "Hello, Miss Grace. You look very smart in your riding outfit this morning. I'm guessing you know your way around a horse."

"Oh, yes. I do!" Grace took his hand, and said to Juliana, "Mr. Logan is going to ride Finnegan today, because that name sounds most like Fingal, his own horse's name."

Juliana nodded and allowed Grace to hurry them out the door. Grace led the way to the stables, skipping happily along in front of them, leaving Logan and Juliana to follow behind, locked in an uneasy silence.

It was, unfortunately, a hint of things to come. Once they were all mounted and riding through the estate grounds, Grace continually darted off to explore whatever caught her eye, leaving Logan and Juliana to drown in the sea of awkwardness between them.

Juliana opened her mouth a dozen times, and closed it a dozen more without venturing a word. How had it gotten as bad as this so quickly? Back at Castle Kinross they'd always had plenty to say to each other, even when they'd been arguing. This abyss between them, this deafening silence, was unbearable. She had to do something, say something—

"Aunt Juliana!" Grace had ridden ahead, but she paused now and waved a beckoning hand toward Juliana and Logan. "Come this way, and see the last of the bluebells!"

Juliana waved and started to make her way forward, and Logan brought Finnegan into step beside her horse. "Everything you said about Grace is true. She's as lovely as you told me she is."

Juliana turned to him in surprise. Logan hadn't offered her more than half a dozen words over the past three days, but if there was one subject on which they could talk easily, it was Grace. "She is. Now you see why I came all the way to Scotland on her behalf. She's worth every single one of the six hundred miles between Surrey and Inverness."

Logan's mouth turned down. He struggled with himself for a moment, but then a harsh laugh tore from his chest. "You didn't come all those miles just for Grace."

Juliana glanced at him and saw the polite mask he'd been wearing for days had cracked a bit around the edges. Her heart began to pound. "Why did I come, then?"

He let out another short, hard laugh. "Come now, Juliana. We both know why. You came for Fitz, of course. Your betrothed. Pity that didn't work out."

It had been some time since Juliana thought it a pity—nearly from the first moment she'd laid eyes on Logan, in fact. "Do you suppose *I* think it's a pity, Logan? Or are you referring to your own feelings?"

He shrugged, but he didn't meet her eyes. "Your father would have thought so, otherwise you wouldn't have lied and told him you'd married Fitz. The Duchess of Blackmore, remember, Juliana?"

There it was, the dark, ugly thing she'd put between them with her lie. "I told you once before, Logan. I don't care about being a duchess. That was my father's dream for me, but it was never mine."

"What about Fitz, Juliana?" he asked quietly. "Was *he* part of your dream?"

He turned to her then, and Juliana gasped at the raw pain she saw on his face. She reached out a hand to him. "Logan, I—"

"Aunt Juliana?" Grace was waving impatiently at them. "Aren't you coming? I'm riding ahead!"

Juliana tore her gaze from Logan's face and called to Grace, "No, I don't like you getting so far ahead where I can't see you. Wait for us, please."

Grace frowned, but she lowered her riding crop and obediently brought her horse to a halt.

Juliana turned back to Logan, her heart rushing into her throat at the lost look on his face. "Fitzwilliam was never a part of my dream. Not in the way you mean it. I care for him, and I always will, but—"

Juliana broke off suddenly, her gaze jerking back to Grace. Had she caught something out of the corner of her eye? Some sharp movement that made foreboding shoot up her spine? Had Grace made a sound, or had Juliana somehow sensed something was coming, in the way of a parent always on the alert for her child?

She didn't know. Even much later she couldn't say how she knew something awful was about to happen, but she stopped mid-sentence and whirled toward Grace.

And what she saw…what she saw…

A scream tore from her throat. "Grace!"

Logan jerked his head toward Grace. They were only a few yards away from her—close enough so they could both see every moment as it unfolded with painful clarity.

But not close enough to stop it.

The small mare Grace was riding had taken a sudden fright to something in the grass—a snake, most likely. The mare lunged forward, nearly throwing Grace over her head, but then with a terrified whinny she reared back, her hooves stabbing at the air.

Grace let out a sharp cry and grabbed for the horse's mane. She might yet have held on if the mare hadn't regained her balance only to dance sideways, trampling at something at her feet. The snake that had spooked her flopped lifelessly between her hooves, and she reared up again in a panic.

"Grace!" Juliana screamed again, her voice hoarse with terror.

Logan surged forward. Juliana darted after him, a prayer on her lips as he got closer and closer to Grace, but just as he drew close enough to grab her around the waist and tug her free from the panicked horse, Grace's fingers tore loose from the horse's mane. The momentum sent her flying backward, and she was falling, falling...

Dear God, she seemed to fall forever, but at the same time too quickly for Logan to be able to do a single thing to stop it.

The next thing Juliana knew, his shouts were ringing in her ears. A sound was clawing its way up her throat, but before she could scream a third time, Grace hit the ground with a brutal slam. Logan leapt from his horse and ran toward her. Juliana didn't recall dismounting, but her feet crashed into the ground as she ran after Logan, praying with every step she took the mare wouldn't trample Grace under her pounding hooves.

Instead, the mare bolted. Logan shot forward and fell to his knees beside Grace.

Juliana didn't remember running. She didn't know if she sobbed, or if any tears ran down her cheeks. Later, all she could remember was Grace, one arm twisted beside her head, and blood—very red against her pale face—trickling from her nose.

* * * *

You need to forgive him...

These words in Logan's soft voice kept repeating over and over in Juliana's head. He hadn't spoken for hours, yet she could hear him as clearly as if he'd just said the words aloud.

She wasn't sure why these words should be haunting her now, unless it was simply that it was impossible to ignore the similarities between this moment and the last evening of her father's life.

She and Logan were in a dark room, sitting beside Grace's bed. Juliana held one of the child's small hands tucked inside her own, but Grace's other arm was secured in a sling. The surgeon who'd come in to set the broken bone had assured them it was a simple fracture, and Grace would suffer no lasting effects from the injury. They'd had the doctor in as well, but he'd been optimistic about the knot on the back of Grace's head, predicting with a calm smile the worst struggle would be keeping the child confined to her bed long enough for her to heal.

Since this morning, Juliana hadn't spared a thought for anything other than Grace. Her father and even Logan had receded to the back of her mind while she waited in agony to see how severe Grace's injuries were.

When the doctor told her Grace was going to be just fine, the relief was like nothing Juliana had ever felt before. It did something to her—shook something loose inside her, and the evening of her father's death came crashing down upon her again.

And with it, something else. Something Logan had said to her that day in the carriage, before they'd arrived at Graystone Court.

She'd told him her father had given her everything, but Logan had shaken his head. Then he'd said something she hadn't understood at the time.

He didn't trust you. That's a difficult thing to forgive in someone you love.

Juliana found the outlines of Logan's face in the shadowy room. It had taken time, but now she thought she understood what he'd been trying to tell her that day. Somehow, he'd known how she felt before she did herself.

Until this moment, she'd struggled to understand why she couldn't forgive her father. He'd been ill when he amended his will—not in his right mind. Juliana knew that, yet even after his death she could feel a hard, cold knot of anger in her chest when she thought about the last few months of his life.

She'd told herself she was a selfish, ungrateful daughter—that only a monster would withhold forgiveness in the face of a beloved father's death. She'd told herself over and over again he'd only wanted her to be safe, to protect her, yet she still hadn't been able to let go of her anger and resentment toward him. She hadn't known why at first, but as the days passed her confused thoughts started to untangle themselves in her head.

Her father had loved her dearly. He thought her perfect—a diamond of the first water, destined to become a duchess. He couldn't have been prouder of her charm and intelligence. She was everything he ever wanted in a daughter, and he saw her as a credit to him.

But he'd never really seen *her*. And she...well, she'd seen herself through his eyes, hadn't she? An accomplished, charming, decorative lady of fashion. For a long time, she'd believed she wanted the same things for herself her father wanted for her.

But that wasn't the truth. It never had been.

The truth was, until she'd been forced to act to save Grace, she hadn't had any more faith in herself than her father had. Deep down, she'd doubted herself. There was a part of her father that hadn't believed she was capable of taking care of herself and Grace, and a part of her had wondered if he was right.

But underneath the trappings that were so important to her father, there was a great deal more to Juliana than either of them had suspected. A woman of strength, of determination and grit. That was the part her father had never seen. He'd never even suspected it was there.

But Logan had.

Never once, since she chased him from Inverness to Castle Kinross, had he ever underestimated her. She hadn't let him.

This man—this fierce, maddening Scot—he'd helped bring out another side of her. The side that was willing to struggle for what she wanted, to fight for what mattered to her. He'd made her pursue him, made her meet every challenge, because nothing less than everything she had, everything she was, would ever be enough for him.

"I never wanted to be a duchess," she said suddenly.

Her voice sounded loud in the quiet room.

Logan's head snapped up.

"I never wanted to be a duchess," she repeated softly, more to herself than to Logan. It was the truth. The titles, the properties, the fortune—none of it had ever mattered to her the way it mattered to her father.

Logan said nothing, and more words rushed to Juliana's lips. She had so much to say to him, so many words locked away inside her heart. "I always imagined I'd marry Fitzwilliam. He was one reason why I came to Scotland. You're right about that. I've always loved him."

Logan remained silent, but she sensed the sudden tension in him.

"At one time I might even have said I was in love with him, but that was a long time ago. I've known for years I love Fitzwilliam in the same way I loved Jonathan. Not as a lover or as a husband, but as a brother, and a treasured friend."

She could feel Logan's gaze on her face, but still he didn't speak. A brief silence fell, and Juliana gathered in a breath. She'd finish what she had to say, because the time had come to be brave enough to tell the truth. She wouldn't turn coward now.

In the end, it was much easier to say it than she'd thought it would be.

The truth always was, wasn't it?

"I never loved Fitzwilliam the way I love you, Logan. I've never loved anyone the way I love you. I'll always regret I didn't have the courage to tell my father that before he died. I never meant to hurt you, and I—I'm sorry I did."

Logan sucked in a breath, but Juliana didn't wait for him to speak. She'd come this far, and her heart already felt lighter for it. "My father might have thought it a pity I never became a duchess. Maybe you think so, too—think it's a pity we married, I mean. But I don't, Logan. I don't want anyone but you."

Still, Logan didn't say a word. Juliana waited, but when another few minutes passed in unbroken silence, she raised Grace's hand to her lips, pressed a kiss to her palm, and rose from the chair.

She did look back—just once—before she left the room.

Logan sat motionless beside the bed, half-lost in the shadows.

Chapter Twenty-one

Juliana was sitting in front of her looking-glass when Logan entered her bedchamber. Her hair fell in a mass of golden waves over her shoulders, with long locks of it trailing down her back. Pins were scattered across the table. Juliana's brush was in her hand, but she wasn't using it. She was perfectly still, staring at her reflection in the glass as if she no longer recognized herself.

Did she know how beautiful she was? How strong? Did she know her father's blindness to that strength didn't make it any less true, or any less a part of her?

Does she know how much I love her?

Logan closed the bedchamber door quietly behind him. As he made his way slowly across the room toward her, he drew off his cravat, his coat, and his waistcoat and let them fall heedlessly to the floor.

He was nearly close enough to touch her when she raised her gaze from her reflection, and her green eyes met his. She didn't say a word, but Logan saw her long, pale throat move in a swallow, saw the way her pulse fluttered wildly under that fine, soft skin.

He slid his suspenders over his shoulders, then tugged his shirt over his head. When he reached her at last his bare chest was heaving, as if he'd run miles—days—just to reach her.

She was watching his reflection in the mirror, her gaze following his every breath, his every move, but when he touched her at last—the softest touch only, his hands landing gently on her shoulders—she squeezed her eyes closed.

"No. Look at me, Juliana." He slid his palms over her shoulders, settled them in the curves of her neck, and waited.

Her eyelids fluttered open, and then her green eyes were on him, burning him everywhere they touched. How had he ever thought he could leave her? What a fool he was, to imagine he'd survive a day without that gaze on him, warming him. He could as soon go without breath, without sunshine.

He gathered the thick mass of her hair in his hands and raised it to his lips. "Did you think I wouldn't forgive you, *bòcan*?" He closed his eyes and buried his face in her hair, hungry for her springtime scent. He inhaled deeply, until his head was swimming with the dizzying scent of crushed leaves and sun-warmed grass.

A soft sob tore from her throat. "I didn't know if you...I wasn't sure."

Logan opened his eyes. He watched as long, silky stands of her hair floated through his fingers, then his gaze met hers in the glass. "Don't you know, Juliana? I'd forgive you anything. All you need to do is ask me, and I'll do anything for you."

Another sob broke from her lips. Tears started in her eyes, but Logan caught them on his fingertips before they could fall. She'd cried so many tears this week. He knew she'd cry many more before she'd spent all her love, anger, and grief over her father.

But not tonight.

He slid his hands over her shoulders again, but this time his fingertips drifted beneath the neckline of her night rail. He eased the fragile material aside to stroke her throat and the tops of her breasts. Logan watched the two of them in the mirror, mesmerized by the sight of his big, rough hands against her fair skin. She was too fine for a man like him, but he was selfish—selfish and greedy—because she was *his*, and he couldn't get enough of her.

Her breath caught as his hands slid lower, dipping under the thin linen of the night rail to stroke the tips of her breasts. They hardened instantly against his calloused fingers. He dragged his fingertips over them, circling and pinching gently until Juliana moaned, and her head fell back against his chest.

"Look at yourself, Ana." Logan tugged gently on the muslin so it pulled tightly against her breasts. Her nipples were hard and flushed a deep pink from his caresses, and Logan groaned as he plucked at them, flicking his fingernail over the eager nubs. They strained against the white material, reaching for his teasing fingers. "*Mo Dhia*, you're so beautiful, Juliana. Every inch of you."

Just that simple caress had left him hard and aching for her. His cock pressed insistently against his falls, and he felt as if he'd die if he couldn't see all of her, touch all of her. Every creamy inch of skin, every curve, every wet, tender fold. He lowered his hands to her thighs, grasped handfuls of the material and dragged it up over her hips. His lips found her ear. "Raise your arms for me, *bhean*."

Her arms rose in the air and he tugged the flimsy night rail over her head. She was bare underneath. Logan stroked his palm over her belly, groaning with need when a spray of goosebumps rose to the surface of her skin in the wake of his touch. He reached lower, playfully circling her belly button, then lower still...

"Open your legs for me, Juliana."

She stared at him in the mirror, her lips parted, a flush darkening her cheeks.

He let his hand drift lower, slowly stroking over the soft skin of her belly until his fingertips found her fair curls. "Open, *beag bòidhchead*."

She opened, a soft moan leaving her lips.

"Yes, Ana. Just like that. Now lean back against me, *neach-gaoil*."

She was trembling, and he helped ease her backward so her head was cradled against his chest. Logan made certain she was balanced securely, then he trailed his hands down one of her thighs to the back of her knee and shifted her position, so the sole of her bare foot rested against the edge of the dressing-table.

She raised her head from his chest, her green eyes going wide when she understood what he intended to do. "Logan..."

"Shhh." He scraped his teeth over her earlobe, nipping at the soft flesh. "Let me see you."

Logan's cock was so hard he felt ready to explode, but he waited, his breath held, for her to give him permission to touch her like this.

Finally, she nodded once.

Logan arranged her other leg as he had the first. When she was spread open in front of him he sucked in a hard breath, mesmerized by the sight of her. "*Mo Dhia*, just look at you."

He couldn't take his eyes off her. Her skin was flushed, her nipples still peaked for him. He let his gaze drift lower, to that most intimate place between her legs, where her damp, tender pink skin seemed to beg for his touch.

He reached between her pale thighs and stroked a fingertip over her. Just a single stroke with one finger, his touch so light.

Juliana gasped.

So, he did it again, and then again, his fingers circling and teasing until she was writhing in the chair, soft whimpers and pleas falling from her lips.

Logan's gaze was riveted on her, everything inside him focused entirely on her pleasure. "Does that feel good, Juliana?" His mouth was hot against her ear. "Do you need more, *beag bhean*? Look at me, and I'll give you everything you want." Juliana was rolling her head from side to side on his chest, her eyes tightly closed, but he took her chin gently in his hand and turned her face to the mirror. "Watch. Watch me touch you."

She watched, her mouth open, her green eyes nearly black. She arched her back when Logan cupped his hand over her and slid one finger inside. "*Logan.*"

Her hips rose, and he growled against her neck. God, it drove him mad to see her like this, her pink flesh swollen, her body arching and twisting under his hand. She let out a sharp moan when he sank a second finger inside her. Her arousal coated his palm, driving him so close to the edge he couldn't wait another moment to taste her.

"Lower your legs. Feet on the floor." His voice was deep and hoarse, almost savage.

She did as he asked, and when he sank to his knees in front of her, he could see her legs were trembling. His hands were heavy, possessive when they landed on her inner thighs and he held her open for his mouth. He lost control the moment his tongue found her sweet flesh. He became frantic, snarling like an animal as his tongue lashed over her again and again, devouring her.

"Logan!" She gripped his hair with clenched fingers, tugging mindlessly as she panted and moaned her way through her release, her thighs shaking. He stayed with her, his lips and tongue stroking insistently until he'd wrung every last tremor from her. He slowed then, caressing her thighs with long strokes of his hands as he lapped gently at her, bringing her down until she went limp, spent.

Logan lifted her into his arms and carried her to the bed. He laid her down on her back and she threw her arms over her head, a sleepy, seductive smile on her lips as she watched him tear off his clothes.

He was mad for her, his cock pulsing with need, but he paused to gaze down at her, his fingers on the buttons of his falls. "You look satisfied, *bhig galla.*"

"I am." Her gaze lingered on his bare chest, then dropped lower, to the evidence of his arousal. Her lips curved when she met his eyes again. "For the moment, that is."

Logan groaned as he struggled out of his boots and stripped off his pantaloons. Nothing excited him more than having her eyes on him, knowing she wanted him. He tossed his clothes aside and joined her on the bed, sighing with relief when he had her in his arms again, with her warm curves pressed tightly against him. "I missed you," he murmured, dropping a kiss onto her temple.

She gazed up at him, her green eyes serious. "I missed you, too. I waited for you. Every night that I lay here alone, I hoped you would come to me. I ache for you, Logan." She took his face in her hands and pressed a sweet, hungry kiss to his lips.

He buried his hands in her hair with a groan and took her mouth harder, his tongue slipping between her lips to tangle with hers. The soft heat of her mouth, her silken skin against his, her breathy sighs in his ears—it all made him mindless with desire and love.

I can't wait any longer...

He eased his hips between her thighs, took himself in hand, and pressed his swollen head against her. She let out a deep sigh and wrapped her legs around him, urging him to go deeper. Logan's mind went hazy as he slid inside. He knew only *her*—her soft, welcoming heat, her pleading whimpers in his ears, the slightly salty taste of her skin as he opened his mouth against her neck.

She moaned when he began to move, her legs tightening around him. Logan sank deeper inside with one measured stoke, then went still, his back bowing from the exquisite pleasure of her heat wrapped around him. "I want you to come for me again," he whispered, with another nudge of his hips.

She panted as he nudged into her again, slowly at first, but then harder and faster as his release slid closer. "Come, Juliana. Come with me inside you."

Her body strained against his. "I—I can't, Logan. Not again. It's too much."

Logan reached down between their bodies, hissing when his fingers found her damp core. "Yes, you can. You're so wet, so ready." He rolled the pad of one finger over her tender nub, moaning when it grew harder under his touch. "Come for me, *breagha bhean*. I need to feel you."

His other hand slid up her body to her breast, his thumb finding her nipple. He worked her with both hands, petting and teasing even as he continued to thrust into her, and God, she was so hot, so sweet, her body clenching around his, greedy for him. He stroked into her harder, urging her on with his fingers. His spine started to tingle, and he could feel his release sliding closer, then closer still, and he couldn't wait, couldn't wait any longer...

Just as he was tumbling over the edge with a guttural moan, Juliana stiffened beneath him. Her breath caught on a sob, and then she was coming apart for him. He dimly registered her breathless cries in his ears and her body squeezing his, contracting around him until everything else faded but the agonizing pleasure of being buried inside her.

It seemed to go on forever, shaking and tossing them in its grip until at last Logan felt the tension drain from her body. She went slack, melting against him. His hips ceased their relentless thrusting as the pleasure slowly faded away, leaving them both breathless and sated.

Logan tightened his arms around her and trailed his lips over her neck before collapsing onto his back against the bed. He took her with him, dragging her close so her head was on his chest, and one of her legs thrown over his.

After a time, their breathing evened, and the sweat cooled on their skin. Juliana shivered and burrowed closer, and Logan reached down and drew the coverlet over them.

They didn't speak, but lay quietly together, wrapped in their warm cocoon. Juliana pressed soft kisses on his neck and stroked his chest, but eventually she went still.

Logan continued to stroke her back long after she'd fallen asleep.

He didn't sleep. He held her in his arms, his thoughts in turmoil.

This business with Cowden had to end.

He'd returned to see the man three times since that initial visit, and each time he'd been ushered into his lordship's presence readily enough. Cowden seemed to relish his visits. He was always unfailingly polite—solicitous, even. He offered Logan his finest port, and encouraged him to remain well into the night, chatting or playing at chess or cards.

Cowden was clever, amusing, charming—the consummate host. Anyone watching the two of them together would have imagined they were the best of friends.

Logan knew better.

Cowden was simply toying with him, lying in wait for Logan to make his next move. He knew damn well Logan intended to get the land in Perth, no matter what it took. So, he bided his time, his cold gray eyes scrutinizing Logan's every move, his every breath, and waited for their inevitable clash of swords.

It would come sooner than he expected. Tonight, Logan would visit Lord Cowden one final time, and when he left, he'd take the rights to Cowden's Scottish land with him.

He needed to finish this. He had Juliana and Grace now, and he wanted to begin his life with them as soon as possible, without any shadows or secrets hanging over them.

The sooner he put an end to Cowden's game, the better. The man was dangerous, and this battle with him was going to keep getting uglier until it was resolved. He didn't want Juliana or Grace anywhere near it.

Juliana stirred in her sleep, and he tightened his arms around her and pressed a kiss in her hair. She sighed, nuzzling her cheek against his chest. He gathered her closer against him and waited, eyes open, for morning to come.

Chapter Twenty-two

Juliana got up several times throughout the night to check on Grace, and ended up waking much later the next morning than was her habit. A quick glance out her window revealed it was nearly midday.

Logan was already gone. His coverlet trailed on the floor, and his side of the bed was cold. Before she had a chance to wonder where he was, she heard the soft sound of the connecting door opening, then closing again.

A moment later, Logan appeared at the entrance to her bedchamber. He saw she was awake, and a slow smile curved his lips. Juliana's breath caught, and she knew she would never become accustomed to how handsome he was. Every time she looked at him, her heart beat in a wild frenzy inside her chest.

"Good morning, *mo bhean*." He leaned his hip against the door frame and crossed his arms over his chest. "You look deliciously rumpled and sleepy." His hot blue gaze moved over her face and down her neck, then lingered on the upper curves of her breasts peeking over the edge of the coverlet.

A slow, intense heat washed over Juliana, leaving her flushed and breathless.

"That's a seductive blush, Ana." Logan dropped his arms and straightened away from the door. "You make me want to see how far it goes."

Juliana lifted the sheet and peeked underneath. When she met his gaze again, her lips were quirked in an inviting smile. "Farther than you imagine."

"Oh?" He prowled across the room toward her, blue eyes glittering, and sank down onto the edge of the bed. "Show me."

Juliana let the coverlet drop to her hips and leaned back against the pile of pillows behind her.

A soft hiss left Logan's lips. "How are you so beautiful? You look like a wicked angel, with your wild hair falling everywhere." He caught a long lock in his fingers and drew it over her shoulder so the wavy ends brushed against her nipple. His eyes darkened as he watched it harden, then he leaned forward with a groan and took it into his mouth.

Juliana's back arched sharply under the teasing caress. "Logan." She reached for him and tried to pull him down beside her, but he caught her wrists and pinned them to the bed. He didn't say a word, but teased and licked at one of her nipples, driving her out of her mind with each stroke of his hot tongue.

"Logan..." She tried to move her hands, to tug free so she could sink her fingers into his hair, but again he resisted, holding her down gently as he continued to pleasure her. When he'd worked her nipple into a rigid peak, he dragged his mouth across her chest, dropping a half-dozen kisses there before his lips closed over her other nipple.

Juliana whimpered and squirmed under his relentless caress as he suckled her. When she was gasping and boneless, he released one of her hands and smoothed his palm down her stomach, drawing closer and closer to the place where she wanted him most.

She opened her legs and arched her hips for him, but when he reached the top edge of her curls, his hand stilled. He lifted his head from her breasts and watched her face as he drew lazy circles on the gentle curve of her lower belly. "Will you come for me like this, *mo bhean*?"

"I—I don't know." Dear God, she was going mad from his teasing, every inch of her body taut as she waited for his fingers to stroke her. "Touch me, Logan."

His eyes had gone heavy-lidded. He dragged one harsh breath after another through his parted lips, but even as he grew more aroused, he continued to deny her. He toyed with her, letting his fingers play in her curls, circling closer, but each time he stopped just shy of her center.

"*Dhia*, I could come to release just watching you." He released her other wrist and leaned over her, his breath hot against her ear. "Take my hand, *bòcan*, and put it where you need it."

Juliana didn't hesitate. She pushed his hand down and pressed it directly against her core.

Logan sucked in a harsh breath. "So wet, Juliana. It drives me mad, feeling how wet you are for me." He stroked between her warm folds and gently pinched her aching bud between his fingers. Juliana cried out, and then Logan's lips were at her ear again, his voice a low growl as he urged her on. "Yes, Ana. This is what you want. Now let me give it to you..."

He slid his fingertip over her, and at the same time bent to suck a nipple into his mouth. His tongue stabbed at the turgid peak, and that was all it took. Juliana's back bowed, and a second later she was tumbling headlong into a breathless release.

He stroked and sucked as she shuddered through her climax, his movements ceasing only when she collapsed into a sated heap on the bed. "Every morning, just like this, Juliana." He smiled at her dazed nod, brushed her damp hair away from her face, and leaned down to kiss her forehead.

She gave him a lazy smile, her body so relaxed she might have fallen asleep again if she hadn't wanted to see Grace.

Logan watched her stretch and twist, and a groan fell from his lips. "You make me want to lie in bed with you all day."

"Then why don't you?" He was still breathing hard, and his cheekbones were flushed. Her gaze drifted lower, and...yes, he was fully aroused, his hard length straining against the front of his falls.

"Not today." He brushed the back of his knuckles over her cheek, then rose from the bed.

Juliana sat up straighter against her pillows. For the first time, she noticed he was dressed for riding, and anxiety swelled in her stomach. "Logan? Where are you going?"

"I need to take care of some business," he muttered evasively.

Juliana frowned up at him. "What business?"

His face closed. "Nothing important."

Julian stilled. Business? He had business in Surrey? Was this mysterious business what had kept him here, then? What would happen once he finished it?

Logan blew out a breath. "It's nearly finished, so it's nothing you need worry about."

But Juliana *was* worried. "Why can't you tell me what it is? Perhaps I could help you—"

"No," he said, his tone clipped. "I don't want you involved in this."

Juliana worried her lower lip. She could see argument was useless. She hadn't been with Logan long, but she already recognized that stubborn set to his lips. "It is...dangerous?"

Logan reached forward and gently pulled her lower lip free of her teeth. "Don't harm it. I may want to bite it myself later."

He gave her that slow, seductive smile that usually distracted her, but this time Juliana held onto her wits. "I don't like this, Logan."

His face softened. "You don't need to worry for me, Ana. I'll be fine."
He hesitated, then added, "But I'll be late getting back to Graystone Court.
I hope to return tonight, but it might be early tomorrow morning."

Tomorrow morning? What kind of business would take him away for
an entire day and night?

She opened her mouth to ask, but Logan pressed a finger to her lips to
hush her. "You'll have your hands full with Grace today. I've just come
from seeing her, and the doctor was right. It'll be difficult keeping her in
bed. Take care of her, and I'll be back before you've even missed me."

He raised her hands to his lips, then rose and went to the door.

She watched him, a chill rushing over her skin. She had the strangest
feeling once he walked out that door, she'd never see him again. "I
will miss you."

Logan stopped and turned back to her. "What did you say?"

"I said, I will miss you. I always do."

Logan heaved in a breath, then let it out again. He gazed at her, his
blue eyes soft. He looked as if he was struggling to find the right words
to tell her something, but when he did speak he said only, "I'll miss you
too, *bhean ghràdhach.*"

Then he was gone, and Juliana was left alone.

* * * *

Logan had been right about Grace. By mid-afternoon there wasn't a
single storybook, game, or toy left in all of Graystone Court that could
distract her. She fretted and squirmed and whined like a regular demon
imp until Juliana was nearly driven to distraction.

Grace was generally a sweet, cheerful child, but her aching arm and
the long, dull day spent in her bed had driven her right into a temper. By
the time the sun set at last, she'd worked herself into such a state there was
nothing left for her to do but burst into a flood of tears.

"Where's Grandpapa? Why hasn't he come to see me?"

Juliana sighed. She'd explained to Grace her grandfather had died,
and she knew Grace understood this meant he wasn't coming back, but
understanding a thing and feeling it in one's heart was not the same thing.
"Your grandfather is in heaven now Grace, with your papa and mama. We
won't get to see him anymore. We'll miss him, but we can still love him
even though he's not here, and he'll always love us and watch over us."

Tears stained Grace's cheeks, and her lower lip was trembling. "You mean he won't be able to play with me anymore?"

"No, Gracie. He won't. I'm sorry, sweetheart."

Juliana gathered Grace against her and soothed her with kisses and whispered words until at last Grace cried herself into exhaustion. Juliana tucked her snugly into bed and pulled the coverlet up to her chin.

"We're not going to live here anymore, are we?" Grace stared up at her with big, fearful dark eyes.

"No, darling, we're not. We're going to go live at Rosemount. You remember Rosemount, don't you?" Juliana had taken Grace there a few times in hopes her niece would grow to love the place as much as she did. "There's a stream with a little bridge over it, and the prettiest little walled garden."

"The one with the yellow flowers?"

Juliana smiled. "Daffodils, yes, and dozens of other pretty ones."

"Are there bluebells there?"

Juliana cocked her head. "Hmm. I'm not sure, but we'll certainly go searching for them next spring. Would you like that?"

Grace didn't answer. She was fussing with her coverlet, twisting the corner between her fingers. "Is Mr. Logan coming to Rosemount with us?"

Juliana stilled. It made her chest ache to see how much Grace already loved Logan. Grace's heart was so open, so loving, just as her mother's had been. But Grace had already known so much loss. If she'd learned to love Logan only to have him leave, how would she bear it? How much loss could Grace endure before her heart closed?

"Aunt Juliana? We won't go without Mr. Logan, will we?"

Juliana didn't know what to say. Grace was carefully avoiding her gaze, as well—a sure sign the answer mattered very, very much to her.

But Juliana didn't know the answer.

Logan had been wonderful yesterday. If it hadn't been for his quick actions, Grace's injuries would have been much worse than they were. Juliana hadn't any doubt Logan loved Grace as much as Grace loved him.

After last night, she would have sworn Logan loved *her*, too—that he was as deeply in love with her as she was with him. But if he loved her as she thought he did, why was he still keeping secrets from her? She'd been asking herself that question all day, and as afternoon and early evening wore on without his return, she grew more and more disillusioned.

With every hour that passed, it became harder for Juliana to believe he'd remain in England with her. He'd have to give up everything to stay with her and Grace. Scotland, and his home and his clan. He was laird now, and Juliana knew better than anyone how devoted he was to his people, how seriously he took that obligation.

Their marriage was never meant to be forever. She was his wife now, yes, but she had no real claim on him. If Logan chose to return to Scotland, she had no right to stand in his way.

"Mr. Logan is coming to Rosemount with us, isn't he?"

Tears were filling Grace's eyes again, as if she dreaded hearing the answer, and it tore Juliana apart to see them. Grace had given her heart to Logan as surely as Juliana had. It would be such a cruel turn of fate if she lost him, too.

But Juliana had never once lied to Grace, and she wouldn't start now. "I don't know if he'll come to Rosemount, Grace, but I hope he does."

Grace's face twisted, but she raised her chin bravely and held back her tears. "I hope he does, too." She hesitated, then asked, "Do you love him, Aunt Juliana?"

Juliana reached for Grace's hand and gave it a gentle squeeze. "I do. Very much."

Grace sighed, and her eyes fluttered closed. Juliana thought she'd fallen asleep, but then she felt Grace's little fingers wrap tightly around her hand. "I do, too."

* * * *

Logan didn't return to Graystone Court that night. He'd warned Juliana he might not, but as the hours dragged on, she found that to be little comfort.

She remained beside Grace's bed long after the child had fallen asleep. She must have slept herself, because at some point she woke with a start. The room was dark, and it took a few moments before Juliana could make sense of where she was.

Grace's bedchamber. Grace had had an accident, had broken her arm, and—

Everything else came flooding back then.

Just last night, she'd sat in this same chair with Grace's hand in hers. She'd tried to talk to Logan, to tell him what was in her heart. Had she failed? He'd come to her last night, but then he'd left her again this morning without explaining where he was going, or why.

She patted at Grace's sleeping form until her hands found the child's forehead. Grace's skin was cool, and she was sleeping soundly. She was healing quickly, just as the doctor had promised. Perhaps tomorrow Juliana could let her leave her bed for a brief walk in the garden.

Or maybe it was already tomorrow?

Juliana rose and fumbled through the dark to the window on the other side of the room. She drew the drapes back to peek outside.

It was dark still, but the moon had sunk low, and the sky was already lightening. Juliana watched as the moon sank from view, giving way to the first tentative rays of the sun.

It was tomorrow, and Logan still hadn't returned.

Chapter Twenty-three

The blood was going to be a problem.

It was everywhere. His chest, his arm, his face—even his hair was matted with it. Damn it, there was no way he could hide this much blood from Juliana.

A blood-soaked husband wasn't the sort of thing a wife overlooked.

Logan hadn't realized how gruesome he was until he wandered into the stables and the lad who was mucking out the stalls caught a glimpse of him. The boy's face turned white, and the rake in his hand slipped through his fingers and landed in the hay.

"Zooks, sir, ye look like ye been in a right dust up!" He gaped at the bloodstains on Logan's shirt, his eyes wide.

Logan winced. If the stable boy was shocked at his appearance, Juliana was going to fall into a faint when she saw him. Or worse, she might burst into a flood of tears. Logan shuddered. He'd rather take another knife wound than see Juliana cry.

It would be less painful.

"Ye been in a brawl, sir?" The stable boy was young enough to think any brawl was good sport, but particularly such a wonderfully bloody one.

"It was something like that, ah…what's your name, lad?"

"James, sir."

"James. Would you be so kind as to take my horse?" Logan handed over the reins. "He's been out all night, so make certain he's rubbed down and well fed."

James took the reins, but he was assessing Logan's injuries with the narrow-eyed fascination of a devoted follower of the fancy. "That yer blood, or 'is?"

Logan looked down at his shirt. "Mine."

"Oh." James looked disappointed, but he added generously, "I'm sure ye done well enough, just the same."

Logan couldn't help but grin at that. Boys were bloodthirsty savages. He'd been no different at James's age. "I may be bloody, lad, but I was the only one of the two of us left standing by the end of the brawl."

"That right, then? Plant 'im a facer?" James rubbed his hands together with unmistakable relish. "Sounds like a right good mill."

"Good enough." If it weren't for the blood running down his arm, Logan would consider last night's visit with Lord Cowden a resounding success. Then again, what were a few drops of blood compared to ninety-six acres of fertile land in Perth? Nothing at all. Not even worth thinking about.

Still, his wounds stung like the devil, and they were the least of his problems. His blood-soaked shirt would frighten the wits out of Juliana if she happened to catch sight of him, and that was to say nothing of the uproar that would follow if Grace saw him.

Well, then. He'd simply have to make sure that didn't happen. Graystone Court was a large estate, with dozens of doors. How hard could it be to sneak inside without being seen? "Tell me, James. Have you seen your mistress yet today?"

"Yes, sir. She were out a bit ago with Miss Grace, walking in the garden, but they went back inside." James leaned closer and lowered his voice. "Ye'll want to avoid 'er, I 'spect, ladies not being keen on blood. No gennelman wants that sort o' mill, does 'e?"

"Not if he can avoid it." Logan knew he wouldn't be able to hide his wounds from Juliana forever, but it would be far better for them both if he could wash and change before she saw him.

James nodded wisely. "Well, I can't say fer sure, ye see, but I 'spect her ladyship is with Miss Grace, in Miss Grace's bedchamber. If ye go 'round the back to the music room and go up that staircase, I doubt she'll see ye."

Logan breathed out a sigh of relief. "You're wise beyond your years, James."

"Ye sure ye can make it all that way yerself, sir? Begging yer pardon, but ye're looking a bit peaked." James nodded at Logan's arm. "Yer bleeding all over yerself."

Logan glanced down at his arm, his brows drawing tight at the fresh spurts of blood staining his shirt. It had soaked through the white linen sleeve, and was now doing its best to ruin a perfectly good pair of buckskin breeches. He'd tied his cravat in a tight knot above the gash, but it must be deeper than he'd realized. Clean, too, with smooth edges. A sharpened six-inch blade would do that.

Damn thing would take ages to heal.

His other injury wasn't nearly as bad, though it stretched from under his arm all the way across the left side of his chest. It was a shallow cut, but bloody enough. For all that it wasn't much more than a nasty scratch, it looked as if someone had sliced his chest in two and torn his heart out through the gap.

Very well. Taken together, it was more than a few drops of blood.

"I'll be fine, but be a good man, James, and help me into my coat." The brawl with Cowden's manservant had left him bathed in sweat, and he'd been foolish enough to take his coat off. Later, when he'd been riding home and he'd become chilled from the blood loss he'd tried to put it on again, but his arm had grown so numb and stiff from the injury he hadn't been able to manage it.

"Yes, sir. Good thinking, sir. Yer coat will hide most of them bloodstains, eh?"

"That's the idea, James."

James held up the coat so Logan could slide into it, but it was tightly fitted to his arms and shoulders. Squirming into the cursed thing turned out to be a more painful business than Logan had anticipated. Worse, it opened up the wound in his chest, which started bleeding like the devil again.

"P'haps this weren't such a good idea after all, sir." James eyed him doubtfully. "Ye looked like ye been drubbed when ye came in, and ye look even worse now. Bloodier, I mean."

Logan didn't doubt it. These weren't the worst injuries he'd ever sustained, but they were bad enough to disorient him. By the time he'd got within a few miles of Graystone Court he was shivering with cold, and so dizzy he was obliged to brace himself to keep from toppling off his horse.

He drew his arm free of the coat with a grunt of pain. "Kind of you to say so, James."

"Beg pardon, sir. Mayhap I should help ye inside? Ye don't look steady-like."

Help him? If he dallied any longer, James would have to carry him. "No, no. I'm fine. Thank you, James."

"Aw right, sir." James grimaced as Logan swayed unsteadily. "If yer sure, sir."

"I'm sure."

Logan *had* been sure too, right up until he reached the house and tried to climb the stairs to his bedchamber. If they'd cooperated instead of tilting under his feet it might not have been such a challenge, but no amount of cursing would make them be still. By the time he'd staggered to the top he'd broken out into a cold sweat, and his vision had gone blurry.

No sign of Juliana or Grace, though, and salvation was mere steps away.

He stumbled down the hallway, found his bedchamber door, and managed to get inside and close it behind him without falling to his knees. He rang a servant, then went to the looking glass to assess the damage while he waited for someone to appear.

His eyes widened when he saw his reflection.

It was…a bit worse than he'd thought.

Cowden's servant had succeeded in landing a meaty fist on his jaw before Logan had felled him. It was now swollen to twice its size, and it had turned a disturbing shade of mottled red.

As for the blood…

Mo Dhia. How was he still standing?

The first swipe of the blade had caught him in the upper arm, and his entire shirt sleeve from the shoulder to the wrist was soaked in blood. His chest was a mess as well, the stark white linen smeared with streaks of red gore. And on the side of his head, was that a…?

Damn. How had he not noticed until now that the blackguard had tried to slice his ear off? He hadn't succeeded, thankfully, but not from lack of trying. There was enough dried blood on Logan's temple and in his hair for him to see it had been a near thing.

Ah, well. Wagering was an ugly business, and here was the proof of it.

Cowden had welcomed Logan into his home the evening before with the same apparent pleasure he always did, and he was as solicitous of Logan's comfort as he ever was. Nothing but the best port and the most comfortable chair nearest the fire would do for Mr. Blair. Cowden couldn't have been more charming if Logan had been Prinny himself.

Right up until the moment Cowden began to lose money, that is.

Lord Cowden was skilled at cards, and careful with his wagers. He didn't drink while he played, his attention never wandered, and he didn't let his nerves affect his strategy.

Again, not until he began to lose. When Logan took several hundred pounds off him in one game, Cowden's charming smile had dimmed. When the hundreds turned to thousands, his forehead had beaded with sweat. That was when his lordship's icy control began to desert him.

Just as Logan had predicted it would.

He'd been watching Cowden over the past few days, carefully assessing his strengths and weaknesses. There weren't many chinks in Cowden's armor, but he had the one failing common to those addicted to wagering.

As so often happened with gamers, a big loss led to panic. Panic led to recklessness, and recklessness led to even greater losses. When Logan offered Cowden a chance to win back the thousands he'd lost with a single high-stakes game of piquet, Cowden hadn't hesitated.

He'd wagered, and he'd lost.

As it turned out, Lord Cowden wasn't a gracious loser.

He hadn't wielded the blade himself. Knife fights weren't gentlemanly, and they tended to be messy, what with all the blood. No, Cowden had sent a manservant after Logan instead. He was a big, hulking fellow, the sort who was handy in a brawl.

Not as handy with a knife, though. Much too slow. Likely as not the man rarely had to resort to the blade, given the size of his fists. He was skilled enough to have drawn Logan's blood, but if Cowden had sent the fellow after him to retrieve the paper he'd been obliged to hand over to Logan at the end of the evening, his man had not, alas, been skilled enough to accomplish it.

The slip of paper with Cowden's vowels remained safely tucked away in Logan's coat pocket. He'd had to reduce Cowden's manservant to a bleeding pulp to keep it there, but brawls and bloodshed aside, Logan was several thousand pounds closer to getting what he wanted. For that reason, he was inclined to call the evening a success.

He doubted Juliana would see it that way, however.

He studied his reflection in the mirror with a grimace. Even he was shocked at his appearance, and God knew this wasn't his first brawl, or even his first knife wound. The thought of his tenderhearted wife seeing him in such a state made him sick to his stomach.

Where was that damn servant? He yanked on the bell again, then went back to the mirror. The cravat he'd tied around his upper arm was stained with blood. He didn't dare remove it for fear it would start oozing again, but he'd been smart enough to tie it under his shirt sleeve instead of over it.

Right. He'd just have to remove his shirt himself.

He got the hem free easily enough, but he couldn't stifle a soft hiss of pain when he tried to pull the shirt over his head. Lifting his injured arm was agony. To make matters worse, the linen was stuck to his lacerated skin with dried blood, and nothing short of a hard tug would loosen it.

By the time he'd gotten free of his shirt he was shaking. He gripped the edge of the table with one hand, waiting for the dizziness to pass, but the room was still spinning when the bedchamber door opened behind him.

Logan looked up, hoping to see the servant he'd summoned.

It wasn't a servant.

"Logan?" Juliana's voice was a strangled whisper, and she was staring at him with her hand over her mouth.

It was his wife.

She looked so horrified Logan's head snapped toward the mirror again, and he let out a silent groan as he saw himself the way she must be seeing him. It couldn't have been worse. If he'd spent the entire ride from Cowden's to Graystone Court trying to come up with the best way to terrify her, he couldn't have succeeded any more brilliantly than he was right now.

The bloody cravat, the slashes on his arm and chest. The swollen jaw, the gash in his ear, the blood in his hair...damn it, he hadn't even managed to hide the blood-stained shirt from her. It was still clutched in his fingers.

He tossed it aside, and held up his hands. Then he remembered they too were covered with blood, and he quickly shoved them behind his back. "It's all right, Ana. I'm not hurt."

I'm not hurt? Christ, was that the best he could do? His wife wasn't a fool. Anyone could see he *was* hurt—people with blood smeared across their chests generally were. "That is, I am hurt, but it's not as bad as it looks."

She was shaking her head, her other hand now pressing against her stomach as if she feared she would be sick. Something dark descended on Logan as he stared at her, something he'd never felt before.

Helplessness.

He'd done this to her. He'd put that look of horror on her face. He wanted to go to her, to take her into his arms, but the thought of staining her with his blood made him recoil.

He couldn't comfort her. He didn't know how to help her.

Not once had Logan ever failed to justify his clan's faith in him. Illness, injury, sick or lost children—whatever the crisis, his clan turned to him when despair threatened, and he found a way to take care of them.

But now, faced with his silent, trembling wife, he didn't know what he could say or do to take care of *her*. Her, the one person in the world he wanted to protect more than any other. Why couldn't he care for her? How could the powerful love he felt for her make him so weak?

His helplessness overwhelmed him, nearly knocking him to his knees. It was stronger than anything he'd ever known. Stronger than the ferocity that had saved his life tonight. Stronger than the four long years of anger and grief he'd carried inside him since the day he watched Rosal Township burn. Stronger even than the will his father had instilled in him, the loyalty and devotion that made him fight to protect his clan.

Strong enough to defeat him.

It all caught up to him then. The burning pain he'd been denying, the blood loss, the long ride from Lord Cowden's, the chill he couldn't overcome—it all slammed down on him at once, and he staggered from the blow.

A soft cry tore from Juliana's lips. Logan's gaze darted to her face. He could see the exact moment when she put aside her confusion and fear, and focused on the one thing that mattered the most to her.

Him.

In an instant, her entire demeanor changed. She dropped her hands to her sides, flung her shoulders back, and pressed her lips together with determination. "Logan."

He was fading in and out, but Logan felt her hands slide around his waist, the brush of her fragrant hair against his shoulder. She was speaking to him, saying something else, but he couldn't hear her. He knew only that she was supporting him—*she*, his wee wife, supporting *him*.

His arm must be so heavy across her slender shoulders, but they were moving together, slowly, across the room toward the bed.

He fell onto it with a grunt. The ceiling above him was spinning and weaving, and he couldn't feel Juliana beside him anymore. He reached out for her, a plea on his lips, and then she was there again. Her small hand slipped into his. He heard her voice, saying something about a basin of water and bandages, but he couldn't make sense of it.

Bandages…who needed bandages? Who—

He shot up, struggling to rise from the bed. Grace. She'd fallen off her horse. She was hurt, and he had to get to her before her horse trampled her—

"No, Logan. Lie down."

Soft hands were holding him to the bed, and the sweetest voice he'd ever heard—*her* voice—was low in his ear, murmuring to him. He couldn't tell what she said, but he went still, listening eagerly. A cool hand stroked his hair back from his face as the room darkened and faded to black around him. She leaned over him, still whispering soothingly, and he knew then, in a way he hadn't known before…

If he was given the chance, he'd listen to her voice forever.

Chapter Twenty-four

"Let me see if I have this right, Lady Juliana." The doctor snapped his bag closed and rose from the chair beside Logan's bed. "First Miss Grace tumbles off her horse, and now Mr. Blair finds himself at the wrong end of a blade, all in the space of two short days?"

Juliana grimaced. Had it only been two days? It felt as if weeks had passed since Grace's fall. "I'm afraid so."

"A broken arm, a mild concussion, and now a half-dozen knife wounds." The doctor shook his head. "I don't know what's come over you all, but I advise you to take the greatest care of yourself, my lady. We don't need any more injuries at Graystone Court."

"No, indeed we don't," Juliana agreed, glancing down at Logan. He looked much better now he was no longer drenched in blood, but between his chest, arm, and ear he was half-smothered in bandages.

"Good. Now, how does Grace get on? Healing properly, I trust?"

Juliana nodded. "Properly, and quickly. I'm amazed at how much energy she has already."

"That's the way with children. She'll be running about before Mr. Blair here is." The doctor turned a stern look on Logan. "Remain in bed until your chest injury heals. It's an awkward place for a wound. If you don't take care you'll tear it open, and then we'll have a festering infection on our hands."

Logan didn't argue, but Juliana recognized the obstinate twist of his lips. It was going to be a battle, keeping him immobilized. A small six-year-old child was one thing, but an enormous, stubborn Scot quite another.

"I'll see myself out." The doctor waved Juliana away when she moved to follow him to the door. "Keep an eye on our patient, my lady. He looks like the sort who'll be out of that bed as soon as you turn your back on him."

Juliana crossed her arms over her chest, eyeing Logan. No doubt he'd do his best to escape, but she was just as stubborn as he was. She'd lock him in this bedchamber and station her two largest footmen outside the door if she had to, but Logan would *not* be stirring from that bed.

She'd had quite enough of this. Logan was keeping a secret from her, and she intended to find out what it was before it killed him.

The doctor closed the door behind him, and Juliana crossed back to Logan and perched on the edge of the bed. A dozen questions were racing through her mind, but she didn't venture a word. She simply looked Logan in the eye and waited. She'd used this same tactic on Grace before, and really, men weren't so different from children when it came to illness or injury, were they?

If she held her tongue long enough, he'd confess. The guilty always did.

Logan looked down at his hands, then toward the window, then he made a great show of inspecting the dressing on his arm, but at last he could stand it no longer and his pleading blue eyes met hers. "It's not as bad as you think."

"Oh?" She folded her hands in her lap. "Tell me, Logan. What do I think?"

He grimaced at her tone. "You think I got into a brawl."

Juliana raised an eyebrow, but said nothing.

Logan squirmed in the bed. "That is, I *did* get into a brawl, but not for the reasons you think."

Another eloquent raise of the eyebrow. "And what do I think were your reasons for this brawl?"

Logan kicked at the covers, but didn't answer.

"If you're quite finished with telling me what I think, then I'd be pleased to hear the truth. Tell me where you've been going the past few days."

The obstinate twist returned to Logan's lips. "There's nothing to tell. By this time tomorrow it'll be over, and it won't matter any—"

"No."

"*No?*" Logan's brows pinched together. "What does that mean?"

"Look at me." Juliana leaned over him, forcing him to meet her gaze. "Yesterday morning you left without a word of explanation. This morning you returned—a full day later—covered in blood and bruises. Now you're telling me it doesn't matter, and it sounds as if you're planning to go off tonight to let whoever stabbed you finish the job. Well, I won't have it, Logan. You're my husband, and you owe me an explanation."

Logan dropped his gaze, a guilty flush on his cheeks. "I knew you'd worry if I told you, and I didn't want—"

"Do you suppose I *didn't* worry because you chose not to tell me? I spent the entire night waiting for you, hoping every moment for your return. But when you did return at last, you..." Juliana's voice hitched. "How do you think I felt, seeing you hurt and bleeding? I thought you were—"

"*Please* don't cry." Logan took her hand. "I'm sorry I worried you, *bhean*. For the past few days I've been working to fulfill a promise I made to Fitz before we left Castle Kinross. It should have been an easy enough task, but it turned ugly. I don't want you involved in it."

"What did you promise?" Fitz hadn't said a word to *her* about any promise, and now Juliana was beginning to see why. "What did you tell him you'd do?" When Logan didn't answer right away, Juliana drew her hand away. "No more secrets. I have a right to know."

Logan blew out a long breath. "Fitz wants to buy some land in Perth. He asked me to make an offer on it, but the blackguard who owns it refuses to sell. He's planning to toss Clan Murray aside to make way for Cheviot sheep."

"What blackguard is this?" Juliana asked, but a shiver of fear was already creeping down her spine. No, it couldn't be. Fitzwilliam knew how dangerous Benedict was. Surely, he wouldn't ask Logan to risk his safety.

"Lord Cowden." Logan spat the name. "He owes thousands of pounds in gaming debts. Every gentleman in England holds his vowels. Fitz hoped the debts of honor would induce him to sell, but Cowden refused."

Juliana wasn't surprised. As well as Fitzwilliam knew Benedict, he'd never really understood how deep Benedict's malice went. No practical concern like money could ever outweigh Benedict's thirst for revenge.

Benedict would never sell. Not because he gave a fig for the land. No, he'd do it for the pleasure of thwarting Fitzwilliam. He would act against his own interests to keep Fitzwilliam from having something he wanted. That was the sort of man Benedict was.

"I've been calling on him this past week to see if I could find a way to persuade him to sell, but he's held fast. So, last night I challenged him to a wager, and—"

"And he lost," Juliana whispered, her voice unsteady. She knew better than anyone a loss wouldn't stop Benedict. It would only make him more desperate, more ruthless, and more dangerous. He'd never give up that land to Fitzwilliam, no matter how many wagers he lost.

"He lost." Logan took her hand again. "Two thousand pounds, on a single game of piquet."

"*Two thousand pounds!*" Juliana gasped. Dear God, it was a fortune.

"Aye. He wasn't pleased. I left with his vowels in my pocket, and he sent his manservant after me to retrieve them. We got into a, ah…scuffle."

"A *scuffle*! Is that what you call it? You came back here carved up like a Christmas goose!"

Logan grinned at that description. "It's not as bad as all that. But aye, the scoundrel had a blade, and he managed to get in a few slices before I left him bleeding in Lord Cowden's stable yard."

Juliana shook her head. Logan considered the matter settled because he held Benedict's vowels, but the opposite was true. This business between Benedict and Logan had just begun. "What happened to Lord Cowden's vowels? Did his manservant get them back?" If he had, it might put an end to this, but if he hadn't…

"No, of course not." Logan looked offended. "The paper is in my coat pocket. I don't want the money, just the land in Perth. Cowden has too many debts to be able to meet them all, even with his wife's money. He loses another wager with me and he'll have no choice but to settle his debt with the property."

No choice? A man like Benedict—the sort who'd stop at nothing to win no matter what it cost—always had a choice. "What do you intend to do now?"

Logan shrugged, as if the thing were as good as settled. "Go back to Cowden's tomorrow, challenge him to another wager, and then another until he gives up the land in exchange for his vowels. That will finish the cursed business."

Oh, no. A chill rushed over Juliana's skin. It was madness to suppose Benedict would simply give up the Perth land without a murmur, no matter how many thousands he lost. He was far more likely to order his manservant to attack Logan again. He'd done so once. What was there to stop him from making a second attempt? How far would Benedict take it, before he'd admit defeat?

Juliana couldn't be sure, but she knew this: he'd take it much further than she'd ever willingly let Logan go.

She clutched at Logan's hand, dread lodging in her stomach. "You don't understand who he is, Logan. He won't behave honorably. What if he loses again, but refuses to settle the debt?"

Logan let out a short laugh, but his blue eyes were hard. "I don't plan to give him a choice, *mo bhean*."

Juliana swallowed. Benedict would be equally as determined not to give Logan a choice. It would end with another brawl, or worse. She hadn't the slightest doubt of it, and with Logan in this weakened condition…

He might brush off his injuries, but he was pale with exhaustion and blood loss, and he was in a good deal of pain. He was trying to hide it from her, but his lips were white at the edges, and every time he stirred in the bed she saw him wince. Logan was a big, powerful man, but as strong as he was, he was still flesh and bone. There was no way he could withstand more injuries.

If this manservant should attack him a second time…

Juliana thought quickly. There had to be another way to settle this, one that didn't involve any more brawls, or another stabbing. Something civilized, like some sort of trade, or exchange. Not money, though. Benedict would always choose revenge over money, no matter how deep his debts. No, it had to be something else. She had to offer him something he knew it would hurt her to lose—

Juliana sucked in a quiet breath. There was only one thing she had she was willing to offer him. One thing it would cause her so much pain to lose, it would be enough to satisfy even Benedict.

Bile flooded her throat at the thought of seeing him again. She was no coward, but there were some people it was wise to fear, and Benedict Reid was one of them.

Logan squeezed her hand. "I've dealt with much worse than this, Juliana. It's going to be all right. I promise you."

Juliana gave him a vague nod, but her thoughts were in a whirl. It would need to be done at once, this afternoon. Logan would insist on returning to Benedict's tomorrow. She wanted the business settled well in advance of that.

She hadn't any doubt Benedict would receive her. He wouldn't be able to resist.

All she needed now was for Logan to go to sleep and she'd duck out. She'd be back at Graystone Court before he even knew she'd gone. If he knew what she intended to do, he'd stop at nothing to prevent her.

She rose from the bed, reached behind him to plump his pillows, and pulled the coverlet over him. "You need to rest, Logan. Go to sleep."

She began to move away, but he grabbed her hand. "I don't feel like sleeping. Come to bed, *galla*."

Juliana stared down at him, openmouthed. "You must be jesting."

"I'd never jest about something so important." He drew her toward him with much more strength than she'd expect from a man in his weakened state. She tugged her hand free, but a smile rose to Juliana's lips. He really was incorrigible. "Later." She leaned over and pressed a kiss to his forehead. "After you've rested."

"A man doesn't want a rest after a brawl. He wants his woman," he grumbled, but he allowed her to ease him back against the pillows. She took the chair beside the bed and stroked his hair until his eyes grew heavy, and his breaths became slow and even.

Once he was asleep, Juliana crept across the room and took up his coat. She found the paper with Benedict's vowels tucked into one of the pockets.

She found something else, as well, and drew it out, frowning.

It was a stone, with a rough carving etched into its hard, flat surface. Juliana held it up to the light of the window, trying to make out what it said. It almost looked like...

It was. The letters J and L, and underneath them a date.

Their wedding day.

She ran a fingertip over the rough carving, sudden tears gathering in her eyes.

Logan had made them an oathing stone. Somehow, Juliana knew he'd carved it himself, though he'd never mentioned it, and he'd never shown it to her. She turned back toward the bed, and her gaze landed on Logan's face. She couldn't say exactly when it had happened, but somewhere between Castle Kinross and Graystone Court, his face had come to mean the world to her.

Her fingers closed around the stone. She wanted to slip it into her own pocket and take it with her for luck, but after thinking about it, she reluctantly returned the stone to Logan's coat pocket.

It wasn't hers. If he'd wanted her to have it, he'd have given it to her.

* * * *

Benedict liked to keep people waiting. It made him feel powerful.

Still, Juliana wasn't surprised when he appeared in the drawing room soon after she arrived. She'd predicted he'd be eager to toy with her, and she could see by the gleam in his cold gray eyes she'd been right.

"Lady Juliana. Why, what a delightful surprise. It's been months since I had the pleasure of your company, but here you are, as lovely as ever." He took her hand and raised it to his lips, his eyes flashing with triumph when she flinched at his touch.

"Good afternoon, my lord. This isn't a social call, as I'm sure you're aware. I have some business to discuss with you." Juliana's words were clipped. If he could, Benedict would do everything in his power to drag out this moment between them. She wouldn't allow it. The sooner she could escape his drawing room, the better.

"Business?" He took a seat on the settee, sitting far too close to her. "I can't imagine what sort of business you could have with me."

Juliana shifted away from him. "Come now, Benedict. We both know that's not true. Let's be honest with each other, shall we?"

He didn't answer. Instead he pressed the tips of his fingers together under his chin, and regarded her with that icy stare.

Juliana suppressed a shiver. She never could bear to look into Benedict's eyes. It was like looking into an abyss. She dropped her gaze, reached into the bag at her side and retrieved the slip of paper she'd taken from Logan's coat pocket. She held it out to Benedict. "Does this look familiar to you?"

Benedict didn't take the paper. His gaze flicked to it, then back to her face. "Perhaps it does."

"They're your vowels, Benedict. It seems you owe my husband two thousand pounds."

The moment she mentioned Logan, a cruel smiled drifted across Benedict's lips. "Ah, yes. Mr. Blair. I'm relieved to find he made it home safely after our game last night. My man Rowley mentioned something about a disturbance. You should warn your husband to be more careful, Juliana."

Juliana managed a casual shrug, but her heart was pounding. "Perhaps you should deliver the same warning to your manservant. From the account I heard, he got the worst of it."

Benedict didn't care for that reminder. His smile faded and his eyes narrowed, but when he spoke, he was as cool and charming as ever. "I can only hope your husband's good fortune continues."

Juliana recognized Benedict's words for the threat they were, and her mouth went dry. "That's what I came to discuss with you."

"What, your husband's good fortune, or the lack thereof?" Benedict laughed. "My dear Juliana, what can I possibly have to say to it?"

Juliana didn't bother to answer that question. Instead she nodded at the slip of paper with Benedict's vowels, which she'd placed on the table between them. "You know very well my husband doesn't want your money. He wants the land in Perth. I do wonder, though, whether that really matters. It occurs to me, Benedict, you may not honor the debt."

Benedict gave her a mocking smile and laid a hand on his chest. "You wound me. I'm a gentleman, Lady Juliana. A gentleman always honors his debts."

Juliana looked at him, a loathing unlike anything she'd ever known burning in her chest. This man had tried to force her to marry him. He'd taken advantage of her father when he was too ill to defend himself. Benedict had done everything he could to take Grace away from her, and last night he'd sent his manservant out to hurt Logan. If Benedict got the chance, she hadn't the slightest doubt he'd do it again.

He wasn't a gentleman. He was a monster, and she was done pretending otherwise. "But that's just it, Benedict. You're *not* a gentleman. We both know you haven't the least intention of letting go of your Scottish lands, because that would mean giving Fitzwilliam something he wants. You'd sooner send your man after Logan again than do that, wouldn't you? Tell me, Benedict. Just how far will your thirst for revenge take you? Will you stop short of murder?"

"How melodramatic you are, Juliana." Benedict laughed, and Juliana could see by the malicious glitter in his eyes he was relishing every moment of this confrontation with her.

"No, I don't think I am. You forget how well I know you." She nodded at the paper again. "But I don't intend to find out how far you'll take this. I've come to collect the deed to the Scottish lands from you. In return, I'll give you back that paper, and something else, as well. Something you've always wanted."

He laughed. "You flatter yourself, my lady. Perhaps there was a time I wanted something from you, but that time has long since passed. You don't have a single thing I desire, Lady Juliana."

"But I do, my lord." She reached into the bag she'd brought, pulled out some papers, and dropped them on the table on top of Benedict's vowels. "I have Rosemount."

Juliana couldn't hide the quaver in her voice when she said it. She and Fitzwilliam and Jonathan had spent so many happy times there when they were children. Jonathan had taken Emma there after their marriage, and later, after Grace was born, they'd all gone together as a family. They'd wandered in the tiny garden admiring the wild roses, and lingered on the bridge to throw stones into the stream below.

So many of her happiest memories were tied to Rosemount. It had always felt like more of a home to her than Graystone Court, perhaps because it was her only connection to the mother she'd never known. She'd wanted so badly to take Grace there, and make a home with her.

To lose Rosemount to Benedict—to think of *him* in that beautiful place, poisoning it with his presence—was enough to make her gasp with pain.

That, of course, was the reason Benedict wanted it.

He didn't have any use for Rosemount. He had a dozen or more other properties, some of which he'd never even bothered to visit, many of them much grander than Rosemount. In monetary terms, the estate was no more valuable to him than the carpet under their feet, or the fine porcelain vase resting on the end table.

In emotional terms, however, it was priceless. Benedict knew it would break her heart to give it up, and that was why he wouldn't be able to resist taking it from her. He'd always been that man—the one who gloried in taking what he had no right to, for the sheer pleasure of keeping someone who loved it from having it.

"Rosemount?" Benedict looked shocked. He hadn't expected she'd offer him Rosemount. "You'd actually give up your mother's estate for some remote patch of scrub brush in the Scottish Highlands?"

No. She'd give it up for Fitzwilliam, who'd treat Clan Murray with the respect they deserved. For Logan, and for the people he loved.

She didn't tell Benedict that, however. She simply stared at him and waited, until at last he shook his head. "I accept your offer, Lady Juliana. Indeed, how could I refuse?"

For the first time since she'd entered his house, Juliana smiled. He *couldn't* refuse. Perhaps another sort of man could, but not Benedict. She'd known that before she crossed the threshold.

Benedict studied her for a moment, then his lips curved in a mocking smile. "You love him, don't you? The Scot. Ah, my lady. I thought you were smarter than that. Indeed, I pity you."

He pitied *her*? Juliana flicked her gaze over Benedict's face, then looked away. How predictable he was. "That's just what I'd expect a man like you to say."

Half an hour later she was riding away from Benedict's estate, the deed to the land in Perth tucked safely into a saddlebag. She cast nervous glances over her shoulder the entire way back to Graystone Court, but no one followed her. Not Benedict, and not his knife-wielding manservant. Perhaps there was a line even a villain like Benedict wouldn't cross. Perhaps he did retain a meager shred of his humanity, but Juliana wouldn't wager on it.

Benedict would never be able to comprehend the kind of love that would make a person give up something they cherished, something it hurt them to lose, for another person.

There was nothing she had she wouldn't give up for Logan's sake.

Not even Logan himself.

Once he had the deed to the Perth land in his hand, there would no longer be anything keeping Logan in England. As soon as he was healed enough to travel, there was every chance he'd leave Surrey behind.

And with it, Juliana and Grace.

She given up Rosemount today, but that wasn't the loss that was tearing her heart to shreds.

It was that she might also have given up Logan.

Chapter Twenty-five

It took Logan half an hour to struggle free of the heavy sleep that had held him pinned to the bed all afternoon. When he managed to drag himself into consciousness at last, he made several unwelcome discoveries.

He was in a bed in a darkened room, his arm was screaming in pain, and Juliana was gone. He sat up and dragged a hand down his face as his sluggish brain fought to process all these mysteries at once.

Something was wrong. He felt as if someone had beaten him with a fireplace poker. His ear stung, his jaw throbbed, his chest was burning, and his arm...*Mo Dhia*, what was wrong with his arm?

He twisted in the bed to get a look at it. A low groan left his lips as pain sliced through him, setting every inch of skin above his elbow on fire. He blinked down at the blood-stained bandage wrapped tightly around his upper arm, confused.

Blood. There'd been blood, hadn't there? He remembered being surprised at how much of it there was. He'd been covered with it, his shirt soaked in it. He hadn't wanted Juliana to see him, but she'd been there, her low, sweet voice in his ear, her fingers stroking his hair, caressing his face—

Cowden.

Logan struggled for breath as memories of last night and this morning crashed down on him. The wager, the brawl with Cowden's manservant, the ride back to Graystone Court, and Juliana, always Juliana...the horror on her face when she'd seen him, her hands holding him gently against the bed, his crushing sense of helplessness...

She'd had the doctor in to dress his wounds, but that had been hours ago. Why was it so dark? He couldn't have slept the entire afternoon and into the night. He squinted at the window, and saw Juliana had drawn the drapes closed before she left him alone.

Logan grunted with pain as he rose from the bed and padded across the room to the window. He pushed the drapes aside, cursing as another arc of pain shot across his chest.

It wasn't nighttime, but late afternoon. Juliana was likely with Grace.

He turned away from the window, frowning at the empty room. There was no telling how long she'd been gone, or when she would return. What was he meant to do until she did? Damned if he knew. He hadn't spent an afternoon in his bed since he'd poisoned himself with the laburnum when he was a lad.

Not alone, that is.

Logan wandered back across the room to the side of the rumpled bed, eyeing it with distaste. Juliana had told him to sleep, but he'd never been one for lying about. A few cuts and scratches weren't going to change that.

He could eat. He wasn't hungry, but a meal would distract him until Juliana returned. He went to pull the bell to summon a servant, but paused when he saw the coat he'd worn last night tossed over the back of a chair.

He'd left Cowden's vowels in the pocket. Any one of the servants could have wandered in here and taken the coat away while he was sleeping. Even bloody knife wounds didn't excuse such carelessness.

He took the coat up and rifled through it, searching for the slip of paper. It wasn't there.

No, it was impossible. It had to be there.

He searched through it again, digging deep into the pockets, but once again the search revealed nothing. He turned the coat upside down and shook it, wincing at the pain in his arm. Something dropped to the floor with a thud, and Logan reached down to pick it up.

It was the oathing stone he'd made for Juliana.

He stared down at it, a thousand different emotions flooding his chest at once. He hadn't known it at the time—or at least he hadn't yet admitted it to himself—but he'd been in love with her when he carved this stone.

Just as he was in love with her now.

Logan closed the stone tightly in his fist. He'd brought it all the way from Scotland with him. He'd kept it with him every day since then, tucked into the breast pocket of whatever coat he was wearing. All this time, he'd kept it close to his heart.

Just as he meant to keep Juliana close to his heart. Her, and Grace. They were *his* now.

And he was theirs.

He should have told her that the night before last, when they'd made love. He should have given her the stone then, and explained that he'd made it for her. That he'd loved her even then, all those weeks ago.

Logan gazed down at the stone, heavy in his palm. Heavier than it should be, because it didn't belong to him. It belonged to her. It always had. As soon as she returned to him he'd give it to her, and with it, his whole heart.

But first, Cowden's vowels. They had to be here. Logan drew in a deep breath and forced himself to search the pockets again, slowly and methodically.

He turned up nothing. The slip of paper was truly gone.

Logan dropped the coat back onto the chair. It didn't make sense. The oathing stone was right where he'd left it, but the paper was gone. If someone had dropped the coat—if the paper had fallen out by accident—then the stone would be missing, as well.

It could only mean one thing. Someone had taken the paper deliberately. Juliana? It must be. He'd told her he had Cowden's vowels in his pocket. No one else knew that paper was there, aside from…

Aside from Cowden, and Cowden's murderous manservant.

Logan's blood went cold.

No. Again, it was impossible. Even Cowden wasn't that brazen. And if he was, how would he manage the thing? It wasn't as if he could march into Logan's bedchamber and rifle through his coat until he found it.

No, but a servant could. It would be the easiest thing in the world for a servant to wait for Juliana to leave, then creep into his bedchamber and take the paper while he slept.

Could Cowden have bribed one of Juliana's servants?

If it were anyone but Cowden, Logan would dismiss the idea as ridiculous. But was it really too far-fetched to imagine a man who'd sent his manservant after Logan with a blade would draw the line at bribery?

Or worse.

What if Cowden was in even greater financial troubles than Fitz realized? If Cowden was desperate enough to send his man to open Logan's throat, what else might he do? How far might he go? Was he desperate enough to try and hurt Juliana, or Grace?

There was only one way to find out.

Struggling into his clothes was harder than Logan had anticipated. The boots were the worst, but he managed it. Juliana was going to be furious when she caught him out of bed, but he couldn't wait for her to return to his bedchamber. He needed to see her at once, as much to find out if she'd taken the paper as to reassure himself she and Grace were all right.

But a search of the house didn't turn up either of them, and none of the servants knew where they'd gone. Neither Juliana or Grace had been seen for several hours.

Damn it, where were they? Grace was injured, and though she was recovering quickly, she still grew tired in the afternoons. There was no way Juliana would have taken her far from Graystone Court.

Not willingly.

Logan's heart pounded as he made his way as quickly as he could to the stables. By the time he got there he was out of breath, and his arm was bleeding again. He called for James, and to his great relief the lad appeared at once.

When he saw Logan standing there, he winced. "Begging yer pardon, sir, but shouldn't ye be in yer bed?"

Logan waved this off. "No. I've been in bed all day. I'm looking for Lady Juliana, James. Have you seen her?"

"I did see 'er, yes. She and Miss Grace was out again this afternoon, wandering about in the rose garden. That were some time ago, though."

"How long?"

James's face creased in thought. "Hour ago, maybe? Maybe more."

An hour? That was an eternity. If Cowden was intent on harming someone at Graystone Court, an hour was plenty of time to accomplish it. "Think carefully, James. Where were they exactly the last time you saw them?"

James caught the panic in Logan's voice and his eyes went wide. "Toward the woods, I think, sir. Miss Grace likes the bluebells—"

The woods. Anyone could have come upon them there, and no one in the house or the stables would be any the wiser. "Saddle Finnegan for me, James. Quickly, lad."

James swallowed. "Yes, sir. Right away, sir."

Logan waited in an agony of impatience as James ran off to do his bidding.

Lord Cowden was either going to be very surprised to see him, or not surprised at all.

* * * *

Logan returned to Graystone Court less than two hours later. It hadn't been a pleasant visit. At least, not for Logan. Lord Cowden had seemed to find it much more satisfying.

His lordship had been overjoyed to find Logan once again in his drawing room, and no wonder. To have the chance to tell Logan, in explicit detail about the bargain he'd made with Juliana—a bargain Logan clearly didn't know a thing about—had likely given Lord Cowden more pleasure than any other moment in his life.

It rankled, but that was the least of it.

Logan went straight to his bedchamber upon his return. Juliana was there waiting for him, pacing and wringing her hands. She whirled around when he opened the bedchamber door and started to rush toward him, but when she saw his face, she stopped. "Logan! I was worried sick! Where have you—"

"Where were you and Grace this afternoon, Juliana?" Logan was more upset than he'd ever been in his life, but he took great care to keep his voice calm.

Juliana's gaze swept over him, and her green eyes went wide with shock. "You've been out *riding*? After the doctor specifically told you to stay in bed? Why, Logan?"

"I went to call on Lord Cowden. We had an interesting talk. But you haven't answered my question, Juliana. Where were you and Grace this afternoon?"

Juliana didn't seem to hear him. Her gaze darted between his arm and his chest, her face going pale when she saw the blood that had seeped through the white bandages. "You've opened your wounds again. You're *hurt*. Why, Logan? Why would you go there again? He nearly had you killed this morning! Don't you understand what he's capable of? He's dangerous—"

"Stop it, Juliana." Logan crossed the room and grasped her by the shoulders. "I *know* how dangerous he is, so you can imagine how terrified I was to find you went to see him earlier this afternoon, alone, without telling anyone where you were going!"

He jerked away from her and crossed to the other side of the room, his hands clutching his hair. *Mo Dhia*, he couldn't remember ever being in such turmoil in his life. Part of him wanted to shout at her, and the other part wanted to snatch her to his chest, bury his face in her hair, and beg her never, *never* to risk herself like that again.

Juliana didn't answer. When Logan turned around she was standing where he'd left her, as white and still as a marble statue.

Logan struggled to take in a calming breath. "I'm not going to ask you again, Juliana. Where did you take Grace this afternoon?"

"The rose garden, then the bluebell wood," she whispered.

The bluebell wood, just as James had said. If he'd simply gone to the wood he would have found them there, but instead he'd rushed off to Cowden's like a damn fool. He saw his mistake now, but at the time he'd been so hazy with panic he couldn't think at all. "Did it occur to you, even for a moment, I might be worried when I couldn't find you?"

"I—I didn't think you'd wake up so soon."

"But I did wake up, Juliana. I woke up and found you, Grace, and Lord Cowden's vowels all missing. I thought…" Logan didn't want to say what he'd thought, or ever think about it again.

She took a hesitant step toward him. "I'm sorry. I never meant to worry—"

"You gave Cowden Rosemount." Logan's voice was flat, his chest heavy with anguish. "Damn it, Juliana. *Why?*"

The words tore from his throat. Juliana recoiled at his harsh tone, his clenched fists. Once again Logan fought for breath, fought for calm, but he knew it was futile. There wasn't enough air in all of Surrey to reconcile him to what she'd lost.

No, not lost. Given up. For *him*.

"I didn't *give* it to him, Logan. I traded it for the land in Perth. I was going to explain everything to you this evening, after you woke. I never intended to keep it from you."

Logan let out a bitter laugh. "You could hardly hide it from me, could you? According to Cowden, you have the deed to the Perth land!"

She reached out a hand to him. "Look at me, Logan. Why are you so angry?"

Logan did look at her, and the plea in her green eyes nearly undid him. He ached to take her hand and draw her against him, but he didn't move. "I told you I'd take care of this business with Cowden, Juliana. Did you think I couldn't manage it on my own? Is that why you went to him behind my back?"

Juliana looked shocked. "No! How can you think so?"

It hurt Logan to think she'd doubted him, but even that wasn't the worst of it.

The worst part, the part he couldn't bear thinking about, was that Juliana had endangered herself for him. She'd lost her mother's estate—a place that had been a home to her, a place she cared deeply about—for *him*.

He was supposed to take care of *her*, to protect *her*.

That she'd lost something so precious to her for his sake was unbearable.

"You and Fitzwilliam want the Perth land, and I knew Benedict would never give it to you." Juliana's voice had gone high and thready. It was the voice of someone who was desperate to be understood, and was afraid she wouldn't be. "Don't you see, Logan? You could have bested him in wager after wager and won thousands of pounds, and he still would have found a way to keep you from getting that land. It never would have ended."

"Why were you so desperate for it to end, Juliana? Was it because you knew I wouldn't leave England until I got the Perth land? Are you that anxious to be rid of me, that you'd give up so much?"

His words landed with a deafening crash between them. Juliana's throat worked, but she said nothing, and a heavy silence fell between them. For the first time since he'd come into the room, she didn't look distraught. Her shoulders went rigid, and the paleness in her cheeks gave way to bright spots of color.

She wasn't sad or distressed or confused anymore. She was angry. "Is that what you think, Logan? That I gave up my home to a man I despise because I want to be *rid of you*? You truly can't think of any other reason why I might have done such a thing?"

Juliana wasn't just angry, she was furious. Her eyes were on fire, and her entire body was trembling. Logan ran a weary hand through his hair, then let his arm fall limply back to his side. Christ, he didn't know anymore what he thought. His chest was bleeding again, his arm hurt like the devil, and he couldn't make sense of any of this. "I don't pretend to understand why you did it, Juliana, but if it was a ploy to get rid of me, you've made a grave miscalculation."

"A miscalculation?" A bitter laugh fell from her lips. "What does that mean? That my nefarious plan to be rid of you has failed, and you're not going back to Scotland?"

There was a strange, hard quality in her voice that worried him, but Logan was too exhausted to work out what it meant. "Oh, I'm going. We all are. You, me, and Grace."

She stared at him, too stunned at first to say a word. "Logan," she began, but he cut her off.

"If you think I'm going to leave you and Grace here where Cowden can get at you, you're mistaken, Ana. You're *mine* now, and I take care of what's mine."

Juliana said nothing, but her beautiful green eyes were so shadowed with hurt he had to look away from her.

"As soon as Grace and I are healed enough to travel, we leave for Scotland."

Chapter Twenty-six

Three days later

They traveled from Guildford to London, then continued north past Leeds and York. Then further north still, to Edinburgh and Perth, and from there to Dalwhinnie, Etteridge, Newtownmore, Aviemore, and, at last...

From Aviemore to the Sassy Lassie in Inverness.

Juliana had taken the same journey twice before. Once when she'd been on her quest to find Fitzwilliam, then again with Logan, except in reverse. They'd traveled this same route, on these same roads, and spent the night at the same inns along the way. It was astounding really, the sameness of it, when everything else in her life had changed so drastically.

The return to Scotland should have been a joyous occasion. If she'd been returning for any other reason than the one she was, she would have been ecstatic. In the short time she'd been at Castle Kinross she'd grown to love everything about it. Ruthven Burn, the Laburnum Arch, the wild blue poppies. Emilia and Fitzwilliam, the Robertson brothers, Mrs. Craig with her gooseberries, and Fiona, with her soft, woolly white head.

A return to Scotland should have filled her heart with delight, but as it was...

As it was, Logan had ruined everything.

Juliana glanced at him, seated across from her in the carriage. His mouth was tight, his blue eyes bleak. They hadn't spoken more than a handful of words to each other during the entire journey. They stopped each evening at twilight, dined together, then bid each other a polite good night and retired to separate bedchambers. Juliana slept with Grace, and Logan slept alone.

"Grace." Juliana tore her gaze from Logan's face and turned to her niece. "Please stop kicking the seat. Be still, won't you?"

Grace's mouth pulled into a sulky line, but otherwise there was no reaction. Since they'd left Dalwhinnie early this morning, Grace hadn't spoken a word to either Juliana or Logan, and now she made it clear she didn't intend to listen to a word, either. The small foot continued to swing, the tip of Grace's boot rhythmically striking the opposite cushion.

"Grace. Your aunt asked you to be still. You will do as she says." Logan's voice was stern.

Grace did as she was bid, but her little face crumpled. Juliana took Grace's hand in hers, but for the first time in Grace's young life, Juliana didn't know what to say to comfort her.

She had no reassuring words for Grace, or for herself. She'd find the words again—tomorrow, perhaps—but at the moment she was simply too exhausted to come up with more than a half-hearted squeeze of Grace's hand.

Grace had been thrilled when she'd found out they were going to Scotland. She'd spent the first few days of the journey bouncing excitedly on the seat, asking questions and chattering happily about every sight that passed by her window.

But like most children, Grace was sensitive to the moods of those around her. It hadn't taken long before she became aware of the tension between Juliana and Logan. As the days dragged on, Grace's spirits sank lower and lower. She grew quieter with every mile, until they'd reached Dalwhinnie. That was when her morose silence had disintegrated into open rebellion.

Grace had spent every minute since fretting over one thing or another. She kicked, squirmed, argued, and complained, and when that failed to relieve her hurt feelings, she wailed. In short, Grace was furious with both of them, and she threw her whole heart into making Juliana and Logan aware of her displeasure.

By the time the coach pulled into the inn yard at the Sassy Lassie, Juliana was so miserable she nearly leapt from the carriage before it stopped moving. Dusk had set in by then, but it wasn't yet the dinner hour. The crowd was thin, but a handful of people were about, most of them locals who'd come for a pint of Fergus's special dark ale and a game of chess or darts.

The first person Juliana saw when she entered the inn was Fergus McLaren, holding court behind the bar. The second was his daughter Alison, who was serving pints of ale and flirting with the customers.

Juliana's mood darkened even further, especially when the beautiful raven-haired girl rushed over to greet Logan, her red lips curled in an inviting smile. "Logan! Ye're back from England already? We didn't expect to see ye this age."

Juliana stiffened when Logan stopped to greet Alison, but she didn't have the energy to fall into a temper over it. So, she simply turned her back on them, took Grace's hand, and led her over to a small table in the corner.

Fergus came out from behind the bar, but to Juliana's surprise he paused only for a moment to slap Logan's back before he made his way over to her and Grace. "Well, Lady Juliana Bernard. Here ye are again. Who's this pretty wee lassie with ye?"

Juliana managed a wan smile. "This is my niece, Miss Grace Bernard. Grace, this is Mr. McLaren. He's a friend of Mr. Logan's."

"How do you do?" Grace gave Fergus a shy smile.

Fergus grinned down at her. "Ye don't look much like yer auntie, little lass. With that dark hair, I'd say ye've a bit of the Scottish in ye."

"I look like my mama," Grace offered uncertainly. "Was my mama Scottish, Aunt Juliana?"

"No. Both your mama and papa were English, but Mr. McLaren is right. Many Scots have lovely dark hair, just like yours."

Logan, for one. Alison McLaren, for another. If Juliana and Grace hadn't been sitting right here, perhaps they'd be running their fingers through each other's lovely Scottish hair even now.

Juliana blew out a breath. She was being ridiculous, of course, but the anger that had been simmering inside her for days was suddenly threatening to boil over. Perhaps she'd only been waiting for an excuse to indulge it.

Alison McLaren had just given her one.

It was much easier to be angry at Logan for flirting with Alison than for the real reason. Not fair, perhaps, especially since Logan wasn't flirting with the girl at all, but after days of holding her tongue, Juliana no longer cared about being fair. If Logan could pretend to be angry about one thing when he was really angry about another, then so could she.

Ever since their argument about her bargain with Lord Cowden, Juliana had been furious with him. Not because he'd shouted at her, or because he'd presumed to order her about as if she were a child. She hadn't cared for either of those things, but she could forgive them.

What she couldn't forgive was Logan saying she'd given up Rosemount to get him to leave England. He'd hurled that ugly accusation not twenty-four hours after she'd told him she loved him. That she didn't want anyone but him.

He hadn't said such a hurtful thing to her because he believed it was true. No, that was just an excuse. He'd said it because he'd been angry at her for giving up something she loved for him. Whether he realized it or not was anyone's guess, but from the moment the accusation had left his lips, Juliana had recognized it for what it was.

A plea, and a warning.

Don't ever risk yourself for me again.

Because apparently Logan was the only one in this marriage who was permitted to make sacrifices. *He* could take care of her, and *he* could take care of Grace, but if anyone tried to take care of *him*...

Oh goodness, no! That wasn't allowed.

Juliana's hands clenched into fists under the table. Every time she thought about it, her entire body went rigid with anger. She'd known before she married him Logan had trouble accepting help from others. He'd been raised to be the rescuer, the savior, the one everyone depended on. He hadn't the vaguest idea how to let someone help him.

Which might have been acceptable, if she hadn't been his *wife*.

His *wife*, damn him. What kind of marriage could they have if he refused to see her as his equal? She wasn't some fragile piece of porcelain, too delicate to stand beside the husband she loved. If that was what he thought, then what made him any different from her father?

She could forgive her father for it. That sort of overprotectiveness was natural in a parent.

In a husband, it was patronizing. Dismissive. Especially from Logan, who knew better than anyone what she was capable of.

"What brings ye back to Scotland so soon?" Fergus asked.

"My husband." Juliana jerked her chin at Logan. "He ordered us back to Scotland. He's every inch the laird now, you see. Whether he truly *wants* us here, well, that's anyone's guess, Mr. McLaren."

Well. Perhaps she wasn't too exhausted to fall into a temper, after all. There'd been a decidedly waspish note in her voice.

Fergus heard it too, and one of his bushy eyebrows shot up. "If he didna want to bring ye, why would he bring ye, lass?"

"Oh, *that*." Juliana waved a causal hand in the air, but she'd been holding her tongue for days. The more she talked, the more the words she'd been struggling to keep inside fought to get out. "Well, we can't be expected to remain in England *alone*, can we? It's far too dangerous for two helpless creatures like ourselves."

Juliana didn't realize her voice had risen until several heads jerked in her direction.

Including Logan's.

Ah. So, it *was* possible to drag his attention away from Alison McLaren. All she had to do was start shouting in the middle of the Sassy Lassie.

Suddenly, there was nothing Juliana wanted to do more. The one thing that could have stopped her was Grace, but when she glanced at her, she found Grace regarding her with a smile far too knowing for a child her age.

Despite Juliana's untoward behavior, Fergus's eyes were twinkling. "Oh now, lass. I wouldn't say as ye're helpless. Not but what some English lasses are, ye see, but ye're more the wily, stubborn sort of Sassenach, wee as you are."

"You have no idea how stubborn I can be, Mr. McLaren. But how refreshing to hear you say so. My husband seems to regard me as decorative rather than useful, despite what I must insist is ample evidence to the contrary."

"Juliana." Logan was staring at her from across the room as if she'd lost her mind. "What the *devil* are you shouting about?"

Juliana shot him a look that made his mouth fall open. "Don't you *dare* curse at me, Logan Blair! If it wasn't for you, I wouldn't be shouting at all!"

Logan strode across the room toward her, and Juliana leapt to her feet to meet him. She didn't care if she only came as high as his shoulder. She'd climbed him once, and she'd do it again, even without the rats.

He closed his hand around her upper arm. "What's this about, Juliana? I'm sorry if you didn't want to come to Scotland with me, but there was no way I would ever leave you—"

"Not come to Scotland with you! Logan, how can you be such a…such a…eejit?" Juliana had no idea where that word came from. It was out of her mouth before she realized she'd even thought it.

A murmur went up around them. Juliana heard one man ask in hushed tones, "Did that lass just call the laird an eejit?"

Fergus was delighted. "Aye, she did! That's it, lass! We'll turn you into a Scot yet!"

"Did you just call me an eejit?" Logan asked her. He looked stunned.

"I did, because you are! Of course, I wanted to come to Scotland with you! Grace and I both did, didn't we, Grace?"

Grace nodded, eyes wide.

"Even now we might be having a delightful time if you hadn't made such a mess of things, but you had to ruin it over that business with Lord Cowden!" Juliana snatched her arm free of his grip. "You didn't even *want* us to come!"

She sucked in a hard, painful breath. Those words felt as if they'd been dragged from the deepest part of her, torn loose from the very depths of her soul. As soon as she said them she recognized them at once as the deepest of the wounds inside her.

Did Logan even want them here? If she hadn't given Rosemount to Lord Cowden, would they be with him now? Logan had said only she was *his*, and he took care of what was his. He hadn't said a single word about her and Grace coming to Scotland with him until after Juliana gave up Rosemount. He hadn't said a single word about love.

"Lord Cowden?" Alison McLaren was watching the scene unfold with an open mouth. "Who's Lord Cowden?"

Neither Juliana nor Logan answered her. They were too focused on each other to pay any attention to anything else.

Logan took her arm again, his fingers tighter this time. "You should never have gone to Cowden in the first place! You had no business risking yourself like. *Mo Dhia*, every time I think of you alone in a room with him…why did you do it, Ana?"

"I told you why. I wanted it over! He was never going to let it end!"

"So, you ended it for us. But why Rosemount, Juliana? Of all the properties you could have offered him, why did you give him that one?"

He already knew why. Juliana could see the knowledge in his face, but for the first time she realized she needed to say it aloud, that too many doubts hid in their silences. "Because he knew it would hurt me to give it to him. He was never going to be satisfied until he hurt someone, and so I—I let him hurt me."

He stared down at her, his blue eyes wild. "*Why*? Why should it have to be you?"

Juliana was horrified to feel tears pricking at her eyes. Not because she'd lost Rosemount. That hurt, yes, but not nearly as much as Logan was hurting her right now. How could he not see she'd done it for him? After all they'd been through, how could he not understand she wanted to protect him as much as he wanted to protect her?

The words gathered in her throat, but they were slow, so slow, to come to her lips. When they made it at last her voice was so soft she wasn't sure if Logan could even hear her. "So it wouldn't be you. It had to be me, Logan, so it wouldn't be *you*."

Silence. The longest silence Juliana had ever lived through. She couldn't bear to look into Logan's eyes, so she lowered her gaze to the floor. The tears that had gathered in her eyes spilled onto her cheeks.

No crying. Not here, not now…

Gentle fingers touched her chin. Logan raised her face to his, and the tenderness in his blue eyes stopped her breath.

* * * *

It had to be me, so it wouldn't be you.

Logan gazed down into the green eyes he loved so well, his heart thundering in his chest. His wee wife was stronger than anyone he'd ever known. So strong she could take care of him when he wasn't strong enough to take care of himself.

All he had to do was let her.

How could he not have understood that until now? How could he ever have thought his love for her made him weak? It wasn't weakness to turn yourself over, body and soul, to the person you loved. It wasn't weakness to trust them to take care of you.

His love for her didn't make him weaker. It made him stronger.

His strength *came* from her, just as surely as hers came from him. He'd never been stronger in his life than he was since he'd fallen in love with her. He was astounded by her—in awe of her. It struck him then, what Fitz had told him weeks ago, when Juliana had first come to Castle Kinross.

She's everything a man could want in a wife...

She was everything he could ever want, and more—so much more— than he deserved.

But he'd keep her for himself, no matter whether he deserved her or not. He'd keep her locked tightly in his arms, and thank God every day for her.

"Ana. *Mo ghaol, mo cridhe. Chan eil caoineadh.* Don't cry, *neach-gaoil.*" Logan wiped her tears away with his thumbs, then cupped her neck in his hands and dropped his forehead against hers. "Shhh, *alainn bhean. Mo bhog bòcan. Tha mi duilich.* I'm sorry."

Juliana sucked in a shaky breath as he continued to whisper to her, a mix of words in Gaelic and English. He knew she didn't understand all of what he was saying, but it didn't matter. She could hear the tenderness, the love in his voice.

"I want you here, Ana." He brushed his lips against her forehead. "You're my wife, and I never want to be apart from you. You and Grace, you're my family now."

Juliana choked down a sob and nodded, her forehead still against his.

"Fergus?" Without taking his eyes off Juliana, Logan reached out, caught Grace's hand, and eased her against his side. "Is our carriage ready? My family's tired. I want to take them home."

"Aye, it's ready." Fergus hurried to the entryway, leading them out into the stable yard. The carriage was waiting there for them, fresh horses in the traces. Fergus opened the door for them, and waved them inside with a flourish. "Ye'll come back and see me soon, won't ye, Miss Grace?" he asked, as Logan lifted Grace into the carriage.

"Yes, I will," Grace promised, scrambling across the seat.

Fergus stuck his head inside the carriage and met Logan's gaze. There was a good deal of humor twinkling in Fergus's blue eyes, but there was seriousness there, too. "I told ye ye'd have yer hands full with this one." He nodded at Juliana. "These sassy, wily sorts make the best wives, ye ken?"

Logan nodded, his gaze drifting back to Juliana's face. "Aye, Fergus. I ken."

"Well then, lad, I s'pose I'll let ye take her home." Fergus was still chuckling to himself as he closed the door.

They were halfway to Castle Kinross when the sun set. Grace went quiet, and when Logan glanced over, he saw she'd fallen asleep. He wrapped his arm tighter around Juliana's shoulders, and she nestled into his side.

Logan pressed his lips into her hair. "I have something for you, *bhean*." He reached into his coat pocket and drew out the oathing stone. "I made it weeks ago. I wanted to give it to you on our wedding day, but now I'm glad I waited."

He held out his hand to her, the oathing stone resting on his palm. Juliana took it up with trembling fingers, and ran her fingertip over their carved names, her breath catching on a sob.

"It's not much of a wedding present, but I thought you'd—"

Juliana pressed her fingers to his lips to hush him. "It's perfect."

He kissed her fingertips. "*Tha gaol agam ort, breagha bhean.* I love you, Ana."

She raised her hand to his cheek. The carriage was dark, but he could feel her green eyes caressing his face. "I love you too, Logan. So much."

He leaned over her, and his lips met hers. When he pulled away, they were both breathless.

"Logan," she whispered, after they'd been quiet for a moment. "Are you ever going to teach me Gaelic?"

He laughed. "I will someday, but not tonight."

He took her warm lips again. She melted against him, and every thought fled his mind as he gathered her close to his heart, safe and warm in his arms. "*Bhean ghràdhach,*" he murmured, pressing his lips to her hair. "*Agaibh mo chridhe.* You have my heart."

Epilogue

Six weeks later

"Logan Blair, you owe me an explanation!"

Juliana burst into their bedchamber, ready to take Logan to task for his most serious transgression yet, but as soon as she caught sight of him, she stopped short. "Oh. What are you doing in the bath?"

She hadn't seen him since they'd woken this morning. He and Fitzwilliam had been fishing with Grace and Duncan Munro all afternoon. Duncan and Grace had met not long after they'd arrived at Castle Kinross. The two children had taken one look at each other, decided they were long-lost souls, and become the best of friends.

"Fitz dumped an entire bucket of herring on me. He claims he tripped and it was an accident, but I know he was lying. Grace and Duncan nearly laughed themselves sick."

Juliana grinned. No doubt Fitzwilliam had been lying. He and Logan had grown closer over the past six weeks—so close they now treated each other like the brothers they were. In other words, they tormented each other relentlessly. They were so merciless Juliana and Emilia had decided they were making up for their lost youth together, starting at about age nine.

Of course, there was nothing else remotely juvenile about Logan, and at no time was that more evident than when he was in the bath. Juliana's eager gaze moved over the smooth, slick flesh stretched tight over his hard muscles, and her cheeks heated.

Logan was leaning against the back of the copper tub, his dark hair slicked back from his face. He noticed her blush, and a wicked grin crossed his lips. "What's the matter, *neach-gaoil*? Haven't you ever seen a man in the bath before?"

She had indeed seen a man in the bath before—she'd seen *this* man in the bath—but it was a sight that never failed to render her speechless. His spread arms rested on the rim of the tub, leaving the hard, muscular plane of his bare chest completely exposed to her hungry gaze.

When she didn't answer, he gave her a lazy grin. "Come closer, *bhean*, and I'll explain anything you like."

Juliana's gaze snapped from his chest to his face. Oh, yes, that's right. She'd come to demand an explanation from him, hadn't she?

She crossed her arms over her chest and did her best to look outraged. "I had a most enlightening conversation with Emilia just now. She overheard me call Grace *bhig galla*, and do you know what she did, Logan?"

The playful grin she loved so much hovered at the corners of Logan's lips, but he didn't answer. Instead he crooked his finger at her, beckoning her forward.

Juliana swallowed. His wet skim gleamed, and the sprinkling of dark hair on his chest made her think of that alluring trail of hair low on his belly. It was just as well that half of him was submerged in the water, or else she'd never get this scolding over with.

"Her eyes went as round as tea saucers, and she asked me where I'd heard that phrase. I told her you called me that, and *then* do you know what she did, Logan?"

The grin widened, but Logan only crooked his finger at her again.

Juliana hesitated. Well, perhaps it wouldn't do any harm to take a tiny step closer. "She *laughed*, Logan. She laughed so hard I began to fear she'd give birth right there in the drawing room." Juliana inched another step closer to him, but took care to remain out of his reach. "It seems *bhig galla* isn't the sweet, loving endearment I thought it was."

"Closer, *dùr bhean*."

Juliana edged a bit closer, but she was enjoying teasing him too much to give in just yet. "Well? What do you have to say for yourself? *Bhig galla*, indeed."

"Closer, Ana, or I'll have to come get you myself."

Juliana took two tiny steps forward, until she was mere inches away from the edge of the tub. "She also told me what *beag deomhan* means, so don't think you've gotten away with that one. Really, Logan, what sort of husband calls his wife a little demon?"

"The sort of husband who has a little demon for a wife. Take your hair down, *leannan*."

"Ah, now *leannan* is much better. Sweetheart is a proper endearment for a wife." To reward him, Juliana began to draw the pins from her hair. She gave him a teasing smile as she dropped them to the floor, one by one. When she'd discarded every pin she shook her hair loose, letting it fall over her shoulders and down her back in thick waves.

Logan's blue eyes darkened as he watched her. When he spoke, his voice was low and husky. "Now your dress. Take it off, *àlainn bana-bhuidseach*."

Juliana was about to obey, but her fingers paused on the button at the back of her neck. "*Alainn bana-bhuidseach*? You've never called me that before. What does it mean?"

Logan's gaze swept over her and an impatient growl rose from his chest. "Take off your dress, Ana."

"No."

Logan raised an eyebrow at her. "*No?*"

"That's right, no. Not until you tell me what *àlainn bana-bhuidseach* means."

Logan's blue eyes glittered at the note of challenge in her voice. "It means beautiful witch. Now take your dress off."

Beautiful witch? She hadn't expected that. It wasn't really a proper endearment, but his rough voice and heated gaze made a shiver of desire dart down her spine. Juliana quickly loosened the few remaining buttons and slid the dress off her shoulders.

Logan stared as she slowly worked the dress down, his gaze devouring every creamy inch of skin as it was revealed. "Your chemise, too."

Juliana drew her chemise over her head.

Logan's lips parted in a groan when she stood bare before him. "Yes. Now come here, Ana." He shifted in the tub, drawing his legs open, and nodded at the space between them. "Right here."

"I can't. There's no room," Juliana teased, biting her lip.

Logan patted the water in front of him, sending it sloshing against the sides of the tub. "There's more than enough room for you, wee wife."

"Hmmm. I don't know. Isn't the water cold?"

"No, but even if it was, I'd soon warm you." Logan crooked his finger at her again, and his lips curved in a seductive smile.

Juliana gazed at him—the damp, dark waves of his hair, one lock now lying across his forehead, his taut, muscular body, the smile in his hot blue eyes—and she gave up the fight. There was simply no resisting her husband.

Logan took her hand as she stepped daintily into the tub. They both sighed when she was nestled against him, with her back pressed against his broad chest and his long legs wrapped around her.

He ran his hands through her hair. "So, Emilia told you what *bhig galla* means?"

"Yes. It means little vixen." Juliana tried to sound affronted, but there was a smile on her lips.

He chuckled against her ear. "Aye, it does. What else did she tell you?" Juliana shivered at the warm drift of his breath. *"Beag deomhan.* Little demon. Really, Logan, you're incorrigible. To begin with, I'm not little—"

"Shh." He nipped gently at her earlobe to quiet her. "Did she tell you anything else?"

Juliana tilted her head to the side to give him access to her neck. "No. She tried to, but I couldn't pronounce any of the others well enough for her to understand me."

Logan ran his palms down her arms, then lower to stroke her stomach. *"Mo bhean uasal* means 'my lady.'"

Juliana arched into his touch. "Well, that's not *so* awful, I suppose."

"Bhean means wife. *Dùr bhean* means stubborn wife," he went on, a smile in his voice.

"Humph." It was hardly flattering, but Juliana couldn't really argue the point. She *was* stubborn. Almost as stubborn as her husband.

Logan was quiet as he traced rhythmic circles on her stomach with his fingertips. When he spoke again, the teasing note had left his voice, and it was hoarse with emotion. *"Àlainn* and *breagha* both mean beautiful. *Breagha bhean. Àlainn bhean.* What does it mean, Ana?"

"Beautiful wife." Such a simple phrase, but it made Juliana's heart swell in her chest.

"Bòcan means sprite. *Uaine air leth-shùil* means 'green-eyed.' *Uaine air leth-shùil bòcan."*

"Green-eyed sprite," Juliana whispered.

She tried to turn in his arms them, but he slid his hands up to her shoulders and held her gently against him, stilling her. *"Neach-gaoil* means beloved. *Bhean ghràdhach.* Beloved wife," he murmured, his lips against her neck. "That's what you are to me, Ana. *Tha gaol agam ort, bhean. Tha thu mo chridhe."*

I love you, wife. You are my heart.

This time when Juliana turned to face him, he let her. She cradled his face in her palms. "How do you say 'my husband' in Gaelic?"

He smiled. *"An duine agam."*

Juliana traced his lips to feel the words. *"Tha gaol agam ort, bhean. Tha thu mo chridhe, an duine agam."*

She stumbled over the words, her pronunciation clumsy, but Logan didn't seem to mind. He drew her tightly against him and took her lips in a kiss that left her breathless.

Juliana made up her mind right then and there to learn Gaelic. "How do you say, 'Kiss me again'?"

"*Pòg mi a-rithist.*" Logan's lips hovered over hers.

Juliana gazed up into the blue eyes that had mesmerized her since the first moment she saw him and whispered, "*Pòg mi a-rithist.*"

He did, until the fire died to embers, and the bathwater ran cold.

Gaelic Glossary

Agaibh mo chridhe – you have my heart
Àlainn – lovely
Àlainn bòcan – beautiful sprite
An duine agam – my husband
Beag bòidhchead – little beauty
Beag deomhan – wee demon
Bhean – wife
Bhean ghràdhach – beloved wife
Bhig – petite, little
Bòcan – sprite
Breagha – fine, beautiful
Chan eil caoineadh – don't cry
Dia tha – God, yes
Dùr – stubborn
Fhìnealta – delicate
Fuilteach ifrinn – bloody hell
Galla – vixen
Leannan – sweetheart
Maoth-chridheach – tenderhearted
Mo bhean uasal – my lady (title)
Mo chridhe – my heart
Mo Dhia – my God
Mo ghaol – my love
Neach-gaoil – beloved
Tha gaol agam ort – I love you
Tha mi duilich – I'm sorry
Tha thu mo chridhe – you are my heart
Uaine air leth-shùil – green-eyed

Author's Notes

Highland Clearances

The Highland Clearances were a brutal period in Scottish history in which large portions of the indigenous population were forcibly, and in some cases violently, evicted from the land they'd farmed for generations. Because the Clearances took place over an extended period of time (roughly the 1750s to the 1880s), and because the reasons for it are so complex and varied, there's a great deal of scholarly dispute regarding the reality of the Clearances. Putting the academic arguments aside, and although exact numbers vary, it is certainly true that hundreds of thousands of native Scots were evicted from their homes to make way for much larger and more lucrative sheep farms.

Like Logan Blair in *To Wed a Wild Scot,* there were landlords who didn't callously toss the people off their land and leave them to fend for themselves. A merciful clan chief might have assisted his tenants to emigrating to North America or Australia, or helping them relocate to the Scottish Lowlands or England. Some landlords, like Logan, simply shifted some of their tenants to another part of their estates, or to neighboring estates.

In the worst cases, however, the Highland Clearances were a tragic period in which families who'd occupied the land for generations were suddenly and sometimes cruelly evicted from their homes. It was not unheard of for hundreds of families to be evicted at once when entire villages and townships were cleared en masse.

In part a response to overpopulation and famine in the Highlands, the collapse of the clan system, and the changing social and economic landscape that took place during Britain's industrial revolution, the Highland Clearances remain one of the most heartbreaking periods in Scottish history.

Strathnaver Clearances

The Strathnaver Clearances are notorious for being one of the most brutal in Scottish history. Between 1807 and 1821 more than ten thousand people were removed from the Sutherland estates at the behest of the Countess of Sutherland. Tenants were forcibly evicted and left to stand by and watch while their homes and possessions were burned to the ground.

In *To Wed a Wild Scot* Logan witnesses the particularly vicious clearance of Rosal Township, one of the largest townships in Strathnaver at the time.

Patrick Sellar

Patrick Sellar, a Scotsman born in Moray in 1780, was the Countess of Sutherland's factor from 1814 to 1816. Sellar was responsible for, among others, the Rosal Township evictions mentioned in the prologue. Sellar was put on trial in Inverness in 1816 for arson and the culpable homicide of two victims who perished in Rosal Township in 1814. One of these was ninety-year-old Margaret MacKay, who died from severe burns after the roof of her son-in-law's croft was set afire with her still inside. Sellar was found not guilty of the charges.

Gretna Green Marriage

In chapter Three Logan tells Juliana a scandalous tale about a lord who eloped to Gretna parish with his housekeeper. This story is true. In 1818, Lord Erskine, a gentleman sixty-six years old, eloped to Gretna Green with Miss Sarah Buck, his much younger housekeeper/mistress. Lord Erksine's son Thomas, scandalized by the affair (and likely concerned about his inheritance!) pursued the fleeing lovers to the King's Head Inn in Springfield, in the parish of Gretna. According to the gossip of the time, Lord Erskine disguised himself in ladies' clothing to confuse his son and thereby elude pursuit. Whether his lordship was wearing a bonnet at the time of his marriage, as Logan insists was the case, is a matter of speculation.

Drum Castle

The description of the chapel at Castle Kinross where Juliana and Logan are married was inspired by the beautiful chapel at Drum Castle in Aberdeenshire, Scotland. Drum Castle's chapel dates from the sixteenth century, and is famous for the arched stained glass window behind the altar that depicts the Crucifixion. Drum Castle is open to the public.

Sources

"Oh, What a Scandal!" Jane Austen's World, October 31, 2015: https://
janeaustensworld.wordpress.com/2015/10/31/oh-what-a-scandal-a-gretna-
green-elopement-marriage-and-divorce/

"POWiS, Places of Worship in Scotland," Scottish Church Heritage
Research Ltd.: www.scottishchurches.org.uk/sites/site/id/478/name/
Drum+Castle+Chapel+Drumoak+Grampian

Sawyers, June Skinner. *Bearing the People Away: The Portable
Highland Clearances Companion.* Sydney, Nova Scotia: Cape Breton
University Press, 2013.